House of Dreams

Fanny Blake

First published in Great Britain in 2015 by Orion Books,
an imprint of The Orion Publishing Group Ltd
Carmelite House, 50 Victoria Embankment
London EC4Y 0DZ

An Hachette UK Company

3 5 7 9 10 8 6 4 2

A CIP catalogue record for this book is
available from the British Library.

ISBN (Trade Paperback) 978 1 4091 5986 5
ISBN (Ebook) 978 1 4091 5988 9

Typeset at The Spartan Press Ltd,
Lymington, Hants

Printed and bound by the CPI Group (UK) Ltd,
Croydon, CR0 4YY

The Orion Publishing Group's policy is to use papers that are natural,
renewable and recyclable products and made from wood grown in sustainable
forests. The logging and manufacturing processes are expected to
conform to the environmental regulations of the country of origin.

www.orionbooks.co.uk

*For Julie – great friend, travelling companion
and chauffeur extraordinaire*

THURSDAY

Before . . .

The house was ready. Under the vine-covered pergola, the table was laid for lunch. The huge cream parasol was up, shading the garden chairs on the other side of the terrace. Indoors, everything was just as it had always been – only a little tidier, perhaps. Upstairs, the beds were made and the rooms aired.

Lucy adjusted the position of a jar of white roses on the table then stepped back to admire her work before moving into the sunshine, feeling its warmth on her skin. She stretched out her arms to either side of her. Today, the air was so clear she could see all the way south to the coast, beyond the rock of Gibraltar, across the straits to Africa. Bailey, her mother's grey-and-white shaggy mongrel, padded down the stone steps in front of her and collapsed, panting, in the shade of a twisted olive tree.

A painted lady butterfly flittered over the pots of red and white geraniums, past the cream parasol and chairs and out towards the garden. Bees hummed in the lavender below the terrace wall. A couple of buzzards hovered over the fields below. Somewhere a cock crowed. Lucy checked her watch. Her sister and brother should have landed by now. They would be here soon.

Even though she had been back here for a few days, preparing for everyone's arrival, Lucy still hadn't got used to her mother not being there. Occasionally, out of the corner of her eye, she would imagine Hope in the garden, cajoling a plant to do better, or framed by a doorway. Sometimes she would be sitting at the piano, her spectacles on top of her grey curls, or in her sewing chair, hands busy. She might be announcing a plan for the day, wondering where she had put something, or opening a bottle of wine. Her presence was here even now, weeks after her death.

Hope had died in England but had asked for her ashes to be scattered at the place she loved most in the world, where she had been her happiest. Her three children were making sure that wish was granted, and Jo was bringing her home in accordance with her final wishes.

And when it was all over, the house would be sold. Lucy gazed around her, unable to believe there would be a time when none of this would be theirs.

I

The Arrivals Hall was a huge dimly lit barn of a place with large green signs pointing the way to the rental car desks in the basement. The passengers had left behind the bright posters welcoming them to sunny southern Spain and entered a utilitarian, cavernous netherworld chilled by the over-efficient air con. Whoever said hell was other people was right, Jo reflected, clutching the map of local attractions that a tourist guide had pressed into her hand as they emerged into baggage reclaim. She missed the heat and the distinctive smell of the rough Spanish cigarettes that years ago had made landing here so distinctive, so special. Now arriving at Malaga was just like arriving at any big modern airport anywhere else in the world.

The airport carousel was loaded with baggage from their flight, but Jo's case had yet to appear. She turned to check that Ivy was still sitting on the empty trolley. Her four-year-old daughter, adorable in her pink leggings and flowery top, hadn't moved except to stare at a family of children whose mother was handing out multi-coloured lollies. One of the children, a girl about the same age as Ivy, saw her watching and came over, trailing her wheelie backpack. The two of them sized each other up. Ivy stayed put, her small face creasing into a scowl. She was reliable like that. Jo wished she hadn't left the packet of Haribo, bought for just this sort of a moment, at the checkout of the Gatwick WHSmith. She refocused on the circulating luggage. Heavily taped cardboard boxes, children's buggies and a variety of cases, rucksacks and holdalls rumbled past – but no sign of the well-travelled green case with the distinguishing purple padlock.

Around the carousel, families were revved up in holiday mood. Children raced around parents driven to the end of their tether. Tempers were already fraying as cases were heaved on to trolleys and children scrambled up the piles to sit triumphant at the top, leaving others disappointed or angry at the bottom. A couple of teenagers sat bent over their phones, thumbs moving rapidly over the screens. A hen party, which had brawled during the flight and been separated by the crew, was split into two miserable groups, backs to each other, their glittery pink antennae drooping. A few moony couples stared at each other, oblivious to the surrounding chaos. Older couples with walking shoes and sticks had grabbed their rucksacks from the carousel and were marching purposefully towards customs and the exit.

Jo was shoved to one side as a man grabbed at a large cardboard box stuck over with labels and caught her shin with its corner. She swore under her breath. He muttered an apology, leaving her to rub her leg while willing her case to appear. She turned again to Ivy, feeling that familiar rush of love that still surprised her with its intensity. Who would have thought that having a child so late in her life would give her so much?

'Won't be long,' she said. 'Our case'll be here in a minute, then we can go. You OK?'

Her daughter's scowl had deepened and she said something that disappeared into her sucked thumb and Bampy, the worn toy rabbit that Ivy insisted went everywhere with her, her brown eyes large above the animal's embarrassingly grubby head.

'What was that?' Jo bent over to make out what she said.

'I want a lolly.' Ivy's eyes travelled to the bright-coloured lollies being sucked by the family beside her.

'Can I have a lolly, please.' Jo corrected her daughter automatically as she rummaged in their rucksack, praying that the packet of Haribo would magically materialise. Oh God, she hadn't got

6

anything that would do as a substitute. She pulled out a couple of carrot and apple sticks from a Tupperware box. 'We've finished the biscuits. Have these instead. Yum.' How half-hearted that sounded, even to her.

Her daughter's face screwed up. 'No, no, no, no! I want a lolly.' Bampy hit the ground and Ivy was on her feet. Surely, the whole airport could hear her. Heads were turning.

Oh God, not a tantrum. Please, not now. 'Just eat these for the moment. We'll get one later. I promise.' Jo spoke clearly and calmly despite her gritted teeth.

'No, n-o-o-o-o-w,' Ivy wailed, pushing away Jo's hand and hurling herself to the floor.

'As soon as we've got our bag.' Jo resisted the almost overwhelming temptation to resort to physical force to get Ivy back on the trolley. Everyone was watching them. But Ivy was beyond reason. She lifted her head, face red, eyes screwed up, mouth open for another loud wail, the epitome of absolute misery. And not a tear to be seen.

Aware of everyone's eyes on them and judgement being passed on her for being a bad mother, unable to deal with her own child, Jo squatted and took Ivy's arm, trying to calm her in a loud whisper. But, feet drumming on the ground, Ivy didn't hear. All the while cases were passing them by, not one of them with a purple padlock.

'Would one of these help?' A voice came from beside them. Jo looked up to see the mother of the neighbouring family holding out a round lolly with a deep-red rose emblazoned in its creamy centre. 'I know what it's like. I always have these with me for emergencies. They never fail.'

Jo glimpsed her Samaritan's three small children, all staring wide-eyed at Ivy, each with a stick protruding from their mouth and sucking furiously.

'Thank you so much.' Jo took the proffered lolly. As she did, she could hear her nanny Sue harping on about the throbbing mass of E-numbers and sugar that promised a lifetime in the dentist's chair. But it offered blessed peace and quiet as well. Which was more important: the immediate present or the unknown future? No contest. Ivy's wails had already scaled back to the occasional whimper as her eyes fixed on the prize. Jo could imagine stickler Sue's tutting disapproval. Keeping up with her shared nanny's exacting standards was a constant trial. All the more so now Ivy had learned to talk and could give away the full extent of her mother's backsliding.

'It's my fault,' the woman admitted. 'I should have offered her one when I dished them out to keep mine quiet, but I didn't like to. Stranger danger, sweets, all that.'

'Oh no. You shouldn't . . .' Jo registered the woman's evident exhaustion, her face a blur of shadow and softened edges, her hair straying from a scraped-back ponytail. 'I should have brought some of—' But, before Jo could finish, the woman had turned to her husband who had just brought over the last of their luggage and was hurrying them away. More grateful than she had a chance to express, Jo passed the lolly into Ivy's grasping hand, then lifted her and put her back on the trolley with the rucksack. Pushing the trolley into a space close to the carousel where the crowd had thinned, she resumed her watch, her anxiety mounting.

'Once we get the case, we can go,' Jo explained again, but Ivy was too focused on the changing colours of her lolly to bother to reply.

There were only a few cases left from their flight by now. Hers was not among them. She closed her eyes and sent up a small prayer. The case could not go missing. Not now and especially not with what was inside it.

What could she have been thinking when she packed their mother? However practical a solution it might have seemed at the time, if the box of ashes was lost the repercussions would be pyrotechnic.

The demands of the budget airline had made packing

impossible. Jo had tried fitting the eight-by-twelve-inch cardboard box provided by the undertakers into her backpack along with everything else. But however she tried, not everything would fit. Something had to go in the hold. Not Ivy, obviously – though the flight might have been more relaxing without her – and therefore not the things that would amuse her during the flight; books; colouring books and crayons; iPad for those more desperate moments; and of course Bampy. And not her change of clothes in case of accidents. And not their picnic, either. Nor Jo's own laptop – too precious and too fragile. She might not get the chance to check her work emails over the weekend, but she felt better knowing she could if she wanted to. That had only left the box of ashes.

Originally she had intended to carry her mother on board with her even though the idea had slightly freaked her out, especially as Ivy would be with her. She had imagined being stopped at Security and having to explain in front of her daughter that the plastic bag of fine pasty-white ash was all that was left of Granny Hope. Ivy could be traumatised forever. Of course Jo didn't want that. The subject of death was already a too-frequent topic of conversation between them since her mother had died. No, the living had to take priority over the dead – even if the dead was your own parent.

Airline regulations probably demanded human remains be carried as hand luggage – but who would know that she had packed them? With luck, no one. And certainly not her mother. In fact, Hope would probably have laughed if she had known. She would have made a joke about how being wrapped in her favourite sea-grass green pashmina and tucked into a comfortable case was infinitely preferable to being squashed among the cabin baggage, jammed between everybody else's bits and pieces. 'Much more me, darling.' Jo could almost hear her voice ringing through Malaga airport.

One more revolve and then she would have to abandon hope.

She smiled at her own pun. Hope could be winging her way to another destination altogether, safely wrapped in her pashmina, warm within a freezing aircraft hold. Jo remembered how she would lament, 'Living in Spain spoilt me. I wish I'd seen more of the world.' Well, perhaps her dream was about to come true.

However difficult it was to accept this was happening, Jo had only one option. She would have to report the missing case and hope for the best. Pushing the contented lolly-licking Ivy on the empty trolley, she began the long walk to find the left-luggage desk. Once at the front of the so-called queue, she registered her missing case in swift, fluent Spanish then waited patiently, giving the relevant details while the appropriate form was filled in, aware that Ivy's lolly had almost come to an end and the little girl was getting fidgety again. As she omitted to mention the crucial contents of her case, Jo's mind fast-forwarded to the rest of the family waiting for their arrival. Compared to her sister Lucy's weeks of caring for their mother in her final swift decline, bringing Hope's ashes home had hardly been a difficult task. But she had royally screwed it up.

The rest of the family would have to be told that she had lost her mother in transit. She pictured the shocked disbelief that would greet her when her brother and sister heard what had happened: Lucy's distress, Tom's anger and his wife's familiar I-told-you-what-would-happen-if-you-let-her-do-it expression. By now, they must nearly be at the house where Hope's last birthday party and the scattering of her ashes was due to take place. Casa de Sueños – House of Dreams – their childhood home. Jo hadn't been there for at least a year and, until this moment, had been looking forward to being back, despite the sadness of the occasion.

Turning tail and catching the next plane home was not an option. Besides, the case would surely turn up eventually. She tried to put the countless stories she had heard of missing luggage never being seen again right to the back of her mind – and failed.

As she fished into her pocket of her denim cut-offs for a tissue to wipe Ivy's cerise-stained mouth, Jo's fingers closed round her phone, stuck to a half-sucked sweet. Of course. If she called Tom and told him now at least she wouldn't have to watch his expression change or hear Lucy's gasp of horror. He could break the news to the others before Jo and Ivy arrived. A plan.

She prised off the lime sweet from the back of the phone and for want of anywhere else, put it into her mouth before calling up her brother's number. Ivy kicked off a shoe so Jo set off across the gleaming marble floor to get it. Rather than start a game she hadn't the heart for at that moment, she tucked the shoe into the rucksack. Ivy's mouth opened in protest.

'Shh,' Jo ordered, as the continental ringtone beeped in her ear.

Surprised by her mother's firmness, Ivy was quiet and concentrated instead on kicking off the other shoe. Equally surprised by her daughter's compliance, Jo was free to concentrate on the best way to explain the current situation.

2

In the back of the car, Ethan and Alex were attached to their separate electronic devices. Although Ethan's iPad was on silent, he accompanied whatever shoot-'em-up he was playing with grunts of triumph and frustration. Alex was curled against the window, earphones in, head half-hidden by his black hoodie, glued to the screen of his Kindle. Both of them were oblivious to the drama playing out in the front seat, never mind the scenery flying past the window.

To the south of the motorway lay the continuous concrete sprawl of Fuengirola, Marbella, Estepona, and all the property developments that linked them. In the distance lay the Mediterranean: an iridescent blue carpet stretching away to the pale horizon, the sun glinting off its surface. One or two tankers sat stationary in the distance while white yacht sails sped east and west. To the north, the mountains of the Sierra Bermeja rose towards a clear cornflower-blue sky.

In the passenger seat, Tom cut off his sister's call and replaced his phone in the breast pocket of his short-sleeved check shirt. 'Can you believe that?' He turned to look at his wife. Belle was sitting in that curiously rigid posture she always adopted when driving, her body tilted forward at a twenty-degree angle, chin out, hands at ten to two.

She turned her head. Her sleek new bob, the colour of a ginger biscuit, swayed with the movement, catching the light. 'Yep. I can.' She focused her gaze on him for a second, her dark eyes large in her carefully framed face, before returning her attention to the tunnel they were approaching. She was still an attractive woman, though he couldn't help thinking that she had been even more so before the merciless Brazilian straightening of her naturally wavy hair, and before the grey hairs were ruthlessly and chemically eliminated. Their joint bank account and her suspiciously unlined face suggested that she might have undergone a touch of facial work, but nothing had been said and, truth be told, his more squeamish side didn't really want to know. What mattered was that she was happy.

Tom knew what she was thinking but he refused to rise to any more scrutiny of his sisters' good and bad points. They'd been through them too many times and he knew exactly what Belle thought of Jo and Lucy. They'd clashed all too frequently over them. He was allowed to criticise his family, but if anyone else – even his own dear wife – dared to, he would defend them to the hilt. He didn't need Belle to spell out her opinions again, especially not while on the way to spend a long and no doubt emotionally tortuous few days with both sisters.

The next tunnel swallowed them up, the darkness lit by the flare of oncoming headlights and an unforgiving neon ceiling strip. Tom felt a movement inside the padded carrier on his lap. Ferdie, Belle's miniature smooth-haired dachshund, was making himself comfortable. The tiny animal had been chipped and passported so he could go wherever Belle went, so go he did despite their sons' sneers. Tom shifted his own position in response and turned up the air con a notch from freezing.

'Whatever possessed her?' Tom muttered to himself, blinking as they emerged into the bright sunlight. Of the three of them, Jo had always been the least predictable, the least conformist, the most frustrating. And yet she had still managed to forge a successful career in advertising, eventually co-founding her own agency with Richard Fowler. Tom was proud but intrigued by her achievement, only imagining that she must split her personality in two: one for work and another for the rest. 'And if the case doesn't turn up?' he asked. 'Sometimes they don't for weeks.'

'Then we'll have to scatter the ashes another weekend. Have you got change for the toll?' Belle was a perennial pragmatist. Tom was granted another glimpse of her face, thinner now after her strict dietary regime that seemed to consist of nothing more than a series of unpleasant-smelling, filthy-looking bowls of gloop. He wrestled in his trouser pocket for cash that she could slip into the machine. After a second, his change rattled into the outlet and the barrier lifted.

'But this would have been Mum's seventieth birthday. It's all planned exactly as she wanted it.' The last thing he wanted was for them to let her down.

'We'll just have to unplan it then.' A grim little smile was shot in his direction as Belle tightened her grip on the wheel. 'Trust Jo.'

'We can't do that. Everyone's coming. Birthday party on Saturday, scattering on Sunday.' He took a deep breath and pinched the skin between the thumb and index finger of his left hand until it hurt: a technique that Frank his occasional therapist had suggested for distracting himself.

'Hope's hardly going to know, is she?'

'That's not the point.' His panic began to recede. 'Perhaps we should turn round?'

'Why?'

'We could help Jo find the case. Moral support.'

No.' His wife's chin jutted out a centimetre further. 'If she can't find it, we won't be able to. Besides, Lucy's expecting us at the house. We're already later than we said we'd be.'

Belle was right, of course, but he couldn't let the subject go. 'All she had to do was carry Mum with her. It's not as though she takes up much space any more.' The gallows humour amused him despite Belle's disapproving shake of the head.

Belle kept her eyes fixed on the road. 'I said you should carry her yourself.'

'But Jo offered because she wanted to do her bit. After all, Lucy looked after Mum for all those weeks while we paid most of the bills.' That resentful inner child that he sometimes found hard to control when in the vicinity of his family was elbowing its way into the open again.

'Which bills?' Belle's antennae were immediately on high alert. Anything to do with money and she was on it like a hawk. They had a straightforward arrangement that suited them both when it came to their finances. As a successful chartered surveyor he made the money and, as an accountant, she managed it (and spent it too). He wasn't complaining.

'Nothing that you don't know about,' he justified himself hastily. 'If there'd been anything else, I'd have told you.'

She nodded her head, satisfied.

Once through the Casares tunnel, they paid the last road toll and took the A-377 inland. They passed the row of giant wind turbines that turned slowly, shining white against the sky. Belle reached out and patted Tom's thigh with a soft hand tipped by immaculate lacquered pink nails. He covered it with his own hand but after a minute she edged hers out and returned it to the wheel. 'You will ask the girls about the ring, won't you?'

Tom nodded. 'Mm-hmm.' He knew the ring she meant and wished she would stop going on about it. Walter, his and Jo's stepfather, had given it to their mother when Lucy was born. A little bit of art nouveau bling that Walter's grandmother had left him for when he met 'the one': two bands of bright diamonds circled the central ruby like two glittering waves. Tom and Jo used to watch the light dance through the stones as their mother turned her hand in the Spanish sunshine. 'Look what Daddy gave me,' she'd say, then laugh as they reached for it and she'd wave it away.

'She wanted me to have it,' Belle insisted.

Tom found it hard to imagine Hope wanting anyone to have it but Jo, who had admired it for so long, or Lucy, whose birth the gift had marked. But their mother set such little store by her possessions and had become even less predictable towards the end of her life, so perhaps... 'Did she actually say that?' he asked.

'As good as,' Belle said, lifting a hand from the wheel, her own solitaire diamond sparkling above her wedding band. 'When we were last all here together.'

The previous October they had come for half-term, ignoring the boys' complaints. Despite Tom's encouragement, they didn't appreciate the outdoor idyll of their father's childhood. They preferred a holiday hanging out indoors or down at the local mall with their mates, watching the premiership games on TV with them, playing endless computer games, listening to music, loafing in the squalor of their rooms on Facebook or whatever it was they used these days. Tom despaired, despite Belle's assurances that this was all part and parcel of modern boyhood. At least Alex read. Or at least Tom thought he did, although, thanks to the Kindle, he couldn't be sure how improving what he read was.

None of them had known then that Hope would be dead less than six months later, diagnosed with terminal colon cancer that had spread through her body. If they had, would they have behaved differently? He felt ashamed remembering how his mother's laissez-faire attitude towards everyday life had sent him spiralling into the anxiety he'd felt as a child when faced with her unpredictability. You never quite knew what to expect from her next. How she managed to attract visitors to the B & B when she was so undependable was a mystery to him – sheer force of personality, he supposed. And of course she relied on Rosa and Luisa, from the village, to get breakfast out on time and to clean the rooms. Belle had responded to his mood by becoming increasingly tetchy as she tried to get Hope to stick to some sort of schedule, while trying to persuade Tom that if they didn't eat until after ten o'clock, no harm would be done. Meanwhile,

Ethan and Alex bounced around between them, Ethan sullen and unhappy with whatever arrangements were made to entertain them, Alex anxious to please though never happier than when left alone with his Kindle or his phone.

As if on cue, there was a shout from the back seat. 'Don't do that!'

Out of the corner of his eye, Tom saw Alex's arm flail in Ethan's direction.

'Stop that right now! You'll make Mum crash the car.'

'No they won't!' Belle protested in an undertone as they lurched over a huge pothole.

'Shit,' breathed Tom, thinking of the car's undercarriage.

'Don't say a thing,' Belle warned, eyes on the road.

'What are you doing, Ethan?' Tom tried to contain his irritation as he turned round to see what was happening in the back seat.

'He kicked me!' protested Alex, rubbing his shin.

'I did not.' Ethan extended a long leg into the gap between the front seats and flexed an unfortunately sockless foot. 'I've got cramp. This car's too fucking small, that's what.'

'You can stop that sort of talk, right now,' said Belle. 'And put your shoes on, for the love of God.'

'Well, it is,' insisted Ethan, stretching his long arms and legs as far – which was not very – as he could. He yanked Alex's hood off his head.

'Get off me!' Alex protested, running a hand through his flop of brown hair. 'Leave me alone.' He squished himself into his side of the car as if hoping he might disappear into it.

'You're such a nerd. What are you reading?' Ethan snatched at his brother's Kindle. In trying to keep it out of his reach, Alex swiped the back of Tom's head.

'Boys!' Tom roared, raising his hand to the spot on his head. 'Is it too much to ask you to behave in a civilised way until we

17

get there?' He could see Belle's knuckles whitening on the steering wheel.

'Sorry, Dad.' Alex stuffed his Kindle down the front of his hoodie out of Ethan's reach.

Ethan withdrew his leg and made a great fuss of reorganising his angular body until he was comfortable. He refocused on his iPad.

'You did bring that new shirt and the trousers I laid out on your bed, didn't you?' Belle's thoughts followed a pattern of their very own.

There was silence from the back, then a 'Yes!!' as someone or something was no doubt shot down in flames. Should they be encouraging this delight in violence, Tom briefly wondered.

'Ethan?' she insisted.

He paused his game and raised his head. Tom saw so much of Belle in his older son's face, in the turn of his mouth, the determined jut of the chin. His son shook his head. 'You didn't say pack the trousers. I never wear trousers here. It's too hot.'

'This is different. This is your grandmother's last birthday party. Looking smart's a mark of respect.' Belle's eyes left the road to glance at her son in the driving mirror. She moved her hands to twenty to four on the wheel. Ahead of them, a heat haze shimmered above the gleaming tarmac.

'I don't suppose it really matters,' said Tom. 'No one's going to judge them. Mum's friends aren't exactly slaves to convention.'

'Of course it matters,' said Belle, lifting her hand for a moment and smacking the wheel. '*I* want them to look smart. We'll just have to go to Ronda and buy some more.'

'I'm not shopping there,' muttered Ethan. 'Anyway, Gran wouldn't mind. She never fussed about what we wore.'

There was no point in reassuring Belle it didn't matter. Appearances were important to her. Tom gasped suddenly and flapped his hand over the carrier. For a small dog, Ferdie could produce the most pungent of smells. Even Belle's nose wrinkled up as she turned towards him.

'Belle! Watch where you're going!'

She turned the wheel just in time to avoid a white four-by-four hurtling towards them. A hand emerged from its window, flipping them the finger.

'Bloody cheek! What's he doing in the middle of the road.'

Tom stared out at the yellow drifts of Spanish broom flanking the road and sighed.

Belle pulled over and stopped the car. She opened the door and got out. The heat invaded the chill of the car like a warm blanket. 'Let's all calm down.' She shut her eyes and took a long yogic breath in, then out, and stretched her arms to the sky, tipping her face to the sun. 'Why don't you all get out and stretch your legs?'

Grateful to be outside, away from the asphyxiating smell, Tom pushed Ferdie's carrier across the hot car bonnet so Belle could give him a walk. Ethan was first out of the back, unfolding his long legs then shaking the others. Alex made less fuss and walked away from the others, setting himself apart, waiting till they were ready to continue. While Ferdie sniffed around the dried grass and wild flowers edging the road, Ethan took himself off into the scrub to have a pee. Belle looked away, before reaching for her wide-brimmed hat on the back ledge of the car.

She arranged the hat at the right angle, checking her reflection in the side window. 'I thought I could rely on him.' She tipped her head towards her oldest son.

'What he wears is less important than Mum's ashes being there. Don't worry.' Scratching his head, Tom felt his new close cut, designed to disguise how follicly challenged he was but that he suspected only emphasised the fact. The sun beat down on his scalp, making it tingle. He reached inside the car for the bush hat that he'd bought in Australia a couple of years earlier.

'I get that.' Belle jumped back and flapped at a large airborne black beetle so it blundered on to a different flight path. 'But she'll turn up. She wouldn't miss her own party.' She pulled on the pink extendable lead, reeling Ferdie back in like a yo-yo so that she could incarcerate him in the bag again. She held him up like a baby, cradling him against her chest. He licked her chin and she smiled.

Tom looked at his watch. 'I'd better call Lucy. She'll be wondering where we've got to.'

He walked towards the glinting metal struts of a telegraph pole. Sweat was beginning to run down his spine. At a distance where he wouldn't be disturbed he took out his phone and called up the house number. It rang for a while. As he was about to hang up, a man's voice answered. '*Dígame.*' He sounded out of breath.

Antonio. He was the one person Tom would rather not talk to. He always felt uncomfortable in his company, never quite certain what his relationship to Hope really was. All he knew was that his mother had always been an incorrigible flirt, enjoying the company of men. Tom wasn't a prude – not by a long chalk. Of course not. But the thought of a man not much older than himself in bed with his mother . . . well, frankly, it was all wrong. Not that he knew it had come to that, but Antonio was around so often and they got on like nobody's business. Antonio was the one who had held the fort ever since Hope had decided to go to the UK to die with her children round her. They couldn't all have abandoned work to be with her at Casa de Sueños, so they should all be grateful that he kept the place going as well as managing the hotel he looked after on the coast. Even so . . .

'Antonio. It's Tom.'

'Ah. You wanna speak to Lucy? I'll get her.'

Tom heard footsteps clicking on the floor, then a shout. At the same time, he heard Belle's voice loud and clear: 'You won't forget – about the ring, will you.' He raised a hand as if she was stopping him hearing someone speak.

Then Lucy came on the line. 'Tom? Where are you?'

'Nearly there. We've stopped because things were getting a bit heated in the car – you know.' He wiped his forehead. 'Mark you, it's bloody hot out of it.'

She laughed. 'Those boys?'

'Partly. But not helped by Jo.'

'Jo? I thought they were coming separately. Didn't their plane get in after yours?'

'Yes, but she's stuck at the airport. They've lost her case.'

'Oh, no. Poor her. But lunch is cold, so it doesn't matter.' She understood Tom would want his on time.

He hesitated. Perhaps it was better to tell her now. Then she could get used to the news while they finished their drive. 'Just one thing.'

'Yes, what?'

He turned to look at Belle. The boys were standing side by side raising small clouds of grey dust as they scuffed the stones at their feet.

'The ashes were in it.'

There was a silence. Then, 'You mean...'

'Yes, Mum's gone AWOL.'

A noise came from the other end of the phone that sounded as if Lucy had burst into tears.

'I'm sorry,' he said. 'I just thought you should know. I should have brought them myself. I didn't think for a second that she'd be so idiotic—'

Another noise interrupted him. All at once he realised that she wasn't crying. Those were great big hysterical jags of laughter. 'That's so fu-funny!' She squeezed out the words between bouts. 'We've got the family and her old friends coming on Saturday and she won't even be here.' Then suddenly she was crying.

Tom didn't think it was worth pointing out that Hope wouldn't *actually* be there anyway. He could see Belle signalling at him, tapping at her ring finger. Why couldn't she just wait? Sometimes he thought this family of women would be the end of him.

'Er, Luce, there's one more thing.'

'Yes?' He heard something that sounded like a sniff.

'That old ring of Mum's. The ruby one. Apparently she promised it to Belle. Could you look it out for her?'

That was definitely a sniff. 'She did?'

'I think so.'

'Well, OK.' She blew her nose. 'But I thought we were going to do all this together when you and Jo were here. I've got the stickers ready, like you asked. But if you think that's what Mum really wanted, I'll look it out for her.'

What a relief. Now all he had to do was convince Jo that that *was* what their mother wanted. The important thing was not to let Belle get involved in the discussion, otherwise it would only end in tears. With a small sigh, he clicked off his phone and began to walk back to the car.

3

Lucy let a tear slide down her cheek. She didn't bother to wipe it away. Over the last few weeks, she had got used to these unprompted displays of emotion that came from nowhere. By now, she just continued with whatever she was doing, tears streaming down her cheeks, as if there was nothing wrong. She sat on the low wall that surrounded the terrace, stretching out her legs, putting her phone beside her, remembering.

All her life, Hope had been in a hurry to get things done, out of the way, ticked off, and dying was no exception. As with every-thing else, once she knew it was inevitable, she was impatient for it to be over. When it was clear she only had a little time left, she had flown home to England 'to be with my children'. The three siblings had made all the necessary arrangements for her. Everyone agreed it would be best if she stayed with Lucy until the point when something else might have to be organised.

'You won't mind will you, darling?' Hope had cajoled. 'Jo's so busy with Ivy Rose. And she's got the agency. I don't know how she does it.' She shuddered. 'And Tom's house is full with Ethan and Alex. Besides, Belle's enough to make a grown woman tear her hair out. Death's one thing, but being driven mad is quite another. Besides, Art's away so much filming, I'll be company for you.'

How could she object, even if she had wanted to? And of course she didn't. She would do anything to help her mother have the death she wanted. But over the weeks that followed she listened to Art's mutterings about how Jo and Tom took advantage of her, about how she always was the one who stepped up to the plate when their mother needed help. It was true that she had lost count of the number of times she had flown out to help with the B & B in high season when Hope couldn't cope. Lucy tried to defend her brother and sister who both had busy, full-time professional lives. They couldn't be expected to drop everything at a moment's notice, whereas she, a childless, self-employed professional cook, could put a line through her diary, drop everything and help as long as Art was working. So she did.

'Bailey! Come on!'

The dog raised his head from the grass where he was lying for a second only, then gave a long groan as he stretched out all four legs.

'Bailey!' She was sterner this time, clicking her fingers. 'Come inside where it's cool. Come on. I'm going to find that ring before I forget. When they arrive it'll be chaos.'

Reluctantly, the dog got to his feet and followed her inside but got no further than the cool terracotta tiles just inside the doorway. He lay down out of the shaft of sunlight with another drawn-out groan. Lucy left him there and headed upstairs.

She had only once been into her mother's room since she'd been back home. As everywhere else in the house, things were as Hope had left them. Luisa had been in there to sweep the tiles, shake out the goatskin rugs and re-knot the mosquito net over the wide double bed, but everything else looked untouched. Glancing up, Lucy realised that even the heavy oak beams that interrupted the otherwise completely white-painted room had been dusted. Before Luisa, cobwebs would swing from them unnoticed, but Hope had at last found a stickler of a cleaner.

Lucy crossed the room to pull back the pink-sprigged cotton curtains, the curtain rings rattling in the silence. Light flooded in. A square bottle of Chanel No. 5 stood on the old dressing table next to the little glass dish that Lucy had bought years ago as a present on her mother's birthday. It had lived here ever since, receptacle for Hope's hairgrips. Several grey hairs were caught in the bristles of the old hairbrush. Lucy picked up the perfume bottle, unscrewed the lid and tipped a little of the scent on her wrists, then with a finger dabbed it on the pressure points beneath her ears. She closed her eyes. It was just as though her mother had entered the room. Her breath caught and she sat on the end of the bed, burying her toes in the goatskin rug, unable to bear the thought she would never see Hope again. A memory flashed through her mind of herself aged four or five bouncing on this same bed and leaping into her mother's waiting arms.

But the ring.

Lucy remembered her mother's hands glittering with silver, and the line of rings lined up on the windowsill of the kitchen when she was cooking. Long ago, Hope had learned to make jewellery from a Swedish silversmith who lived in Gaucín for a few years. By the time he left, she was selling her designs through shops in Ronda, Estepona and Marbella. That lasted sometime. Then suddenly she stopped silversmithing and stopped wearing her rings at the same time. There they were now, tarnished and stacked on the fingers of two wooden ring holders in the shape of hands. Strings of beads hung off the corner of the dressing table mirror. Her box of loose beads must be around somewhere: a perfect gift for Ivy. Silver bangles overlapped in a green ceramic dish. Lucy picked up the wooden incense box, its side decorated with two inlaid brass elephants, a pattern of holes in its arched lid. Inside there were a few pairs of simple earrings, but not what she was hunting for. On the bedside table, a dog-eared copy of *The Poisonwood Bible* lay abandoned. Some nail clippers. As she leafed through the novel, a piece of paper fluttered to the floor. She picked it up. Her mother's schoolgirl italic writing listed dishwasher tablets, tomatoes, onions, pork fillet and white wine.

She looked at her watch. The others would be here soon. She crossed to the mahogany chest of drawers, opening one drawer at a time, with zero results. Not surprisingly, the basket of flip-flops and espadrilles under the bed yielded nothing, but you never knew with Hope. The only place left was the wardrobe. Lucy caught sight of herself in its clouded mirror, red-eyed and harassed. A hand through the unruly curls she had inherited from her mother only made her look more unhinged than usual. Hesitant, she approached it, knowing that the moment she opened the doors a flood of memories would be released.

When they were kids, Tom had claimed that he'd found a door at the back that led into another world – 'not Narnia but just like it'. Lucy had soon found out that wasn't true. She must have been about six when she had crept in there during a game of hide-and-seek. She had pulled the door to as the sound of Jo's counting grew fainter. She reached out with a hand, searching for the secret door, feeling for a handle, pushing the wood, hoping for a hidden catch, but there was nothing there. Disappointed, she made herself a space among the shoes, curled up as small as she could, knees to chin, hardly daring to breathe. The hems of her mother's skirts brushed her head, giving off that familiar scent, making her feel safe in the dark. The empty metal hangers shivered on the rail when she moved. She had heard the other two dash into the bedroom. 'Coming, ready or not.' There was the sound of drawn curtains, of them scuffling under the bed, then the door closed and silence fell. The minutes grew longer and longer. She grew hotter and sleepier, unable to keep her eyes open. Eventually she was woken by Hope. The other two had got bored with the game almost as soon as they had started it and had wandered off to do something else, forgetting all about her. Nobody had even noticed she was missing for at least an hour. Sometimes she felt that was the story of her life.

The door creaked as she pulled it open. So many familiar clothes hung in front of her. Seeing them was like being confronted by her mother's recent history: the jacket she wore for gardening, threads snagged by her English roses; the pairs of Walter's corduroy trousers that she insisted on wearing during the winter ('Ridiculous to throw them away and, besides, they remind me of him') gathered round her waist secured by a belt or a piece of string. They were muddled up with the lighter trousers she wore in the early spring. Once the sun came out, she would change into skirts and dresses that her old hippy self refused to let go. Feeling like an intruder, Lucy started moving from one item of clothing to the next, dipping her hand into every pocket she came to. This was all wrong, as if she was somehow betraying her mother's trust, invading her privacy. But it had to be done. Belle and Tom would only moan if she didn't look. She came up with plenty of bits of old tissue, clothes pegs, corks, seed packets, seed markers, but no ring.

Below the clothes was a jumble of the smarter shoes Hope wore on special occasions – not that there were many of those – glittery sandals, the pair of staid navy courts she had worn for Ivy's autumn christening in London, leather boots for the winter. Above, was the shelf used for her few handbags. She didn't have much use for them either, usually slipping her purse into one of the large reed baskets hanging on the wall of the back porch. Refusing to give up, Lucy pulled down what she found, bringing with them a couple of shapeless wide-brimmed sun hats and the blue-and-aquamarine pillbox hat that Hope wore at Lucy's wedding to Art. So long ago.

As she felt inside a jet-beaded evening bag, she felt something hard against her knuckle. She unzipped the pocket and fished through the loose change only to find the object of her search. Such was the care Hope took of Walter's present! Surely her mother hadn't really promised this to Belle? That was so wrong.

She tried the ring on but soon realised that if she pushed it past her knuckle, she'd never get it off. Dropping it on the bed instead, the ruby shone like a bead of blood against the white bedspread. She shoved everything else back where it came from and shut the wardrobe doors, relieved not to have to look any further. Picking up the trophy she went downstairs to put the finishing touches to lunch. Belle was bound to be on some sort of weight-loss jag – Lucy couldn't remember a time when she hadn't been trying to improve her appearance in one way or another. The two boys had at least moved on from a diet that allowed nothing but sausages, chicken and chips. And Ivy – she stopped short. Ivy. Just the thought of the little girl made Lucy aware of the great aching void inside her. Not for the first time in their lives, Jo had got the one thing that Lucy had always wanted more than anything. When she married Art they had seen a future together full of children – their own family – but Fate had other plans for them.

She went into the kitchen to finish the last-minute preparations. Tom and Co. wouldn't be long. The minute hand of the kitchen clock clicked on to twenty past one. Having lunch any later than two would throw her brother out of sorts. She reached for the blue-and-white apron hanging on the back of the door. Aware she was repeating one of her mother's habitual gestures, Lucy felt the lump in her throat, the tears sting her eyes yet again. She took the diced green and red peppers, the chopped olives and chopped hard-boiled eggs from the fridge and tipped them into identical blue-and-white ceramic bowls. Slugging some olive oil from the can into the frying pan, she lit the gas and waited till the oil was hot enough for the small cubes of bread that began to sizzle on contact. She shook the pan, flicking them over and over until they were thoroughly browned. Lifting them out with a slotted spoon and resting them on some kitchen towel to make sure they were crisp, she went out to the terrace to check the table.

A pair of dark-green lizards skittered away over the top of the low white wall as she straightened a chair. She had found and washed the white tablecloth and napkins, polished the glasses and got out the round rush mats. This was a long way from Hope and Walter's heyday when no one bothered with such niceties and the bare table would be littered with plates of food, wine bottles, glasses and ashtrays filled with dog ends of untipped Celtas cigarettes or Walter's black 'cheroots'. Hope had always loved company, the louder and wilder the better.

Not even Belle could find fault with this. Lucy adjusted the muslin cover over the water jug so the coloured beads clinked against the glass. She would fill it with iced water when they all sat down to eat. Over her head the vine leaves moved in the gentle breeze.

Back in the kitchen she unpacked the slices of *chorizo, jamón Ibérica, salchichón* and *lomo* and arranged them on a platter. She gave the hunk of manchego cheese a plate of its own, cutting a chunk of quince jelly to sit beside it before taking the salad of big beefy tomatoes from the fridge, and slicing some avocado into the green salad in the olive-wood salad bowl and tossing it in garlic dressing. There. Just as she finished, the crunch of a car's tyres sounded on the drive outside.

Car doors were opened and slammed shut. Footsteps sounded through the house. 'Lucy! Where are you?'

'In here,' she called, wiping her hands on her apron. 'Coming.'

But before she could go out to greet them, Tom was standing in front of her. He swept her up into a hug. 'Hey, Sis. Cooking up a storm, I hope.'

She hugged him back – at the same time squeezing shut her eyes to stop the tears that were threatening again. When she opened them, Belle was standing behind him, Ferdie by her feet. Lucy pulled away from the comfort of her brother's arms.

'Belle. Great to see you. I like the hair.' She went to embrace her sister-in-law. Hugging her was like hugging a steel rod – not an inch of give.

Belle took a step back, cupping the bottom of her bob with her hand. 'Do you? My colourist persuaded me on the colour. I wasn't so sure at first.' She bent to scoop up Ferdie who was in danger of being trodden on.

'Yes, it's . . . well, it's different.' Lucy struggled to find the right word to describe the ginger helmet. 'And you've lost weight since last time, too.' That was always a compliment that went down well.

'I'm getting there.' Belle preened, resting her hand on the round of her stomach that she was clearly making a superhuman effort to hold in.

'Why don't you put your stuff upstairs while I get lunch on the table?' Lucy suggested. 'I suppose we should just start without Jo.'

'God knows how long she'll be.' Tom shook his head as he went out to the car. 'I should have brought Mum myself.'

'That's what I said,' Belle threw over her shoulder as she and Ferdie trotted after him without offering to help with lunch.

Resigned, Lucy took the iced water from the fridge.

Only seconds later a sharp bark came from the hall, followed by a scream and the sound of claws scuffling on the tiles. Then a crash of something hitting the floor.

'Bailey!' Tom roared. 'No!'

Lucy raced through to be confronted by two backsides, one large and one small, in the air in front of the oak chest. Belle's was on the left, her slightly too-tight pink Capri pants in imminent danger of splitting at the crucial seam. Beside her, Bailey's wagging hindquarters. Belle was on her knees, with her nose virtually on the floor. The pink lead ran from her hand and disappeared under the chest. Bailey had adopted an almost identical position: front legs outstretched on the ground, nose down, ears pricked and shaggy tail like a pennant in a gale-force wind. The rug had been swept to one side and the pewter letter plate had been knocked to the floor, scattering the unopened post. At the door stood Ethan and Alex, grins splitting both their faces, making no move to help.

'For God's sake, someone get that dog out of here!' Belle shrieked, looking up at them for a second. 'Ferdie won't come out. Come on, baby,' she coaxed, giving the pink lead a couple of tentative pulls. 'He's absolutely terrified, poor little thing.'

'Bailey probably thinks he's a rat. He'll eat him most like.' Ethan nudged Alex and they fell about laughing.

'I don't care what he thinks. Do something, someone. Ferdie, sweetie, it's OK...'

As Lucy put a firm hand on the larger dog's collar and yanked him away, Belle gave a short sharp tug and Ferdie shot out from the shadows like a cork from a bottle of cava straight into Belle's waiting arms. Bailey lunged forward, dragging Lucy with him, barking, excited.

'Shut up, Bailey!' Lucy regained her balance and jerked him backwards.

Belle was on her feet, clutching her diminutive treasure to her chest. 'I can't have that dog in the house with Ferdie,' she shrieked. 'You'll have to tie him up outside.'

'I'm not doing anything of the sort,' Lucy protested. 'This is his home. Sit!' To her surprise Bailey obeyed, although his eyes stayed glued to his potential new plaything. She took a deep breath. This was only the start of the weekend. She would not let things go wrong so soon. 'Perhaps it would be better if you all slept in the *casita* after all. Ferdie'll be safer there.'

'I thought we were all going to sleep in the main house just this last time?' Tom said. He sounded anxious, though Lucy could tell he knew what her answer was going to be.

'Not if that animal's going to be in it,' insisted Belle. 'I won't be able to sleep knowing Ferdie's not safe.'

'Oh, Belle...' Tom despaired.

'*That* animal is Mum's dog,' Lucy pointed out. 'Bailey's lived here since he was a puppy, ever since she stopped Carlos from drowning the litter. You know that. He's not going anywhere.' At the mention of his name, Bailey made a sudden bid for freedom, only to be almost throttled by the hold Lucy had on his collar.

'Bailey! Sit!' she repeated.

His tail thumped on the floor, as his attention switched to her for the briefest of moments.

'Lucy, please...' reasoned Tom. 'We said we would. For the last time.'

'No, definitely not. As long as Ferdie's here, you can't sleep in the house.' If she wasn't firm now, the weekend would be in constant uproar. Tom's sentimental streak would have to take a back seat to the accommodation of his wife's ridiculous pet. After all, nobody had asked them to bring Ferdie. Couldn't they have left him with a friend? 'It's going to be crazy enough without having dogfights thrown in every five minutes,' she reasoned. 'And what if someone got bitten? Ivy, for instance.'

Belle was already out of the door, heading towards the car. 'Let's just stay in the *casita*, Tom. It really doesn't matter where we sleep.'

The two boys trailed behind her while Tom gave Lucy a look that was far from happy. She ignored it, shut Bailey in the sitting room until the coast was clear, and went back to putting lunch on the table.

4

As Jo turned off the road into the drive, the sight of the old house brought all sorts of memories flooding back. The upper right-hand window, above the deep-red bougainvillea that turned the corner of the house above the vine-covered pergola, was dark green framed like the rest, and marked what had once been her bedroom. She knew all its secrets: the way the window jammed after a rainstorm – Tom had once put the heel of his hand through the glass trying to open it again for her; the floor-board that could be lifted to reveal the space where she hid her diary and her running-away money; the wonky book case that would only carry a certain number of books before they all fell to the floor; the marks on the door where she had tried to screw in a bolt before Hope found out and took it away. Even though Hope had long ago redecorated, covering the marks where she had stuck her posters and postcards on the walls, she hoped Lucy would have put her and Ivy in there together, in where she once belonged.

From below, the white-washed farmhouse was partially hidden by the modest olive grove that had stood there for as long as Jo remembered. Harvest time meant Walter and a couple of local farmers gathering and taking the fruit to the small, family-owned factory outside Ronda to make their own olive oil. From this angle, the white houses of Gaucín were only just visible on the ridge of the mountain above, the ruined Moorish castle standing watch over them. Jo stopped the car and turned off the engine, enjoying this moment of peace. She glanced in her rear-view mirror. Ivy was slumped in the child seat, sound asleep, sweat sticking her hair to her forehead, cheeks pink with heat, mouth only just open. Bampy was hanging from the edge of her seat. That rush of love again. Nothing could quell that.

Looking back towards the house, Jo stared up at the two-storey building bright in the sunlight, the pale-ochre pantiles on the slight angle of the roof, the two square white chimneys capped with bird guards. She could just see the front terrace, the pergola shading the table ready for lunch. To the left of the house was her mother's garden. Hope loved telling how when she announced she was going to have an English garden everyone had laughed at her. '*Un jardín Inglés! Aquí?!*' The locals' disbelieving laughter would come with much head shaking. But with careful planting and attentive gardening, she had proved it could be done. This was Hope's little piece of England. In contrast to the wild flowers that sprang up everywhere else, white roses bloomed alongside larkspur, aquilegia, hollyhocks, valerian and silvery lamb's ear. Jo couldn't remember her mother lavishing such care and attention on anything else – including her three children. She would notice every new shoot, watering and encouraging the plants throughout the summer and, in the winter, after poring over seed catalogues and planning the next year's look, would send off her orders waiting impatiently until they arrived.

'Come on,' Jo said to herself. 'Get on with it. They'll be waiting.' Except she knew they wouldn't be. Tom would never wait for anyone if it meant him being late.

She turned the key in the ignition and drove very slowly up the drive, past the meadow vivid with wild flowers and the olive grove before parking alongside Tom's silver hire car. Getting out, she paused for a moment, letting the heat of the day wash over her. She hauled her backpack from the boot of the car and dumped it by the side of the house. That could wait. Manhandling Ivy out of her seat proved more of a problem. Woken from a deep sleep, her sweaty and very cross daughter resisted every attempt to wrangle her from the car.

'Come on, sweetie. Help me a little, here. Lucy's inside and she's dying to see you. And after lunch we can have a swim.' *And if you do this for me without a fuss, life will be so much easier.*

'Don't want a swim!' Ivy's right foot caught Jo hard on the chin.

She bit back the urge to shout, knowing it would only make things worse.

As she struggled with her protesting daughter, Jo became aware of someone watching them. She looked up to see Tom standing at the corner of the house, smiling, looking as though he knew what she was thinking. She grinned back at him, glad to see him. His napkin was tucked into the open neck of his shirt. Holiday informal already. His hair was shorter than ever but, with those round specs, that sort of French philosopher look rather suited him. The bump in his nose where a tennis ball had hit him at full pelt during one of their matches had never gone away.

'Did you find her?' He took a step towards the car. 'You should have phoned.'

'I'm sorry. My bloody battery died. And then I had to get the car. With a four-year-old who didn't want to be there, it was a nightmare.' Waiting in the heat of the airport basement, willing the queue for the car rental desk to fill in their interminable forms had been hell on earth. Ivy was not the only child growing ever more fractious. And she had been one of several parents losing patience with the system.

She gave up the current struggle with Ivy, leaving her to get out in her own good time. Instead Jo walked towards her brother, aware Ivy was watching them. They kissed on both cheeks.

'You have found her, haven't you?'

She took a step back. 'Nope. 'fraid not.'

His whole body tensed, a frown creasing his forehead. 'You *are* joking?'

'They've tracked down my case and promised it will be with us by this evening,' she reassured him. 'They promised.'

'We've started lunch.' Tom didn't look reassured as he changed the subject rather than argue.

'You go back to the others. I'm just going to take Ivy in through the kitchen and give her a drink on her own. She'll be better after that.' Ivy was at that moment clambering off her seat and out of the car, screwing up her eyes against the sunshine. She stood by Jo, clinging on to her leg as she peered up at Tom, clutching Bampy and sucking her thumb.

'Hello, Ivy,' Tom gave her an avuncular smile as he squatted down. 'Did you like the plane?'

His question was met with a suspicious stare before the child buried her face in the back of Jo's thigh.

'Want some lunch?' He tried again but was this time met by a shake of the head and an even more furious bout of thumb sucking.

'We'll be there in a minute,' Jo said, her hand stroking Ivy's hot head. 'Won't we?' As she watched him turn the corner of the house, she lifted Ivy on to her hip. 'Oof! You'll be getting too big for this soon.'

In the kitchen, Lucy was crying over a half-empty bowl of gazpacho. She looked up as Jo and Ivy came in, wiping her eyes with a corner of her apron. 'I thought you'd never come.' They kissed over the top of Ivy's head. 'Hey, Ivy. Want a drink?' She blew her nose.

Ivy nodded, still stunned into uncharacteristic silence by her new surroundings, clinging even more tightly to Jo's neck. Lucy moved over to the fridge and poured her a glass of orange juice. 'This OK?'

Ivy nodded and reached for the glass as Jo put her down on a chair and straightened her top.

'Tell me you found Mum?' Lucy mouthed over Ivy's head. 'Please. I couldn't bear it if—'

'She should be here by tonight. They promised me.'

Lucy gave her a watery smile and sagged with relief. 'Thank God. Losing her now would be terrible.' She hugged her sister. 'I'm so glad you're here. It's been awful so far.'

'Already?' But Jo knew exactly what her sister meant.

'She's brought that bloody dog—'

Jo put a finger over her lips and nodded in the direction of Ivy who was watching Bailey sniffing about the floor, hoping for titbits fallen from the table. 'Walls have ears.'

'I'm not a wall!' Ivy protested before finishing her juice.

'What I meant was that she's brought the dog!' Lucy made a face. 'I've had to put them in the *casita* and ban it to their room so Bailey didn't have it for lunch. Talking of which . . .' She ladled gazpacho into two bowls and put them on a tray. 'Ivy, you'll eat this, won't you?'

The little girl nodded. She gave Lucy a stern once-over before asking: 'How old are you?'

Lucy smiled. 'How old do you think I am?'

Ivy scrutinised her again, slow and careful, then made a decision. 'Ten,' she said, with all the solemnity she could muster.

Lucy laughed and bent to kiss her on the cheek. 'I think you and me are going to get on just great this weekend. That's the nicest thing anyone's said to me so far!'

Jo took a glass from the open shelf and went to the fridge to pour them a glass of wine each. The others could wait for a moment while she heard what Lucy had to say. She pulled out the chair next to Ivy and prepared for the latest in the catalogue of Belle-related moans that had grown to an unexpected length over the years.

'I made this fantastic gazpacho. She asked me what was in it and when I mentioned the bread and oil you'd have thought she'd been stung by a hornet. "Bread!"' Lucy lowered her voice as she imitated Belle's shrill horror. '"The carbs! But don't worry, I've brought something with me." She disappeared to their room and came back with some kind of filthy food replacement muck that looked like strawberry vomit!'

'Well, *we're* here now,' said Jo, 'and we're starving, aren't we?' She looked at Ivy.

Ivy nodded again.

'Then let's put all this on a tray and join them. They'll be wondering where we are.' Lucy picked up the tray and led the way.

They walked through the hall, and out of the open French doors to the terrace. Unused to seeing the table so spruced up, Jo did a double-take. 'Oh, Lucy. You've done us proud. Those white roses are perfect.'

'Glad you think so. Antonio's been looking after the garden. The roses are beautiful this year. Mum would have been proud.'

'Jo! At last.' Belle looked up from her plate, her face half-covered by the most enormous sunglasses. 'We thought you'd be right behind us. What happened?'

'You know perfectly well,' Jo fired back. 'Hi Ethan, Alex. How are you guys?'

They both mumbled something that could have meant anything. Jo decided to give them the benefit of the doubt and helped Ivy into a chair.

Belle inclined her head. 'Mmm. Well, I did say . . .'

Ethan elbowed Alex in the ribs, then pushed his chair back. 'Think we might go for a swim,' he said.

Given an excuse, Alex jumped off his chair, obviously as keen as his brother to get away from a tableful of adults.

'Too soon after the meal, boys.' Belle shook her head so the ginger helmet swung. She pushed the right side back behind her ear.

'Mum, that's so old school,' said Alex. 'Nobody believes that any more.'

'Tom?' Belle appealed to their father but he only answered with a shrug of his shoulders as he helped himself to a slice of manchego. He ignored his wife's raised eyebrow: a silent comment on the size of the piece he had cut for himself.

Jo had a mouthful of the chilled soup that was, as she had known it would be, absolutely delicious: rich, tomatoey, garlicky and thick with bread. 'This is fabulous,' she pronounced. 'Don't you think, Ivy?'

Ivy nodded, still overwhelmed by her new surroundings. Meanwhile, the two boys sloped off to their room to change.

'I thought we might talk about what we're going to do with all the furniture this afternoon, or what's left of it,' Tom said, getting straight to the point. 'I've got an estate agent coming round on Monday morning.'

'You never told me about that,' said Lucy, her eyes refilling with tears.

'He *is* the executor of your mother's estate,' Belle pointed out.

'But we're *all* her children,' Jo restricted herself to saying.

Belle tightened her lips and turned away, stretching out her bare legs into the sun.

'I'm just trying to get on top of all this. We're only here till Tuesday, so I thought you'd want me to get on with things.' Tom rubbed a hand back and forth over the stubble on his head.

'I thought you'd talk to us first, that's all,' said Jo, at the same time helping Ivy to some meat and salad, avoiding the cucumber her daughter had suddenly decided to hate the week before.

Lucy nodded her agreement.

'Mum wanted us to sell the place so there'd be no arguments over what we should do with it,' he reminded them. 'So let's not have one now. We've only just arrived.' He pinched the skin between his thumb and forefinger.

Belle laid her hand on his, proud of her husband's diplomacy. That, or she was preventing him from helping himself to more cheese. He moved his hand away and cut himself another sliver of manchego with a splodge of quince jelly to the light accompaniment of Belle clearing her throat.

Ivy pulled at Jo's sleeve. 'Can we go swimming?' Her courage was returning.

'Later, sweet pea. I've got some important things to talk to Tom and Lucy about first. Why don't you do some drawing and then we'll swim.'

Ivy produced her finest pout. 'But you promised!'

'I could take you,' offered Belle, reaching out her hand. 'If that's all right?' She turned to Jo who nodded, guilty about the relief that coursed through her at the offer of help. But she wouldn't say no, even to Belle.

Ivy was transfixed by the sparkling diamond, the pink nails, so unlike her mother's workmanlike hands. She looked unsure.

'We could stay in the shallow end and then we could go and see my dog,' Belle coaxed her. 'You could even hold his lead. He's just the right size for you.' She held out her hands as if she was boasting about a fish she had just landed. That was the clincher. Looking at Jo for the approval that she got immediately, Ivy slid off her chair and held out her hand to Belle. 'Isn't it bloody any more?'

Belle looked puzzled. 'What ever do you mean?'

The two sisters held their breath. Jo, about to explode with laughter, kicked Lucy under the table.

'Lucy said he was a bloody dog.' Ivy's voice was crystal clear.

'Did she?' Belle glared at Lucy.

'That's not what I meant, Ivy.' Lucy started collecting up the plates. 'It was a silly joke I was having with your mum.'

Belle's mouth straightened in a narrow line of disapproval. Or was it disappointment? Jo couldn't tell.

'Ferdie's a nice dog,' Lucy went on. 'You'll love him, and he'll love you.'

Jo gave her a glance as if to say 'Don't overdo it,' before turning to Ivy. 'Let's see if we can find some armbands. You can show Belle how well you can swim now.'

*

Twenty minutes later the lunch was cleared away and Jo, Tom and Lucy sat in the sitting room together. The sounds of distant laughter carried in through the open doors. Tom took Walter's old wing-back chair, still in its same place by the fireplace, while Lucy and Jo sat on the faded red sofa, dislodging the cream mantilla embroidered with large red flowers that hung over its back. Soot marks from years of winter fires stained the chimney breast.

Jo leaned back, enjoying being back home, despite the circumstances. In here, they were surrounded by Walter's paintings, abstract landscapes characterised by his bold use of colour and confident brushstrokes that she had always loved and admired. This was what he painted before he started churning out local scenes for the tourists, when the money started running out. In the bookshelf were rows of well-read paperbacks that she recognised only too well.

A pair of swallows swooped in and out of the wide French windows that led on to the terrace, unperturbed by the human visitors as they visited their nest that was tucked under one of the beams. Hope would never chase them away, believing their annual visit was a lucky omen. Lucy had been exactly the same, and Jo had understood why when one year she saw a row of plump little heads peering out at them, waiting for a parent bird with food.

'What if they don't find your case?' Lucy finally dared say what everyone else was thinking.

'They will. They promised. They put it on a flight to Barcelona instead – all they have to do is get it back here.' Jo made herself sound confident, not wanting to share her uncertainty.

'In the meantime, we might as well get on.' Tom picked up the pad of paper on the coffee table, and gave them both a pack of different coloured adhesive spots: yellow for Jo, blue for Lucy and red for himself. He tapped his Biro on the table as if bringing them to order. With a sudden insight Jo understood this military efficiency was a way of managing his grief. It gave her pause. For all of them, however differently they interpreted their pasts here, getting rid of Casa de Sueños and everything in it meant the end of so much. This was the last time they'd revisit their childhood haunts, be able to relive those memories. But this was what Hope had chosen, and she was a woman used to things being done her way.

Jo turned the packet of stickers in her hand. 'Now what?'

'We divvy everything up. Decide who gets what and get rid of the rest. Simple as that.'

She stared at her brother. This was a bit like the mind games they had played with each other when they jostled for advantage as kids, trying to be noticed first. Jo had the feeling that there was going to be nothing simple about this at all. And she suspected Tom knew that, but neither of them would be the first to admit it. 'What?' she asked. 'You mean we have to go round stickering what we want?'

'Exactly,' he replied, pleased with his plan. 'It's what a friend of ours did when his father died and he said it made everything much easier.'

'What if two of us want the same thing?'

'Then we trade.'

He made the process sound so obvious but the idea of bartering over their parents' possessions seemed too mercenary to Jo. However, she hadn't got a better idea.

'You know she's left us all presents, don't you?' Lucy produced another tissue and blew her nose.

'Presents?' Tom sounded alarmed. Presents were not part of his plan.

'Mmm. When I came out to bring her to England in January, she spent ages wrapping things up before we left. Something for each of us and something for everyone on the party list. She knew she wouldn't come back here again.'

'What sort of things?' Tom was immediately suspicious. Like

42

the other two, he knew how whimsical and self-indulgent their mother could be. 'Is that even legal? Can she do that outside probate?'

'No idea. But she has. She locked them in the chest in her room and gave the key to Antonio. He's got strict instructions not to bring it here until Saturday.'

Tom put his head in his hands. 'Oh God.'

'It might not be that bad.'

Jo and Tom exchanged a look. Knowing that Lucy always took the side of her mother in a disagreement was one thing that had often united them: the half-brother and half-sister against the doted-on baby of the family.

'She always had to be the centre of attention and she's still managing things, even from the other side. Why couldn't she just let us sort things out ourselves?' Tom spoke for both of them.

'You don't know what the presents are, do you? They might be something we really want. Sometimes she got it right.' Jo remembered years of presents that had brought both joy and disappointment. She'd never forget when Tom got the catapult they both so desperately wanted, and she got a measly girly dressing gown. She had smarted for months, even though Tom let her have a go at target practice in the woods whenever she wanted. But she had so badly wanted her own.

'If it was anyone but her, I'd agree. But you know what she was capable of. Remember the saga of the bike? That huge box?'

That was a bit of memory lane Jo hadn't been down for a long time. Inside the box had been another and inside that another. Jo's excitement diluted with every layer until she opened the final one, only to find a copy of *Alice in Wonderland*. She had put it on her shelf and never read it, in protest. Hope had been delighted with her own joke, while Jo hid her feelings and began a subtle war of attrition until she wore her mother down. 'She gave in the

43

following year though.' The bicycle had been a shiny blue second-hand boy's bike with a pennant attached to the handlebars. It was magnificent, and it was Jo's. Hope had paused in her efforts to tame her tomboy daughter for a while after that. 'Who's coming to the party anyway?' she asked. 'Have you kept a list?'

'Yes. I've got it somewhere upstairs.'

Lucy sounded as if she was about to snap so Jo went to her rescue. 'Let's do one thing at a time,' she suggested. Why don't we get this over with first and then concentrate on the party? Where do we start?'

Tom raised his head. 'How about with her jewellery? Luce – did you find the ruby ring she said Belle could have?'

'The one that Walter gave her?' Jo was astonished. 'Belle can't possibly have that. Mum always meant Lucy or me to have it. You *know* that.'

'Well, perhaps she changed her mind. Apparently she told Belle she could have it when we were last here.'

'Did you actually hear her?' Jo ignored the look Lucy was giving her: a silent plea for her to keep quiet.

Tom shook his head.

'Then I simply don't believe it.' Jo smacked the sofa arm. 'She wouldn't be so inconsiderate.'

'Jo! Belle wouldn't lie.' No one could insult his wife. 'She knows how difficult this is for all of us.'

'Then she must be mistaken. Mum would never have said that.' Jo was not going to let this go. 'Walter gave her that ring when Lucy was born. Remember how she used to flash it around? If anyone should have it, Lucy should.'

'I don't mind. Really.' Lucy said.

'Well, I do,' Jo insisted, incensed by the perceived injustice. 'It's yours by right. If you won't stand up for yourself, I will. Where is it, anyway?'

Both she and Tom turned to stare at Lucy who fumbled in

her apron pocket. 'I found it in her wardrobe but I was rushing to have lunch ready for you lot and I thought I put it in here.' She shook her head. 'I must have put it down somewhere in the kitchen.'

Tom and Jo exchanged a well-practised glance of resignation, assuming their childhood fall-back position of superior older siblings.

'Shall we just get on?' asked Tom. 'We'll settle this later, when Luce has found the wretched thing. In the meantime, there's a whole houseful of stuff. If we're going to be like this over every-thing, we'll take forever.'

'Why? What else has Belle been "promised"?' Jo was straight back on the attack.

Tom looked ruffled. 'Nothing. I just meant if we argue over everything.'

'I'm not going to argue over anything else,' said Jo, pacified. 'I don't want anything much.'

'Well, that's a relief.' Tom sat back in his chair.

'But, Jo, you must have something,' Lucy insisted. 'There's so much here that you should have.'

'I don't need any more stuff, honestly. I just want a token or two. Believe me, I've got a lifetime of memories that aren't going anywhere.' Before they had a chance to say any more, from outside came the sound of screaming. Jo leaped to her feet. 'That's Ivy!'

Belle came in from the terrace carrying the little girl whose bright-red face was streaked with tears. As soon as she saw Jo, she stretched out her arms.

Belle relinquished her. 'She's trodden on a bee and only you'll do.'

'Shh.' Jo stroked the hair from Ivy's face. 'Lucy, have we got anything?'

'Baking soda and ice cream. They're in the kitchen. I'll come with you.' She took Ivy's hand, unfolded her fingers and kissed the palm of her hand. 'Shall I tell you about the time your mum sat on a wasp? She screamed her head off and she was much older than you!'

That was the end of the afternoon's stickering.

5

Lucy was happy pottering in the kitchen again, chopping onions and peppers ready for her and Jo's supper. To her relief, Tom and Belle were taking Ethan and Alex into Gaucín so it would only be the two of them. As hard as she tried to get them to communicate, those teenage boys sucked the energy from whichever room they were in.

As soon as Lucy had told Tom she had booked supper at the Mirador for the following night's dinner, she saw Belle and Tom exchange a look. Most recently, Hope's favourite restaurant had been El Lateral but, without Hope there, Lucy had wanted to go somewhere different. Surely Belle could understand that? She stabbed at the onion under her hand. She bet they were going to check the Mirador out, make sure it was good enough. If only they would relax and trust her. The one thing she was really good at was knowing the best places to eat, and the best food to provide. After all, she'd made a career out of it. At least they'd soon be leaving for the village. But before they did, Tom was keen to make a start with his stickers. As soon as Ivy was in bed they were going to try again. 'Just one room, but then at least that's one less for tomorrow.' He flicked a finger at the packet in his hands, keen to get on.

The thought of splitting up their childhood home upset Lucy more than she had anticipated. The others seemed to be much tougher about facing up to what they had to do. Within moments of Tom and Jo's arrival at the house, she had felt herself slipping back into the role of the little sister whose opinion mattered least. She had to pull herself together.

She stopped what she was doing. A balmy evening breeze was blowing through the open window, cooling the kitchen. The house had been just as it was for as long as she could remember. Things might have been moved around and cleaned up a bit once Hope started letting rooms over the summer, but its essence had remained the same. Stickering its contents was just so wrong. Trust Belle. Tom would never have thought of that himself.

Jo came in, her hair wet from the shower. 'Phew! She's asleep at last. If anyone had told me how hard it was having a child, I wouldn't—'

Lucy's longing for her not to go on must have been written all over her face.

'Oh Luce, I'm sorry.' Jo came into the room and put her arm round Lucy's shoulders. For a moment neither of them spoke. Then Jo lifted her head from Lucy's. 'I wasn't thinking.'

'Doesn't matter.' Lucy shook her off. But of course it did. Terribly. Everyone knew that the one thing Lucy had wanted for years was a family of her own. 'Don't worry,' she said turning away, their closeness broken. 'Really. Some things just aren't meant to be. Drink?'

'Water, for now. But I'll get it.' Jo went to get one of the big plastic bottles from the floor of the larder. She poured them both a glass. 'Are you still trying?'

'Not really. There's no point. We've done everything, as you know. Even IVF. Months of feeling rough for nothing. And let's face it, I'm getting on a bit now. Art won't talk about it any more. In fact, we hardly talk at all.' She swiped the onions into the frying pan, determined that she was not going to cry again. 'I shouldn't have said that. It's just one of those bad patches. Forget it.'

'How can I?' Jo looked at her with concern. 'Is that why he isn't here?'

'He's coming tomorrow. He's been tied up on set in Bristol,

but they've arranged things so he can have a twenty-four-hour pass for Friday and the weekend.'

Jo took the wooden spoon from her and stirred the onions. 'That's good, isn't it? I haven't watched for ages, but have they recast him or something? I didn't realise he was so important.'

'No, he's still Steve the charge nurse but they're filming some crucial episode where the hospital's bombed.' Art had explained to her in some detail but it had gone in one ear and out the other as she had carried on planning the menu for what had turned out to be the last private dinner she had catered for. He had struggled with his acting career for years, doing bits of teaching and gardening on the side. Then he had got his break in *Emergency*, one of the nation's top soaps. The day he got the part, they had been over the moon but that was over four years ago now. Four years of weeks that Art spent working in Bristol while she held the fort at home outside Cambridge, getting her catering business off the ground as she started to build a list of regular clients. After years of working in restaurants or for other private chefs, she had finally decided to go it alone. And that was a problem. Having such separate lives led to their increasing independence from one another and decreasing interest in what the other got up to.

'It must be hard if he's only at home one or two days a week.'

'Which? Our relationship or the no baby situation?' As she asked, Lucy felt the familiar tug at her heart. To be denied the family she had wanted so badly when her sister got pregnant by accident seemed so unfair. Especially when Jo had always said she didn't want children; that her work kept her busy enough.

'Either. Both?' Jo pulled out a chair and sat down.

'To begin with everything was great. Whenever we got the chance, we were at it like rabbits! But I never got pregnant, then he got the job, and now . . . well, let's just say the fire's pretty much gone out.' She flicked off the gas under the pan.

'Maybe having time together here will help.'

Jo didn't really believe that any more than she did.

'I think we need more than a couple of days,' Lucy said. Whatever they could achieve in that time would be like sticking a plaster over a gaping wound. 'I suppose this was all a bit inevitable and it's difficult for us to accept. We'll have to make the best of it.'

'Oh, Luce. I'm sorry. What will you do?'

'Don't be sorry. I'll be fine. Art's not going to leave the show. Too much to lose. And I've let my business go over the last few months with Mum so I'm thinking of starting something new. I like the idea of setting up my own B & B and offering cookery lessons – that'll keep me busy.' As she said it, she wondered whether she really would. Making plans was one way of displacing her hurt, her intense sense of failure at not being able to conceive, just as helping and then looking after their mother had been. But plans were one thing, action was another.

'Right! You two ready?' Tom yelled from the hall. 'Is there anything either of you want from the kitchen? If not, let's start in here.'

Lucy and Jo looked at each other and burst out laughing. Suddenly the atmosphere changed – there they were, two sisters united again for a brief but powerful moment.

'Here we go. Better keep the old boy happy.'

Lucy gazed at the well-used pots and pans hanging over the hob, at the collection of 'useful' baskets on the fridge, at the piles of bright ceramic plates and cups on the dresser and shelves. 'Let's do in here later. There's stuff that definitely might be useful for me. Let's do what Tom wants for now.'

They found him in the sitting room examining a painting. 'I've always liked this one. All that grey and the blue and green underneath remind me of a storm brewing. Belle rather likes it, too,' Tom mused.

'But I don't want to get in the way of anything.' Belle looked down at her lap where Ferdie was snoozing, evidently having recovered from his traumatic start to the stay. 'I mean . . . If neither of you want it, then the colours go perfectly with our dining room.' Belle never knew when to stop. 'We could give it a good home.'

'I bet you could,' muttered Jo so low that only Lucy could hear. Imagining Walter's noisy outrage at hearing his paintings being judged by whether or not they fitted in with someone's colour scheme only made Lucy smile.

She couldn't look at any of them. Instead she walked across to the table by the window and picked up a blue-and-white ceramic jar with a full-bellied body that tapered to a narrower base. On its top sat a domed lid.

'I thought we might put her ashes in this.'

'If we had them.' Tom murmured. He had insisted that he be the one to phone the airline to check the case had been found. He hadn't bothered to hide his lack of faith in Jo, or his angry frustration when he heard the case had yet to arrive in Malaga.

'Jo gave it to Mum one birthday and she loved it.' Lucy carried on. 'It's lived here ever since. Remember when we all went to Morocco? Our last family holiday away together. Didn't you get it then?'

'I did, and then I had to carry it back without breaking it.' Jo crossed the room to join her. 'We stayed in that riad with the pool in the courtyard and candles all around at night. Do you remember we swam there in the dark? So beautiful. And the party that year was the time they all went skinny dipping? I must have been about nineteen. All those ancient wrinkly bodies! I was used to Mum and Dad but all the rest – and all at once!' She laughed. 'Back then I thought they were horrendous, so embarrassing. Now I just think, good for them. Oh my God, look at this. I'd forgotten it was here.' She picked up a framed photo from the table. 'Mum and Walter.'

Lucy gazed over her shoulder, feeling another tear slide down her face. Captured in the olive grove about twenty years earlier,

Walter was squinting into the sun. The sarong he always wore for painting and his dark tanned chest were daubed with paint. He had pulled his greying hair back into a ponytail. A paintbrush was tucked behind his ear. An untipped cigarette in his hand sent a trail of smoke drifting upwards. This was the quirky, demanding but loving father she wanted to remember. Beside him, their much younger, tanned mother stood with an arm around him. She looked as good then as she had at any time earlier in her life. She wore a bikini top, a long floaty skirt, and her sun-bleached shoulder-length hair was pulled back off her face that was shaded by the brim of her floppy straw hat. Her face was turned, slightly tipped, towards his, her smile caught for eternity. 'They did love each other, you know.'

'In their own way,' added Jo. 'If you don't count those rows they used to have. Remember that time she hit the bottom of the tray of drinks he was carrying and the whole lot went flying?' She laughed. 'That must be why I've stayed single. If they taught me anything it was that commitment is way too difficult.'

Belle cleared her throat.

'Any decent relationship has its ups and downs,' said Lucy. 'You need the bad times to make you appreciate the good.' She felt Jo's eyes on her. 'It's true. And anyway, they always made up.'

'That was all part of it, I guess,' said Jo. 'Though I didn't see it at the time.'

'Don't let's forget he was a great father to us,' Tom pointed out. 'Given he wasn't yours or mine.'

'Whenever we asked her who was, she'd just go, "Oh darling, that was sooo long ago."' Jo imitated their mother's airy way of answering any awkward questions. '"How do you expect me to remember?"'

'You did love him though, didn't you?' As she asked, Lucy realised she wanted to be the only one who truly loved him: he was hers, not theirs and that knowledge was impressed into her psyche. It gave her importance and meaning.

'Of course we did,' said Jo, putting the photo down. 'He gave me my first easel. I'd never have gone to art school if it weren't for that. I loved the hours I spent in the corner of his studio...' She paused, a far-off look in her eye.

Lucy stared at her. Jo had it wrong. The small easel in there was hers. She had been the one allowed to paint in the corner of the studio surrounded by her father's chaos: canvases were stacked against the wall, screwed-up paper, empty tubes of paint, boards used for mixing colours littered the floor. The room smelled of turpentine, linseed and oil paint mixed with the smell of cigarette smoke. And in the centre of the room was the larger easel and usually Walter, cogitating, stepping back to consider his work in progress, tutting with frustration as he worked to get a detail, a shade of colour just right... Then he'd come over and see what she was doing, show her how to improve a line, change perspective, try a different colour. She'd bask in his attention.

'Can we get on with this?' Tom broke into their thoughts.

Belle looked at her watch. 'We've only got half an hour.'

'So,' Tom encouraged the other two. 'Is there anything either of you specially want in here? What about the piano?'

Jo went over, lifted the lid to the keyboard and played a couple of notes. The battered old upright hadn't been used for a family singalong for years. There had been a time when no party was complete without Hope playing along with Walter on guitar and everyone else joining in the old favourites. 'I wish I had room,' she said, plinking another couple of notes. 'But anyway, I can't imagine it anywhere else but here.'

'Neither can I,' said Lucy, at the same time watching Belle's eyes travel towards the desk where Hope could be found on a winter evening writing letters or angrily paying the bills at the last possible moment. Belle gave an almost imperceptible nod towards Tom.

'I'd like the desk,' said Lucy before she even had time to think. 'And everything in it.' With some satisfaction, she saw Belle purse her lips and slightly narrow her eyes as she was outflanked. At the same time, Jo glanced at Lucy in surprise and she felt herself crumple. 'I'm sorry,' she said, as tears ran down her cheeks. 'I can't help it.'

Two hours later, Lucy and Jo were settled on the terrace under the huge cream parasol, glasses of white wine in hand, a bowl of pistachios on the table. It was cooler now. The sun had dropped below the horizon leaving the silhouettes of the hills outlined against an orange glow as the sky gradually darkened. The scent of lavender drifted in the night air. Around them swifts dipped and soared, punctuating the air with their screeches.

'I didn't want the bloody desk at all,' Lucy admitted. 'But I can't bear the idea of Belle picking and choosing. She's such an effing mercenary.'

'Complete with her new helmet!'

They both laughed.

'At least it's only her. This is just the calm before the storm. Wait till the others start arriving tomorrow, we'll wish it was today all over again.'

'I know we will. And however difficult she may be, she does make Tom happy – strange as that might seem to us.' Lucy stretched out her legs and rested her heels on the low wall.

'Strange indeed. But at least we've finished one room. To-morrow, I'm going to suggest we do it on our own. I know how hard this is for you.'

'It's not the division of spoils, it's more what it represents. It feels so final. It's the end of Mum and Walter. It's the end of our childhood. It's the end of everything I had here after you both left for your sixth form and uni—' She was interrupted by the phone.

'I'll go.' Jo got up to go inside. 'Let's hope it's the airline. Tom's going to have a coronary if Mum doesn't get here soon.'

Lucy leaned back in her chair, hands clasped behind her head. Bailey gave a series of high-pitched yelps as he shifted his position on the ground beside her. His legs trembled as he chased rabbits in his sleep. Or Ferdie. Lucy rested her hand on his side. He raised his head then laid it down again, stilled. The cicadas shrilled around them. On evenings like this there was nowhere else she would rather be in the world. Without either of her parents there, the place had assumed a kind of peace it hadn't known for years. Together they had entertained, partied, argued, made up. Alone, Hope entertained, partied, argued, made up. All that was over now bar the last birthday party of all.

She was interrupted by Jo's return. 'That was Adam. They're arriving tomorrow, but won't see us till the evening. I told them we'd meet them at the Mirador between eight thirty and nine. OK?'

'Yes. He knows the drill after all these years.' Lucy picked up a pistachio and forced open the shell with her thumbnail. Every year for as long as she could count, their cousin and his family had come for the weekend to celebrate Hope's birthday, spinning the time into their annual holiday. Every Friday night, they all had dinner at a local restaurant. That was the prelude to the Saturday party: the party always so carefully planned by Hope. And this weekend was no exception.

'I'm not going to sit next to him, even if the only other choice is between Ethan and Alex. Last year I was catatonic with boredom.'

'Well, don't look at me. I'm just as allergic. How come the other side of Dad's family is so dreary and conventional? I'm sure I've heard everything Adam's got to say on the subject of reinsurance.'

'Look at Tom. You can't get much more conventional than him. I guess it just depends on how you react to the way you're brought up.'

'I suppose. But a gene or two must be thrown in for good measure, surely.' Lucy could almost hear her parents and friends sitting around the table on the terrace. Voices raised in debate. Loud laughter. The clink of bottles against glasses. The smell of simple peasant cooking coming from the kitchen. Their mother, always at the centre of things, loving the company, welcoming any waifs and strays – 'The more the merrier,' was her counter to any objection. 'Actually I wanted to ask you something while Tom and Belle are out.'

'Ask away.' Jo sipped her wine and stared at the sky.

'Mum's room.' She immediately had Jo's attention. Hope's room was in the same small building as Walter's studio. Hope had once argued that if Walter was having his own space then she should have hers too, so they converted what was once one of the original farm's outbuildings into a room each. Way back, she used hers for meditation – or so she claimed – and then it became her retreat whenever she had had enough of whatever was going on at the house. In any event, the room was strictly off limits to anyone else, even Luisa the cleaner. 'I can't go in there by myself. It would feel all wrong.'

'Has Tom said anything?'

'No.'

'Have you ever been in there? I never dared.'

Lucy was surprised to hear that. Jo was the boldest of the three of them and definitely the one most likely to have snuck in there without Hope's permission. 'No, never,' she said. 'I've tried to look through the windows, but the curtains were always drawn.'

'Actually, I could never find the key or I might have,' Jo admitted. 'Have you got it?'

'I know where it is.'

'Shall we?' Jo poured them both another glass of wine.

Lucy hesitated. They would have to go in there at some stage. But was now the right moment?

'Come on.' Jo got to her feet. 'We won't have time tomorrow and anyway, Belle will be stalking us. Imagine what Walter would have said if he'd heard her talk about his painting as a design accessory?' She laughed. 'We should do this together. Mum would have wanted us to.'

6

There was something about breaking into Hope's private sanctuary that made Jo feel like a naughty child all over again. As she turned the key in the door, she half-expected Hope to be barring the doorway, arms outstretched, hands on the frame. 'You know you can't come in here, girls. This is my private place. Nobody comes in but me.' Jo's heart was slamming against her ribs as the door swung open on to darkness. She was aware of Lucy standing close behind her, heard her taking a nervous sip of her wine, as she reached inside, trying to find a light switch, patting up and down the wall, feeling the roughcast plaster under her palm. Shadowy objects materialised as their eyes got used to the darkness.

The sudden electric light dazzled them for a moment. Then Lucy gasped. Instead of the disorder that had attended so much of their mother's life, here was a tidy, organised space. A Moroccan brass lampshade sent geometric patterns of light and shade across the ceiling. Along the left wall was a sofa covered with a rust-coloured woollen throw and cushions galore. In front of it a sea grass mat covered most of the tiled floor, while on the wall behind hung a faded Indian batik of water lilies. A floor lamp was tilted in the right position for reading. She went over and switched it on. An empty white mug sat on the nearby mosaic coffee table: shiny rich red octagons were surrounded by a band of emerald rectangles and diamonds. Beside the mug lay an uncapped pen – a Sheaffer – and an open paperback novel, face down.

It was as if Hope had stepped out only a moment or two earlier. Jo felt a pinch of sadness knowing that her mother would never find out how her book ended.

A long mirror hung beside the glass doors at the back of the room. On the other side was a faded wicker chair, its floral cushion bleached by the sun. Opposite the sofa, on the other side of the room, was a low, wide bookcase. Three thick white candle stubs sat on its top, their wax melted over it. But the picture that hung above them was what held Jo and Lucy's attention. An ornately framed portrait of a young woman dominated the room. She lay back, naked, on an unmade bed, a cigarette in one hand, the other hand on her breast, touching her nipple. Beside her a table held a bottle of wine, a glass, an ashtray, a book. She was half smiling, the tip of her tongue visible against her lower lip. Her head was inclined to one side so her curls tumbled over her lower shoulder. But it was her eyes that were the focus of the portrait: eyes that gazed out at the viewer, teasing, inviting, seductive.

'Wow!' Jo was the first to speak. 'I don't know what I was expecting but it wasn't this.'

Lucy crossed the room to stand in front of the painting. 'This is fabulous! It really catches a moment. She's beautiful. I wonder who she is.'

'Isn't it her?' Jo smacked a mosquito then scratched her arm as she joined Lucy. 'Look at her eyes. Mum's were that same greeny-blue. It's not one of Walter's though, that's for sure.' She leaned forward to see if there was a signature anywhere. 'Nothing. Odd.'

'Well, whoever painted it obviously knew her pretty well. Shall we take it into the house? That bluey background might tone in with one of Belle's decorating schemes.'

Jo laughed. 'Perhaps we should. Do you think Tom will want it?'

'Shouldn't think so. Why? Do you?'

'I like the idea of remembering Mum like this – look how at

ease with herself she is. She looks so happy. I wonder who the painter was.'

'Did she ever tell you anything about her life before Walter?'

'Only the sketchiest details, even though I was part of it. Tom, too. I know we left England and went to Ibiza when I was a baby. But we left the island when I was four. Same age as Ivy. Tom was two by then, and of course she'd met Walter. He took us to Dorset to live near his parents, but she must have found that stifling. Then, when the family company was sold to Cadburys, the resulting money meant that Walter was given enough to support them for a while.'

'So that's when you all came here?'

'We stayed in a friend's house first, further along the coast. But then they found this place – Casa de Sueños – Mum's House of Dreams – where you were born and everything was going to turn out for the best.'

'And it did.'

Yes,' said Jo, once again looking up at the young woman her mother once was, full of hopes and dreams for her future. 'I guess so.'

'Art encouraged me to worm more out of her when she was staying,' said Lucy. 'He said it was our last chance. He thought I should record her for posterity but I knew she'd freak out at the idea. Anyway, she was too weak by then.' Lucy flopped on to the sofa. 'I did try to talk to her but I never got anywhere. It was as though she'd drawn a line through her past and didn't want to remember anything about life before Walter. What do you think can have happened?'

'I haven't a clue. Wish I had. I've wondered for so long. But she couldn't get rid of Tom and me, of course – just everything else for whatever reason. I don't think she realised how unfair that was on us.'

'What was unfair?' Tom came through the door. 'I saw the

light on and came over. Well!' He paused, taking a look around. 'Not what I was expecting.'

'Mum's silence about who we are. You and me. Our fathers. Now she's dead, we'll never know who they were.'

'But she thought Walter was enough. And he would do anything for her, including taking us on. He even moved from England because she couldn't settle. He wanted her to be happy. Us too. And look at us – we've survived. That's enough for me.' Tom patted Jo's shoulder. 'And it should be for you too, after so long. Let it go.'

He had no idea of what was going on in her head, of how much she wanted to know who she was. Was that too much to ask?

Tom's hand dropped as he stared at the painting. 'God! Is that her?'

'Yep.' Jo caught his fingers and squeezed. 'We thought you might like to give her houseroom.'

'I'm not sure what Belle would say.' He gave a little laugh. 'My mother, naked in our living room...?' He let the thought sit there for a moment. 'Er, I don't think so.'

They smiled at one another, imagining Belle's embarrassment.

'I thought more the dining room,' said Lucy. 'I can just see you all eating under her nose.'

'Don't!' said Tom. 'It's not her nose I'm worried about.'

'Well, if neither of you want it, I'll take it,' said Jo, whipping the packet of stickers from her pocket and placing a yellow dot on the frame. 'There. At least one of us will have her.' They stood together, gazing up at the woman their mother once was, lost in their private thoughts.

'Why couldn't you tell us, Mum?' Jo broke the silence as she addressed the picture.

Tom sighed beside her. 'Perhaps she was shielding us from something?'

'Or protecting herself?' Abandoning speculation, Jo got up and went over to the glass doors. 'Shall we look at the terrace? See if there's anything out there.'

Lucy moved the chair as Jo turned the key, then pulled the doors open until she could release the catches on the louvred shutters. Outside was a small private terrace, east-facing and divided from Walter's by split-pine fencing. Jo could imagine Hope sitting out here under the vast canopy of the sky, star-gazing, alone with her thoughts. Above them, the sky was a dark velvet cushion, pinned with stars. As she gazed up at them, one shot towards the horizon leaving a brief bright trail. Without thinking, she hummed a bit of 'Catch a Falling Star', one of the songs Hope used to sing with them when they were little.

Lucy heard her and joined in. '*Save it for a rainy day.*'

A bat dived low over their heads, then up and away into the night sky.

'Anyone for tea?'

The peace was broken. Belle's footsteps sounded on the court-yard stones on the other side of the room. 'Are you in here?'

Without a word, the three siblings went back inside.

Jo lingered in her mother's room while the other two went through to the yard to head off Belle. Funny that instinct made them all want to preserve the privacy of their mother's sanctum – at least for this first time. Their intrusion was one thing but even Tom understood the need to keep it to themselves for the moment.

'What have you found?' As she listened, Jo could picture Belle's nose twitching with interest.

'Nothing much,' came Tom's voice. 'Mum must have cleaned the place out before she left for England.'

'Oh well.' Belle lost interest straight away. 'Lucy, I want to talk to you about the Mirador. Are you sure it's going be big enough?'

'The upstairs outside terrace takes twenty people comfortably. It'll be fine.' Jo heard the control Lucy was exerting.

'And if it rains?' Belle insisted.

'It won't. The forecast's good until Sunday. And if it's cold,' Lucy pre-empted the next criticism. 'There'll be blankets to be on the safe side.'

'Some of us might rather sit indoors. Tom?' Belle had clearly decided the arrangements weren't going to suit everyone and had no intention of resting until they did.

'That's completely fine too,' Lucy cut in. 'Anyone who prefers to sit inside can. That's not a problem. It's meant to be a very relaxed family affair – the usual thing. I don't think any of us mind who sits where. So if you two want to sit inside, do. Although of course it would be much nicer if we were all together.'

Touché! Hats off to Lucy for handling Belle just right.

'But I—'

'Didn't you say something about tea?' Tom asked. 'Shall we go in?' Their footsteps disappeared in the direction of the house.

How Tom had changed. As a teenager he'd had a short fuse: a boy who flipped whenever something went wrong. But marrying Belle had changed him. The long practice and compromise of marriage, Jo supposed. Something she had no intention of discovering for herself now. Or perhaps he had recognised something in Belle that responded to a need that had always been inside him. Other people's relationships were so often a mystery.

Lucy turned back to her. 'Aren't you coming?'

'That was neatly done!' They high-fived. 'But I think I'll stay for a minute and lock up. I won't be long.'

Lucy raised an eyebrow. For a moment, she looked as if she was about to say something, then thought better of it. 'See you in a minute then.'

Alone at last. Jo was drawn back into Hope's room. She left the doors to the terrace open, switched off the main light and sat on the sofa. A moth fluttered round the lamp, battering its wings against the shade. She stared at the portrait, angling the light so she was left in the dark and it shone on the young Hope. The eyes of the woman in the portrait fixed on her.

'Why did everything have to be such a mystery?' Jo asked, her voice loud in the empty room. 'Why was it so hard to tell us what we wanted to know?' She went over to look closely at her mother's mercurial young face as if she might learn something from it.

'Oh, how I hate you sometimes!' she said suddenly, spitting out the words into the empty room. And then, feeling guilty, she immediately retracted them. 'No, I don't. Of course I don't. I'm sorry. I just wish you could have talked to us before it was too late.'

After a few moments of silent contemplation, Jo went and knelt by the bookcase. Unlike the shelves in the house where books were stuffed in at random, some lying horizontal on top of the rest, these were neatly shelved in subject order. She ran her eyes along the rows. They were mostly self-help paperbacks: books that would put Hope in touch with her inner self, improve her mind, improve her body. Some of them must have been read and referred to time and again, their spines broken, their corners curling.

'Does any of this stuff really help? Did it help you?' She pulled out a paperback and flicked through. '*The Untethered Soul*,' she read aloud and shook her head before returning it to its place. 'I don't believe you really bought into all this.'

The eyes in the portrait were fixed on her.

Taking out a small hardback, she turned it in her hands. '*The Prophet*,' she read aloud. On the first page was an inscription. '*Besos, R.*' R? Stuck between the endpapers was a photograph, the back spotted brown with age. She stared at the faded brown image of a young woman in a loose dress, walking on a beach, windblown, holding a toddler by the hand. The child was a dead ringer for Ivy. The woman was laughing at the photographer, saying something, her hand waving toward them. Jo took the picture over to the light where she could see it better. The woman was Hope – those curls and her eyes gave her away and the girl could only be her, Jo. They must have been somewhere in Ibiza, but she didn't know where. For a second she imagined dark seaweed smothering a long empty beach, a one-storey white cottage, a big blue washing-up bowl on a wall, dust. Then the memory, if that was what it was, disintegrated.

As far as Jo knew, Hope hadn't kept any photos from those days. If she had, she had kept them hidden. 'I thought I could remember everything I needed to,' she would say. 'How wrong I was.'

Jo had always been envious of her friends whose parents, often to their child's embarrassment, could produce albums of photos that catalogued every stage of their development. These landmarks and pointers all helped make up their memories: the sort of memories that were unavailable to her.

'Well, I'm keeping this one,' she said aloud and put it next to one of the candles. Perhaps there were more hidden between the pages of other books. She took out one after another, shaking out the pages. After she had been through two of the three rows, she had only found a pressed buttercup and what looked like forget-me-nots tied with a piece of blue ribbon – but no more photos.

'Jo!' Lucy's voice travelled across the courtyard. 'Your tea's getting cold.'

She would continue her search in the morning. But for what? And would she recognise it even if she found it? And how much did any of it really matter now? Perhaps Tom was right to accept things as they were. What good did raking up the past do?

She closed the terrace shutters and doors. As she locked the door behind her, she looked at the photo again under the yard light.

'What's that?' Lucy had come out to get her.

Jo passed it to her. 'Mum and me, I think.'

Lucy took it and peered at it under the outdoor light. 'That's so sweet.' She took Jo by the wrist. 'Belle's making tea and talking about going to bed. But I fancy sitting out for a bit longer with another drink. You?'

'Good plan.' This might be the last opportunity to have the terrace to themselves for the next couple of days. 'Let's make the most of it.'

FRIDAY

7

'I'm not coming to Ronda.' They were both in their bathroom, getting ready to start the day so Tom had to shout to make himself heard over the shower.

'Don't be such a misery.' Belle put her shower-capped head round the glass divide. 'We won't be there for long.'

'I'm not being a misery. I've just got other things to do. And Ethan really doesn't need new trousers. So *you* don't need to go.' But once Belle got an idea into her head it was hard to budge it. That was one of his wife's more testing traits. He leaned forward to examine himself in the mirror. Not too bad, he supposed: slim enough, but the matching luggage beneath his eyes didn't do him any favours. Nor did the deep vertical creases between his eyebrows or the lines bracketing his mouth. Shame about the lack of hair. What else did age have in store for him? On the rare times he stopped to look at himself like this, he occasionally wondered if there was anyone else in the world who resembled him: a father? A half-brother? But he never wondered for long. Jo had got him thinking in ways he didn't want to think any more. Aware of Belle still watching him, he retrieved his razor from his sponge bag with a sigh then squirted some shaving foam on to his hands.

'I think he should look respectable, that's all.' Assuming she'd had the last word (another of those singular traits), Belle withdrew to her shower. The bathroom filled with the smell of her shower gel. Hyacinths? Bluebells? Tom watched her pink silhouette performing her ablutions then drew the razor up from his Adam's apple and under his chin. If he didn't look like his mother he must – no, he *might* – look like his real father.

'No you don't.' He raised his voice to be heard again. 'You're just making a point because he didn't pack what you asked. The boys don't need to dress up. That's the last thing Mum would have expected. All she cared about was the turnout, not what they wore.' If Belle heard any of that, she ignored him and carried on washing her hair. He swore as he nicked his skin. A bead of blood appeared on his jaw. He heard the water being turned off, looked at his watch. Seven thirty. Time to get on.

Belle emerged, wrapped in a large stripy towel. '*I'd* like them to look their best, even if your family don't notice.'

'In that case, you'll have to get the train. I'll take you to the station and I'll come and collect you later.' How much more reasonable could he be?

'Do you think Jo and Lucy might need my help to get the place ready for the party?'

He tried to translate the question. Was she saying she wanted them to need her or was she dying to get away for the day? Tom rinsed off the last of the shaving foam as he decided how to answer. He'd love her to get on better with his sisters, but even he had to admit that she got it wrong with them more often than she got it right. No wonder they tended to give her short shrift. She probably wanted the answer to be yes but he knew exactly what his sisters would say if asked. 'No,' he said, patting his face dry. 'I don't think you need to worry. It's not as if we haven't done this before.'

'I know, but it's the last time, so it's important to get it right. We don't want to run out of paella like we did last year. I wonder if Lucy's ordered enough soft drinks?'

'I think it's best to leave that to her.' Tom wondered whether it was too late to train for the diplomatic service. Negotiating his way between his wife and his sisters when they were all together was like walking a tightrope, his heart in mouth most of the time. One wrong step and it could all go pear-shaped. But he was practised at it.

'I just thought that it might be too much for her. She's so upset.' Belle kissed him on the back of the neck as she went past him into the bedroom.

'She'll be fine. Cooking's how she copes.' Even he understood that about his younger sister. Neither Lucy nor Jo seemed to think he got what made them tick, but he was used to paddling in the undercurrents that swirled around this family. He knew more of what was going on than they imagined. He listened to Belle murmuring to Ferdie, rolling up her exercise mat, heard the blast of air from the hair drier. He brushed his teeth, ran a hand over his head, the stubble surprising him yet again, and left the bit of tissue he had used to staunch the blood stuck where it was. He checked his watch again. Time for breakfast.

In the bedroom, he dressed quickly. So easy out here. Shorts, shirt, sandals. Boom. 'Boiled egg?' he shouted over the noise of the hair drier. But Belle was concentrating on her hair. He took her silence as a yes. Taking the sponge bag that doubled as their medicine bag, he headed out to the house. The boys would stay asleep until they were woken. He would leave that pleasure to Belle. If she was so keen to take Ethan to buy an unnecessary pair of trousers, she could suffer their son's brooding silence for the rest of the day. Tom would rather not have words with his children unless it was absolutely essential. There seemed to be so many opportunities these days, why force it?

In the kitchen, Lucy was already making a big jug of coffee. Bread was sliced and waiting to be toasted. 'Morning.'

Tom found a corner on the worktop for his and Belle's armoury of vitamin pills, herbal supplements, Wellwoman supplements, cod-liver oil and the all-important glucosamine supplement to ward against joint stiffness. Lucy said nothing, just gave one of those looks. He knew the family laughed behind their backs about his and Belle's health fads. 'If you've got a decent diet, you don't need any of that stuff.' He could hear Hope saying it now. Who knew who was right? He took his choice of pills and put them in an eggcup. He'd rather not risk it.

He was putting on the water for the eggs when Jo and Ivy came in.

'We've been for a walk already.' Jo was carrying a wilting bunch of harebells and scabious. 'Show Tom what you found, Ivy.'

Ivy held out her hand. In it was the broken speckled shell of a bird's egg.

He bent down. 'I think that's a blackcap's egg,' he said. 'I used to collect—'

Before he had a chance to say any more, a car scrunched to a halt outside. The slam of a door was followed by footsteps. 'Belle!' they heard a familiar voice say. 'The other in-law. You got here before me. Where are the others?'

Tom noticed that as Lucy looked up from pouring milk into a jug, there was a momentary clenching of her jaw, the suggestion of a frown. They disappeared as quickly as they had come. He had also clocked the beady way Jo was watching their sister. Carefully? Protectively? So what was going on there that they hadn't told him? Thoughtful, he went towards the door.

'Art!' he bellowed. 'Welcome! You're just in time for breakfast. Come in.'

Art appeared in the doorway, letting Belle in front of him. He was a handsome man, some years younger than Tom. His smile revealed a mouthful of expensive, even white teeth in a tanned face. His hair fell forward in a boyish flop. His T-shirt was tight enough to reveal that he was no stranger to the gym. Tom held in his stomach for as long as he could in an automatic response. But there was nothing he could do to make his arms match the solid biceps and triceps and God knew what other muscles that were on display. Art was every inch the Hollywood star apart from the fact that he had never been near Hollywood – and probably never would go. *Emergency*, despite the occasional surge in viewing figures for a Christmas special or a multi life-threatening disaster, was not the most likely catapulting point.

'Lucy?' Art made her name sound like a question.

Lucy put down the jug, went over to him and kissed his cheek. 'You made it, then. Good.' Whatever was troubling her before had gone.

'Left Bristol at three and caught the first flight out. I said I would, didn't I?' He brushed down his T-shirt with both hands as if checking his six-pack was still in the right place. He gave a small nod of satisfaction.

'I know, but I wasn't sure whether it would really happen.' She put the coffee on the tray with the cups and saucers and headed through the hall and out to the main terrace.

Art shrugged. 'Who's rattled her cage?'

Jo stepped in before Tom had his answer ready. 'We're all a bit churned up this weekend. You can imagine. But it's especially hard for her. She spent more time here than either of us.'

Art shrugged again, his expression giving little away. He followed Lucy outside. Tom hesitated. Should they allow them a moment alone? But before he had time to answer his own question, Belle had gone ahead of him.

By the time breakfast was over, the whole family was present and correct but the atmosphere was anything but relaxed. Art and Lucy had barely exchanged a word, the boys were monosyllabic and to compensate Belle kept up an over-cheerful stream of chatter that tripped and stumbled into the gaps left by the others. To top it all, she had brought out another bowl of yellowish dietary gloop for breakfast that smelled of synthetic bananas. Lucy had just made a face when she saw it, picking the largest piece of toast for herself and loading it with butter and jam.

An angry-looking Ethan brightened marginally over a couple of pieces of toast and an over-boiled egg. Despite Tom's pointed suggestions, he refused to take off his porkpie hat. Keeping it on all day was a ridiculous affectation in Tom's eyes whatever the

73

current fashion. Beside his brother, Alex looked as if he needed another day in bed. The side of his thin pale face was still creased from where it had been pressed against the pillow, his eyes were puffy with sleep but at least he mumbled a bleary, 'Good morning'. More than his brother had managed.

Eventually Belle herded them both into the back of the car and Tom drove them to the station at El Colmenar. 'Won't take long to get the trousers then we can explore.' Belle's excitement about what they would do when they arrived in Ronda was met with a heavy silence. Ethan and Alex were as enthusiastic as a pair of ostriches with their heads in the sand. Tom almost felt sorry for her.

They waited on the green tarmacked platform until the train arrived. Once he had waved his family off, Tom crossed the village square to Mesón Las Flores where he sat outside under the awning and ordered himself a *cortado*. When it came, he took his time, stirring in the sugar that Belle would frown at, adding one more spoonful for the hell of it, then making the milky coffee last as long as he could while watching the world go by.

After half an hour to himself he was ready to go home and face the day ahead. Jo and Lucy might not like dividing up everything in the house but the job had to be done. Hope had made him executor of her will for a reason, and he was determined to prove to her that he was worthy of the responsibility. That old childhood desire to please was rearing its head again. As a child he had rarely managed it, or so he felt. Being in the beam of Hope's pleasure was like nothing else. But she was like a lighthouse: that radiant light would move away from him, leaving him in darkness till the next time. There were no half measures. Hope had never really understood his marriage to Belle or why he didn't want the disordered life of his childhood. He liked the settled – no, the *ordinary* existence he had now. Unlike his mother, he didn't like surprises. He liked to know where things were going to be when. His mother's ashes going missing had unsettled him. Of course they hadn't arrived the previous evening. He would have to phone the airline again when he got back, unless Jo had already. And then he would have to find the right moment to mention the money Hope owed him, something he should have brought up much sooner than this.

Back in the car, he drove up the road that wound like a mouse intestine out of the valley past olive groves, fields of scrubby pasture grazed by horses and mules, lush green oak forests. Above it all was the vast blue bowl of sky. He tuned into a radio station playing classical music. In the absence of his treasured DVD collection, that would have to do. With no one to ridicule him for being out of tune, he started to hum along.

The house was silent when he returned. The doors were all open, Bailey snoozing in a corner of the terrace in the shade of a chair. Someone must have just watered all the plants in pots, leaving a trail of water between them. Bees buzzed among the lavender that grew below the wall of the terrace. He walked through the house, turning off the radio in the kitchen.

Looking across the courtyard, he saw the door to Walter's studio was open. Jo looked up when he came in. 'Art's gone for a snooze. Lucy's taken Ivy to Gaucín with the promise of the playground. They're getting on like a house on fire – I'm so glad. And I'm mooching with a purpose. I thought I'd do a bit of stickering on my own but it's more difficult than I thought it would be.' She brandished her pack of stickers towards the paintings. 'What should we do with all these? It feels all wrong to throw them away.'

Tom looked at the canvases stacked against the wall. 'Are they worth anything?'

'I shouldn't think so. At least, certainly not the "tourist trash"—'

'Steady on!'

'Well, that's what Dad called them. That or "painting by numbers". Don't you remember how he'd go on and on about how he was compromising his talent by having to paint to make money once his had run out?'

Tom shook his head. 'You were the one who had all that time with him in the studio.' All he remembered was how excluded he felt when Jo and Walter were squirreled away together painting. He had never felt encouraged in the same way.

'But you never showed any interest.' Jo dismissed his complaint without a thought. 'At first you were always too busy collecting eggs or feathers or bones – remember how cross Mum was when you boiled that sheep's head in the kitchen and it stank the whole house out? – and then later you were off playing football or hanging out with Fernando and the gang.'

'Nobody ever asked me.' How petulant he sounded, even to himself.

'Oh, Tom!' Jo looked up from yet another painting of a white village. People liked the bold colours, the gaudy representations of white villages and dramatic skies that reminded them of their holidays. Walter did not. His forced compromise was the source of some of his and Hope's most blistering rows. 'You've never said anything before.'

'And now it sounds ridiculous. It's so long ago. What does it matter?'

'All the same . . . I never knew.'

Embarrassed, Tom dismissed her concern. 'Too late now. Anyway, I probably would never have been any good. You and Lucy were the artistic ones.'

They began to work through the stacks, sorting out the recognisable beauty spots and white villages.

'He must have painted more views of the Ronda viaduct than he had arguments with Mum. They're better than any photograph,' Tom put yet another on to the pile, 'however much he hated doing them.'

'Necessity,' Jo said. 'And it kept him busy. But look at this.' She held up an abstract in blues and greys with an uneven streak of deep carmine slashing through its centre. 'This is what he was really about. I love it.'

'Then take it. Use that yellow spot.' Tom picked up another smaller viaduct and made a face. 'Jo . . . ?'

'Mmm?' She was concentrating on the job in hand.

'Is Lucy OK?' As soon as he asked the question, he wondered whether he should have kept quiet.

Jo lifted her head from the paintings. 'Why? What makes you say that?'

She obviously knew something he didn't. But how much did he really want to involve himself, so he hesitated then found himself going on. 'She didn't seem pleased to see Art, and the atmosphere at breakfast . . .' He tailed off, watching his sister as she put the canvas down. He braced himself for whatever she was about to say, wishing he hadn't brought it up in the first place. He should leave his sisters' love lives to them. Observing from the sidelines was what he did best. After years of being Jo's confidante when they had left university and were kick-starting their lives in London, hearing the anguished detail of her tangled affairs that one by one ended in separation until she had met Jake, her one love, he had vowed to steer clear of further involvement. After all, his own life was hard enough to keep tabs on.

'*Holá!* Anyone here?' a woman shouted outside. Someone was walking round from the front of the house and down towards the pool.

They shook their heads at each other. Neither of them recognised the voice. But unexpected visitors were quite usual at Casa de Sueños, especially in the run-up to one of Hope's parties.

Jo smiled. 'Lucky escape. You didn't really want to know, did you?' she asked affectionately. She had always been able to tell what he was thinking.

'In here,' she called, as she went outside and turned in the direction of the pool. Then she gasped. 'Oh my God! Maria?

What are you doing here? We haven't seen you for *years*. You look amazing.'

Tom froze where he was. Maria. It couldn't be. That voice – it was richer than he remembered, less Spanish and more American. He sat back on his haunches to steady himself as his stomach turned over. Who would have thought that after all this time just hearing her name would be enough to make him react like this? But she went to America – what was she doing back here?

'I know.' She spoke again. 'Too long. I was so sad to hear about Hope.'

'Thanks,' said Jo. 'It all happened very quickly. Would you like some coffee? I was just about to make some.'

It must be more than twenty years since he last saw her. That moment when he had turned as he went through the departure gate was etched on his memory. She was standing stock still on the other side of the barrier, one hand lifted in farewell, her face a study in misery. Her long black hair was pushed off her face so her distress was there for the world to see.

He could picture her as clearly as if it were yesterday. She wore a faded green T-shirt, loose, patterned harem pants, an ankle chain, leather flip-flops. Round her neck was the silver bird on a chain that he had bought her in Seville. They had spent the previous night together, consumed by a last flare of passion that was like nothing Tom had ever known – before or since. Even now, he could conjure up how it felt: her legs wrapped around him; her back arched, pushing against him; her face thrown back as she came; the intensity of their shared pleasure as they made love for the last time. The following morning they had drifted about Casa de Sueños as if drugged with grief, waiting until it was time to leave. Hope had kept out of their way. Maria drove him to the airport, hardly saying a word. Everything that needed to be said had been said the night before. There was no more talking to be done. No more explaining. They said goodbye for the last time.

He had walked through the barrier, knowing she was watching him. It wasn't too late. He could still change his mind. He stopped. He had to see her again. Had to. He turned. In that moment he had been tempted to run back, to change the course of his life forever. But something inside him insisted leaving was the right thing. He had raised his own hand in reply, then torn himself away. A path not taken.

He had buried these memories for years. Deep and ever deeper.

He had heard that she had left Spain shortly afterwards to make a life in America where her uncle lived in Boston. He, on the other hand, had flown home to the UK and into the waiting arms of Belle and a new and very different existence. Home and Belle: the two cornerstones of his life. Maria could never have given him the peace of mind he found with Belle. She was too volatile, too dangerous, too bohemian. They had never been in touch since although, and this was the first time he had wondered, perhaps Jo had kept up with her without saying anything to him. Their affair may have been a lifetime ago, but the sudden stab of jealousy he felt was definitely part of the present.

'Tom!' Jo called from outside, breaking into his whirling thoughts. 'It's Maria. Come and say hello.'

'Won't be a moment,' he called. He had to steady himself before he could see her.

'Tom?' he heard Maria ask as if surprised. But, to his relief, she didn't come in. Instead the women moved away towards the house.

Tom paused. Was this one of Hope's 'surprises'? Had she invited Maria? He wouldn't put it past her to give a last mischievous stir to the pot. But why? He stacked another couple of white village paintings, feeling his heart beating too fast. Additional stress was not good for him. He was already worrying about having to explain Maria away to Belle. Naturally, he had never confessed to two-timing her as he dithered over his future, unable to make up his mind between the two women. Impossible to imagine of himself, but true. He was ashamed to remember how he had treated both of them but had always believed that they would never find out. And perhaps they still didn't need to. After all, Maria had once been Jo's closest friend. Maybe that was enough. Jo would never tell on him.

He found them on the terrace, sitting under the garden parasol. Jo had made coffee and found some biscuits. Maria had her back to Tom as he came through the door. The straight black hair he remembered had been cut into a longer, more relaxed version of Belle's new style. Otherwise, from behind, she looked just as she had when he had last seen her: same upright posture, same slim frame.

Hearing his footsteps, she turned and stood immediately, a broad smile spreading across her face. He stared at her, transfixed. She looked older, of course. The flash of white hair that fell from her side parting was new, as were the signs of a life lived, but the face was the same. Those full lips, high cheekbones, flashing dark eyes. What was different was the clothes. A chic sundress and heeled strappy sandals replaced the hippy gear of so long ago. A gold band circled her ring finger with the flash of a precious stone. She was sophisticated, groomed – and married. Beside her, he felt like the awkward Englishman he was. He desperately wished he wasn't wearing his shorts.

'Tom! It's been such a long time.' She came towards him, kissed him on either cheek.

Recovering himself, he returned her kisses. Her perfume was rich and exotic, an expensive version of the musky patchouli that she used to wear.

'Let me look at you.' She took a step back. 'You haven't changed.'

Standing in the sun, he could feel the sweat running down his back. He dug his sun specs out of his pocket and slipped them on.

Jo coughed. 'Oh, come on. Maria, you mustn't be too kind!'

They all laughed.

'But I thought you were in America. Married?' Tom heard his voice as if it was coming from a thousand miles away.

'I was.' She gave him that generous smile he remembered so well. 'I mean I am. But I'm visiting our daughter Christina, who's studying in Madrid. Then when I heard from Hope, I realised the timing of her party coincided with our visit to Fernando – you remember my brother? Of course you do. I wanted to show Christina where we grew up. Besides, I wanted to pay my respects. Your mother was a great woman and we always loved coming here.'

'What a nice thing to say,' said Jo. 'Of course we loved coming to yours for exactly the opposite reasons. Your mum seemed so calm, in control, whereas we never really knew where we were.'

Maria laughed. 'Do you remember that time we waited at the station in the rain for over an hour because Hope was trying to catch one of the chickens and forgot all about us?'

'That pretty much sums it up.' As Tom pulled a chair into the shade beside them, he caught his shin on the pot of geraniums. He hissed in pain but was glad the others pretended not to have noticed. Sitting down, he resisted the need to rub his leg where he was certain a bruise was already forming. He put his sandaled feet under the table where they couldn't be seen and helped himself to a biscuit: *galletas Maria*, his favourite. Lucy had remembered.

As the two women began to catch up, Tom listened with half an ear. So Hope had been intent on mischief-making from beyond the grave, despite there being nothing to achieve by bringing Maria back into their lives. It made him nervous about what else she might have stored up . . . He would ask Lucy for the list of party guests immediately she got back.

8

Tom kept flicking his wedding ring with his thumb as he talked, avoiding looking directly at Maria. His body language gave away exactly how ill at ease he was; in contrast, Maria looked quite at home. Jo was intrigued. Their tempestuous – a word impossible to associate with Tom these days – affair was over and done years ago and Belle had won the prize. Jo remembered the long nights spent with her brother in her shared London flat with him bending her ear over his dilemma: Maria or Belle? Belle or Maria? He had been torn in two for ages until he finally made his choice. Then, it was a choice she understood. Whether Jo liked her or not, even she could see that the love and stability Belle offered was what her brother needed then – and probably now. Would he make the same choice today? The thought briefly crossed her mind before she dismissed it as ridiculous. You can't escape the choices you make in your twenties. Maria had been his first true love.

Jo, on the other hand, was pleased to see her. They might have lost touch but seeing her again, the time lost had concertinaed into nothing. The day the two of them met was as clear as yesterday to her when eight-year-old Jo slid behind a desk in the back row of the class on her first day at school in Estepona. She was lost among the sea of Spanish children and, worse, felt marked out as different. Just her blonde hair was enough. Her atrocious Spanish made it worse. As she waited for the teacher to appear, all she wanted was to be transported back to her old school in Dorset and her friends in England. Especially Rosie. At the first break she had stood in a corner, not knowing what to do with herself, biting the inside of her trembling lip, determined not to cry.

Then: 'Come with me.' A small, olive-skinned girl with bright eyes and shiny black hair pulled tight into a single plait that fell down her back took her wrist and pulled her towards the lockers, showing her where to put her things. At the next break, she had kept her company, experimenting with her shaky English as Jo tested out her equally inadequate Spanish. The seeds of their friendship were sown.

What they had in common were their two English mothers. However, against Hope's scattiness, Sally was a model of organisation. Despite being married to a Spaniard, she had not embraced the Spanish concept of '*mañana*'. At Las Almendras, meals came at regular intervals, tempers rarely flared, and children were noticed and encouraged, never forgotten or ignored. Where Maria loved the benign neglect and the freedom on offer at Casa de Sueños, Jo and Tom had longed for the reassuring order of her family's lifestyle.

Jo and Maria's friendship continued through school and even after Jo was packed off back to England for the sixth form on Walter's insistence. When she returned for holidays she found that Tom and Maria's friendship was closer than ever and when his turn came for an English sixth form, that friendship began to change into something else. They often did things as a threesome until Jo realised she was no longer really wanted and was being edged out of the way. After university, she started a life for herself in London, but when it came to his turn, Tom found the transition more difficult. After only two terms at Manchester, he abandoned his degree and came home to Maria. It took some time until Walter finally persuaded him to give his education one more go, and to try again in Edinburgh. While he was there, he met Belle. Jo remembered again the months and months of anguish as he tried to make a choice between his two very different women. But all that was years ago and no longer of any importance. They had been young then.

'I heard you were married?' Jo had her eye on the showy engagement ring.

Maria inclined her head.

'Is he here?' Jo asked, hoping they would meet the man Maria had snared. After all, until she got together with Tom, the two of them had spent many an hour debating the merits of the same boys, devising the best ways to get off with them. Saying that Maria was staying with them at Casa de Sueños meant Sally never knew how they hung around the beach bars or dared each other into the darkened discos where the Euro-pop was so loud you couldn't hear yourself speak. Hope just assumed they were old enough to take care of themselves – if indeed she even noticed they were missing.

'No, he's way too busy.' Maria looked into the distance. 'He's the CEO of a molecular diagnostics company in Boston and couldn't get away.' She paused while they looked suitably puzzled and impressed. 'What about you?'

'I thought I might once, but it all fell apart. Since then I've never met the right guy.'

'And she's tried plenty of them,' chipped in Tom.

'Do you mind?!' Jo took a playful swipe at his arm and missed. 'But I do have a daughter. One of the best mistakes I ever made.'

'I'll meet her tomorrow, then.' Maria put down her coffee and picked up her bag.

'You're not going already? There's so much to catch up on.' But was there really? Her pleasure in seeing Maria was giving way to the realisation that they probably had little in common now except a bond from the past and the memories that went with that.

Maria was on her feet, bending over and kissing her goodbye. 'You both must have so much to do. We can catch up after the party. I just wanted to say hi and to make sure you were expecting me. I didn't want to turn up unannounced – or unwanted.' She looked at Tom for affirmation, but Jo answered for him.

'Of course you're wanted. And why don't you bring Christina with you? We'd love to meet her. She can hang out with Tom's boys.' Maybe she'd even brighten up their stay.

'Teenage boys?' Maria asked. There was a pause as, for the first time, she and Tom exchanged a glance that he disengaged from fast. 'How did we get here? Seems like yesterday that we were only that age ourselves.'

Tom looked down at his feet, curling his toes in his sandals.

Arm in arm, Jo walked Maria towards her car, asking about which of their once mutual friends she had kept up with, reminiscing, laughing. When she returned to the terrace, Tom was sitting where she had left him, staring towards Sierra Crestellina. The mountain was crowned with a light drift of cloud and he was frowning, lost in thought.

'I thought you'd be back at the stickering,' she said, picking up the tray to take inside.

Tom emerged from his trance. 'Did you know she was coming?'

'Who? Maria? No. But I'm quite glad she has, aren't you? It's been a long time.' She took a second look at him. 'Tom?'

'Mmm.'

You haven't still got a thing for her, have you? You can't have.'

Tom shook himself. 'Of course not! Don't be ridiculous. It's been years. Just surprised to see her, that's all.'

But seeing Maria had awoken ghosts of the past for Jo too. Tom wasn't the only one to leave his broken heart in Spain. When he and Maria had finally hooked up together, Jo lost her heart to one of the many young men who frequented the beach bars in the summer. Kristian – blond, blue-eyed, body of a God. There was never any question of her settling down with the Norwegian student who holidayed there for two summers and Easters in a row – everyone knew what was said about holiday romances – but the intensity of their relationship had been hard for both of them to let go. She had even visited him in Bergen for a weekend before they acknowledged continuing was pointless. Wasn't that what they said about first love? You never forgot.

They finished going through the studio, speeding up now the morning had almost gone. The pictures were sorted into stacks – the ones they wanted, the local views and the rest. Tom wanted nothing else but Jo couldn't resist stickering the child-sized easel that she unearthed in a corner. 'Ivy will love this. I spent hours standing at it copying whatever Walter was doing. He'd organise a table so I could line up my paints and a jam jar of water.' When she had visited the reconstruction of Francis Bacon's studio in Dublin, she had felt quite at home.

'You don't think Lucy will . . .' Tom hesitated.

'What would she use it for? Maybe it got passed on to her when I got too big for it, I don't remember, but I'm sure she'll be fine. If not, she can always object.' She wouldn't, though. Jo was sure. She picked up a metal tube and unscrewed the top. Inside was a complete set of unused sable-haired paintbrushes. This was what she had come home for. Walter would want her to have these. She peeled off a yellow dot and stuck it on the lid. 'Do you remember how he would get us to buy him new brushes and pigments from Cornellisens?' The art shop in London's Bloomsbury was a cornucopia of artists' materials. How she had loved those missions to find everything Walter had ordered. She would hover over the drawers full of pigments picking out the ones he wanted to mix his own colours. Tempted by the tubes of oil paints and acrylics, she would study the different colours, enjoying their names and what they conjured up: Alizarin Crimson; Burnt Umber; Viridian; Ultramarine. 'You're OK if I take these, aren't you? I might even start painting again, you never know.'

'Fine by me.' Despite, or perhaps because of, his upbringing, Tom didn't have an artistic bone in his body whatever he said. 'The rest of this mess can go, though. Agreed?'

'Once Lucy's had a look through, yes.'

'Let's move into the house.' He looked at his watch. 'She'll be back soon so she can have a look then. When are we expecting Antonio?'

'He's bringing Brad from the airport some time late this afternoon.'

Tom groaned at the thought of Hope's half-sibling. 'Why's he coming?' He locked the studio door behind them, and they crossed the courtyard together. 'It's not as though Hope's going to be here to welcome him.'

'Don't start! We didn't invite him to the funeral so this is his way of saying goodbye. She wanted him to be here.'

'But they barely knew each other.'

'That's not fair. You know how much trouble he took to track her down when their dad died a couple of years ago.'

'Yes, and she didn't really want to know. Remember those frantic phone calls begging us of think of diversion tactics for her? She tried everything until she had no choice but to meet him. He belonged to the part of her life she'd left behind.'

'But she must have been intrigued. Otherwise she would never have agreed to meet him. She flew over especially in the end. Anyway, he's coming so we're going to have to make the best of it. And he's staying here.' She produced the last sentence like a magician pulling a rabbit from a hat.

'Here!' Tom was appalled. 'What's wrong with the Casablanca? Why are you being so protective of him? You don't even know him.'

'Tom! He's family. He asked if he could stay and Luce and I thought it would be OK. It's only for a couple of nights.'

He grunted as he hung the key back on the rack inside the kitchen door.

Hope had coerced Jo into going with her to meet Brad for half an hour in a London hotel. The meeting was brief. Tucked into a discreet corner of a lounge, cups of tea on the table in front of them, Hope had found it impossible to relax, unwilling as she was to unwrap the past and talk about their father. She couldn't get out of there soon enough. 'That was a mistake,' she had said as they found Jo's car in the car park. 'I'm sure he's a decent man but meeting him was like opening a barrel of worms. He reminds me of too much that I'd rather not remember.'

Jo wanted her to say more, but Hope had clammed up after that. She would never have chased Brad up while Hope was alive but she had her own reasons for wanting him here now. At some point she would find an excuse to ask him the questions she'd been thinking about. She would pick his brains about Hope's parents – her grandparents – and how and why they ended up in Australia. Why hadn't Hope gone with them? If Hope wouldn't break her own silence, perhaps Jo could begin to crack it now her mother was no longer here to stop her.

Art was in the kitchen, rummaging in the larder. His swimming shorts allowed a generous glimpse of his finely honed physique. There was only one way to get pecs and a six-pack like those, and that was devotion. While Jo had to tear her eyes from his body, Tom made a point of looking anywhere but.

'Where's the coffee?' Art sounded as exhausted as he looked. 'I need a quick hit, then a swim, and I'll be right as rain.'

'Let me.' Jo did the honours while Art lounged decoratively against the worktop, and watched. Tom went upstairs. A door opened and shut and footsteps sounded above them.

'Thanks. Where's Lucy?' he asked as he took the cup of coffee from her. 'Mmm. Smells good.'

'Gone to get some last-minute bits and pieces. She's taken Ivy with her. They're getting on like a house on fire.'

He turned away from her. Their failure to have a child had clearly hurt him too.

'They shouldn't be long. One of us has got to go to Gibraltar to pick up Elaine.' Lucy's godmother was flying in from London that afternoon. She began to wash up the milk pan. 'I'm surprised so many people are making such an effort to come. Hope would be thrilled.'

'That's why, I guess. She was one of those life forces, even at the end.'

Jo was surprised. She had never heard Art talk about their mother like that before. Her surprise obviously showed.

'I hardly saw her, of course. Working in Bristol and all that...' He stopped. 'But when I did, she was still firing on all cylinders even though she was so tired most of the time. She loved my dry Martinis almost to the end!' He smiled. 'I learned the knack from an American actor on set.'

'Yes, she was pretty extraordinary at times.' Jo stopped herself from saying how infuriating she could be too. 'That's why people kept coming back to stay. Although running the B&B was a hell of a lot of work, she loved having them here. It was like a never-ending party during the summer.'

'She had Antonio to help, didn't she?'

'With Luisa and Rosa, yes. We're indebted to him, whatever Tom may think.'

Art grinned. 'Of course. Weren't they lovers? You've got to hand it to her!'

'Who knows?' This wasn't something she wanted to discuss with Art. 'I doubt it, though she certainly didn't mind anyone thinking they were. I never asked. Didn't want to get the wrong answer!' Not for the first time, she resolved to be a more ordinary mother for Ivy.

Art downed his coffee and disappeared down to the pool, trailing a towel over his shoulder, armed with his Kindle and suntan oil. Jo went upstairs. Now Tom and family were in the *casita*, she wanted to make sure the other spare bedroom in the house was ready for Brad. She needn't have worried. Lucy was a step ahead of her. If she didn't know, she would never have guessed it was once Tom's room. There wasn't a clue to give away its history. Instead the beds were newly made with white sheets, pillows piled against the blue and white striped headboards. A couple of paintings of local beauty spots adorned the walls. Above the white dressing table hung a mirror framed with shells. A posy of wild flowers was on the chest of drawers. Everything was uncharacteristically straight and matching, neat and tidy: nothing like her mother's usual vibe. She threw open the French doors on to the tiny veranda, breathing in the summer air. Somewhere, Bailey barked.

Satisfied everything was ready, she left the room and put her head round her mother's bedroom door. The familiar smell of Hope's scent prompted a wave of sorrow, reminding her that she would never see her mother again, never argue with her again about current affairs, about art, about how she should be living her life. Hope refused to understand why Jo hadn't settled down. 'What do you mean you haven't found the right man?' she would ask, her voice rising in disbelief. 'Find one that might do and sculpt him into the one you want.'

That might have worked for her, but not for Jo. Besides, she had found one once, but let him go. Hope couldn't grasp the fact that her daughter enjoyed her own company most of the time. It was inconceivable to her that a woman could exist happily without a man. Or exist at all. But Jo didn't feel lonely or deprived. Since Jake had gone, she had never met a man who she would want permanently in her life. She didn't want to follow the example set by Hope and Walter. Instead, she found that the pleasure she took in the relationships she had was heightened precisely because she had a private place she could go to when she wanted to. As years went by, she valued that privacy more and more highly. She was too set in her ways to change now. Except she *had* changed. Everything had changed with the advent of Ivy.

She thought she heard the sound of a car so ran downstairs, anxious for her daughter's return, longing for her company again. But the sound must have travelled up from the road. There was no one there.

Tom was at the desk in the sitting room, rummaging through the drawers. 'Lucy can have all this if she wants but I just want to be sure there's not something important here that we need to know about.'

'Like what?' Jo slipped off her shoes to feel the cool of the floor tiles on her feet: a heavenly contrast with the heat outside. 'She'll tell us if there is.'

'She might not recognise it.' Tom pulled open another drawer and dumped its contents on the desktop.

'Aren't you being a bit obsessive? Looks like a load of old bills and letters to me.'

Tom ignored her question and kept leafing through the papers. 'Look at this.' He passed her a slip of paper. She recognised Walter's writing.

'Whoopsy-Doo, I love you. I can't imagine my life without you. All my love, darling Hope,' she read. 'The old romantic! Who knew? That's so sweet.'

'And here's a postcard you sent her from Dublin.'

'Let me see.' A miniaturised Guinness poster. 'God, I sent this years ago. Fancy her keeping it.' She had posted it near the university, anxious to get back to the hotel room where her lover Enda was waiting. She had made a brief sortie to buy some tights, some Rizlas and to send the postcard. That had been quite a weekend! She wondered what had happened to him. Once he started wanting more than a long-distance affair, the fun began to go out of things and they agreed to part. She heard he got married six months later. She wasn't invited.

'She kept quite a lot.' He nodded towards a small pile of papers. 'I'm sorting them out. That's not the only one from you.'

'Really? How funny. I never imagined she'd keep them.'

'Of course she did. She loved getting them.' Tom paused for a moment. 'Lucy won't mind if I take the ones I sent, will she? They're funny little reminders, like snapshots of our past.'

Jo glanced at him. He was turning one over, and she caught

the bright colours of an Asian street market. 'I'm sure she won't. But you can ask her. That sounds like them.'

There was a sound of car doors slamming, a shout, then running footsteps. Ivy charged into the room, hurtling towards Jo who swept her up into the air and kissed her on the cheek. 'Did you have a good time?'

'*Magnífico!* That's my first Spanish word.' Ivy wriggled to be put down and bounded out to Lucy who was walking through the hall. 'Where is it? Where is it?'

'Let me put these in the kitchen first.' Lucy was lugging a couple of bags of shopping with her.

'Let me help.' Jo went through with her. 'I thought as Antonio was on the coast he was going to Mercadona for anything else we needed?'

'He is.' Lucy began to pull out loaves of bread, rice, turmeric, washing-up liquid. 'But you know what happens. I thought I only needed the washing-up liquid and then I got a bit carried away!' Beside her Ivy was clutching onto the table edge, jumping up and down. 'Here it is.' She passed a brown paper bag to her.

'Oh Luce, you shouldn't.'

'What? Spoil my only niece? What other chance do I get?' She squatted down to help Ivy pull a box out of the bag.

'Look, Mummy.' Ivy brandished the box in her face. 'A princess dress!' She started ripping the cardboard apart. Out fell a confection of vivid-purple net with a gold bodice emblazoned with the plastic picture of a Disney princess, and a glittering, gaudy tiara. 'I must put it on now.' She sat on the floor to take off her shoes.

'It's lovely.' Jo helped her undo her shoe. 'But won't you be a bit hot?' She really didn't like this sort of gender stereotyping but, at the same time, she didn't want to hurt Lucy's feelings. And besides, what was the harm if it made Ivy happy? 'I thought we might have a swim.'

But Ivy was deaf to distraction. Off came her shorts, her

T-shirt, and on went the dress. She held out the tiara to Lucy. 'Can you?'

'Of course. Let's go and get a hairbrush. You're going to look sooo pretty.' The two of them left the room holding hands. Jo heard them go upstairs. No, Ivy was not going to look sooo pretty, Jo said to herself. She was going to look ridiculous and girly, and it would be impossible to persuade her to wear anything else now. But what could she do? She might want an idealised old-school childhood for Ivy where the toys were educational, the food nutritional and the TV and Internet had no role to play, but the pressures of a twenty-first-century childhood were impossible to resist. She had decided they would have a much easier life together if she just rolled with the punches. If it made Ivy happy to be dressed like a Disney princess, then so be it. And if Sue, her nanny, didn't like it – well, which one of them was Ivy's mother?

She pulled her phone out of her shorts pocket and challenged herself to a game of Scrabble.

9

The inside of the car was like an oven. Lucy could feel the sweat pooling at the base of her spine as she turned on the air con. Driving down to the coast was the last thing she wanted to do, but she was looking forward to seeing her godmother again. Besides, Tom was so set on his stickering – let him, he could have what he wanted if it made him happy – and Jo obviously wanted to spend time with Ivy. Lucy sympathised. Being a working mother must mean that the hours Jo had with her daughter were particularly precious. Lucy had always imagined herself being more of an earth-mother type, the calm, giving centre at the heart of a frenzied family life – but it was pointless her thinking that way any more. She had to accept her life for what it was now, not what it might have been. As for Art, she had left him by the pool, having refused her suggestion that he might come with her. Yes, she was trying to be a good wife again. But he had just raised a lazy hand, his oiled body gleaming in the sun.

'Give a guy a chance to recover,' he drawled. 'I'll help you when you get back. There's something I need to talk to you about.'

The hand had dropped and he turned his face away in the direction of the sun.

To talk? Why couldn't they just have had the conversation there and then? Besides, what did they have to talk about? There had been a time when they knew everything there was to know about each other's lives. They would spend chunks of their weekends together catching up with what had happened in their separate weeks. Not any more. Now there were huge gaps in their knowledge. Lucy couldn't remember the last time Art had asked how her business was going. But that was as much her fault as his. When had she last asked him about what was happening on set or behind the scenes? All she knew of his fellow cast members was what she saw on the screen or paraded in the Mail Online's sidebar of shame. She didn't ask him any more because, somehow, she had let herself slide to the periphery of his life. It was though she existed in the shadows. What's more, a little bit of her was frightened to find out what really went on when he was in Bristol. He had another life there in a world that had nothing to do with her. And she had let that happen. When he got the role of Steve, neither of them had dreamed that he would become such a staple part of the soap. While perhaps not quite the nation's darling that he imagined he was, he was certainly popular enough to attract the paps. Being followed by them was enough to turn anyone's head, she supposed.

Having reached the petrol station in Gaucín, she was turning out on to the main Gibraltar road when a motorcycle zoomed past her, the rider wearing red, white and blue racing gear crouching low over the handlebars.

'Maniac!' she shouted. Of course he couldn't hear her, but she felt a whole lot better. 'Idiot!' she finished off, turning away from the knot of people in the café who were staring at her and laughing.

As she drove, she barely heard the music on the radio. She was too preoccupied by the thoughts chasing through her mind, too disordered and speedy for her to be able to get a hold on any of them. The state of her marriage; precious Ivy who couldn't help underlining her own sadness at what she would never have; Casa de Sueños, Hope's 'house of dreams' and her childhood home where many of her own dreams were born; her own future – she had no answers to any of them. And then there was Antonio.

She hadn't dared to think about Antonio since the rest of the family had arrived. But without him, the last few days would have been torture. His company had made being at the house much easier, making her feel that she wasn't alone. The sense of connection she felt to him had surprised her as much as it certainly would Tom and Jo if they ever found out. She couldn't help a smile as she imagined Tom's face. But Antonio had to have felt it too. She stopped herself short. How could she even begin to think of him in that sort of way? Her mother's dear friend! But he and she were the two people in the world who had helped Hope have the end she wanted. The two of them had been drawn together by Hope's death. And he was closer to her age than he was to her mother's. She shook her head. Stop it! She was married, for heaven's sake, and she took her vows seriously, however difficult that could sometimes be.

She'd been so relieved when Antonio had disappeared the previous day on the pretext of not wanting to be in the way of the family, of having some work to do at the hotel, of going to the supermarket for her. Too many pretexts, in fact! But Tom had never made a secret of his dislike of Antonio's presence at the house, despite him being a godsend to Hope, helping her with so much. Out of the blue, it struck Lucy for the very first time that perhaps their relationship had really been more platonic than any of them had thought. Hope would have loved everyone imagining there was more to their friendship than they saw. And Antonio was perfectly capable of playing up to that just to amuse them both.

Lucy arrived at the airport, parked, and made her way to the Arrivals gate on autopilot, having done this so many times before. She stood among the waiting holidaymakers, tour reps and drivers holding up passenger names on pieces of card. Every time the doors opened, she looked out for Elaine's bird's nest of blonde hair.

Just as she was beginning to wonder whether she had got the arrival time wrong, there was a wild shout. 'Lucy!' Heads turned towards the woman who was coming through the door. Elaine's streaked-blonde hair, grown wiry with age and chemicals, was organised into some approximation of style, aided by a couple of large hair combs. The dark glasses that hid most of her face were large and round, with wide black and white frames. Her lips were bright carmine red. Long necklaces, bracelets and rings livened up the loose black dress she wore. Lucy was aware of several men gazing at her godmother who looked like a magpie on overdrive. Her handbag and camera had slipped off her shoulder and were dangling beside the handle of her case. Under her arm were some magazines, and a couple of bottles of champagne in a Duty Free bag hung from her spare hand.

Lucy smiled as she edged round the barrier to help. Once she had offloaded as much as she could, they kissed.

'Darling, how are you?' But before Lucy had time to reply, Elaine swept on: 'Such a flight! I honestly thought we were going to come down over the Bay of Biscay. Talk about turbulence. Never known anything like it.' She pulled a face. 'Anyway, it's over now. So what's been happening? Are you all at each other's throats yet? I know how divisive death can be. I still don't talk to my brother – he made such a song and dance over what he felt was his due, we almost ended up in court.'

As they made their way out to the car, Lucy was subject to such a barrage of chat, she didn't have a chance to get a word in edgeways.

They piled Elaine's luggage into the boot of the car and climbed in. 'They're all looking forward to seeing you,' Lucy managed to squeeze the information into the briefest of gaps in Elaine's monologue.

'Is it hell?' Elaine untangled her necklaces, ordering them over her chest. 'When we cleared out our parents' house, I thought I'd never get over it. All that stuff. And that's all it is, of course. But all of it – even the smallest thing – suddenly has such importance because of who it belonged to. Throwing anything away is so permanent.'

Lucy manoeuvred the car out of the space and on to the road. 'Well, Tom's in charge of all that.'

'I'm sure he is. I've never known a more organised man. I bet he's got you all using stickers.'

'How did you guess?'

Elaine's bracelets clicked together as she raised her hand to straighten her sunglasses. 'I've known him too long.'

Of course she had. She was another of Hope's friends who had always treated Tom like the little prince of the family: something that used to gall Jo and Lucy. When, at sixteen, he had gone to school in England too, Elaine took him under her wing alongside Jo. When they didn't have to visit the Dorset relations or go home to Spain, she would take them both out of school or university and up to London where she spoiled them as much as she could: cinema, shopping, meals out. When it was Lucy's turn, Elaine had done the same for her. She had been a part of their lives for as long as they had lived at Casa de Sueños and was considered one of the family.

During the drive back, Lucy relaxed as she listened to Elaine's colourful account of what was going on her life. Having met Ted, an Englishman who would no more settle somewhere out of his motherland than fly to the moon, she had left Andalucía years ago to live a comfortable life in London. She became a journalist and ended up editing a minor but successful fashion magazine, feted and blessed alike. But she had never given up her friendship with Hope. She visited whenever she could and brought Ted, and their children Chloe and Jonathan, with her. 'They're both gutted not be here but Chloe's due to pop at any second – her third, can you believe it? And Jonno's in New York on business. I'd never pictured him as a music mogul – but there you go. They send their love, of course.'

'They wrote—' Lucy began.

'Of course they did. They loved Hope as much as I did. I can't bear to think of her gone.' She removed her sun specs, wiped her eyes, then put them back. 'But life does go on. It has to, I suppose. I didn't think I'd ever get over Ted's death, but in the end I bounced back.' She turned to look at Lucy. 'So much to do and so little time. Did I tell you I was taking photography lessons – University of the Third Age, have you heard of that? Marvellous – such a dear man who's trying to drill the technical side of things into us. As for Photoshop...'

When they pulled up at the house, Lucy was up to speed with pretty much everything in Elaine's life. Once her godmother had recovered from the excitement and sadness of arriving back here, it would be her turn. For all her bluster, Elaine would have sensed Lucy wouldn't want to talk when she was driving. Instead, at some point, they would find a quiet spot where nothing could distract them, and then she would kick back and listen.

Antonio's battered white Renault van was parked away from the other cars, tucked in beside the garage. So Brad must have arrived too. Lucy wondered where they were, before remembering Art and the talk he had wanted them to have. She must focus on getting her marriage back on track. Elaine was right. Life *did* have to go on and time *was* marching past. She hadn't been fair to Art. Perhaps Jo had a point too: a few days here might work wonders for them whatever the circumstances. The sun so often made things better.

Lucy felt those wretched tears threatening again. The touch of a hand on her sleeve made her turn round. Elaine removed her sunglasses to show that she understood the emotional swings and roundabouts her god-daughter was riding. 'She wouldn't want you to be sad,' she said, driving Lucy even closer to the brink of tears. 'She would have loved to think of you all celebrating her birthday again. Just like the old days.' She heaved a sigh and began to open the car door. 'Oh, don't. You'll get me going in a minute.'

'Except she's not here.' Lucy wiped her nose with the back of her hand. 'And she was always the one at the centre of the party.'

'We can do it without her. We must. That's what she would have wanted.' Elaine climbed out to a rapturous greeting from Bailey, who had ambled out from the house at the sound of the car.

'Elaine! Good to see you.' Tom was walking towards them. 'Let me help you with your bags. Bailey, you clown. Get down!' He picked up a half-chewed tennis ball and tossed it into the olive grove.

The dog put his head on one side and looked at Tom as if to say, 'What? Me? Chase that? In this heat? You're having a laugh.'

'You're in the *casita* with us, I'm afraid. We'll try to keep the noise to a minimum, but the boys... well, you know. I'm just about to head off to meet them from the train. They've spent the day in Ronda with Belle.'

'In this heat?' Elaine fanned herself enthusiastically with her hand as Lucy opened the boot. 'She must be crazed. But how are you, dearest Tom?' She embraced him and began regaling him with the details of her flight, at the same time as concentrating on detaching one of her necklaces from one of his shirt buttons.

Lucy hid her smile as she followed the two of them over to their rooms. They took no notice of her as she put down Elaine's magazines and Duty Free. Did she have time for a quick swim and a shower before the evening began?

In the house, Jo was talking to Brad. Lucy hadn't realised how good-looking Hope's half-brother was – still. Did that make him her half-uncle? He lived right up to the Australian stereotype: an outdoorsy, fit-looking man with startling blue eyes that shone from a weathered face crowned by thick greying hair that stood on end. He had his iPhone in one hand, a battered old cricket hat in the other.

'Hello, Brad. Can I help?' she intervened.

'Brad's mosquito net has a hole in it,' explained Jo with a look of undying gratitude.

'And the little buggers love me,' added Brad with a laugh.

Lucy submitted herself to a hug, breathing in his sandalwood and spice scent. His room was the only one with a net. She had meant to sew up the hole but with one thing and another... Besides, nobody usually used them up here. 'I'll patch it before we go out tonight. Promise. Though I think it's still a bit early for them. Did you have a good journey?'

'Good but long. I thought I'd have a quick zizz before supper tonight, if that's all right with y'all.'

'Yes, of course. I'll do it now then so I won't need to disturb you.' She went into the sitting room where Hope's sewing chest sat beside her favourite chair. Before she even had time to think about what she was doing, Lucy pulled her stickers from her pocket and marked both the chair and the chest. Her mother had sat in that chair every winter, darning or sewing, a blanket on her lap, sometimes with the luxury of a hot-water bottle underneath despite a fire roaring in the grate. She would have a glass of her favourite Rioja on the top of the sewing chest and, in the bad old days, an ashtray. 'Just the one, darlings. That can't do me any harm.'

Lucy opened the lid. Inside was a jumble of coloured threads and wools. She disentangled a measuring tape and a small blue tin of pins. Underneath everything else she found a reel of white cotton and a packet of needles containing only one needle that was threaded with red. The fleeting thought that the last person to have touched this was her mother was almost unbearable. She pulled out the thread and tucked it into her pocket, before sticking the needle into the top of her T-shirt.

Brad was waiting, sitting on the edge of his bed, concentrating on his iPhone again. 'Cricket scores,' he said.

'We're so glad you've come...' she started.

'It's the least I could do.' He got off the bed. 'Although we didn't know Hope well at all, she's still my sister. I wanted to be here.'

Lucy wondered why Hope had never had the same desire to connect with her extended family? When asked about them, all she had ever said was: 'After my mother died my father got married to someone much younger than him. I hated her. They left me in England and asked his sister, my Aunt Jean, to keep an eye on me. I was sixteen – lonely, stubborn, frightened – and determined to prove I could manage without them! They were unhappy, confusing times. And that's as much as I want to remember and all you need to know.' She clamped shut her mouth, not willing to be drawn any further.

'Didn't you see your dad again?' Lucy had persisted, shocked.

'Never. He wrote and sent guilt money – an allowance that he went on paying for years. If it weren't for that, I'd never have survived. I have to give him that. But I couldn't forgive him for leaving me. Couldn't they have waited a few more years, at least until I had left school? Don't ask me any more. I really don't want to think about it.' After that she had clammed up, refusing to talk about him or her stepmother any further.

'It's lucky your party coincided with a business trip to the UK,' Brad said as Lucy licked the end of a piece of thread and slid it through the needle's eye. 'We've got two restaurants in Sydney that specialise in Australian grub and now we want to open in London. Amber, my wife, is flying into Heathrow on Monday. She couldn't get away any earlier because of the kids, but I wanted to come over for this first. Then I'm joining her.'

'So quite a family affair,' she commented as she made quick work of the hole in the net.

'Well, if you've got the talent there, you might as well use it.' He rumbled with laughter. 'Aren't you the cook?'

'I am indeed.'

'Maybe we can find a role for you in London. Amber's looking for someone to oversee the operation once it's gets up and running.'

Was this the opportunity she had been waiting for? Lucy tried to imagine herself braising kangaroo bollocks, grilling alligator steaks or making emu pies – maybe a bit too recherché for her. 'Sounds fun,' she said, and bit off the thread before shaking out the net to make sure it was in one piece.

'Well, talk to Amber. It'd be a joy to have you on board.' He bent over to undo his trainers and remove them and his socks. 'And now I must get one over the jet lag.'

'Of course.' She glanced at her watch. 'And I must have a swim. There's just enough time before Tom and the others get back.' She was aware she was putting off having that word with Art, but the thought of being in that water was too enticing. Just a few moments on her own was all she wanted. But maybe Jo and Ivy would be in the pool. She allowed herself a small sigh.

10

The real heat of the day was giving way to the makings of a pleasant evening as the light grew softer. Ivy was in the shade of the trees by the pool playing some complicated game that involved a plastic cow and a horse left behind by a previous lodger. She had refused point-blank to go swimming. Nothing was going to persuade her to take off the princess dress that was slightly too big even with a T-shirt underneath. Her tiara had slipped to a rakish angle over one ear. Every now and then a few words drifted in Jo's direction, enough for her to know that her daughter hadn't moved and Jo could lean back on her arms and enjoy the sensation of sun on her body, the cool of the water on her toes, eyes half-closed but alert in case—

A noise made her look up. Lucy was walking towards them. Seeing her in the dark-blue swimsuit, Jo realised for the first time how much weight her sister had lost since the previous summer. Her collarbones were too prominent and her upper arms were super lean. Her dark curls were kept off her face by the sunglasses she had pushed back on the top of her head, emphasising her cheekbones.

Ivy spotted her at the same time and dashed over, abandoning her animals, almost tripping on her purple net skirt. 'Luceee! Come and see me swim.'

Lucy swept her niece in the air and swung her around, both of them laughing. 'Princesses don't swim in their clothes, do they? So let me have a quick go while you change. Then I will.'

Ivy raced back to Jo. 'I need to take this off. Now.' She couldn't keep still from excitement.

Typical. Jo had only been trying to persuade Ivy to take the wretched dress off all afternoon but whenever she suggested it Ivy wouldn't hear of it. Jo wondered where this stubborn streak came from – surely not from her! When she had suggested Ivy put on her Crocs, Ivy had wailed. 'Nooo! They can't go over my glass slippers.'

'Only so you don't cut yourself or get stung,' Jo insisted.

'My slippers are on my feet already.' Ivy held out her bare feet so Jo could see. 'Be careful,' she shrieked, 'or you'll break them.' In the end there was no alternative but to let her have her way. She had already completely forgotten the insect sting of the day before.

Unlike her daughter, Jo had never forgotten being stung here. It was one of those things that had lodged in her memory for various reasons. That particular night the grown-ups had been so involved with their card game that they ignored her yells until they could ignore her no longer. Walter then insisted an unwilling Hope gave him her hand to play while she dealt with the crisis. She took Jo inside, got out the baking soda, dabbed it on and gave her a hug but, in her eagerness to get back to the game, forgot the all-important ice cream: usually the crucial part of any cure. Instead she left Jo to be comforted by Tom while she rushed back outside to her game. Furious at being deprived of her compensation, Jo had made him come with her while she raided the freezer. They finished all the ice cream they could find, eating it straight from the tubs before replacing them where they came from. Afterwards they went round the back of the garage where they shared a cigarette she had nicked from a packet in the hall. They coughed their guts out and were horribly sick. She had never smoked again, and was furious that Hope never mentioned the ice cream.

There was a splash as Lucy dived in, disturbing the translucent expanse of blue and sending ripples lapping against the pool's edge. She surfaced into a leisurely breaststroke before rolling over on to her back and wallowing like a seal. A pair of iridescent turquoise dragonflies gleamed in the sun as they darted above her, wings catching the sunlight.

'Quick!' Ivy was standing with her arms in the air waiting for the dress to be pealed off her.

'More suntan cream.' Jo fumbled for the tube that was somewhere under her towel.

'No, no, no – I'm going swimming.'

'Then you'd better wear your T-shirt. The sun might still burn you.'

'I don't want it to get wet.' Ivy's chin wobbled.

Don't shout, Jo told herself. Exercise all the patience you've got.

'T-shirt and pants are pretty cool,' said Lucy who had arrived at their end of the pool. All they could see of her was her sleek head, eyes large in her face, and her fingers holding on to the side. 'I'd wear them, if I were you.'

Ivy looked doubtful. Jo took advantage of the moment by threading on the old armbands she'd found in a cupboard, making it too hard to remove the T-shirt quickly. Her point!

'Lucy!' Art roused himself from his lounger at the side of the pool, carefully angled to get optimum sun. 'Have you got a moment?' He slung a towel around his sunburned shoulders.

'Of course, in a minute. I promised Ivy. Then I'm all yours.' Lucy took the little girl by the waist and lifted her into the water. 'Are these your armbands?'

'They're in the suitcase,' said Jo, sounding world-weary. The bloody suitcase that Jo was beginning to think might never turn up at all. The last girl she had spoken to at the airline had been so unhelpful too. To her, it was just another lost piece of luggage, no different from anyone else's. She had no idea of the significance of its contents and Jo couldn't explain to her. She smiled at Ivy, who was hanging on to Lucy. 'She's quite a water baby though, aren't you?' That was the proud result of hours spent in the local pool with other competitive mothers keen to give their children every possible advantage in the world. 'She knows never to go in on her own, don't you?'

Ivy nodded and clung on to Lucy's neck like a limpet, her legs tight round her waist. Lucy's smile was beatific. Out of the corner of her eye, Jo could see Art watching what was going on. He had rolled onto his side and propped himself onto his elbow, one leg bent. His aviator sunglasses meant she couldn't see his full expression but he looked thoughtful. There was definitely something of Jude Law about him.

'So this is where you all are.' Elaine came through the gate having exchanged her black dress and jewellery for a garish lime-green swimsuit covered by a loose see-through lemon tunic. 'How warm's the water?' She went to dip a toe in the water. 'God, it's freezing!'

'Once you're in, it's lovely,' encouraged Lucy. 'Come on.'

'I've heard that before.' But without wasting another second, Elaine had stripped off, dived in, surfaced and was shaking her head. 'Brrrr! And I trusted you! I'm surprised my heart hasn't stopped.' Then, without further ado, she struck out in an efficient crawl, cutting through the water for one length after another. The others looked on amused. Every time she came close to Lucy and Ivy, she slowed down so as not to splash them, then turned and sped away again. Jo had lost count of the number of lengths by the time Elaine emerged up the steps, rough-dried her hair and wrapped herself in a towel. She took the lounger beside her and angled a parasol so the sun would finish the job.

'Good for the soul, I dare say,' she said, lying down with a long sigh. 'Now, tell me all about you and Ivy and what's happening in your life.'

As they began to catch up on each other's news, they watched Lucy and Ivy sploshing about in the shallow end, shouting with pleasure. The horse and cow had been brought into the game, with Lucy repeatedly diving down to rescue them whenever Ivy dropped them.

'I'm going in, Lucy. I'll see you inside.' Clearly tired of waiting for her, Art stood up, gathering his Kindle, suntan oil and towel to take in with him. He had barely spoken to Jo while they'd been by the pool together. Once he had lain down, he had started reading, making it quite plain he didn't want to be disturbed. After a while, giving in to the heat, he lay back and closed his eyes. He hadn't moved again until Lucy appeared. Jo decided to give him the benefit of the doubt – the poor sod must have been working hard and be exhausted. She had left him to himself.

Moments later, Lucy and Ivy climbed up the steps out of the pool, water streaming off them.

'I'm going to have to go in. I'll see you later, Ivy Rose.' Lucy bent forward and shook her head, showering Jo and Ivy with water. Ivy laughed and tried to do the same.

'We should go in too,' said Jo. 'Elaine, you must be gasping for a drink.' She wrapped Ivy in a towel and began to tickle her until they were both weak with laughter. By the time they stopped, Elaine and Lucy were laughing too.

'Well, I wouldn't put it quite like that but . . . What about the champagne I brought?"

'Yes, let's.' The four of them began to walk back to the house when Ivy remembered she had left her animals by the pool. Her towel was flung on the ground as she dashed back to retrieve them while Jo waited. By the time the two of them reached the terrace, Lucy had gone upstairs to find Art but Elaine was still outside admiring the English garden.

'As beautiful as it always was. Hope would be so pleased.'

'All down to Antonio.'

Elaine nodded. 'Smart move having a younger man in tow to help about the house. I don't know how she did it.'

'Nor me.' Jo broke off a white rose that was just passing its best and gave it to Ivy. 'How have you coped?'

'Since Ted died? I've been fine on my own. I get a bit lonely sometimes, but there are worse things than loneliness and it always passes. I see the children as often as they'll allow me to, and the grandchildren, of course. They're the light of my life. Now . . .' She paused. 'That drink?'

'Of course. Come right this way.' Jo paused in the hall, hearing Tom on the phone in the sitting room. So the others were back from Ronda.

'How can you have lost it?' he yelled. 'Yesterday you told me that it had been misrouted to Barcelona and that it would be delivered today! What? Majorca? . . . Well, perhaps you could do me the favour of finding out as soon as possible. It contains some essentials that we need urgently for tomorrow night! Thank you. Yes, I'll be here. Yes, waiting. Goodbye.' There was a silence as he must have put the phone in his pocket. 'Bloody idiots. If they find it and get it here, it'll be a miracle.'

'Calm down.' Belle's voice was calm. 'Getting het-up isn't going to help. This is all Jo's fault and you should let her deal with it. Take a breath.'

Elaine raised an eyebrow at Jo who had to do all she could not to laugh.

'I simply don't believe them.'

The sofa creaked as he sat down.

Jo put a finger to her lips and gestured with a nod towards the kitchen. The last thing she wanted at that moment was to have to face her brother. Losing her mother was her fault but she was every bit as capable as Tom of haranguing the airline. She wished he'd leave it to her. She and Elaine tiptoed towards the kitchen. Then Ivy dropped the horse and let out a squeal.

'Jo! I thought I heard someone.' Belle came to the door of the sitting room, Ferdie pattering behind her. The woman's hearing must be supersonic. 'And, Elaine, you've arrived.'

Ivy went straight to play with Ferdie. Jo looked around for Bailey. He must have taken himself off to the woods or Lucy had shut him in the garage.

'Yes,' said Elaine, kissing Belle on both pale cheeks. 'I got in this afternoon. Where were you?'

'I took the boys into Ronda. We did some shopping and I took them to the bullring.'

'Well, you're here now.' Tom came up behind his wife. 'I've just been on to the airline—'

'I know,' said Jo. 'I heard. I wish you'd leave it to me.'

Elaine turned to her. 'Can't you borrow something from Lucy or me? It's not as though you need much here. What's in the case that's so special?'

And that from a woman who has a new outfit for every occasion, thought Jo, amused. She glanced at Tom who shook his head, warning her not to say anything. A squall of irritation blew through her. Why did he have to assume control of everything as if both his sisters were incapable of taking their share of the responsibility?

'Actually, Mum is.' She spoke in a stage whisper and pointed towards Ivy, indicating that her daughter didn't know. Contradicting Tom's obvious wish gave her a pathetic childlike pleasure.

Tom looked thunderous. Belle laid a restraining hand on his shoulder.

'Hope?' For a second, Elaine looked confused.

Jo nodded. 'Yes. I put the box of her ashes in there because I didn't have enough hands to carry everything.'

'Really? You mean we've nothing to scatter?'

'Exactly.'

Elaine began to laugh. 'That's absolutely priceless! We're all gathering to give her the best send-off ever and she's not even here. That's so like her.' She wiped an eye with the back of her hand. 'Oh, come on, Tom! Loosen up. Can't you see how funny she'd find it?'

He allowed himself to crack a smile but it disappeared as quickly as it arrived. 'I'd feel much happier if she were here. I want her to be.' For a second he sounded like the small boy Jo remembered being so upset when Hope failed to turn up at a school concert where he had a starring role. The one and only time as it turned out. He had been inconsolable, having desperately wanted to prove he deserved her pride. But Hope had got sidetracked before leaving the house by saving a kitten that had got stuck up a tree and turned up as the school hall was emptying.

Elaine controlled herself. 'I'm sorry, Tom. That was wrong of me. Of course it matters, and I'm sure she'll be here. She'd never miss a decent party.'

'Let's hope you're right.' A tinny version of Beethoven's Fifth blasted into the hall. He pulled his phone from his shorts' pocket and studied the screen. 'That's them calling back.' He held up a finger. 'One second.'

None of them moved as they waited, listening. Tom's frown cleared as he heard whatever the person at the other end had to say.

'You have? Thank God for that.' His face brightened. 'Tomorrow? You're sure this time? . . . All right. And it will be brought to the house? You've got the address? Yes . . . Yes . . . That's it, yes, after the bridge on the right, yes. Good. Thank you.' He hung up. 'They've found it and will definitely have it with us tomorrow.' His relief was obvious.

'Well, that definitely calls for a drink.' Elaine was the first one to move. 'Who's for a glass of bubbly?'

Belle arched a perfectly tweezered eyebrow. 'Water for me. I'm driving tonight.' She turned to her husband. 'Or are you?'

'You are,' he said firmly, taking a step away from her restraining hand. 'Let me do the honours, Elaine.'

'I'll take mine to my room while I change,' she said.

Jo saw Belle's eyes widen at the idea of Elaine drinking on her own.

'What about Brad?' Jo wondered aloud. 'Ought one of us to wake him?'

'It's only six. He can have a few more minutes.' Tom followed Elaine into the kitchen. 'Oh!' He stopped dead.

'*Holà. ¿Qué tal?*' Antonio emerged from the larder. 'I was making sure you've got enough fish for the paella. I brought some from the coast but could get more in the morning.'

'That's my job, thanks,' said Tom.

Jo frowned at him. There was no need to be quite so rude. Fortunately Antonio seemed not to notice. 'We're having a drink. Would you like to join us?' she asked.

Tom glared at her, making sure she knew he wasn't pleased.

'Are these all she's got?' asked Elaine, who was getting out some wine glasses.

'No, no. Let me.' Belle went to the glasses cupboard and did the honours.

But Antonio had seen Tom's reaction. 'I have things to do in the garden before tomorrow,' he said. 'Then I'll go home before the supper tonight.'

'Thank you, Antonio,' said Jo, as he left the room. 'I don't know what we'd do without you.'

'Do you have to be so ingratiating?' muttered Tom.

'I'm just being polite to the man who looked after Mum.'

'If you must put it like that.' Tom's face showed how much he disliked the idea.

'Tom, stop it. You don't *know*. Whatever their relationship was is none of our business and he's done a bloody good job looking after the house since Mum left for England. There's no need to treat him like that.'

'Children, children.' Elaine stood between them. 'Shall we at least try?'

'Sorry, how embarrassing. You're right.' Jo leaned down to Ivy, who was standing beside her, shrouded in her towel. 'Come on, princess. Let's find you something to wear.' As soon as the words left her mouth, she knew they were a mistake.

'My princess dress.' Ivy grabbed the net skirt that was scrunched in her mother's hand.

'Let's go upstairs and decide. Then you can come down for a drink too. We won't be a moment.' Could she be fairer than that? For once, Ivy didn't argue but trotted ahead of her up the stairs.

Brad's room was at the turn in the flight. Jo knocked at the door. 'We'll be leaving in a couple of hours. I thought you might want a shower first and then join us for drinks.'

There was a grunt and the sound of the bedsprings squeaking. Then: 'Thanks. I'll be down soon.'

She thought she heard the voice of a radio sports commentator come to life as she turned away.

Going along the corridor, she became aware of raised voices behind Lucy and Art's door. Not them, too? She couldn't hear what they were saying but she could tell that it wasn't friendly. Not something else going wrong? The idea of burying herself under the bedclothes for the rest of the weekend suddenly held huge appeal, except who would look after Ivy? Even disappearing on her own with the pretence of work wasn't an option. Ivy ran ahead to their room. Jo dawdled, trying to eavesdrop on Lucy and Art while pretending she wasn't doing anything of the sort. She stopped by the chest that still contained the remnants of their dressing-up clothes for grandchildren even though Ethan and Alex had never been interested in them. A red spot blazed on its lid. Never! Tom had always poured scorn on her and Lucy's enthusiasm for dressing up in her mother's old clothes. He had no right to it. In one swift move, she removed the spot. In a second, she replaced it with a yellow one.

Having done that, she felt so guilty that she allowed Ivy to put on the princess dress without so much as a murmur.

11

When she followed Art into the house, Lucy was more than ever regretting not having given him the welcome he deserved. She had no excuse for being so dismissive. Although, when he came through the kitchen door, seeing him had been enough to make all her doubts and anxieties about their marriage resurface. He didn't even look like the man she married any more. Back then, he had been just an ordinary guy, good-looking enough, thoughtful, who played tennis every so often and went for the odd run. Now, he was honed and toned out of recognition. Well, as honed and toned as someone over forty could be. Not that you saw any of that when he was in his TV charge nurse's uniform.

When they first met at supper at a mutual friend's, he had fine-tuned the 'resting' side of his career, not having worked as an actor for years. She had just started working for Corrigan Catering, a large wedding reception caterer that seemed so much better than the hotel kitchen where she had been before. Then, he had been an earnest wannabe with a fund of amusing almost-but-not-quite audition stories while she had been working flat-out with her eye on the role of head chef. He funded himself by waitering, tour guiding, anything legal that paid but allowed time off for those auditions. How things changed. Years later, her career was tanking but he was continuously employed, continuously preoccupied by the impression he might be making. He filled the few breaks he did have from the show by doing voiceovers and radio work. She couldn't remember the last time they had been on a proper holiday together. His career came before absolutely everything else – even their attempts to start a family. Anything reliant on her cycle had to be timed round his filming schedule too.

As she approached their room, she noticed the red sticker on the old dressing-up chest. She was tempted to replace it with one of hers, but decided that wouldn't be playing the game. Opening the door, she felt oddly nervous. The first thing she saw was Art's empty leather holdall next to her case. Everything he had brought had been unpacked and put away. His attention to his wardrobe was as meticulous as his attention to his body. On the chest of drawers lay his comb, hair gel and sunglasses. As she straightened the bed cover, disturbed from when he had been sleeping earlier, she heard the shower being turned off.

She took off her swimsuit, hung it out of the window through force of habit, and put on one of the cotton dressing gowns that Hope insisted were hung on all the guest bedroom doors. Once her children had all left home and Walter had died, Hope had discovered her sometimes quite inadequate inner domestic goddess. To survive, she had taken paying guests and certain creature comforts were provided. These small idiosyncracies were what made people return. They liked the little touches, the views, the area, as well as their unusual bohemian hostess.

Lucy stretched out on the bed and waited until Art emerged, trailing a cloud of cedar and citrus in his wake. When he saw her, he stopped dead. 'I didn't hear you come in.'

'I was only a few minutes behind you. I couldn't resist playing with Ivy.'

He reached for his watch and fastened it on his wrist. 'I was beginning to think we were never going to get any time together.'

'I'm sorry.' She patted the bed beside her. He didn't sit down. 'It's all been so difficult and there's so much to do.'

'I thought that's why you came out early.'

That sounded as if he was blaming her. She had expected a

bit more understanding from him than that. She jumped to her own defence. 'I've shopped for food and tidied the house and helped Antonio with the garden but I had to wait for Tom and Jo to sort out the rest. Tom's so sure everything can be done in a weekend. How he thinks that when we're having the party and people keep arriving, I don't know.'

'You should have said. I could have stayed away.' He bent so that he could see his reflection, and ran the comb through his wet hair before turning to look at her. 'After all, I paid my respects to Hope at her funeral.'

'Don't be silly. You know I don't mean you.' Her earlier behaviour must have provoked this strange mood of his.

'But you don't seem very pleased to see me.'

'Of course I am.' This was all so complicated. She was increasingly unsure what she felt and he wasn't helping.

He sat in the corner chair. 'Lou, we've known each other long enough. I could tell by your face when I walked through the door this morning. It was as if you could barely stand to be in the same room as me.'

She started a half-hearted protest, but he carried on, counting out her misdemeanours on his fingers.

'And then you went to town. And then you disappeared to pick up Elaine.' Three fingers raised in the air. 'We should at least do each other the courtesy of being honest.'

However important it was to fix their relationship, this was not the time for home truths. The weekend was difficult enough without that too. Lucy gazed at him, trying to salvage the feelings that she had once had for him. But, however deep she dug, she had nothing in reserve. With a sudden, blinding clarity she realised she was looking at a man more in love with himself than with her. She had taken so long to understand that because she hadn't wanted to. His long absences and their struggle for a baby had eaten away at what they once had until there was very little left. They had protected themselves the best way they knew how, by throwing themselves into their work.

Was he acting now? she wondered. Was he playing a part for her benefit?

'Well?' he said eventually. He clearly had something to say and didn't know how. Instead he was trying to provoke her so that whatever was said would be her fault.

'Yes, we should be honest,' she said, feeling suddenly exhausted. 'In fact we should have been honest with each other a long time ago.'

'What do you mean?' He frowned and came over to sit on the edge of the bed. He'd perfected his concerned bedside manner after so many years in *Emergency*. Or was this him being genuine? She couldn't tell what was real any more.

'I don't think we should do this now, whatever we need to say to each other.' She found herself playing for time. 'Everyone's downstairs and we've got to be at the Mirador at eight thirty.'

'If we don't talk now, when the hell will we? We must.' Art studied his fingers, pushing back the cuticles on his thumbs before looking at her, his eyes unusually bright. 'We never see each other any more. This isn't what I got married for.'

This wasn't acting. This was the real Art.

'What *you* got married for?!' She could hardly believe she had heard him right. 'What about what *I* got married for? This isn't all about you, Art. It's about me as well. You've never heard me complain about the job taking you away. I was pleased for you, pleased that you got your break at last. But have you ever thought about me, about what I've been going through? Have you thought even for one second what it's been like for me living without you, having to deal with not conceiving yet again, yet another failed bout of IVF, never mind trying to keep my business going at the same time? Where were you when all that was going on? We should have been together.'

His mouth tightened and he closed his eyes. His jaw tensed

and relaxed. Then: 'I was earning a living so we could afford all that medical treatment.'

Lucy felt as though she might explode. 'At the same time as fulfilling at least one of your dreams, while mine were falling apart. Lucky you!' She sprang off the bed and into the bathroom. She couldn't bear to burst into tears in front of him.

'Wait a minute!' He followed her and stood in the doorway. 'Don't walk away from me like that. You know that's not how it was. I wanted – I *want* – a family every bit as much as you.'

'Of course, I know. I'm sorry. I really am.' She hadn't meant to be so cruel. She reached out to him but he took a step back. His eyes had never looked so unforgiving. She tried again. 'Don't let's row. Please. This is meant to be a special weekend. However difficult, don't let's make it worse. Let's save this till we get home. And then I promise we'll talk properly.'

Art dropped his towel on the floor and pulled on his Calvin Kleins, then a pair of khaki shorts. 'Look, I'm here because I like your family, I was fond of Hope – all that – but there's something else . . .' He paused.

Lucy's breath caught. Where was she in that burst of affection? Where was the 'and I love you'? She went back to sit on the end of the bed. 'What are you trying to say, Art? Tell me.'

'This is hard and I know it's not the moment but . . . well, I have to.' He caught sight of himself in the mirror and peered closer at his face, reassuring himself there were no flaws.

'Have to what?'

'I needed to see you. I needed to talk to you. When Hope was dying, you were so upset. I couldn't then. But now—'

'I'm upset now,' she said, disbelieving. 'Can't you see that? Whatever you want to tell me can wait a couple of days, surely.' Lucy wanted to put off the moment of hearing whatever he was about to say.

'No, it can't. I was going to wait. Of course I was. I'm not so heartless that I didn't want to wait until all this . . .' he gestured towards the voices they could hear outside on the terrace, '...was over. But something's happened.'

His hedging filled her with an awful impatience to know but one that was hemmed with dread. 'What's happened, Art? What's so important that can't wait?'

He cleared his throat, looked down as he twisted his wedding ring round his finger. Here it came. She held her breath.

'I've been seeing someone else.'

Silence.

They stared at each other, Art waiting for her reaction, not knowing what it would be.

Lucy was pinned to where she was, unable to move, completely numb. Although she had always known this was a possibility, everything felt as if it had been cut away from under her. 'Who?' she managed to whisper.

'Carrie. Carrie Flanagan.'

He didn't need to say more. Lucy remembered when Carrie Flanagan had been cast in the series. The news had made the headlines. In her early thirties (that hurt), she had made her break in a hugely popular historical TV soap, before becoming hot news in theatreland. Lucy had seen her on the front of a couple of women's magazines, innocent-eyed, bee-stung lips, a neat cap of brown hair. Her beauty was elfin-like and extremely photogenic. Casting her in *Emergency* had been a huge coup for the series (or so Art said at the time), one that had done wonders for the viewing figures.

'Isn't she a bit out of your league? A bit young for you?' She couldn't help herself as her feeling began to return.

Art bristled. 'She doesn't think so.'

Before realising what she was doing, Lucy got to her feet and slapped him hard across the face. His surprise could not have been greater than hers. She loathed violence of all kinds, but this felt right. She stepped back as he raised his hand to his face, rubbing his cheek that was stained red where hers had connected.

'You bastard! How long?' Fury rode hot on the heels of the satisfaction of the slap. How dare he do this to her after all they'd been through?

'About nine months.'

She took a breath as a terrible, aching hurt almost overwhelmed her. Nine months. All during the time Hope was dying. No wonder he hadn't come home to give her the support she had wanted so badly. Nine months. Since before Christmas, when he had to return to work on Boxing Day – or so he said. It all made sense. Nine months. The same length of time as a pregnancy. The thought spun through her head.

'Nine whole months and you could have told me any time during them. But no, you choose to tell me at my mother's house on the weekend of her last birthday party when we're scattering her ashes. The perfect moment. Well done. Thinking of others as usual.'

'I'm sorry.' At least he had the grace to say that. And to look shamefaced.

'Why now?' The strength of her hatred for him shocked her. 'Why now?'

He picked up his towel and fiddled with the end of it, unable to look her in the eye. 'Because the story's about to break in the press.'

Lucy's stomach rolled over.

'We've been so careful—'

'Oh, good for you.' She couldn't help herself.

He ignored her. 'But we got papped coming out of her flat. I've been tipped off that the picture's going to run in the press sometime this weekend. I had to tell you before you or someone else saw it.'

'How thoughtful.' Lucy's head was spinning. This couldn't be happening. Not after so long and so much. Not now. Not this weekend. She almost didn't notice when he sat beside her and took her hand. She snatched it away.

'I've wanted to tell you for months. Really. But you've been so preoccupied with Hope and your business, I didn't want to make things worse.'

'What? So this is my fault? But you could have waited till next week. Even that would be better than now. You could have made up some story about going round to hers for a reason and that the press have twisted things to make it look...' She gulped as the tears began. 'You could have—' but she couldn't say any more.

'I couldn't.' He started stroking the back of her hand, a gesture that once would have meant something. Not any more.

She snatched her hand away. 'Why not? Just four more days. That's all you would have had to lie for. What difference would that have made?'

'I'd have given anything not to tell you like this. But apparently we're holding hands, and I think there might be one of us kissing...' His voice tailed off.

Lucy felt sick. 'You could have thought of something.'

'I couldn't.'

'Why not?'

Silence.

In that moment, Lucy knew exactly what was coming. She waited, her nails digging into her palms, wishing she could be transported to anywhere other than this modest white bedroom. She focused on the heart-shaped lavender bag hanging from the bed head and waited.

'She's pregnant.'

Neither of them moved. There was a shout from outside and the sound of a ball hitting a bat. But inside the room, everything was still. Lucy felt as if that moment would never end. There was a rushing in her ears, as everything else around her dimmed. Her first thought was that she was going to be sick. She jumped to her feet and dashed to the bathroom. On her knees, she retched into the toilet until there was nothing left. For a moment, she hung there, her head resting on her arms. She felt Art's hand on her back.

'You OK?'

She shook him off. 'What does it look like? No, of course I'm not bloody OK.'

He squatted down beside her. 'Oh, Lou. If I could have told you any other way, I would.'

'Would you? You've had nine months to say something. Nine whole fucking months! And the only reason you have now is because a picture's appearing in the paper. Well, that'll work wonders for *Emergency*'s ratings.'

'You don't think we've done this on purpose?' He was shocked.

'I don't know, Art. Nothing would surprise me.'

'What are we going to do?' For a moment, he looked uncertain.

'I don't know that either.' She sat back, feeling the cool of the shower divide against her back. 'What do you want to do? You're the one calling the shots.'

'I don't want to upset this weekend any more than we have to.'

'That's nice of you.'

'Lucy, please. I'm trying to make this as easy as possible.'

Lucy had an unbearable urge to laugh. Where did all these lines come from? A bad episode of *Emergency*? Instead, she stood up and went to turn on the shower. Her mind was beginning to clear. This weekend, her family had to come first.

'I'll tell you what's going to happen.'

He looked expectant, like a puppy unsure whether or not he'd done something wrong, waiting to be told what to do. 'I'm going to have my shower. Then we're going to go downstairs and pretend nothing's happened. You are not going to ruin this weekend.'

Art almost managed to hide his relief, but not quite. 'And if the others see the paper?'

'They won't. We're in our own little bubble here. And if they do, then it doesn't matter. We'll lie. But you're going to leave as soon as you can get on a flight. We'll say you've been called to the set or that you've got an audition. You're going to go home and pack and you're not going to come back.' She clasped her hands tight so he wouldn't see them shaking.

'But—'

'I'm sorry but I'm going to have my shower.'

He looked as if he was about to protest but Lucy shook her head, making it clear she wasn't going to listen to any more. Eventually he left the bathroom and shut the door behind him. Letting the dressing gown drop to the floor, Lucy walked round the divide to stand trembling under the shower. She raised her face to the showerhead, her mouth open in a silent scream.

When she returned to the bedroom, Art was nowhere to be seen.

12

Tom peered at his watch, hoping no one would notice, but they were cutting things a bit fine. Unlike the rest of his family, he had never embraced the Spanish notion of *mañana*. Putting off what you could do today until tomorrow was unthinkable to him. It wasn't a way to run your life. His right fist tapped against the palm of his other hand, as he carried out a silent roll call. Lucy and Art were the only ones missing. He tutted to himself. Coming down on time was the very least she could do, given everyone else was here. All hands were needed on deck. He paused, amused by the expression. Whenever Lucy had gone sailing with him as a kid, she was absolutely hopeless. God only knew how many times she'd come close to being knocked out of the boat by the boom. Or just knocked out full stop. She had never quite got the idea of having to do what the captain said when he said it. As a result, they'd spent more time in the sea than on it. He remembered how relieved he had been when she'd decided to hang up her life jacket for good. He'd sailed on his own after that.

Brad had been regaling Tom with the details of his and Amber's last European trip in detail, city by city, highlight by highlight. Tom had broken away when they reached Vienna to come indoors and stand in the sitting room, half-hidden by the wall where no one could see him. Thank God for Elaine who had taken on the role of hostess with Ivy. They were moving among the troops, dispensing olives and pistachios, pouring champagne or white wine. He looked at the time again.

'We're in Spain, Tom.' Jo had crept up behind him. She tapped his watch. 'Time has no meaning any more. *Mañana* is what it's all about. Relax.'

Tom tensed. Was there anything less relaxing than being told to relax? Outside, Belle was laughing at something Ivy had said to her. She would have loved a little girl but they had both agreed that two children were enough. But at least they had made a proper family – more than either of his sisters had achieved. In the meadow Ethan and Alex were playing a game of bat and ball that provided an intrusive backdrop of whacks and shouts.

'Have you seen Lucy?' Jo asked.

'No. She could at least have come down on time.' Tom stopped himself from looking at his watch again.

'Here's Art. She can't be far behind. Ask him, if you're really worried.'

Tom watched as Art went straight out to talk to Belle, picking up a bottle of beer from the table en route. Belle would love the attention, as Art almost certainly knew. One of *Emergency's* biggest fans, she adored the kudos that came with being related to one of the cast. Of course Lucy would come down in her own time – after all, it wasn't as though she hadn't done her bit on the food front. He went outside and pulled up a chair alongside Brad again. 'Can I get you anything?'

'You can wrap up this view and give it to me to take home.' Brad gave a rolling belly laugh. 'I'm so envious of Hope having lived with this for most of her life. Must have done wonders for her soul.'

Tom cleared his throat. 'She loved it here. That's why she called it House of Dreams. But don't tell me it's that bad in Sydney?'

'Just very different. You should visit.'

Tom shook his head. He wasn't going to admit to his recently acquired anxiety about long-haul flying. The hypnotherapist Belle had insisted on meant he had got as far as Spain, but the idea of anything longer than three hours still reduced him to a cold sweat. He was kicking himself for having caved into the pressure she had put on him to take her on a dream trip to Sri Lanka the following spring, giving him no choice but to persevere with the sessions. 'Maybe one day,' he said.

'What are you talking about?' Lucy appeared at the French windows. She looked stunning in a lavender-blue dress. Antonio hovered behind her. 'Shouldn't we be thinking about going?'

'I think we should all go together, don't you?' Belle detached herself from Art. But not far, Tom noted.

'There's plenty of time,' said Jo, offering Brad more wine.

He shook his head. 'No thanks, hon. I'd like to go. I'd like to see the village before it gets too dark.'

'We'd better get on then. Ethan! Alex!' Tom was relieved that the decision was made. However, leaving was a long way off yet. The boys needed rounding up, Ferdie would have to be got ready, Bailey shut in, doors locked then reopened when something was forgotten, cars chosen, drivers allocated. He sighed.

They parked at the top of Calle del Convento and walked down to the Mirador from there. As they passed the convent, Ivy started clamouring to go into the playground next door. To Tom's irritation, Jo gave in. One slide and then they must go to dinner. Tom picked up the pace. They were already running late. Jo took no notice.

As they walked the long street, voices could be heard through the shutters of the closely packed houses. Dogs barked. A snatch of music came from somewhere, the sound of a TV. A few people sat outside the small bar at the fork in the road.

Elaine and Brad trailed at the back. Brad was exclaiming at the quaintness, the charm of the white village and its winding streets, the burst of colour from a bougainvillea or pots of geraniums. They laughed together at the huge brightly coloured model lizards on the walls of houses. They lingered over the laminated bird guides on others, noting aloud the difference between swifts, swallows and house martens, wondering whether he might see a Bonnelli's eagle or a vulture during his stay. They hovered together over the posters advertising Art Gaucín, a weekend when local artists displayed their own work at home. They stopped outside the bars, peering into the darkness inside, greeting barmen, studying the menus.

Ethan and Alex stuck close to Tom. They could be relied on to do that when there was the promise of a good meal in the offing. They had left Belle dawdling with Art. Tom could hear her laughing whenever Art spoke. He wondered what they were talking about.

'Are you sure this is the right way?' Ethan caught him up. He was almost taller than his father already: a fact guaranteed to make a man feel old.

'Yes. I know this town like the back of my hand. Anyway, didn't we come this way last night?' He flipped the brim of Ethan's hat harder than he meant to, so it flew into the gutter.

'Fuck's sake, Dad! Alex, don't!'

Alex had flipped the hat onto his foot and was attempting a game of keepie uppie. Grinning, he gave up and passed it to his brother. 'Only three,' he said.

Ethan grabbed the hat, reshaped it and put it back on his head, just so. 'No, we didn't come this way,' he said. 'We went right after the square.'

Tom turned around to find the others had disappeared. For God's sake! Now where had they all got to?

Another turning to the right and there was the restaurant. The sound of singing emerged from the bar on the corner opposite. Only a discreet doorway and a modest sign marked out the Mirador. Immediately inside was the reception, backed by a gleaming steel and white kitchen that was noisy with activity. Steam rose out of pans, the sounds of cooking and the smell of cooking fish filled the small space as something was flung on to a grill.

Tom waited for a moment as the two boys dashed up the stairs ahead of him. *Breathe.* He didn't want to arrive feeling any more stressed than necessary. It fell to him as the 'man of the family' (Belle's choice of phrase) to dictate the mood of the evening, to make sure it went well. The description amused him. Jo was far more like the man of the family than he was. His older sister knew her own mind and was so sure about how she wanted to lead her life without worrying what other people thought.

He picked up one of the Art Gaucín fliers from the bottom of the tiled stairs and made his way up. Emerging on to the roof terrace, he found the others already there, milling about by the bar. How had that happened? The two large tables laid up and waiting would seat far more people than he thought they had invited. He looked for Lucy.

She was standing by the bar with Antonio. She and Jo had insisted he come. 'Whether you like it or not, he was Mum's dear friend.' Antonio's hand was on Lucy's arm as he gave all his attention to what she was saying. His Spanish complexion, dark from the sun, and his slicked-back black hair made him stand out in this bunch of Brits. His white shirt was open just a button more than necessary in Tom's view. His dark eyes were fixed on Lucy in a way that made Tom feel quite uncomfortable. He made his way through the gathering towards them.

'Here you are! I didn't realise we'd asked so many people.'

Lucy looked up at him. She had obviously been crying again. He put his arm round her shoulder, drawing her towards him. Antonio got the message and moved down the bar to talk to someone else. Lucy put her hand on her brother's chest and gave him a watery smile.

'We haven't. Bernard's booked the other one for his latest walking group. Look at them! They're like a bunch of army commandoes!'

Tom looked over at the all-male group of walkers who surrounded Bernard, a local guide. They looked capable of covering a fair distance every day. 'But I thought we had the place to ourselves.'

'So did I. I'd no idea. He always ends every week's tour with a big dinner for them all but he never said anything about coming here.'

'Shall we see if there's a table big enough inside?' There wouldn't be. The restaurant indoors was already crowded.

'But the terrace is so beautiful.' Above them, the moon hung like a sucked sweet in the darkening sky. Jasmine, passionflower and plumbago wound up the concrete pillars. The silhouettes of swifts darted and wheeled beyond them. 'I should have double-checked, but I didn't think.'

Tom resigned himself to the evening ahead. Belle was right as usual. If he wanted things to be done his way, he should have organised the dinner himself. 'Have you done a seating plan?' he asked, still hopeful.

'No plan. Although I don't think the three of us should sit together, do you?'

He might have known. 'Is everyone here?' He looked around. Just at that moment there was a clatter and a roar from the stairwell. On to the terrace emerged two elderly men, one of whom was supporting a woman unsteady on her feet. Tom recognised them immediately. Bill, Ian and Daphne were the closest of Walter and Hope's old reprobate friends. Ian was a fellow painter, his tatty paint-stained clothes a giveaway, his bibulous complexion in contrast with his thick white hair. Tom rubbed his own head, momentarily envious. Beside Ian, Bill was almost skeletal, tall and thin like a starved plant stretching up for sunlight, with an impressive moustache that would have suited a world-war fighter pilot. Clinging onto his arm was Daphne, larger than life, and larger than most of the people on the terrace. Her loose, multi-coloured dress hung like a tent from her expansive bosom. Her eyes were bright in a face that was as ruddy as Ian's. When she laughed, something she did at the slightest excuse, she shook like a mountainous jelly.

'There you are, Tom.' Daphne waddled over and embraced him. He could barely reach her cheek to kiss it, so much of her came between them. He felt himself cushioned against her body in far too intimate a way. Her generous contours were surprisingly solid. He pulled away as soon as he could, turning his head away from the smell of alcohol on her breath.

'Good to see you, Daphne. Bill. Ian. How are you?' They didn't need to answer since they'd obviously downed a freshener or two before coming. He looked for Jo, wishing she would rescue him. 'Shall we all sit down?'

Bill and Ian murmured kind words about Hope before getting themselves drinks from the bar. They were exactly the sort of companions that Hope loved – unpredictable, dangerous, no strangers to the bottle – and exactly the sort that made Tom nervous. Their company lent the feeling that something unexpected was about to happen.

Determined they should sit down, Tom at last managed to weed their guests from the growing party of walkers crowding round the bar and direct them to the table. By the time he finally got there himself, most of the places were taken. Belle was sitting between Alex and Art, preening as Art draped one of the blankets over her shoulders. The evening was hardly chilly enough for that, Tom thought to himself. Lucy sat at the other end of the table with Elaine while Jo, despite her objections, was enmeshed with cousin Adam and family.

The only place left for Tom was at the end where four seats were left empty. He had no choice but to take his place with Bill, Ian and Daphne. He reached for the nearest bottle of wine and began to pour. If you can't beat them, join them, he thought. Not that he ever drank to excess. But tonight might be the one to drive him to it.

'Whoa!' Daphne put her hand on his arm. 'It's a glass not a bucket.'

He looked down at what he'd done. The wine was almost at the rim of the glass. 'Oh, damn.'

'Let me help,' she said and, without waiting for him to agree, tipped half the contents into her own glass. 'I'll sip at it.'

As the neighbouring table of walkers began to fill up, their voices rose in volume, drowning out those at the family table. Tom looked up at the stars, feeling the evening stretch out ahead of him, and took a long swallow of his wine.

13

To Jo's dismay, Ivy had chosen to go with Lucy to sit further down the table. She watched her daughter with pride. Despite the bedraggled purple princess dress, Ivy looked adorable with her hair tied back in two uneven bunches. Lucy had found a couple of ribbons – one blue and one tartan – in Hope's sewing box. The only place left for her was beside cousin Adam, a reactionary know-all who could bore for England.

'Wine?' Adam was holding out a bottle of Rioja. The light glinted on the ginger hairs on his arms.

'Thanks.' Jo held out her glass. Anything to help her to get through this evening was welcome. Then she remembered she was driving and jerked the glass away without warning as Adam began to pour. The red wine splashed on to the tablecloth and, worse, on to her cousin's neatly creased cream chinos.

'Oh God, I'm so sorry.' She grabbed her napkin and pressed it against his thigh.

Looking appalled at this unprecedented physical contact, he snatched the napkin from her hand and dabbed at the deep red stains himself. 'Don't worry. Accidents happen.' He forced the words through his teeth.

'Salt? Water? White wine?' she offered, reaching for the water jug. 'I never know which is best.'

'I think I'll stick with red,' he said raising his glass and staying her hand with the other. 'Please don't! I'm wet enough. Cheers.'

She laughed and put the water down. So there was a sense of humour lurking in there, after all. But its appearance was short-lived and the two of them were soon struggling for conversation over the tapas, moving in desperation from the weather, to holidays, to the Spanish economy and the effect on expat housing. If she could have driven a nail into her brain to relieve the tedium, she would have. She looked down the table to see if Tom and Lucy were faring any better. All this enforced jollity must be just as hard for them.

At the far end, Tom looked as desperate as she felt. Ian and Daphne were arguing across him, something about British politics, not letting him get a word in edgeways. The expats out here were never shy about holding forth on how Britain should be run even though they hadn't lived there for years. Jo knew exactly how much he must be hating it. Even when things were going well, Tom was uncomfortable in large gatherings. He reached out for something to eat as Daphne passed Ian a plate of meatballs without waiting to see if he wanted one.

'The trouble with David Cameron . . .' Ian thumped on the table. Jo lost the rest of what he said as Brad offered her a piece of tortilla, asking her to explain what the other tapas dishes were.

'The NHS is finished.' Daphne's voice rang down the table, drowning out everyone else's conversation. She slopped more wine into her glass.

'Don't be so bloody ridiculous, woman. It's been going since 1948. Any government who lets it disappear needs its head examining. The country would be up in arms. Any privatising party in power would start losing seats hand over fist.' Bill picked up the nearest bottle as he joined in and poured himself a generous slug.

'Can't you see what's happening?'

Tom caught Jo's eye. He shrugged, with a look of resignation and, with a finger, quickly and surreptitiously mimed cutting his throat. What could he do except pray for the evening to be over soon? Nothing would stop these three once they were on a roll. She gave him a sympathetic smile, rolled her eyes. A noise from the neighbouring table made her look towards them. One of the walkers was trying to organise his friends into a commemorative photo to accompanying guffaws over jokes in a language she didn't recognise. Something eastern European, perhaps.

A shrill laugh brought her attention back to their table. Belle's head was thrown back in delight at something Art had said. He waited for her to finish laughing, clearly pleased with the effect he was having. He loved an appreciative audience. Jo watched, wondering what he was up to. He had barely talked to anyone else but Belle since they'd left the house. And she was lapping up the attention. 'That's not really true?' she twittered when she had recovered herself. 'Is it?' She bent over and placed a protective hand on Ferdie's head that was poking out of one end of the dog bag on a chair beside her. She tickled the base of his ears.

'On my life,' said Art, crossing his heart.

'No, really? What did the director say?'

Art leaned towards her and began to tell her, though they were too far away for Jo to be able to pick up exactly what the director had said. But whatever it was must have been hilarious, judging by Belle's reaction. The others stared at her as she dabbed her eyes with her napkin. Even Ian, Bill and Daphne paused for breath. Tom looked daggers down the table. When she had finished laughing, Art said something else that had Belle's eyes on stalks this time. 'No! But I've always thought she looked such a nice woman.'

Their heads separated as the waitress reached between them with their starters. They had spurned the tapas Lucy had ordered for everyone else in favour of a small salad each that included a suspicion of salmon and avocado. Belle picked up a fork and moved her food around the plate, then refocused on Art who was embarking on another story from the set.

Art and Lucy hadn't looked at each other once that evening. Not once. Usually, they communicated with a touch, a glance or a smile – all those things that couples did. But ever since Lucy had come downstairs in her blue dress – nothing. They had stuck to Belle and Ivy respectively as if their lives depended on them, barely exchanging a word with anyone else at the table.

As if aware of Jo's scrutiny, Lucy lifted her head from her conversation with Ivy and smiled. But the smile didn't reach further than her mouth. Her eyes were sad and looked even more red-rimmed than earlier. She radiated exhaustion and resignation. Jo resolved to find out why when they got home.

The walkers on the next table were growing louder by the minute. Bernard had them passing round a traditional *bota de vino*. One by one, the men held the leather pouch in the air and squirted wine into their mouths, trying to imitate the perfect arc that Bernard had demonstrated. The wine didn't even touch his moustache. Some couldn't get the flow going at all, others missed their mouths completely to roars of laughter while the success of the skilled one or two was met with loud cheers and stamps.

Lucy's table had to shout to make themselves heard. Just as Jo was losing the will to go on, a shriek rang round the restaurant. She knew without looking where it came from. Silence fell as the whole restaurant looked round. Sure enough, Ivy was off her chair, holding a soaking tartan ribbon in her hand. It must have fallen from her chair and landed in a puddle of wine from the next table. 'My ribbon,' she wailed.

Lucy tried unsuccessfully to console her. Her suggestion of cutting the remaining dry ribbon in two was met with hysteria as Ivy grabbed it, yelling,' My ribbon. Mu-m-my!'

Jo excused herself to Adam and Brad and went to her. 'Ivy, give me the ribbon.' She held out her hand. 'We'll wash it and when it's dry it'll be all ready to wear in the morning.'

'But I want to wear it NOW!' Ivy snatched it back and threw it on the table.

'She's exhausted.' Jo excused her to the table as she put her hands under Ivy's arms and swung her on to her hip. Ivy almost toppled them both over as she leaned down for the ribbon. Lucy passed it up to her just in time. Ivy pressed her cheek against

Jo's. Jo relaxed as they fitted together like a jigsaw. Then a small fist hit her head.

'Ow!' Jo grasped her daughter's hand so she couldn't do it again. 'Let's go and see if we can make a bed for you.' She made herself speak calmly, willing herself to be patient.

The next table had stopped staring and returned to their riotous eating and drinking.

'Nooo!' Ivy screwed up her little red face in fury.

'Come with us,' said Lucy, standing up. 'I know a place where we can make a special den just for you. And there might even be ice cream there.'

The bribe worked. Jo kicked herself for not being quick enough to think of it herself, then remembered her nanny Sue's disapproval of bribes. Perhaps they shouldn't. Ivy stopped crying immediately and looked at Lucy with big, watery eyes. 'Ice cream?'

Thank God for her sister.

'Yes, strawberry or chocolate.' Lucy led the way into a quiet corner of the bar, Jo wishing that she had Lucy's way with children. She was a natural, unlike her. One of the waiters helped them arrange four chairs and some cushions into a bed, a thick patterned blanket spread on top. The ice cream was produced and eaten, and Ivy's eyes began to close. With relief and gratitude, Jo produced Bampy from her bag – the finishing touch. Ivy wriggled into a comfortable position under the blanket while Jo stroked away the tendrils of hair that stuck to her damp forehead.

'It's way past her bedtime,' she whispered, in an attempt to excuse her daughter's gruesome behaviour.

'Not an excuse much used in this family!' Lucy whispered, and reached out to touch Ivy's shoulder.

'Do you remember when you were about this age, I once found you sound asleep curled up in one of the dog baskets? God knows how late it was when you'd crawled off there.'

'That's what Mum was like, though. She always let us dance to our own music.'

'Routine? What's that?' Jo sounded almost like Hope.

They smiled at each other, acknowledging their mutual understanding of their mother.

'Well, not having one hasn't done us any lasting damage. She just brought us up the way that suited her. Other things got in the way.'

'Are you OK?' asked Jo, still stroking Ivy's head although her daughter was already sound asleep.

'Of course. The whole weekend's a bit of a strain, that's all.' Lucy gazed at the floor, the toe of her shoe running up and down the join of the tiles.

Jo sensed there was more. 'There's something else, isn't there?'

'I'm really fine. Honestly. Apart from the fact that Ian has kept his hand on my thigh throughout the whole meal.'

'He's such an old goat! Why didn't you say something?'

'Didn't want to make a scene. This is meant to be the traditionally joyous dinner before the party.' She raised an eyebrow.

'Are you serious? I'd have slapped him down.'

'Bet he wouldn't have dared if Mum had been here. You wouldn't swap places, would you?'

'You'd rather sit between Adam and Brad? I'm not sure which is worse.'

'Provided I'm not by Art.' Lucy's screwed up her face as if she wished she hadn't said anything.

So something was going on.

'I don't mean that in that way,' she corrected herself quickly. 'All I meant was that we mustn't sit beside the person we came with. You know how Mum liked us to mix it up a bit.'

Jo was unconvinced. But they had been away from the table for too long already. She would have to get to the truth later. 'OK, then. Let's get back to the fray,' she said, gesturing to let Lucy go first. 'You should talk to Adam anyway – good luck with that.' She mimed a yawn.

Back at the table, she took Lucy's place as agreed, all ready to slap Ian down if he tried anything with her. But he hardly noticed the two sisters had changed places. Instead, he was busy arguing with a waitress who had brought him a plate of sardines.

'I wouldn't order those bony things if they were the last plate of food on earth,' he protested.

'Ian, I think you may have—' began Tom.

But Ian wouldn't hear of it. As he objected, he waved an arm and accidentally hit the plate that the long-suffering waitress was holding close by his head. The offending sardines flew up into the air. A couple of them landed and skidded across the tiled floor but another skimmed by Jo's head. She ducked just in time but the sardine, grilled and served with the restaurant's signature tomato sauce, smacked against Elaine's head, slid down her hair and settled in her lap.

She jumped to her feet with a shriek. 'Oh my God!' The fish fell to the floor, leaving a trail of tomato and oil down the front of her pale-green dress. She grabbed a napkin to take off the worst. 'Bloody marvellous!'

Ian stammered out an apology over the back of the waitress, who was retrieving the fish from the floor.

By Elaine's side Ethan was cracking up with laughter, despite the glare Belle shot at him across the table. He helped himself to a glass of wine. That only earned him another.

Antonio poured a glass of water. 'Would this help?' As he passed it over Ethan's head to Elaine, Ethan jerked upright in response to Belle's gesture telling him not to drink any more. So doing, his head knocked against the glass so water cascaded over his hat, dripping from its brim on to his T-shirt. A loud snort erupted from Alex across the table.

Ethan snatched the hat from his head and shook it dry, sending a spray of water towards Elaine.

The hysteria that had been skimming under the surface of the gathering erupted into the open as most of the table failed to contain their horrified laughter a moment longer. Even Elaine was smiling as she got up to join Ethan on his way to the *servicios* to put things right. 'Come on, Ethan. Let's go and clean ourselves up.'

The only people who ignored what was going on were Bill and Daphne, who were deep in an argument about the England/ Scotland divide. Daphne's distant Scottish relations apparently gave her the inside track and the authority to shout down any- thing Bill contributed to the conversation that might be seen to support the unionists.

'For Christ's sake, Bill. Don't you understand anything? The oil does not belong to England,' she roared as she stood up, glass in hand. 'Where's the Ladies?' she asked the waitress who pointed her towards the stairs. 'I'll be back to explain.' She sailed past Elaine and Ethan, who stopped at the top of the stairs to let her by. As if they had a choice. They looked at each other, and grinned. There was only room for one of Daphne so they would have to wait.

As Elaine took the banister, there was a shout, a crash and the sound of something substantial falling below her. They could hear Daphne shouting something in pigeon-Spanish.

Elaine watched what was going on then announced to the table. 'I think she may need some help.'

But Tom was already out of his seat on his way to the rescue. He rushed past Elaine and Ethan and, a moment or two later, he and a waiter emerged from the stairwell, one on each side of Daphne who was hopping up sideways. With their support, she hopped to the nearest chair amid cheers from the table of amused walkers.

She acknowledged them with a wave. 'Bloody stairs. I need a drink.' She held out her glass to the nearest waiter who took it to the bar. 'Tripped on the mat halfway up and went over on my bloody ankle. Heard it pop. May have broken that table! What a place to put it.' She lifted up her sizeable leg to rest it on the chair that Tom had brought over. 'It'll be fine. Just can't put any weight on it at the moment.'

The barman produced a bag of ice that Tom balanced on her ankle. 'You must keep it up. Don't put any weight on it. Do you want me to call the doctor?'

Daphne gave him a look signifying that of course she knew all that. 'There's no need. I'll be fine in a minute.'

Jo had been watching the proceedings in disbelief. Just when she thought the evening couldn't get any worse, it had done exactly that. 'What do you want to do, Daphne? Finish your supper or would you like me to take you home?' She had known Daphne long enough to know that she wasn't much interested in food when free drink was available.

'No, no. I'll call Ros. She'll come and get me. I don't want to break up the party.' Daphne took a mouthful of her wine. 'But I'll sit here. Can't stand being next to that stupid sod for another second. The union, for God's sake! Good excuse.'

Jo knew Ros, the equally solid Scotswoman who wrote the most surprising and tender short stories that were published by a small local press. The two women had lived together for years, making a modest living from the writing retreats they hosted. Hope had known them well. Jo hoped Ros would get there soon.

Brad and Ian appeared not to have noticed anything had happened; their voices were still raised in heated debate. Val was trying to draw Alex into conversation while Belle was deep in conversation with Adam and Art had transferred his attentions to Elaine who had returned to the table, a large wet stain marking her dress. Their heads were bent together as he explained something, before she reeled back laughing and the two of them burst into a snatch of song.

'In olden days a glimpse of stocking
Was looked on as something shocking'

Brad joined in for the chorus with a rich baritone that Jo hadn't expected.

'Now, heaven knows
Anything goes.'

They all started laughing again. At least someone was having a good time.

Elaine, her face flushed, called over to Jo. 'What a night. I can't help feeling that Hope's got her eye on us and is staging the most memorable weekend yet.'

'It's so weird to think this is the last,' she replied.

But Elaine had already turned back to Art.

Around them the conversations continued. Loud laughter rose from the adjoining table. Puddings were brought and eaten. Coffees were drunk. Antonio excused himself from conversation with Brad to go home. Jo watched him go, saw him cast a last, quick look towards Lucy who didn't notice. Tom tried to draw Ethan and Alex into the general conversation. Alex gave his father no more than he had to Val, obviously desperate to get back to the ebook that he had under the table. By contrast, Ethan was talkative, garrulous even. He had Adam and Val in stitches as he told them about being made to take part in a school sports day and coming last in everything. Jo wondered if she was the only one who had noticed how much he was drinking. Then she saw Belle's face, which told her she wasn't.

Eventually, the evening wound down. For Jo, the time to go home couldn't come soon enough. Good nights were said, lifts were arranged and promises of seeing each other the next day were exchanged. They left the walking group ordering another round of drinks.

14

In the absence of Ros, who had not been able to get away because she was ministering to a cat giving birth, Lucy had volunteered to drive Daphne home. While she went to get the four-by-four, the others rose to the challenge of manhandling Daphne safely down the stairs and out into the street with the restaurant manager fussing on the sidelines. By the time she had been manoeuvred into the passenger seat and Lucy was driving out of town, Daphne was snoring softly. As they reached the main road to Benarrabá, her wine-stained mouth was wide open and the snore was more of a rhythmic roar.

The smell of stale alcohol and garlic forced Lucy to open a window. She was glad Daphne was asleep. The last thing she wanted was company. The night air rushed into the car, bringing with it the faint smell of wild herbs. The road was empty except for a rabbit that crossed their path, its scut white in the headlights. It didn't stop to look at her.

Art. For the first time that evening, she allowed herself to process what he had told her. After all they had gone through together, perhaps because of it, he had finally fallen out of love with her. Perhaps finding comfort with someone who wasn't hurting and could give all of themselves to him was inevitable. Lucy had been so wrapped up in her own disappointment and sense of failure that she had unintentionally stopped letting him in.

The first scene she had seen him and Carrie share flashed into her mind. Carrie was playing the new consultant; beautiful, stern, plain-speaking, who wasn't afraid of making enemies and intimidated the rest of the hospital staff. All except for Art's character, the charge nurse who wasn't afraid to stand up for himself and his colleagues. When they clashed for the first time, sparks flew. There was definitely an electricity between them that several TV critics had recognised. But back then, Lucy had believed the two of them were acting.

What an idiot she had been.

Beside her, Daphne coughed and opened her eyes. 'Sorry you've had to do this, but I couldn't drive.' There was an intake of breath as she adjusted herself, moving her ankle to get comfortable. 'We'll have to pick up the car in the morning.'

'It's not a problem. I'm glad to have an excuse to get away for a bit.' Being alone long enough to sort herself out was what Lucy wanted more than anything.

'You mustn't mind Ian.' Daphne wiped the dribble from the side of her mouth. 'I saw his hand on your leg. He doesn't mean anything by it. He's just an silly old man.'

'So he should know better.' Lucy was immediately cross with herself for sounding so prim.

Daphne rummaged in her bag and brought out a hip flask. She unscrewed the top and tipped a quantity down her throat. 'Just a nightcap. Ros keeps the liquor under lock and key at home.'

Lucy didn't find that remotely surprising. They drove off the road and down a stony track, pale in the moonlight. She pulled up outside an open gate. Beyond it, the door to the house was ajar and a light beamed inside.

'She's up then.' Daphne opened her door then, finding it hard to get out on her own, reeled back as it swung shut in her face. 'She was a nurse in the Paleolithic period, so she'll bandage me up.'

'Let me,' said Lucy, going round to help.

The noise of their arrival had alerted the household. A Jack Russell came tearing out of the door, yipping around Lucy's knees. Music was playing inside: a soft, soulful something that she didn't recognise.

'Django, get down!' Ros, a woman equal in girth to Daphne but lacking the alcoholic blush, stood in the doorway blocking the light. She was cradling a cat to her impressive breast and watched as Lucy helped Daphne round the side of the car. When she saw Daphne unable to put weight on her right leg, she stepped forward. 'I knew you wouldn't be able to keep off the booze. You're hopeless. Wait a second. Let me put Orlando down. I'm keeping him away from Sheba and the kittens – four of 'em.' She disappeared inside to re-emerge a second later, empty-handed, to take Daphne's other side, as gentle as she was huge. 'Let's get you in the house.'

Between them, Lucy and Ros managed to get Daphne inside without tripping over the excited dog nipping between their legs. Once Ros had thrown the occupying newspapers on to the floor, they lowered her into an armchair. Lucy pushed a tapestried footstool towards her while Ros went into the adjoining kitchen for a pack of frozen veg to put on the injured ankle. Their windows were wide open. The light from inside cast long shadows across their much-loved and well-tended garden.

'Coffee? Tea?'

'I should really get home.' But in this shambolic house where everything was abandoned on whichever surface presented itself first, she felt almost relaxed for the first time that day. Having had a mother who could care as little as her friends for her surroundings, this reminded her of the chaos of her childhood home. She didn't want to get back in the car and confront the fears and anxieties awaiting her.

'Just a quick one. Daphne's having one.' Ros was not giving Daphne a choice in the matter. 'It won't take long to make. Come into the kitchen and tell me what happened.'

However forceful a character Daphne was in public, it was obvious who ruled the home roost. Lucy followed Ros into the kitchen where the chaos of the sitting room was, if anything, worse. A female cat was suckling four kittens in a basket. Various bowls of animal food were spread about the floor. Clean plates and cutlery were piled up all over the counter.

'There's no point putting all that away,' said Ros, catching Lucy's gaze. 'They only get used again.'

The walls, painted green many years earlier judging from the numerous nicks and scrapes, were decorated with pictures that mostly hung squint, including one of Walter's wilder abstracts. Postcards were stuck on the wall between them: grateful thanks from writers who had stayed with them and benefitted from being there. Ros set about making the coffee while Lucy told her what had happened.

Ros heard her out, then threw back her head with a loud guffaw. 'I warned you not to meet up with Bill and Ian first,' she shouted towards Daphne. 'And how will you go to the party tomorrow?'

The only reply was a snore.

'She wouldn't miss Hope's last party. Nor would I, even if I have to carry her.'

They both smiled at the picture that conjured up as Ros took three mugs that were stained tea-brown inside. She spooned instant coffee into each one.

'So sad to think that it's going to be the last one. We've had some high old times at their place. What's going to happen to it now?'

'We're selling it,' said Lucy. 'The estate agent's coming on Monday. Tom's got it all sorted.' As she spoke, she felt that same gaping hole opening up inside her again. The house had meant so much to all of them, but especially to her and Hope. Hope had once pinned her hopes and dreams for the future on it while Lucy's own dreams had been born there. Perhaps that was true of the others too. If only there was a way that they could keep the place, so that it would continue being part of their lives. Now Art was leaving her, perhaps she could move here for a while and

145

lick her wounds, start anew in a place she loved. But that wasn't what Hope had wanted and the other two would never agree.

'That's quick. Couldn't you leave it a while? Let things settle?' Ros stole a second look at Lucy, as if there might be more to the story than that.

But Lucy knew that anything she said would be round the local community in a flash. She limited herself to: 'It's what Mum wanted. She was very determined that we wouldn't be burdened with it.'

'I can imagine how determined that would be.' Ros poured the boiling water into the mugs and stirred each one. 'Hope always knew her own mind,' she went on as they rejoined Daphne who roused herself as they sat down. 'She knew what was right, whatever anybody else thought.'

'Last night we were wondering what she must have been like when she was younger, before we ever knew her,' said Lucy. 'What people must have thought of her having three children, each of us with a different father.'

'Shocking, I imagine.' Daphne tried to push herself into a more comfortable sitting position. 'But I don't think anyone really knew here. Not the Spaniards certainly. And those who did, like us, didn't care. After all, one of the reasons we moved from England was to escape from that sort of small-town, small-minded prejudice. She and Walter arrived with their happy family, and that's all that anyone knew. And it was all they needed to know.'

'It's true, we were happy. And Tom was fine with that although Jo still wants to know who her real father was.' She studied Daphne, who seemed to be avoiding her eye. 'Mum never said anything to you, did she?'

'No,' said Ros, refastening the slide that held her fine grey hair off her face. 'We all respected each other's privacy round here. We'd listen if talked to but would never ask. We all had our private reasons for coming here.' She looked at Daphne.

'She would never do anything to hurt Walter.' Daphne pushed

herself into a better sitting position, while Ros put a cushion at her back. 'And by the time he was gone, she felt it was too late for truth-telling. Couldn't face it on her own. Whatever 'it' was. That's all she once said to me.'

'But he was like a dad to the two of them.' Lucy found herself sticking up for her father once again.

'He was. He was a marvellous man and they loved each other to bits. He really supported her and let her lead the life she wanted. And she let him paint. They may have fought like cat and dog when they did, but it always blew over. And you can't have the highs without the lows. We know that!'

The two women laughed.

As she drove back towards Gaucín, Lucy was distracted from her own problems by memories of her parents that had been prompted by the conversation. All the drink-fuelled evenings she remembered observing had merged into one long, hazy reminiscence of Casa de Sueños filled with people. The terrace was hot and crowded, the sounds of talking and laughter rising over the music playing inside. Once a ten-year-old Lucy had watched Hope dancing on her own in a corner of the living room, swaying in time to the music, arms wrapped around herself. Walter came in, spotted her and took her in his arms. They moved to the centre of the room, where they danced together as if no one else was there. When the music stopped, they parted, slightly breathless, and their friends applauded. Lucy had run up to them, and they included her in a family hug. Hope loved being the centre of attention. But what bit of truth-telling couldn't she face? They'd never know now. And Art was just the same. Perhaps that was why they had got on. They recognised how much they had in common. And now he was leaving her too.

When she got home, she found everyone but Art still up and gathered chatting in the kitchen. Belle was making some herbal concoction that she swore guaranteed sleep. As she took the foul-smelling brew out of the room, she checked a little gizmo she pulled out of her pocket, and tutted.

'What's that?' asked Jo.

'My Fitbit. You should get one. Everyone in my walking group has. We call ourselves the Fitbitches.' She laughed at the joke. 'They count the number of steps you take in a day, and I'm way under the mark today.' She didn't wait for a reply, just walked off to the *casita*, Ferdie's bag in her free hand.

Tom and his boys grabbed glasses of water and went to their room to watch a film on Tom's laptop. Elaine and Brad made their excuses and took themselves to bed, leaving Jo and Lucy the only ones up. They sat on the terrace, a bottle of wine on the table between them.

'I'll miss all this,' said Jo, with a gesture that encompassed all they could see: the bulk of Sierra Crestellina to the East, orange and white lights twinkling at intervals all the way to the coast and beyond. The air was cooler thanks to the night breeze. In the distance there was the occasional hoot of an owl, the cry of an animal against the background of the cicadas.

'Not as much as I will.' Lucy took a sip of her drink. 'All my childhood and then all those visits to help Mum out when she needed me? I feel rooted here. I wish we didn't have to sell up.'

There was a pause before Jo spoke again. 'Is everything really all right between you and Art?'

'What makes you say that?' Lucy didn't want to talk about how humiliated and upset she felt. That would only make everything worse.

'I've been watching you both and I can tell something's wrong.' Jo was looking straight ahead. Her profile showed off her tipped-up nose, the scar on the side of her forehead from when she fell out of a tree as a child, always fearless, the one who went first, the one who went highest.

'I've just got a lot on my mind.'

'Mum? This place?'

'Oh Jo, I really don't want to talk about it.' But she knew Jo would worry away at this until she got an answer. Jo still had that occasional big sister's urge to look after her and Tom if they were in trouble. But Lucy didn't want to give her that pleasure, at least not until she had sorted out her emotions into some sort of recognisable order. At the moment they felt too raw to unpack and examine with anyone else.

'But maybe I can help,' Jo insisted.

She would have to say something, just to shut her up. 'It's the business,' she tried. Perhaps that would be enough to satisfy her. 'I haven't been able to pay it enough attention over the last few months and I've lost so many customers. You know better than anyone how you can't let up for a moment if you want things to keep up and running.'

'I certainly do.' Jo gave a rueful laugh. 'I've been checking my emails whenever I get a chance. This weekend we've had to get everyone in on the Flakers Crisps rebrand and I'd be furious with myself if it went wrong – it's a huge account for us that we can't afford to lose – even though Richard's more than cap-able of seeing it through without me.' She examined her hands, turning them in the light: neat squared-off nails, no jewellery. 'But that's not all, is it? You and Art have barely spoken to each other since he's been here.'

'Christ, Jo! Please don't go on. Everything's fine.'

'Lucy, I know you.' Jo gave her one of those know-it-all looks she was so good at. 'Where is he by the way? He's usually up for a last drink.'

'No you don't know me. Not really. It's not like when we were kids and saw each other all the time and knew everything that went on.' But she could feel herself teetering on the brink of con-fession. The temptation to offload everything, to have someone else understand a little of what she was going through, to help her sort it out, was getting stronger, despite herself. 'Probably trying to change his ticket home,' she said.

That made Jo sit up. 'Change his ticket home? Why?'

Lucy picked up the bottle and poured them both another drink. No, she was not going to explain now. Was not.

'You might as well tell me. I'll only find out in the end.'

That was probably true. Jo had an uncanny knack of being able to worm the truth out of people while at the same time keeping her own secrets to herself. The only person who had resisted her every effort was, of course, Hope, who had always refused to tell her the one thing she wanted to know until that last moment that came too late. Perhaps that was why Jo had developed such finely tuned antennae for what was what. Years ago, when Lucy was being ostracised by some of her class and didn't dare say what was happening for fear of reprisals, it was Jo who had worked out what was wrong and had taken the two ringleaders to task on the way home from school. Lucy had never found out what had been said, but they left her alone after that.

The same had happened when she was losing her heart over Juan, a barman in Gaucín. No one in the family could understand why she couldn't eat and spent half her time mooning in her bedroom, dreaming of ways to make him notice her. It took Jo to notice how she behaved whenever they went to town, and Jo to do the detective work to find out that he was twice her age, had a drug habit, was married and had beaten up one of his friends, before Lucy had been persuaded to turn her attention to someone else. And it was Jo who had always been on the end of the phone through those fruitless days of IVF when no one else wanted to know because they didn't know what to say. Yes, she had always looked out for her when she could.

'You might as well. After all I'm the only big sister you've got.' Jo blew her a kiss.

That was enough to topple Lucy's barriers. They might not be as close as they once were but perhaps they could be again. All she had to do was let go. She still didn't want to discuss what Art had been up to until she had got her own head round the fact he was going to be a father without her, but perhaps telling something of what had happened would help her do that. And so she began to talk about her struggling marriage, her failing business. As she did, she felt the relief of letting go of her secrets and of the strain of months of anxiety.

Jo didn't interrupt once, not even when she was being told stuff she knew already. Eventually Lucy confessed that Art was leaving although she still couldn't bring herself to mention Carrie or the pregnancy. She wasn't ready for the intolerable weight of sympathy that would come her way. Nor could she bring herself to explain how the whole affair was about to be splashed all over the press. Talking about it would make it real when she wanted to keep it at bay for a few more days. It would be public knowledge soon enough.

At last she stopped and the two sisters sat quietly in the terrace light with the darkness around them, reflecting. For Jo, there was sadness for her sister and the sense of frustration that came with, for once, being powerless to help her. For Lucy, there was the relieved but played-out feeling of having confessed.

15

They had only been watching the film for about half an hour when Tom realised he was in the wrong place. While Ethan and Alex were sniggering at innuendoes that shouldn't be funny to anyone over the age of about ten, he was balanced on the edge of the bed with his left foot braced against the floor. The screen was only visible if he craned his neck. When he overbalanced and slid off the bed on to the floor, the boys barely gave him a second look.

Alex's 'Where you going, Dad?' got lost in another gale of laughter. Neither of them tore their eyes from the screen. They didn't need him to be there. Long gone were the times when he would sit on their beds reading bedtime stories, being begged to stay for 'just one more'.

Tom felt old and weary. Life was going past too fast. He longed to be able to put a brake on it. He walked along to his and Belle's room and tapped on the door.

'Yes,' she called. 'At least, yes if it's you, Tom. I've been waiting...'

He recognised that tone. She was feeling frisky, but he was absolutely not in the mood. Usually it was the other way round. But the weekend had him on edge and he could not think of anything else. He opened the door and was immediately greeted by the bitter smell of her herbal sleeping concoction muddled with whatever lotions and potions she had been using in her tireless quest to hold back time. He looked at his watch. It was time for bed, especially given the long day ahead but he wasn't tired. These days, he found it hard to sleep for the full eight hours Belle claimed were an absolute necessity for a balanced life. Anxiety often kept him awake but being awake only made his anxiety worse.

Belle was sitting up in bed, her eyes shielded by a tartan eye mask. She raised her hand, as if she was about to lift it from her face. 'Tom?' She sounded nervous, as if she thought he might be an intruder.

Why didn't she just lift the damn thing and look?

Unable to resist, he tiptoed across the room and dropped his voice to a growl. 'I'll huff and I'll puff and I'll *blow* your house down.'

She shrieked and uncovered her eyes, disturbing the perfect fall of her hair. 'For God's sake!' Then she smiled. 'You are silly. Are you coming to bed?' She threw the duvet back off his side of the bed.

Tom had his exit strategy ready. 'I'm really not tired,' he said. 'Do you fancy a nightcap?' He knew what the answer would be.

'No, I'm exhausted. I was about to turn off the light.' She managed to convey just how disappointed she was that he wasn't going to turn in with her. 'And you shouldn't have one either. It'll only keep you awake. Why don't you take one of those valerian pills?' In a huff, she shunted herself down the bed until only the top of her head was visible. 'Good night...darling.'

Perhaps he should think again and join her, but he had left it too late. The moment had passed. She reached out a manicured and creamed hand from under the duvet and switched off her bedside light.

Why bother turning off the light if her eyes were blacked out? He'd only wake her up by tripping over something in the darkness when he came back into the room. He felt his way round the bed, stubbing his toe on its corner. The pain shot up from his nerve endings, bringing tears to his eyes. But even his shocked gasp didn't get the concerned reaction he could usually expect.

He felt his way to his bedside table and flicked on the lamp. Belle shifted her position and growled in protest. He grabbed his thriller, switched off the light and found his way to the door without further injury. He would make himself a drink and read in the living room.

As he walked across the courtyard back to the house, the appeal of a peaceful half hour to himself grew. In the kitchen, he unearthed a bottle of whisky and poured himself a couple of fat man's fingers on the rocks. The doors to the terrace were still open. He listened to the familiar sounds of the night. In the distance, a car. He settled himself in the comfortable chair by the fireplace, picturing Walter in the same place while Hope sewed or played the piano. Moments of domestic harmony. Now, instead of a fire, the grate was full of dusty pinecones from the woods and the piano stood silent, the sewing box shut. He had just opened his book when he heard a voice outside.

Disturbed, he crossed the room to see who was there. His two sisters were still up too, sitting on the terrace despite the cool breeze. Jo was leaning towards Lucy, who was huddled over her knees.

'Still up?' he asked, unnecessarily.

'We couldn't sleep, so we're having a much-deserved drink and a chat. Catching up.' Jo cast a glance towards Lucy, who had pulled her pashmina over her head so just her nose peeked out. Tom couldn't make out her expression. 'Come and join us.'

He went inside to get his drink while she pulled up another chair.

'Should we talk about tomorrow?' he asked. 'Have we got everything ready?' He should have checked hours ago, when reminded by Antonio. Every year since Walter's death, the paella was his responsibility.

'There's not much we can do about it now if we haven't.' His two sisters laughed like the co-conspirators they once were. The mild hurt he'd feel when they used to exclude him from what they were doing rolled back across the years.

To begin with, it had been Jo and he who were inseparable. Lucy's birth had only strengthened their bond. While Walter and Hope were preoccupied by the baby, he and Jo would take off to the woods. They'd spent hours out there, running wild, making dens, climbing trees. They'd spend ages watching trails of ants, making barricades so the insects had to find a way round. Then Jo would lose interest and drag him off to look at a black beetle stranded on its back or a lizard shedding its skin. They grew older and collected birds' eggs and feathers (though Jo quickly got bored with that). They played warriors hunting an unseen enemy. They made traps, digging holes and covering them with grass and twigs – that was stopped the day Walter tripped in one, twisting his ankle. Then Jo started riding at a newly set-up stables nearby. Tom never liked horses – too unpredictable, too dangerous for him. But riding gave Jo the freedom she craved, leaving him to their collections and his solitary nature study. Later, in the summers, when he and Jo returned to Spain in the school and then the university holidays, Lucy had hit her teens and the girls would closet themselves in their bedrooms and it was all hair and make-up, music and boys. Tom would be left on the outside. No wonder he and Maria had eventually been drawn together during those long, hot summers by the pool or at the beach. And then he had chucked in his course and come home. But that was all another world now.

He stood and looked at the stars, the constellations pin-sharp against the darkness. 'Remember how Mum and Dad would sit out here for hours at night, star-gazing? They tried to teach me the names of all the constellations but I could never remember them.'

'That's Orion's Belt,' said Jo, waving an arm towards the night sky. 'At least I think it might be.'

'Where?' Tom tipped his head to look. 'Are you sure? At this time of year?'

As Jo pointed out the stars she was looking at, Tom suddenly remembered Hope and Walter sitting just where Lucy and Jo were. A hot summer day and they'd dealt a game of snap on the low table between them, including a hand for him. An Indian silk scarf kept his mother's hair off her face, its two ends draped over her shoulder. In the heat, her face was slicked with sweat. Walter was topless as usual, a column of ash building up on his cigarette before dropping into his greying chest hair. The game of Snap had been fast and furious, hands smacking on top of each other as they claimed the different piles, voices rising as they shouted 'Snap!' Then, all of a sudden, the mood changed.

'What are you doing, Walt?' His mother's voice was sharp. 'That was mine.'

'I don't think so.' Walter scooped up the pile of cards. 'Don't be such a bad loser.'

Like a child, Hope tipped the table so the cards scattered on the ground. But Walter was having none of it. He picked her up and carried her, laughing and kicking and screaming, all the way to the pool and chucked her in the deep end. He and Tom thought it was the funniest thing. She didn't speak to them for hours afterwards.

'Bailey!' Lucy welcomed the dog as he ambled up to them from the direction of the olive trees. 'What are we going to do with you?'

'I think you'd better sticker him and take him home,' joked Jo. She moved to sit on the low terrace wall and ran her hand over the top of the lavender on the other side, then stopped to squeeze the leaves. She smelled her fingers.

'Hope must have had a plan,' said Tom.

'She thought Antonio would have him.' Lucy scratched the dog under the chin so that he stretched out his neck and wagged his tail with pleasure. 'I think he will.'

'Is he going to be here tomorrow night?' Tom rather hoped not.

'Of course. He's bringing up the key to the chest.'

He groaned.

'It could be worse,' Jo said. 'At least she hasn't organised a treasure hunt this year.'

'Or thought that fancy dress was a good idea. What about that year when we all had to come as something exotic?'

'And Bill came as a banana!'

While the sisters laughed, Tom was worrying about Hope's latest plan. 'What do you think these presents are?'

'Bits and pieces for friends, I should think. One last thing for them to remember her by.' Lucy waited as Bailey rested his head on her lap, then continued scratching his ears.

'But for us?'

'Not a clue. And maybe she changed her mind. I hope we're not going to be embarrassed in front of everyone. I wouldn't put it past her.'

'Oh, Jo,' Lucy's voice was full of reproach. 'She wasn't that bad. She loved us all to bits.' She bent over, taking Bailey's head in both hands, and kissed his nose.

'She had a funny way of showing it sometimes. What about those times when she forgot to pick us up from school because she got caught up doing something else? God, it was hard being the child of such a free spirit.' Jo flung open her arms to the sky, as she took the mickey out of herself. 'Does funny things to you.'

'Being a parent's hard,' said Tom. 'You should know that by now.' He deadheaded one of the geraniums in the pot beside him and started tearing off the dried petals, one by one. 'We all know what Philip Larkin said about being fucked up by our parents. They may not mean to but they do. All of them.'

'I won't fuck up Ivy,' said Jo, quick to leap to her own defence. 'Whatever you do with Ethan and Alex.'

'Oh, but you will,' said Tom, half-smiling into the night. 'You may not mean to but you will. We all do. That's all part and parcel of the human condition.'

'Very deep.' Jo took a sip of her wine.

'Well, at least it's something I won't have to worry about.' Lucy was sounding more robust at last. 'That's a blessing at least.'

'That's very glass half-full,' said Tom. 'But at least you've got your business. How's that going, anyway?' he asked, eager for a change of subject to something less emotional.

Jo laughed. 'You are funny.' She knew exactly what he was doing.

'No, I'm interested. Really. It must have been difficult with Hope staying.'

'It was.' Lucy sighed. 'Not helped by Book the Cooks starting up at the end of last year. I told you about them. Two of them were friends of mine and they opened up their own cookery school and catering company just a few miles away. As soon as I was preoccupied with Mum, they scooped up my clients. Some friends!' She kicked at the terrace wall. 'They stole my idea and then they stole my customers. I won't get either back now – they're too good. That's why I was thinking maybe I could set up a B & B or even a small hotel of some sort.' Her voice wobbled. 'But now things have changed again, and I don't know what I'm going to do.'

'Changed how?' asked Tom but Jo quickly spoke over him. 'Can't think of anything worse,' she said. 'Are you sure?'

'Yes,' said Lucy, sitting straighter. 'I think I'd be good at it.'

'If you're serious, I could help you with a business plan or a projection.' This was where Tom excelled. Facts and figures. Business contacts and a clear head for numbers and priorities – that was what it was all about. 'You'll need a proper forecast.'

'Thanks. Everything's a bit in the air at the moment. But you'll be the first to know.' Lucy got out of her chair, folded her blanket and left it on the back of the chair. 'I think I'll turn in. I've got a lot to think about.' She leaned down and kissed them both good night.

Tom and Jo sat in silence.

'What's she got to think about?' asked Tom when he could wait no longer.

'Don't ask.' Jo finished her wine. 'I swore I wouldn't tell.'

'But this is me,' said Tom. A large part of him shied away from what might be an emotional minefield but he should do his bit by his family where he could.

'What about Maria turning up?' Jo attempted a neat change of subject. 'You're OK about her coming tomorrow?'

'Of course.' He tried to sound as if whether she was there or not didn't matter, but the words stuck in his throat.

'But seeing her again threw you, didn't it? I could tell.'

'No,' he said firmly, meaning yes. 'All that was a long time ago.' If he said it firmly enough, perhaps he'd believe it too. 'We've got our own lives now.' But he had been more disturbed by the visit that he cared to admit.

'By the way, did you see that the old house has been developed at last?'

'What? Not *our* old house?' For years the derelict finca had been his and Jo's secret hideaway. In case of discovery, Jo had the idea of rigging traps that would bring branches crashing down on intruders or make them trip over. They worked hard together making sure they would hear anyone approaching. They brought down stuff from the house to furnish it. Hope never noticed the garden cushions from the garage went missing. The sleeping bags they used when camping in the garden were brought down too. They smuggled out food from the larder and the fridge so they could feast next to the fire they'd light in what must once have been the living room. The roof of the place had long gone so they'd lie on their backs, watching the sky and telling each other stories. It had been theirs for months until, one day, they heard a crash followed by some shouting. Jo had been on her feet immediately. 'It's the boys from the farm. Quick! Grab a stick. We'll fight them off!' But he had grabbed her arm and pulled her out of the back door and on to the track home. They were no match for those boys – or at least he wasn't going to risk himself finding out.

'I was so angry when you made me run away,' she said now.

'That wasn't running away. It was a tactical retreat,' he protested as he had always done when she reminded him.

'I wanted to fight.'

Even in this light, he could see the same gleam in her eye. 'I know you did. To the death. And I wasn't ready for that.'

She laughed. 'You never were. And after that we couldn't get near the place. Sami's traps were way better than ours.'

'Someone must have sold it at last. We should go and look at the place.'

'Let's.' She leaned back in her chair. 'We had a good time here really, didn't we?'

'Yes,' he agreed. 'Over too soon. Growing up doesn't often come like that any more. You'll see. Our boys couldn't be less interested in that sort of thing.' That was the nearest he'd ever come to talking childcare with her.

'I'm already finding that out,' she said and patted his hand.

SATURDAY

16

Jo woke early to the sound of a cuckoo. For a second she
thought she was back in England. But outside the sky was that
perfect blue once again as the sun climbed higher. The sounds
of building work travelled from somewhere lower down the
hillside. A bee buzzed in through the open window, then out
again. She lay on her back, eyes shut, enjoying this moment of
peace, remembering others of Hope's birthday weekends, most of
which had involved some drama of one kind or another. There
was the time Daphne threw a full glass of *tinto verano* over their
neighbour during an argument. When everyone else weighed in,
the only way Hope could stop it was by getting Walter to fire his
air rifle over their heads – nothing like the appearance of a gun
to break up a party quickly. Or the occasion when Hope broke
her ankle when she tripped, dancing around the garden. Another
sure-fire way of bringing a halt to proceedings. Then there was
the time the chessboard was overturned in rage when Ian accused
his opponent of cheating. Hope's parties were never predictable,
never dull, and she had relished every minute of them: the more
drama the better. Jo pulled up the sheet to her chin. Ivy's steady
breathing rose from the mattress in the corner.

They were sharing Jo's old room, just as she'd hoped. For years
Hope had kept it like a shrine to the daughter she had lost, never
understanding her three children's choice to settle in grey old
England, the country she had left far behind her. Had she hoped
they would return one by one when their education was complete? Perhaps, but Walter had spent the dregs of his inheritance

making sure their children had what he regarded as the best start in life. And the best start, as far as he was concerned, was an English education. He didn't trust the local schools to do the job completely. So off they were packed at sixteen to be finished off and polished into university students (English, of course). But by making that choice and setting them free, he forfeited their closeness as a family. The upheaval of leaving and making new friends had been ghastly but they had all survived and made their own very different lives. Even though Tom had broken off his degree and come back for a year or so until he was ready to return, in the end he chose to leave for a life in England. And yet this house had always remained at their centre, the place to which they always returned, however sporadically, the place where they belonged.

When Hope finally accepted her children weren't coming home, the board games and books were stashed in the cupboard, the walls were stripped of the postcards and paintings. Jo's childhood clothes were given away. Her graffiti and wall paintings were obliterated under coats of white paint. The height chart she made on the door frame herself disappeared too. Walter's paintings of local landmarks now hung on the walls instead. Down came the faded cotton curtains to be replaced by pretty floral patterns. The shutters were restored and repainted a deep green. A couple of rag rugs were thrown down on the wooden floor. A new, distressed (one of Hope's later hobbies) chest of drawers was the final nail in the transformation of Jo's childhood lair into an attractive guest bedroom with a view. Tom and Lucy's rooms had received exactly the same treatment.

The only nod to Jo's youth was the old school desk and chair kept in a corner for visiting children. Jo knew every scratch and ink-stained score on its surface. She had decorated it with a yellow spot the night before. That and the loose floorboard. Jo had checked it was there the previous night and was going to share her hiding place with Ivy later.

Breathing deeply, Jo tensed and relaxed every muscle group in her body, starting at her toes and working gradually upwards until she reached the tips of her fingers and finally her forehead. The urge to look at her emails filtered away – almost. Just as she was feeling at one with the universe, floating somewhere just above the bed, her focus was distracted by a thump somewhere to her right. A second later, a weight landed on the bed beside her and a small thumb and finger were prising open her eyes.

'Ow!' She opened them herself before she was blinded. Ivy, still rumpled from sleep, was curled in a ball beside her. 'Come here, monkey.' She lifted one side of the sheet so her daughter could crawl into her arms.

'Love you.' Ivy smacked a kiss onto her cheek.

Jo inhaled the hot, sweet-sour smell of her daughter. One of the best she knew. 'Love you, too.'

'Love you, three.'

'Love you, four.'

'Love you to infinity and beyond.' Ivy leaped from the bed, one arm stretched out above her head in a passable imitation of Buzz Lightyear. 'Let's go find Ferdie.'

Jo clicked on her phone to check the time and groaned. 'He'll be asleep – it's too early.' She could imagine the confined joy that would greet Ivy if she let her loose on the rest of the household now. She dragged her mind into gear. If only she and Lucy hadn't opened that last bottle. 'Why don't you see if you can draw him for Aunty Belle, instead.' Aunty Belle. How odd those two words still sounded when put together. For years, neither she nor Lucy had thought of Belle as anything but Tom's rather trying wife, mother of his boys. But now, after a careless night in bed with a man Jo barely knew, whom she had never seen again since – well, everything had changed and Belle would be forever the aunt of her child.

Despite the beginnings of a headache, she stumbled out of bed to get Ivy's drawing book. On second thoughts, she pulled her iPad from the rucksack. Under Sue's 'expert' nannying influence, Jo was determined not to belong to the band of mothers who settled their four-year-old in front of their iPad or the TV for an hour or two while they snoozed for a bit longer. But on the other hand they made life so much easier. And why shouldn't Ivy enjoy what other kids enjoyed? This was childhood, twenty-first-century style. She found the animal pairing game. And educational, too? She might have come to motherhood late and unexpectedly but she longed, above everything, to make a good job of it. But it was hard. She tried to follow the advice in the childcare books she had read more times than she could count, but Ivy didn't always react the way those children in case studies did. Jo recognised she was a pushover when it came to her daughter and it was to Sue's despair. Getting Ivy to sleep in her own bed had been a job and a half. But what was nicer than having your toddler under the duvet with you? Don't answer that, she warned herself. It had been a while since she'd had a man there. She was discovering that men were wary of single mothers of her age, nervous of being sized up as instant father material.

But Ivy would always come first now. And when the time was right, Jo would tell her who her father was. She would not do what her mother had done to her and squirrel away the information until it became an issue. However, she would have to be so sensitive about the timing and the way she explained things. Thank God Ivy was too young to understand just yet. Or was she? Perhaps Jo was beginning to understand Hope's reticence a little better at last.

On second thoughts, she would go with the drawing option after all. She slipped the iPad back and retrieved the drawing book instead, earning herself a gold star from Sue. Fortunately Ivy seemed not to notice.

Ivy grabbed the pencil case and sat down. 'My desk,' she announced.

'Mmm', murmured Jo as she fell back into bed. She lifted her laptop from the floor where she had left it before she went to sleep and clicked into her emails and began flicking through, checking nothing needed her urgent attention. Her partner Richard had briefed her on what was happening with the rebrand and how he had everything under control. She needn't have worried. She looked towards Ivy bent over the paper, intent on what she was doing. 'Is that Ferdie?'

'Nope.' The intensity of her daughter's efforts doubled after she'd screwed up one piece of paper and started again. 'I'm writing down my name so when Grandma Hope wakes up from her death she'll know who I am.'

Jo was stumped for an answer, so settled for, 'That's nice,' and returned to her emails.

Eventually satisfied, Ivy padded across the room and presented Jo with her name unevenly written in red crayon. As Ivy chose one of the picture books they had brought in the backpack, she said, 'When will I die?'

'Oh, not for a long time.' Jo made herself sound breezy, despite the flip of her stomach. She snapped shut her laptop. Richard didn't need her interfering, whereas Ivy did. Since her grandmother's death, the child had developed an interest in death that was bordering on obsession.

'After you?' She wasn't about to give up.

'I hope so.' Oh God! What was she meant to say? There must be advice for dealing with questions like this but she had left her childcare manual at home. What would Sue say?

'When will you die?' Ivy snuggled into the curve of Jo's arm and gave her *The Gruffalo*, her current favourite, then rolled on to her stomach and rubbed her nose on the pillow.

'I've got no plans to die. You don't need to worry about that.' Keep it matter of fact. Change the subject.

'Where is Grandma Hope?' Ivy crossed her legs.

Good question. Jo sat up straighter. Where indeed was her

mother? Still in the baggage reclaim in Majorca? Or might she have made it to Malaga by now? Tom would be steaming if not. 'In heaven,' she volunteered. Appalled to hear herself giving the one answer she had vowed never to give, she corrected herself. 'Actually, the truth is I don't know.'

'Why not?'

'Because no one knows what happens when you die. Let's read this.' She opened *The Gruffalo* at page one.

'Why don't they know?' Ivy looked at her, resting her chin on her hand. 'I don't want to die.'

Jo reached out to stroke Ivy's tangled hair. 'You're not going to for a very long time. Don't worry. I won't let you.' Another lie, but surely a necessary one. She was way out of her depth here. 'Look at this.' She pointed at the illustration guaranteed to divert Ivy's attention.

'Grandma Hope did.'

For pity's sake! Why wasn't the Gruffalo working his usual magic?

'Yes, well she was old.'

'I don't want to get old.' Ivy rested her head on Jo's shoulder, so she could see the book properly.

'Everybody gets old, Ivy Rose.' Jo tickled her daughter who giggled, then looked inquisitive again. 'Remember how you were three last year and now you're four? That's what getting older is. If we didn't get older, we wouldn't have any birthdays. And you wouldn't like that, would you?' She could see Ivy building up to another question. Quick, think of something. 'Why don't we go downstairs and get some breakfast. We could take Bailey for a walk before it gets too hot.'

'In my pants?!'

'It's your shorts or your pink top until our case comes. You choose. It'll be an adventure.'

'I'll wear the princess dress, then.'

*

168

Belle was, as always, a couple of steps ahead of Tom. Her hair was held in place by a pristine white eyeshade. When she ran, she reminded Tom of a dressage pony. Her head was perfectly balanced, her back was ramrod straight and ever since Ethan had accused her of running like a girl, she had changed her gait to a high-stepping trot. She had dragged Tom out of bed early, convincing him that the early morning was the best time for a run. Not this early! He stole a look at his watch. 6.45 a.m. That late-night whisky was not helping.

The trainers that she suggested he pack 'just in case' were already wearing a sore patch on his heel. He had paid a fortune for them from some state-of-the art running shop only a month earlier when he and Belle had agreed to embark on a new stage in their joint health-and-fitness campaign. This plan included running together – whenever Tom couldn't find a convincing excuse. Out here he didn't have the convenient demands of work to fall back on. Belle might raise an eyebrow but she would never question those. She, on the other hand, had embraced this new regime with the frightening vigour that she gave to every new project. Each morning, she fastened her Fitbit on to her wrist, squeezed herself into her deep-blue Lycra and headed off to the park, waving as he passed her in the car on the way to work – a guilty muffin and a latte on the passenger seat.

His shorts were already chafing his inner thighs. Belle had spent more of his hard-earned salary on Lycra for him too, but wearing it made him feel like an idiot. Even sore thighs were preferable to that. He considered taking off his T-shirt but he didn't want to bare his less-than-perfect physique. Having seen Art flaunting his worked-on body around the house, Tom (and Belle, most probably) was all the more aware of his incipient paunch, his less-than-perfect pecs and flabby upper arms. He had noticed how both Elaine and Belle hadn't been able to tear their eyes from his brother-in-law.

He was falling behind. The band of his baseball cap felt welded to his scalp. He stepped up his pace as Belle turned her head and flashed him a white smile. She started jogging on the spot while she waited for him. It would be uncharitable of him to notice that the running had yet to have an obvious effect on her figure, but he couldn't help himself.

'All right?' she said as he panted up beside her. 'Isn't this beautiful?' She removed the earphone from her right ear, never missing a step.

He could hear a tinny voice floating from her hand into the morning. She must be listening to one of her improving podcasts. Her urgent drive for perfection was admirable even if he did sometimes find it a little wearying.

They had driven up to Gaucín and were running on a trail that looped through the cork oak forests on the other side of the village. The track ahead curved round to the left, past trees that looked strangely naked with the thick cork barks stripped from their smooth lower trunks. The best of the spring flowers were over, but the stony ground was still bright with pink rock roses, scabious and occasional poppies and dandelions.

Tom bent over, hands on his knees, waiting for his heart to resume its normal rhythm, for the burn in his calves to ease. He could see Belle's natty trainers still tattooing the ground as she jogged beside him. When he recovered himself, she stopped to stretch her hamstrings, then her quads.

'Ready?' she asked, shaking out her arms.

'Shouldn't we turn back? I really should be there for when Mum's ashes arrive.' His heel was stinging like nothing on earth. His knees felt distinctly unsteady. He felt a wild need to escape from everything. He wanted to be free, to be himself, to not give a toss. Had he been like that once – or was he dreaming? Then he glanced at his wife and registered that her expression was one of real affection. Despite her occasional infuriating moments, she did love him. Always had.

The pressure of her hand on his back made his T-shirt stick to him. The sweat felt cold against his skin.

'We've got time to do this first,' she said, her hand shifting as she jogged. 'You're always talking about getting priorities right. This should be one of our first. If we don't get fit, we won't be good for anything.'

'You don't think this is too ambitious for me? I'm finding it . . . quite tough.' He deliberately added the 'quite'. He didn't want her to know he was struggling as much as he was.

'Not at all.' She was smiling in that way that meant she knew he was perfectly capable. 'You can always walk a bit, if it's too much.'

No way was that going to happen.

'It'll be too hot soon.'

'Tom! It's not even seven in the morning. We'll be home by eight if we get on. The others will only just be up. Come on.' With that she checked the number of steps she had run, the number of calories expended, gave a small but satisfied smile, and set off again. She was not going to let him off the hook.

She was right. Of course she was. He would be back in plenty of time. Unless he broke his leg or had a heart attack or did in his kneecaps. But if he did, then they would have to manage without him anyway. Besides, Lucy and Jo were just as anxious as he was that everything should be right. He flapped his T-shirt in an attempt to dry it off. Then, with a heartfelt sigh, he took off after his wife, one foot in front of the other, his legs objecting to every step.

As he ran, his mind refused to rest, distracting him from his physical discomfort. Would Hope's ashes be there in time? What would her presents be? Should he make a speech? The thought started in his mind for the first time. Of course he should. How could he not have thought of that before? What would he say? What else could go wrong? Who else would turn up? How would he introduce Maria to Belle? As they dipped down into a valley where the river bed was thick with flowering pink oleander, the demands of his body finally took over so all these questions flew out of his brain at last and all he could do was focus on the path up towards the waving yellow broom ahead of them, and into the woods again.

At last he concentrated on the job in hand, increased his speed to catch up with Belle who was taking the bend ahead of him. It wouldn't do to let her get the better of him altogether. He would never hear the end of it. He would show her he was a match for her. If it killed him.

Lucy had barely slept.

When she had finally got to bed, Art was already tucked up. He lay on his back, hands linked behind his head with his eyes shut. His mobile was on his bedside table with his Kindle. As she moved around the room, he opened his eyes.

'I've checked the flights and I can't get a seat till Sunday.'

Her heart sank. All she wanted was for him to leave so she could concentrate on the rest of the weekend.

'What would you like me to do?' He sounded like an uncertain child.

She was too numbed and exhausted to find the disdain she wanted. 'We'll just have to act as if nothing's happened. Pretend. You shouldn't find that too hard.' She heard him sigh and the creak of springs as he turned over, away from her.

The rest of the night had been torture. She had lain with her back to him, rigid, not wanting to touch him, not wanting him there. She didn't want to be reminded of what they once had, of what he was now going to share with another woman. But how hard it was, feeling his presence, smelling his familiar scent, listening to his breathing. Even though things hadn't been perfect between them for some time, she had never wanted them to end like this.

She went over and over the last nine months, reliving the

things they had done together, looking for signs she had missed. She could find nothing. He had played the part of the husband, the concerned son-in-law quite brilliantly, without raising a single suspicion. Yet all that time he and Carrie had been having an affair. That time he was at home when Lucy and he had gone to dinner with Fay and Edward, they'd gone home and made love, perfunctory as it was. He hadn't behaved any differently. Every walk they had taken, when they'd even held hands once and kicked through leaves, even when he lost his wellie in the mud. All those episodes of *The Good Wife* they'd watched together, those shared bottles of wine over meals she took special trouble over because he was at home again, those jokes he made and she laughed at – small pleasures that she had believed they both enjoyed together, despite their lack of any real communication. All a sham. And then he had to end it this way.

He had only been forced into telling her by the press, not even by his own conscience. Could he have chosen to be any more selfish, more hurtful? If the paparazzi hadn't caught him, when would he have broken the news? Beneath her shock and unhappiness, she felt that first shoot of anger growing stronger. With it came a desire to hit back. However hurt and humiliated she might be, she would hold her head high. She had done nothing wrong. She had tried everything to make their marriage work, to have a family, but Nature was against her. Not just against her, against both of them. Their expectation and longing for that big, happy family had been denied – but not to him. Instead, she would have to reshape her life into something different that she would be equally proud of. Not being broken by this would be her revenge. Finally, with her new but shaky resolve and the whisper of an idea, she had drifted into a disturbed sleep.

Now, moving around the kitchen on autopilot, she willed herself to concentrate on the day ahead. Making a big breakfast for everyone would give her something to do until the others were up. She was peeling some garlic cloves to rub on toast with olive oil when a dishevelled Art appeared.

'You snuck out very quietly,' he said, almost as if nothing had changed.

'Didn't want to wake you.' If she could have arranged it, he would remain asleep until the weekend was over.

'Look, Lou. I really am sorry it's happened this way. It's the last thing we wanted . . .'

We? She froze.

'. . . and I'm sorry I'm stuck here making things more difficult for you. Would you like me to find a hotel? Would that be better?'

She gazed at this man who she had once loved so dearly. Whatever feelings she once had for him had left her. Moving to a hotel would make his life so much easier, but she didn't want him let off the hook that easily. 'It's all right,' she said. 'We'll manage.'

'Will we?' He sounded doubtful.

'Just for one day? I think we can do that.' She didn't know where her strength was coming from, but it felt good. 'Hope would want you to be here. She might not like what you've done, but for some reason that I can't quite think of right now, she was always fond of you. Just stay away from me as much as possible.'

'Have you told anyone?'

Of course that's what mattered most to him – the opinion of others. How had she put up with that for so long? The knife slipped and cut her finger. 'No.'

'Good. I think that's for the best, don't you.'

She held her finger under the tap, her blood running away with the water. She didn't want the attention the news would bring either. 'But I meant what I said. When you get back, take what you need and go before I get home. We'll sort out the details later.' She stopped before her voice let her down. She would not let herself be brought down by this, however difficult that might be.

He took a step towards her. 'Let me.'

'I can manage.' She opened the cupboard where the First Aid box was kept. The last thing she needed was his help or his sympathy. 'Just help yourself to coffee and leave me to get on in here. I've got plenty to do before everyone gets up.'

'OK.' He didn't bother to disguise his relief. 'Then I'll have a quick swim and keep out of your way.'

She didn't look up when he eventually left the room, just watched a tear drop onto the chopping board in front of her.

And so the day began.

17

By mid-morning, the preparations were underway. The gaudy but faded bunting that Hope brought out once a year was strung through the olive trees in front of the house. Tom had lined the drive with candle lanterns and flares to be lit after sundown before hurrying off to make sure he had enough wood for the open fire to cook the paella. Hope's ashes still hadn't arrived despite all the airline's promises, so he was taking his mind off them by keeping busy. He had given jobs to all his immediate family. Alex had been torn from his Kindle and was arranging tea lights on the wall surrounding the terrace, on every ground-floor window ledge. Where Alex went, Ivy now followed. She had transferred her fickle affections for the morning ever since he had read her two stories in a row with the promise of more.

Belle was in charge of the outside seating arrangements so she had arranged all the rugs and cushions she could find on the grass below the terrace. She kept her eye on the rest of her family, checking they didn't need her help. Ethan was down at the pool, fishing out leaves and dead insects. The loungers had been arranged just so (with his mother's interference), towels arranged over their backs in case anyone wanted to swim. More tea lights and lanterns were arranged on the low tables between them. There was a splash as he must have given up his job and leaped into the water.

Jo stood on the terrace, scratching her head as she wondered what they had forgotten. The only thing she could think of that was missing was Hope herself. Gone but hardly forgotten. Tom had been on the phone to the airport yet again, been passed from one person to another until he slammed the phone down in a fit of rage. She wished he would let her take over before he had a heart attack.

In the distance, the African coast was hidden in a bluish haze. A couple of small clouds had appeared in the west, but nothing to worry about yet. Jo fixed on them watching them change until one of them took the form of a pharoah's head. Hope had always been best at that game of seeing impossible shapes in the most ordinary of clouds, but Jo had always prided herself on coming a close second.

Satisfied that everything was going to plan, she returned to the kitchen where Lucy was at the centre of a buzz of activity. She was in her element, handing out tasks to whoever was there and making sure everything met her exacting standards. No one would guess that anything was wrong, and, Jo reminded herself, no one must know.

'Jo! Where have you been? I need someone to chop these squid.' Lucy gestured towards a couple of bags on the worktop. 'I meant to do half of this yesterday but everything else took over.'

'Sure.' Jo grabbed the knife that was thrust at her and got to work alongside Tom who had come in to de-beard a heap of mussels. Elaine was peeling vegetables for Brad to slice. The two of them were absorbed in a discussion about the latest in the tennis, occasionally checking Brad's phone to see what was happening.

'I didn't know you were keen on sport,' said Jo, curious.

'Ah, but I'm a woman of many interests!' Elaine laughed as she passed Brad another carrot.

After his swim and a bite of breakfast, Art had driven off under the pretext of doing some shopping. If anyone had noticed the coolness between him and Lucy, nobody had said anything. After all, this wouldn't be the first time Hope's party would be distinguished by a spot of marital disharmony. These things usually blew over.

As the afternoon began, their guests retired to prepare themselves before the other partygoers began to arrive. Jo managed to persuade Ivy to nap with the promise of a swim and a woodland fairy hunt afterwards. Alex was to thank for that, despite Ethan's scorn. Jo was beginning to realise there was more to her young nephew than she had given him credit for.

But there was still no sign of her green suitcase. No sign of Hope.

She could hear Tom on the phone to the airline again. He, of course, had got there first. 'What do you mean you didn't have a driver? Put the bloody thing in a taxi. Is it beyond the wit of man...' His self-control seemed to have deserted him altogether.

Jo left him to it. What mattered more than the ashes arriving was that they held a party that would not disappoint the guests or let Hope down. At the kitchen door, she stopped. Inside, Lucy and Antonio were standing opposite one another, by a large bowl of cold garlic soup. Lucy was holding out a spoonful to Antonio so he could taste it. As the spoon entered his mouth, he closed his eyes, a look of intense pleasure crossing his face.

'Mmm. *Magnífico*,' he murmured.

As he opened them again, they met Lucy's. She gave a funny little dreamy smile back. For a moment, unaware Jo was there, they stood lost in a world of their own.

Jo cleared her throat. At the sound, Lucy jumped, collecting herself immediately. 'I think that's perfect,' she said. 'Simple but good.'

But Jo didn't miss the flush on her sister's cheeks as she turned away to put the spoon in the sink.

'Jo!' Antonio came towards her to kiss her on both cheeks. She tried not to let her thing against beards get the better of her as his touched her cheek, and kissed him back.

'How are you, Antonio? I'm sorry we didn't chat much yesterday.'

'*Muy bien*. I'm well. Thank you.'

She and Lucy had always joked about his 'bedroom eyes' but she had never really studied them before. They were the colour of woodsmoke, heavy lidded with thick dark lashes. He smiled. His chipped front tooth made a not-quite-perfect smile all the more charming. She had never noticed that either. Hope must have, though.

'This must be difficult for you,' she said.

Lucy raised her head sharply from the salami she had begun to dice.

'I'm all right,' he said. 'We knew our friendship had to end some time and we enjoyed ourselves while it lasted.' That smile again. Surely he wasn't flirting with her, not after what she had just witnessed? She returned the smile with one of her own.

Thank God Tom wasn't in hearing distance. He'd be squirming.

'"Life goes on." That's what she always said.' Antonio turned to Lucy for her agreement.

Did she? Jo didn't remember ever hearing her mother say anything of the sort. But since she'd made her life in England, she and her mother had seen each other infrequently. She made the journey out here less often than the other two – work had been such a drain on her time. But apart from the geographical distance, an emotional distance had grown up between them too, and not just because Jo was forging her own path. She had never been able to get over Hope's refusal to talk about her and Tom's fathers, and now she would never know if this was what Hope was going to change when she asked to see her that very last time. She envied what she saw as Tom's masculine disinterest, but she couldn't get there herself. The not-knowing had always niggled away at her, scritch-scratching against her psyche.

While Tom had been appalled when Antonio stepped into the frame after Walter's death, she had felt nothing but relief. She had no inkling what his relationship with their mother really was and she didn't give a fig. Lovers or close friends – who cared? They seemed to have given each other whatever they needed. All that mattered was that someone had been looking out for Hope and any filial responsibilities could be shelved for a little longer. So, seeing less of her mother than perhaps she should meant she never knew her that well. And she knew Antonio hardly at all. If she had come out here more often than the obligatory once a year, she might have heard more of Hope's thoughts on life and death.

Where were those bloody ashes?

Lucy was nodding, her eyes glassy. 'When she was with me, she was always talking about how you had to jump over the obstacles life puts in your way and keep on going till you reach the finishing tape.'

Jo was amazed. 'Really? She said that?' Then she remembered the bookshelves in Hope's room groaning with self-help books.

'Well, perhaps you didn't know her as well as we did towards the end.'

Jo was unused to the edge in her sister's voice. But she couldn't argue. Lucy had made the effort that Jo hadn't. She had got beyond thinking of Hope as just their mother and had got on with her as any other woman would, finding out what made her who she was: something they couldn't have been less interested in when they were younger, too preoccupied with their own lives.

'Anyway, we *do* have to move on. She's right. There's no point being stuck in the past,' said Lucy with conviction as she turned her attention to the chopped salami that she swept from the board into a large salad bowl. 'Where are those jars of chickpeas?'

Was that remark about the past directed at Jo, at her refusal to give up her desire to know? She watched as Antonio passed her sister what she wanted. Lucy looked away from him as she took it.

Something else was going on here that Jo hadn't seen before. It was as though a second conversation was being held between the two of them in a language she didn't understand. But Art was still here . . .

'What can I do to help?' she interrupted.

Lucy looked around her. 'Antonio's going to do the washing-up.' She gestured at everything piled up by the side of the sink. 'So you could dry, or you could check everything we need's on the table outside.'

'Already?'

'They'll be here in a couple of hours. We'll put the food out last thing but you could just check everything else is there.' She gave the salad a last stir. 'I hope everyone comes. We'll be throwing food away otherwise.'

'Hope always made sure there was enough for everyone too.' Antonio started filling the sink with water. 'Not everyone likes paella.'

'I hope you're right,' said Lucy. 'Or we've wasted a morning on these salads.'

Jo hesitated, but she couldn't help herself. 'What about the key to the chest, Antonio? I suppose we've got to do that the way she wanted, too.'

Antonio fished into his shirt to produce a heavy old-fashioned key hung around his neck. He held it up. 'But I promised her not to give it to anyone.'

'Come on. I'm not going to open it. I just want to know it's safe,' said Jo and put her hand out.

He raised his eyebrows at the unintended slight, shook his head and slid the key back inside his shirt. 'It's quite safe with me, I assure you. I will do all of Hope's last wishes. I promised.'

The awkward silence that followed was broken by Art who came in carrying a couple of bags. He stopped when he saw the three of them and stood looking awkward. 'I got the bread,' he announced, putting the bags on the counter.

'And a newspaper?' Lucy's tone was crisp.

'No. They'd all sold out by the time I got there.' He shifted from one foot to the other. 'If there's nothing else, I'll just see if Tom needs a hand.'

'Why don't you?' said Lucy, not even lifting her head from whisking the dressing. Jo's heart went out to her sister. This must be impossible for her. On impulse, Jo followed Art into the hall.

'Can I have a word?'

'Sure?' He turned towards her, removing his aviators. His face was drawn, the shadows under his eyes making him look more vulnerable than she had noticed before.

Jo could see he was hurting too. Maybe I can help them, she thought. Maybe I *should* help. 'Look, Lucy's told me you two are having problems.'

His hand went to his jaw, his fingers working over his stubble as he stared at her: his eyes a piercing blue but hard, unforgiving.

Jo pressed on regardless. 'This is such a difficult time for all of us, but especially her, I think you could—'

'She told you?' He frowned as he lowered his hand to the end of the banisters as if steadying himself – or stopping himself from lashing out.

'Well, not in any detail, but I just—' She tried to backtrack, wishing she'd thought before opening her mouth, but he wasn't listening.

'Lucy!' When there was no reply Art went and opened the kitchen door. Cooking smells drifted into the hall as he called her again.

'Art, don't! I was only going to say . . .' Jo stopped.

Art was not listening to her. For a moment she thought he was about to walk out of the house but then he turned on his heel and stood framed in the doorway to the terrace, his shadow caught in the shaft of sunlight that sliced across the floor.

Lucy came, wiping her hands on her apron. She stopped to straighten the pewter plate on the chest. 'Yes?' She looked first at him then at Jo, at first puzzled then alarmed.

'I thought we weren't going to tell anyone until after the weekend.' Art's voice was puzzled but accusing.

'We aren't.' Hers shook.

'Well, how come Jo knows? You've obviously been talking to her. What do you think that makes me feel?'

'*You*?!' Lucy's eyes were wide with disbelief. 'What about me? What about what I feel? That doesn't seem to feature on your list of priorities at all.'

He took a step into the house, his face relenting. 'You know that's not true. But after all we said . . .'

'After what you've done . . .'

They both turned towards Jo: Lucy, confused and hurt; Art angry.

'I'm sorry.' Jo tried to cool things down. 'I was only trying to help.'

'But this has nothing to do with you,' said Lucy. 'I asked you not to say anything.'

'I know, but I was only going to say—'

'Something about the baby. I know.' Art looked almost sorry for himself. 'But, this isn't the way I meant it to happen.'

'The baby?' Jo switched her gaze from one to the other of them, puzzled. 'You're pregnant? But you said—' Behind Lucy, she could see Antonio in the kitchen, getting on with the washing-up as if nothing was happening.

'Of course I'm not pregnant.' Lucy sat down on the bottom step of the stairs, and put her head on her knees. 'Weren't you listening last night?'

'Yes, of course I was,' protested Jo. 'But then who?' As she spoke, things began to fall into place like a game of Candy Crush. Oh, why had she ever said anything?

There was a pause as Lucy lifted her head and stared at Art as if she was seeing him for the first time. Then she broke the silence. 'Are you going tell her? Or shall I?'

'You tell her. I'm done here.' His face had closed up, having made that decision. 'I'm going to find a hotel and stay there until I can get the first plane home.'

'You're going?' Lucy lifted her head, something like relief crossing her face.

'Well, I can't stay here now, can I?' He made it sound as if she was to blame. 'I don't know why we ever thought that would work.'

Lucy moved to one side as he crossed the hall to go upstairs, pulling away as he tried to touch her head. He stopped halfway up. 'I'm really sorry it had to end like this, Lou. You don't deserve it, I know. I hope we'll be able to be friends when all this blows over.'

Jo saw her sister stiffen. How was it that Art managed to turn everything into a scene from a bad soap opera?

'Babies don't blow over,' was all Lucy managed to say.

'And, Jo . . . I hope you'll understand.'

She stared at him in disbelief. 'Who wrote your script?'

'Shut up, Jo. If you're going, Art, please get on with it.' Lucy pulled herself to her feet, looking exhausted. 'We'll talk about what happens next as soon as I get back.'

As soon as Art disappeared from view, she turned on Jo. 'Which part of "don't tell anyone until after the weekend" didn't you understand?'

'Art isn't "anyone". I was only trying to help. I'm sorry.' Jo had never felt so in the wrong. Nothing she could say would make this better.

'I don't need your help. Really, I don't. I trusted you.'

'I just thought—'

'Stop it, Jo! Stop thinking. I can stand up for myself now.' She moved to the French doors and stared out before turning round to face her. 'Art's having a baby with Carrie Flanagan, that actress who plays the consultant on the show. He's leaving me for her. That's what this is all about.'

Jo tried to interrupt but Lucy carried on. 'And why did he choose this weekend to tell me? Because there's a story breaking in the press about it. The only good thing to be said is that he had the balls to come and tell me himself and didn't do it in a phone call or an email.' She gave a sad smile. 'I thought we could manage the weekend but perhaps that was stupid. I didn't want everyone to know until I've decided what to do. I don't want anyone's pity or advice. At least not at the moment.' She sat down, put her head in her hands and took a huge deep breath. Bailey got up from his patch of shade on the rug and came over to put his nose against her arm. 'But perhaps you've done me a favour.'

'Nobody else will know. At least not from me.'

Lucy looked up, putting an arm round the dog. 'You mean you *can* keep a secret?'

'I shouldn't have said anything. If I could wind back the clock, I would. I'm such an idiot for thinking I could make things better.'

'Yeah, you are, so please don't try again!' Lucy wiped her eyes with the back of her hand. Bailey licked her cheek. 'But I guess it had to come out sometime.'

'Not from me.' Jo was determined to make amends. 'No one else needs to know. But a baby...'

'Yes, there's no going back.'

Steps sounded on the landing upstairs. They both looked at Art as he came down, carrying his holdall. He was pale, his eyes red too. Lucy jumped to her feet so Bailey went to Art, wagging his tail. Jo wished she could wind back just fifteen minutes and start again or alternatively disappear but all she could do was stand where she was in case Lucy needed her.

Art ignored a disappointed Bailey and went to kiss Lucy good-bye but she took a step back just in time. 'I'll call you as soon as I get home,' she said.

He nodded, chastened. 'Bye, Jo,' he said. As he left the house, he looked broken, as if he was finally realising the implications of what he had done, that there really was no going back.

Jo put her arm around Lucy as they watched him rev the

engine, sending stones spitting from under the wheels of the car as he drove off.

'A weekend of goodbyes,' said Lucy, her voice shaky. 'Not just to Mum. Poor Art wanted a family as badly as I did. I guess I should be surprised this didn't happen sooner.'

'Not this way though. Not this weekend.' Jo could barely speak through her outrage. 'What will you do now?'

'No idea, apart from this.' She removed her wedding and engagement rings and tucked them in the pocket of her shorts. 'I don't want to stay in our house. I'm sure of that at least; too many ghosts. And I'm not going to resurrect my business although I've got to make a living somehow – perhaps I could cook Australian in Brad and Amber's restaurant after all.'

'That's got to be a last resort.' Jo squeezed Lucy's shoulder.

'I'm not really sure bush tucker's my thing. There's got to be something else.'

'Oh well, you've always got us, your fabulous dysfunctional family! We'll help however we can.'

Lucy managed a laugh. 'I know. But right this minute, I'm just going to have to get through this weekend. Don't say anything to anyone. I mean it. Not even Tom. Then I'm going to follow Mum's advice and try to get on with my life as best I can. That's what she would have done.'

But you're not her. Jo didn't say it.

'I'm tougher than I look.' It was though she had read Jo's mind. 'I want her to have the party she planned. I'm going to say Art's been called back by his agent for an urgent audition. I'm going to make myself believe that, and so are you. I'm going to try not to think about what's happened till I get back to England. I'll have plenty of time to feel sorry for myself then – and to plan.' She looked at Jo, her face pinched, her eyes pleading but determined. 'If you want to do anything, then help me do this.'

This was a side to her sister that Jo had rarely seen. She nodded. 'OK.' Anything else would have been redundant.

Lucy tightened her apron strings, straightened her back, breathed out. 'Then let's get back to the kitchen and put this show on the road!' Then, under her breath to herself, 'He's been called away for an audition.'

18

The shower beat on Lucy's head as she tried to rid herself of all thought. That was the only way she was going to get through this. Her new dress lay on the bed. Hope had been adamant that the party should be a celebration of her life. She didn't want a memorial party where the guests wore funereal black and stood, stone-cold sober, sipping cups of warm tea, remembering her with respect. She wanted a party. She wanted surprises. She wanted fun. She wanted to be remembered as she had lived. Lucy had chosen a brilliant-peacock-blue silk that she had bought half-hoping Art would notice her. She stopped herself. He was not even going to see it now. Not ever. Would he have found himself a hotel near the airport, she wondered. Perhaps he would be on the coast, alone in a bar somewhere or on the phone, explaining to Carrie what had happened. Stop it, she admonished herself again. Stop it.

The sooner she was among other people, the better. She veered between wanting company and wanting to be alone but, once the party started, she wouldn't have time to think. She turned off the shower and got herself ready as quickly as she could. The dress slid over her head. She had lost weight since she tried it on in the shop. She still had various finishing touches to do in the kitchen, so she slipped on her blue suede pumps and tied on her stripy apron.

Downstairs, she could hear someone on the terrace doing something with the table setting so she went outside, eager for company. What she saw made her lean against the door frame for support, her heart pounding. Her mother was bent over the table, laying out serving spoons, a small glass of wine in her hand. Her face was turned away from Lucy.

Lucy felt a scream wheeling up inside her.

'I forgot these.' Jo held up the remaining spoons. 'Something the matter? You look as though you'd seen a ghost.'

'You're wearing Mum's dress!' Lucy's heart rate slowed as reality sank in. 'I thought you were her.' She blinked hard to clear the vision.

'It's the only one that I could get into.' Jo pulled at the front of the dress where the buttons strained over her bust. 'Everything I've got's in my case so I had to borrow something.'

'You should have said. I nearly had a heart attack.' Lucy hated the idea of Jo poking through their mother's wardrobe as if it were hers.

'Didn't I? I meant to. I must have forgotten in all the excitement. Anyway, I don't look anything like her.' She flipped a hand at Lucy's curls.

'She wore that at the party last year.' Lucy had a clear memory of Hope presiding over proceedings, the flame-coloured print making her look alight, alive, and much younger than her years. 'And you sort of stand like her.'

'Do I?' Jo straightened up. 'But I'd completely forgotten about the dress. Should I change?'

'Into what? Anyway, I shouldn't think anyone else will remember. Ask Tom if you're worried.'

'Ask me what?' Sweat was beaded on Tom's forehead, smuts of charcoal on the big white apron covering his shirt and shorts. He stopped and stared at Jo as if seeing her for the first time. 'Don't I recognise that dress?'

'It's Mum's. Do you think it's OK for me to wear it?'

'Why not?' He looked in the direction of the fire. 'She's not here to.' His mind was obviously elsewhere or he might have been more circumspect. 'In fact, I'll be astonished if she arrives at all now. What a bunch of cowboys.'

'My case!' wailed Jo. 'I need it.'

'Don't tell me it still hasn't arrived?' Belle came up behind him. A floral sleeveless dress revealed arms turning pink from the sun. Her sunglasses and her burnished fringe hid most of her face. She stared at Jo. 'Isn't that... Isn't it a bit weird wearing your mother's cast-offs today?'

'Not at all,' said Jo, obviously making an on-the-spot decision.

'They're not cast-offs,' said Lucy. 'They're just borrowed for the occasion.'

'Well, if you think it's all right, then I suppose it is.' But Belle's face told a different story.

'Belle...' There was a warning note in Tom's voice.

'I'm just saying, that's all. But fine. Has anyone seen Alex? He's supposed to be helping with the paella.'

'Isn't he reading with Ivy?' Jo had left them on the sitting room sofa with all the books Ivy had brought. Alex had surprised her again by acting out all the parts until Ivy was yelling with delight. She was definitely warming to her nephew.

'He was, but then they came looking for wood with us. We left them having a fairy hunt in the woods. You said they could.' Belle was clearly pleased her son was doing such a good job looking after Ivy.

'You left them there?' asked Lucy, surprised.

'And they're not back yet?' Jo was immediately on the alert.

'I haven't seen them.' Belle didn't seem to think that was important.

'Didn't you tell Alex to be back by now?'

'He knows he has to be here to help,' Belle replied. 'They'll be back in a minute.'

'What if they're lost?' Alarm bells were obviously ringing for Jo. 'What if something's happened to them?'

'They won't be,' said Tom. 'Alex isn't an idiot. He's been in the woods hundreds of times. He knows his way around them.'

'And if Ivy's run off?'

When Lucy turned she saw the terror in her sister's eyes. All the worst possible scenarios must be racing through her head. All she wanted was to know Ivy was safe and to have her there with her. That primal bond between mother and child was so strong and was the one thing that Lucy would never experience now. Never. Finally acknowledging that gave her a strange kind of release. She reached for Jo's hand. 'We'll find her.'

Tom checked his watch, glancing over to Belle for confirmation. 'Alex said they'd—'

But Jo didn't have time to listen. 'Come on! Let's go to the woods and look for them. We can split up when we get there.'

Just then there was a movement at the door of the house. A small voice yelled, 'Mummy!'

They all looked at once. Ivy stood in the doorway, her purple dress hanging lopsided, her beaming face smeared with lipstick. Behind her was Alex. Judging by her face, Jo was experiencing a hundred times the relief felt by Lucy as Ivy ran towards them.

'Ivy!' Jo leaped up the steps and hugged her daughter to her. Ivy immediately smeared a lipsticky kiss on her cheek. 'Where have you been? I was about to go looking for you.'

'We got back ages ago,' said Alex, looking quite smug. 'I went to see if she wanted to come and see Ferdie. She was in your bedroom where I'd left her with her books.' A fleeting look of worry crossed his face. 'I thought that was OK.'

'Of course it was,' said Jo. 'I should have looked there first myself.'

'I was getting ready for the party but you weren't there.' Ivy beamed.

'I thought you were lost,' said Jo. 'Belle said you were in the woods.'

'We found a fairy castle there.' She lifted the bottom of her skirt with both hands and twirled on the spot. 'Alex told me the Queen of the Fairies goes there when it gets too hot. And it is very hot.'

'It's a tree,' Alex explained. 'You know the one near the edge that's got a hollow trunk? The one where Dad always told me the dinosaurs lived.'

Tom laughed at the memory. 'I'd forgotten about that. Walter and I used to hunt dinosaurs there once upon a time. So . . . no harm done. Come and give me a hand, son.'

'Have I done something wrong?'

'Not at all,' said Belle. 'You've been brilliant.' She patted his shoulder.

'I'm sorry, everyone.' Jo was clutching Ivy as if she would never let her go. 'I went a bit over the top. Thanks for looking after her, Alex.'

Alex beamed, then, awkward as the focus of everyone's attention, he looked down at his feet so his hair fell over his face.

'Go on. Get back to your paella.' Jo was smiling as she lifted Ivy onto her hip. 'I think we've got a bit of cleaning up to do.'

As the two of them went inside, Lucy felt suddenly alone. Jo and Ivy made a little unit all of their own that admitted no one else, and had changed Jo's life. Down at the fire, Alex was taking a batch of browned chorizo slices from the pan. Belle was instructing from the sidelines, standing well back from the heat of the flames, flapping her hands to create a breeze. As Tom shoved another branch on to the blazing fire, Ethan came over to join in. A second set of happy families. Lucy swallowed hard and turned back to the house.

In the kitchen, the familiar smells greeted her, inviting her to relax, to think about what needed to be done, not to wallow. This was the place where she could be herself, let go. She took the parcel of sliced Serrano ham from the fridge, pulled at the piece hanging from the parcel so it tore away, and ate it. On the counter sat ten honeydew melons. Putting down the ham, she reached for one of the large serving plates then pulled the first of the melons towards her and picked up a knife and sliced cleanly through the first one.

Upstairs, Jo was wiping Ivy's face with make-up remover pads. 'Next time you want to go looking for fairies, come and tell me.' She was still experiencing extreme relief from having found her daughter. She had made a stupid fuss, but if something happened to Ivy she didn't know how she would go on without her. Of course, Hope would never have reacted like that, confident her children could look after themselves.

'But you said I could go.'

'I know, but you should tell me when you do.'

'The fairies weren't there anyway. Alex said they had gone shopping. Ow!'

Jo rubbed harder at a particularly stubborn smear of lipstick under Ivy's eye. She wasn't even going to suggest removing the princess dress despite the bodice and skirt beginning to separate. If Ivy looked like a waif and stray, so be it. Sue would never know and could smarten her up when they got home. She switched off as Ivy went into a long rambling story about the Queen of the Fairies who was having a party exactly the same as they were. Ivy could talk non-stop for ages whether anyone was listening or not. Oblivious of the stir she had caused, she rattled on, leaving Jo to her thoughts.

She had been single ever since Jake had disappeared from her life, and she had been happy that way. They had parted after seven years of living together when they both admitted they wanted something more in life. He took a sabbatical from his work as a doctor and went travelling. She threw herself wholeheartedly into getting to the top of her career ladder. They had talked about how when he returned, they might pick up their relationship and move it on a bit. But he never had returned, so Jo never had the chance to discover what 'moving it on a bit' might mean.

And she had got on with leading her own life. After all, what choice did she have? He went to work for a charity somewhere in Africa, being fulfilled, giving something back – all those clichés. He might still be there, for all she knew. As it was, her work had expanded to fill the gap he'd left behind and she had never met anyone else who filled his shoes.

Not that her life had been empty. Far from it. She worked hard and she played hard. That was the way she liked it. There had been lovers, of course, but not one with whom she could imagine sharing the minutiae of her daily life. They were men with whom she had fun both in and out of her bed. Some of her affairs lasted longer than others, some of them occasionally even looked as though they might develop into something more. But that was the moment she shied away. As she grew older, she had become more set in her ways and the less she had wanted them overthrown. She was used to living alone, and liked the sound of her front door closing on the outside world.

Other people might think that was strange, but her lifestyle had suited her well until Ivy's unexpected appearance on the scene. Jo had thought, in as much as she had thought about it at all, that her chances of conceiving at her age were non-existent. But she had been wrong, and her perfect world had been thrown into chaos that had taken her some time to adjust to. Joint parenting might be easier, and she could imagine the fun of sharing the responsibility and pride for a child with someone else but she would rather go it alone than compromise over a relationship with any man for that. She loved her life alone with Ivy, even if it did sometimes complicate things.

The sound of a car horn brought her ricocheting back to the present. What was the time? Jo grabbed her phone and checked – 14.50. Whoever it was, was ten minutes early: unheard of round here, however much Tom might have liked things otherwise.

Unless it was the airline at last.

But, looking out of the window, she saw not a delivery van

but a snappy yellow sports car. Out of it stepped Maria and a young woman who could only be her daughter, the resemblance between them was so marked. The obvious difference was the hair. As long and dark as her mother's once was, Christina's was dip-dyed so at the bottom, the darkness became a neon blue, then shiny purple. Tom came up from the garden to welcome them, wiping his hands on his apron. Even from her vantage point, Jo could see his face was flushed. The heat of the fire, or could his feelings be getting the better of him? The two of them leaned in to kiss each other. Maria went to the right, and Tom went . . . to the right. They tried again and both went . . . to the left. They looked as if they were engaged in some kind of curious courtship ritual as they both moved back and in again – this time both to the right. The fourth time they got it right, Maria laughing until Tom trod hard on her foot as their cheeks touched. Then, as she rubbed her toes, they laughed together. Only Jo noticed Belle standing at the fire, watching Tom like a hawk.

'Quicksticks!' Jo interrupted Ivy who was still in full flow. 'Let's go down. The party's starting.'

Ivy jumped off the bed without drawing a breath. 'And the fairy king and the fairy baby . . .' and on she went as she followed Jo out of the room.

When they got downstairs, Tom and Maria were having a stilted conversation about how so little had changed at the house. Belle was busy continuing with the preparations for the paella, waiting for Tom to come back to her.

'And you must be Ivy.' Maria squatted to say hello to the four-year-old who was hiding behind Jo's legs, silent at last. Not waiting for a response, she stood up and turned to her own daughter. 'Jo, meet Christina.'

Christina took a step towards her. Close to, she was even more like a young Maria than Jo had realised. Her extremely short shorts – they could not possibly be any shorter – made the most of her slim, tanned legs. Her coloured hair fell over the strappy

T-shirt that was as brief as it could be, the sparkles round the neckline being the only concession to the party. So the clothes were modern but the real resemblance lay in her oval face, the almond-shaped dark eyes that sparked with life, the generous mouth turned up at the corners, the smooth olive skin and, of course, that hair. She held out her hand.

'I've heard so much about you.' The American accent came as a surprise.

'Yes,' said Maria. 'Ever since we got back here, she's been listening to me going on and on about what we got up to in the holidays.'

'I've heard it all,' chipped in Christina. 'The beach, the river, the woods, the beach – sounds amazing.'

Tom suddenly snapped to and, leaving them to it, tore himself away to return to his post beside Belle.

'Come in,' said Jo. 'Come and meet Lucy. She's finishing off and I ought to be helping.'

'We'll help too,' said Maria. 'We shouldn't have come so early. Very un-Spanish of me. I've lost that *mañana* mentality living in the States.' She shook her head at Jo's objection. 'Come on. It'll be fun. Like old times.'

19

Tom wiped his brow with the tea towel he had stuck in the waistband of his apron. The fire was blazing, the flames licking round the circumference of the giant pan of paella. Steam billowed up from the bubbling mess, carrying with it the smells of fish, chicken and saffron.

As he stepped back from the heat for a moment, he was yet again regretting his years' old offer to take Walter's place as paella maker. Having done it once, the summer after his stepfather's death, it was just assumed that he would do it again. And so he had, without ever expressing the dislike that he then forgot until the next time. Why would anyone in their right mind light an open fire and cook like this in the baking heat of the day? Even if they were protected by the shade of an oak tree.

This had once been his stepfather's moment of glory. Sprung from his studio, Walter would stand by the pan, aloof from the rest of the party – all of whom hovered out of reach of the heat of the fire – stirring the cooking rice with a long-handled wooden spoon. Unlike Tom, Walter relished the heat. No sissy shirts and apron for him. He'd stand in just a pair of shorts or a sarong, oblivious to the danger presented by the spitting fat or boiling liquid. By the time he'd prepared the meat and fish and had begun cooking, the bottle of wine by his side would be more than half empty, the glass still steady in his hand ready for more. But for Tom, being the cook was like standing in the flames of hell. He sipped from his bottle of water.

Belle had taken herself away to the shade of the olive trees where she had found a couple of deckchairs to share with Elaine. She leaned back, absent-mindedly stroking Ferdie who as usual was on her lap. Tom couldn't imagine what the two women might have in common to talk about although he knew Elaine was a good listener. Oh Belle, he said to himself with a reluctant sigh. However steadying and fulfilling she and their marriage had been for him, he couldn't stop himself wondering once again what his life would have been like if he hadn't made the choice to return to the UK and to her when he did.

As he continued stirring the paella, Tom's attention swung to Maria, who was talking to Antonio. She tipped her head back and laughed at something he said, to be rewarded by Antonio's smile. Lucy joined them, gesturing towards the table where she had laid out the tapas. Antonio rested his hand on her back, then took it away. Tom blinked. That man was too familiar by half. Tom still felt there was something untrustworthy about him, and refused to believe he was anything other than a gold-digger. Why else would he have worked his way into Hope's affections? Antonio was clearly attractive to other women like Maria or – God forbid – Lucy. Where was Jo? He should talk to her. But she was nowhere to be seen. Tom watched the three of them walk back towards the house together.

Around them swirled the other party guests, their glasses being filled by Alex and Ethan. Through their legs ran Ivy and a couple of other small children with whom she had made friends. Having settled in and lost her nerves, she reminded Tom of Jo as a girl. Ivy already had that same independence of spirit that he so envied. There was a bark from the garage where Bailey had been shut in with a pig's ear. Nobody wanted another scene between him and Ferdie. Although Tom couldn't help a smile as he remembered Belle on her knees in the hall, trying to coax her beloved pet out from under the chest.

'Drink?' Jo appeared beside him, holding a bottle of Rioja and a jug of Lucy's homemade lemonade. 'I've just been down at the pool. All the lithe young things are down there. Just like we used to be. Anything rather than mix with the oldies. Doesn't it feel weird to be one of the oldies now?'

'Very.' Tom held out his glass for the lemonade. Belle had almost but not entirely convinced him that abstinence was the best route to a long life. It certainly was when she was around.

'You sure?'

He nodded. 'Have you seen Antonio, by the way? He seems very close to Lucy, all of a sudden.'

'Take no notice. He's like that with all the women. He's just not a bundled-up, repressed Englishman, that's all.'

'Thanks a lot!'

She put an arm round his sweating shoulders then removed it straight away. 'You know what I mean! Anyway, we can hardly send him away now. God, it's hot here. How can you bear it?' She took a couple of steps back from the fire.

'It's about done now.' Tom stepped back with her. 'The fire's dying down and I'm going to stop stirring so there's a decent *socarrat*.' He loved rolling that word on his tongue. *Socarrat*. The crusty, caramelised paella bottom was something Walter had prided himself on getting right. Over the years, after watching him, Tom had got the hang of it too.

But Jo wasn't to be deflected. 'You mustn't forget that Hope loved him – Antonio, I mean.'

Tom spluttered on his drink. 'Please!'

'Not in that way. At least, I don't know ... Maybe she did. But he was wonderful with her. For all her faults, I bet she was fantastically good fun. She didn't care, did she?'

'Not about anyone else, that's for sure.' Talking about Antonio and his mother made Tom uncomfortable. He didn't want to think what may or may not have gone on between them. He wiped away the sweat that was running down the side of his face.

'Perhaps if she had, she'd have told us the whole story about who we are.'

'Not again! Why does it matter so much to you still? After all, you're the one who should understand now you've had Ivy.'

Jo's mouth dropped open, her eyes wide. 'Are you serious?'

'Well, yes. I suppose I am.' Tom wished he hadn't started this but the way she was looking at him so expectantly meant he had to go on. 'None of us know who he is, but there's a man out there somewhere who's Ivy's father. Aren't you in danger of repeating history?' He felt a sudden irrational sympathy with whoever Ivy's father was. 'Look what he's missing.'

Jo looked at him as if she couldn't believe what she was hearing. 'The way I'm bringing up Ivy is completely different. I'll tell her all about him when she's old enough to understand.'

'We'll see.' He turned his attention to the fire, kicking at the branches so the flames died down a little. He could sense Jo's fury as she searched for the right words. He turned back to her. 'It may not be as easy as you think.'

'I can't believe you're siding with Mum, that you think what she did was acceptable.' His words had obviously hit harder than he'd meant them to.

'I'm not. And I don't think it was acceptable, but it's what happened. And you still mind about it. I'm just pointing out the facts. Think about them,' he said and turned his back again to signal that the conversation was over.

'Jo! Tom!' Come and get something to eat before we start the paella,' Lucy yelled from the terrace where there was a jam of people around the table. The sound of their voices carried on the breeze. Brad detached himself from the throng and came in their direction, carrying a plate of tapas.

Jo waved at Lucy to let her know she had heard but her face gave away how much the conversation with Tom had upset her.

'I thought you two might like something.' Brad held out the plate. 'I've been in charge of too many barbies back home and

I know exactly what it's like to be stuck out on a limb cooking while everyone else has a good time.'

It would be churlish to refuse, so Tom took a fork and speared a piece of melon and ham. As he lifted it to his mouth, a shriek rang out from the house. Belle? The melon slid from his fork to the ground. On the terrace, heads turned as she ran down beside the garage, clutching Ferdie to her chest. 'There's a rat in there!'

Taking advantage of the door that she had left open, Bailey exploded into the garden in hot pursuit. Belle was waving and shrieking at them to 'Catch it!'

Lucy raced over to collar him but seeing so many people and plates of food, Bailey had no interest in Ferdie. He grabbed a bit of chicken that had fallen to the ground and made off with it into the olive trees.

Tom left a grinning Brad to caretake the paella while he went to the rescue. By the time he reached the terrace, Belle was hysterical.

'Calm down, darling, for heaven's sake. It'll only be a field rat. They're much more frightened of you.'

But Belle was not to be mollified so easily. 'Go and look!' she insisted. 'I only went in to get some ice from the freezer and it ran over my foot.' She stuck out her leg so the sun glittered on her jewelled sandals and her mink-coloured toenails.

'Hazard of the countryside,' offered Daphne who was squeezed into one of the canvas chairs, her injured leg resting on a footstool. She resembled a Turkish pasha in her velvet mirrored hat and voluminous dress.

'I don't care where it's a hazard! I'm not going in there again until you've found it. Tom, please.'

Tom shook his head. 'No point. It'll only find its way back.'

'But we need the ice.'

'I'll get it then. You stay here.'

But before Tom could do anything, the double toot of a car horn turned everyone's attention towards the gate where a small red van was turning in. It drove past the cars parked in the meadow at the bottom of the drive and slowly approached the house.

'Tom, please.' Belle pulled at his arm, urgent. 'I can't get the ice until you've got rid of it.'

But the rat would have to wait. Tom walked down to meet this last guest. Jo was right behind him. They arrived at the van just as it stopped. The driver left the engine running as he got out and went round to the back. '*Holá.*' He threw open the doors and heaved out Jo's green case, its handle decorated with the purple padlock. '*Momento.*' He returned to his seat, pulled out a small machine and held it out for Tom to sign.

Jo took it from him. '*Gracias,*' she said as she wrote her name. 'Hallelujah. She's made it after all.'

'Thank God,' said Tom. 'And not before time.' He reached out to take the case, extending the handle so it could be wheeled up the path. He was not going to risk letting his mother's ashes out of his sight again.

Jo snatched it back from him. 'I can manage, thanks.'

They turned back towards their guests, who were watching what was going on as Elaine explained in rather too loud a voice what had happened, without a thought for Jo's embarrassment.

'Typical.' Jo patted her bag and waved at everyone. 'Trust Mum to make an entrance.'

Twenty minutes later, Hope's ashes had been transferred into the blue-and-white ceramic jar that Lucy had picked for them. This, in turn, had been placed in the middle of the sitting room mantelpiece, somewhere where it would be quite safe yet in full view of the proceedings. Lucy changed the background music to Ella Fitzgerald singing Cole Porter. A party at Casa de Sueños wasn't a party without music.

'I know it's sentimental of me,' she said to Jo. 'But it feels right to play Mum's favourite music even if she can't hear it.'

But Lucy had always been the sentimental one of the three of them. She had been so relieved when Jo eventually appeared again, having changed into a dress of her own. Hope's was back in her wardrobe where it belonged. She looked round the empty room again, imagining it full of people, smoke, the clink of glasses and sound of chatter with the familiar voice of their mother rising over the rest, exhorting the others, 'Let's dance. Come on, everyone.'

As Lucy sat down, sorrowful, she spotted a red dot stuck on the backrest of the tatty chaise longue. 'Look at that.'

Jo made a face of disbelief. 'Tom would never want that un-less . . . Belle must have been having a little go-round of her own while we were getting the food ready. I wonder if he knows.'

'I can still see mum lying there the day after a summer party, hungover, probably still in her dressing gown, hair a bird's nest, sipping a large Fernet Branca – "medicinal, darling". I used to love those post-mortems on the night before.'

'Next time you see it, Belle will have had it reupholstered and it'll be unrecognisable. Or will it?' Jo carefully unpeeled the sticker and screwed it up in her pocket before replacing it with a yellow one of her own. 'That'll teach her.' She exchanged a complicit grin with Lucy and stood up to join her.

In the garden, the guests were beginning to mill around the paella where Brad had begun to dish up. Tom had at last gone to the garage to help Belle with the ice. Their plates laden, the partygoers found themselves places to sit and eat. The older guests made their way back to the house to the chairs under the shade of parasols while the rest were spreading themselves around the rugs and cushions laid out earlier. The hottest part of the day was well over now. The two sisters stood in the doorway watching before Jo took Lucy's hand and squeezed it. 'Courage, mon brave,' she whispered. 'Into the breach.' They stepped outside together as Ivy came barrelling up towards her.

*

As Tom entered the garage, his eyes adjusted to the dim light provided by a single bulb hanging from the middle of the ceiling. No one had parked a car in here for as long as he could remember. Against the walls were shelves of boxes containing everything a handyman might need but never used judging by the amount of dust and cobwebs covering them. Otherwise, there were old lawn mowers, garden tools, an ancient stripy swing seat with a strut that had been broken for years, an old chest of drawers that Hope had never got round to distressing, broken deckchairs, buckets and spades, Bailey's bed and a bowl of water. Against the wall was the old chest freezer.

He went over and lifted its lid. As he did, he saw something scurry behind it. Nothing would make him confess to Belle that rats weren't high on his own list of likes either. He speeded up, reached in and grabbed hold of a corner of a plastic bag of ice, tugging it free. He heard the door of the garage open and close behind him. Belle: come to see if he was doing what she asked. He closed his eyes, resigned.

'Tom?'

He stopped dead, dropping the bag back into the freezer and stood up straight, his pulse racing. 'Maria!'

'I saw you come in here. Can I carry anything?' The American twang in her voice made him smile.

Seeing her, Tom felt an almost overwhelming urge to take her in his arms but he stood rooted to the spot, appalled at himself and at his feelings, trying to bring them under control. Unable to help himself, he took a step towards her.

'No,' he said. 'I—'

'Tom? Are you in there?' The door opened and Belle stood framed in the opening, clearly reluctant to come anywhere near the rat again. She removed her dark glasses. 'Oh!' Her surprise at seeing the two of them together seemed to fill the garage.

Maria remained quite unperturbed. 'Just seeing if I could help, but Tom's got it all under control.' She went towards the door, the skirt of her yellow dress swinging as she walked. At the door, she turned. 'Haven't you?'

'Yep.' He nodded and bent over the freezer again, grateful for the cold on his flaming hot cheeks. He took a deep breath as he yanked the bag of ice into his arms. Nothing had happened. There had been nothing for Belle to see.

'Excuse me,' she said to Belle, who stood aside to allow Maria past, her eyes following her.

Tom couldn't help the tug of lust as he watched the sway of Maria's walk as she headed back to the party. He hadn't forgotten that either.

'Well!' said Belle. 'Who does that woman think she is?'

'An old friend,' said Tom, a little dreamy. 'A very old friend.'

'Really? You've never mentioned her before.' She waited as if expecting him to say something more as he walked past her into the open, lugging the ice with him.

She shut the garage door with a slam. As Tom felt Belle's eyes burning into his back, he remembered how jealous she could be. A few years back, he hadn't wanted to lose Rachel, the best surveyor he had in the business, but when Belle's innuendoes, then her constant questioning and cross-examining about how they spent their working day together got too much, he had no choice. He had quietly advised Rachel to look for a job elsewhere at the same time as putting in a good word for her with a couple of other companies. Of course she was snapped up, and he had replaced her with young Steven, a hard worker who wouldn't say boo to a goose. He missed the laughs he had with Rachel but he preferred a quiet life, an ordered life. That's what he had opted for and that's what he had got.

He paused for a second, so Belle could catch him up then he rested the ice on the ground and took her hand. 'It's all a long time ago. She was a neighbour, a friend of Jo's. There's nothing more to say.'

'Hmph.' Belle scrutinised him closely as if she suspected he might not be telling the truth. 'Yellow's a very difficult colour to carry off.' Satisfied she had had the last word, she pecked him on the cheek.

Tom caught a glimpse of the dress in the crowd. 'Actually, I think it rather suits her.' He used both hands to hoist up the bag of ice, and together they went to rejoin the party. For once Belle was silenced.

20

If anyone had told Lucy that she would have got this far through the day without collapsing under the weight of her sorrow, she would have been astonished. Yet, somehow, she had managed. With so many people milling around the place, she had almost succeeded in tricking herself into believing that her mother and Art were here, somewhere out of sight, that nothing had changed.

She looked around her. Antonio was chatting to a knot of Hope's and his friends from the village. He caught sight of her watching and raised a hand, smiled and winked. Or was that last a trick of the light? She recalled the feel of his hand on her back just before lunch: brief but concerned. She had instinctively leaned back into his touch. Even that slight physical contact had given her comfort, just when she needed it. Antonio seemed to understand what she was going through without having to ask.

Not far from her, Brad sat in a faded deckchair bent over a game of backgammon that Elaine had set up on the grass between them. Nearby, Bailey was wolfing down the leftovers on someone's abandoned plate. The dog looked around him, anxious to see if anyone had spotted him before moving off to hunt for more.

Not far away, Ivy and her newfound friends were climbing an ancient olive tree. She had reached a point just above the gnarled trunk's divide and was squealing for attention. 'Look at me!'

Lucy went over to see if she could help. 'Can you get down?'

'Of course.' As Ivy slid to the ground, there was a ripping sound as the back of the purple net skirt finally detached itself from the golden bodice. But she didn't notice. Trailing fabric behind her, she ran over to her mother who was on one of the rugs, talking to Adam and Val, keeping half an eye on her daughter at the same time. Jo lay back against a cushion so she could take the brunt of Ivy's weight as her daughter hurled herself at her.

'Can we go swimming?'

Jo groaned. 'Not again! Don't you want some pudding?'

'No.' Ivy pouted. Lucy was about to offer to take her, liking the idea of a temporary escape route from the party, when a man's voice spoke behind her.

'We were so sorry to hear about Hope. She was very special to lots of us here.'

Lucy spun round to see who was talking to her. An elderly man leaning on a stick had separated himself from the crowd. Watery blue eyes alleviated the grog-blossom red of his face. His lips stretched into a thin smile. On his arm was a woman whose skin was ravaged by sun damage. They were more expats, local friends of Hope who she barely knew.

'Sandy. Isabel. I'm sorry not to have seen you earlier. But thank you. It's good you could be here.'

'Wouldn't have missed it. You've got quite a turnout up here to pay their last respects. All the locals.' He extended a claw-like hand, its arthritic knuckles swollen, to grasp her arm. By his side, Isabel simpered. 'Hope always said the last party would be one to remember.'

'For the right reasons, I hope,' said Lucy, her eyes stinging with tears again.

'Of course,' said Isabel, fishing in her bag for a tissue that she passed over. 'I'll never forget how she used to look after everyone, making sure that we were all having the best possible time.'

'Yes, she was the life and soul,' Sandy agreed.

To Lucy's relief, Tom shouted something from the terrace, beckoning everyone to come closer, cutting off their conversations. Somewhat reluctant to move after the tapas and paella, the party heaved to its collective feet and drew near. The teenagers hovered on the edge, waiting to make their escape back to the pool.

'I'm sorry to disturb you all.' Tom raised his voice for everyone to hear. Jo, Lucy – do join us up here.' The two of them went to where he was standing with Belle who had Ferdie tucked under her arm, out of Bailey's immediate reach. Behind him, the house stood solid, its windows gleaming in the early evening sun, the doors open in welcome. The deep-red bougainvillea at the right corner behind the vine-clad pergola, planted as a sapling by Hope, reached up to the upper windows. From the sitting room came the soft sound of music, turned down so Tom could be heard. On the terrace, long shadows stretched from the pergola, from the lights dangling over the table, and from the two large cream parasols. Someone would take them down later, after sunset.

Jo lifted Ivy from her shoulders and put her on the ground. Ivy grasped her mother's finger, and leaned close against her legs, dodging behind her then out again. Lucy and Jo stood on either side of Tom, Jo standing a little too close so that she was just in front of Belle, edging her out of the way. Lucy heard Belle's murmur of complaint as she was forced to step sideways, but this was their moment, not hers.

'I meant to say something earlier but the rat rather got in the way.' Tom looked over his shoulder at Belle with affection while his audience laughed. She gave an embarrassed smile back. 'Anyway, all I really want to do is to say welcome to you all from all three of us and thank you for coming.'

As Lucy clasped her hands together, trying to focus on what he was saying, she couldn't help noticing that the varnish had chipped on one of her nails. She started picking at it.

'Losing Hope . . .'

You'd think she was a dog, as if she might wander in through the gate at any moment. Well, in a way she just had . . . Lucy let her mind drift. Mistake. She was presented with a clear picture of her Cambridgeshire home, empty of Art and his clutter. The bookshelves in the sitting room were stripped of his precious collection of first-edition war-poets; his framed black-and-white photographs (another of his short-lived enthusiasms in the years when he was 'resting') left empty squares on the walls; no more shoes to trip over; no more scripts left open on the sofa; no more Saturday football blasting through the house; the garden demanding attention; the bed permanently cold and empty. Scared by this vision of her immediate future, she forced herself back into the present.

'. . . but she's here in spirit.' A ripple of appreciation went round the crowd. 'So bearing that in mind, we'd like you to enjoy yourselves in the same ways as before: the table tennis is in the barn as usual; croquet in her beloved English garden; *pétanque* on the drive. And if anyone's feeling really energetic, we've strung up the rather holey badminton net over there.' He pointed towards the side of the house where the ground was flat. 'And, of course, there's always the pool. We've put plenty of towels down there.'

'And board games indoors,' Jo added. 'Chess, backgammon, Cribbage – you name it.'

'And music for dancing,' chipped in Lucy. That was her favourite part of the party – in past years, as the sun slipped towards the horizon, the doors of the house would be thrown open as they were today, the light spreading into the garden along with the sound of music. From below the terrace when she was young, she'd watch her parents' friends dancing together, apart; stray figures coming outside for a cigarette, kissing, talking, dancing more. As she grew older, her friends would be found there, too, then her and Art. Inside the music played non-stop unless Hope changed the track to something she liked better, taking no notice of any objections. The atmosphere would be hot and sticky, the carpet rolled back, smoke wreathed over the heads of the dancers, glasses covering every surface – everybody having fun. That was how Hope liked it. When she was small, Lucy would join in or sit on the big cushion in the corner of the room where she often woke in the morning, having gone to sleep unnoticed.

'Yes, and music for dancing.' Tom loaded all his well-known dislike for this one activity on to the last word. There was a roar of laughter. 'And of course it wouldn't be one of Hope's parties without plenty of food and drink. Please help yourselves to more. And if you can't find anything, just ask one of us. Now . . . We're here to celebrate our mother's life. That's what she wanted us to do, so let's do that. So for the last time, can I ask you to raise a glass – to Hope, long life and happiness.'

That was the traditional toast that Walter then Tom had made year after year. And now, never again. Lucy turned for a glimpse of the blue-and-white jar on the mantelpiece inside.

'To Hope, long life and happiness,' echoed their guests, raising their glasses so the lowering sun danced off them.

As they drank, there was a kerfuffle to the side of the terrace. Antonio was pushing his way backwards towards Tom. His face was dark with the effort of carrying the chest with Juan, Luisa's husband. They almost dropped it at Tom's feet. Antonio straightened up, a hand on the small of his back, grimacing with pain. The guests murmured with curiosity. What was going on?

'Not now, Antonio.' Alarmed, Tom tried to move everyone away. 'Let's get on with the party.'

'But Hope wanted me to bring it out here now,' Antonio protested. 'I promised her.'

'Maybe but *I* don't think this is the time.' Tom stood firm. 'We'll look at this later. Jo?' He appealed to his older sister.

She looked at Lucy. 'What do you think, Lucy. Should we?'

'It's what she wanted,' Antonio reminded them. 'Didn't she say to you that she wanted the presents given at the party?'

With all eyes on her, Lucy hesitated. Then, 'She did,' she agreed, aware that she was going against their brother. 'But nobody has to unwrap them now.'

'And they're for her friends,' Antonio added, putting his hand on the domed lid of the chest. 'Hope wanted everyone here to have something from her.'

'Oh God.' Tom massaged his temples with his thumb and fingers of one hand, as if he had a terrible headache starting.

'Open the box!' shouted someone. Lucy thought she recognised Ian's voice. Sure enough, when she looked up, he and Bill were propping each other up, drinks in hand: two grizzled old roués who had made not the slightest concession to the occasion. They wore what they had always worn to Hope's parties: tatty shorts, deck shoes (not that there was a boat in sight), untucked shirts, sleeves rolled up; almost identical but for their different heights, Bill's moustache, and the ancient cricket hat sported by Ian.

'Let's just do it,' said Jo. 'Sooner it's over the better. And look, everyone's waiting now.' She took Ivy's sticky hand in hers.

Indeed, faces were turned towards them, waiting to see what was going to happen next. Was this Hope's last surprise? To the side of the party, Lucy spotted Alex and Ethan sloping off with the other teens in the direction of the pool, having no interest in what was going on here. Ethan was sneaking out a bottle of wine and a couple of glasses. He looked over his shoulder, guilty but leading the way, Christina not far behind him. There were others in the small group she didn't recognise, lit cigarettes tight between their fingers. She looked to see if Belle had noticed but, like everyone else, her sister-in-law was concentrating on the chest.

Antonio reached under his open-necked white linen shirt and, with a flourish, pulled the key, now on a black ribbon, from around his neck. He lifted it over his head and, ignoring Tom's outstretched hand, slipped it into the lock.

Lucy's pulse was racing. A sense of foreboding meant she didn't want to look but, at the same time, she couldn't tear her eyes away. What special gifts could Hope possibly have left them? She caught her breath.

The key refused to turn. Antonio pulled it from the lock then tried again.

'Let me!' Tom reached out for a second time, clearly unhappy that Antonio had taken the limelight.

But Lucy understood. Hope had entrusted this final act to Antonio, and he was determined to fulfil her wishes. He was doing this for her. She put her hand on Tom's shoulder. 'Let him do it,' she whispered. 'For Mum.'

With bad grace, Tom grunted his assent, shook off her hand and took a step back. He could be relied on not to make more of a scene than necessary in front of their guests.

Jo gave Lucy a look of thanks. Ivy started to say something but Jo squatted down and put a finger over her mouth. 'Shh. A pirate chest. Look.'

Ivy's round blue eyes moved from Antonio to the chest as the key turned and the lid creaked open. The guests standing nearest craned their necks to see what was inside. The three siblings and Belle leaned forward.

All Lucy could see was lots of small parcels wrapped in garish, patterned paper. On top lay a long, foolscap envelope.

'Oh God.' Tom groaned under his breath, massaging his temple again. 'Do we have to do this?'

It was Jo who reached in to pick the letter out. 'What's the worst that can happen? This is her final curtain. We might as well let have her way for the last time. Look. It's addressed "To everyone here". At least there's nothing for us, after all.'

The words were written in Hope's familiar scrawl. These must be the last words that she'd dashed off before coming to England, written when she knew she was dying. The thought tore at Lucy's heart.

'I'll read it.' Tom cleared his throat. Jo was ripping open the envelope, then took out the letter and passed it to Tom without looking at its contents. He took his reading glasses from his shirt pocket and perched them on his nose, peering over them at his waiting audience.

Lucy didn't take her eyes off the paper trembling in his hand.

Tom raised his other hand for silence. 'I won't take up much of your time. Now – I know none of us will forget Mum . . .' He paused, as there was a murmur of agreement that gave him time to collect himself. Belle stepped forward to put a steadying hand on his arm. He glanced at her and visibly relaxed a little as he cleared his throat.

'She was always the life and soul of this party, and she's just made sure that she is again. She's left presents for everyone . . .' He paused for the whispers to die down. 'And a letter.' He waved it at them. 'This is what she says.'

Lucy felt as if her heart was about to fly out of her mouth. She couldn't take her eyes off Tom while Jo crushed her hand in hers.

'"My dearest friends and family,"' he read.

'"I know I'm dying and I haven't got long. I'm leaving here and going to England to be with my children for the last few months, or even weeks. So I shall almost certainly miss this year's party. I can imagine you all gathered on the grass under the terrace and on the terrace too. I wish I could be there with you."'

There was a strangled sound. It took a moment for Lucy to realise that she was the one responsible. She covered her mouth with her spare hand, pressing her fingers hard against her lips, feeling her teeth against them.

'"I don't want you to forget me . . ."' Tom read on.

'Typical,' whispered Jo, so low Lucy only just heard. Tom frowned at her.

'". . . so I'm going to give you each a little something to remember me by."'

'Well, we were warned.' Jo's voice was louder.

This time Tom's stare would have silenced a lorryload of hecklers. She mumbled an apology and stroked the fine strands of hair off Ivy's face. Tom coughed and continued.

'"If I were there, we would have had a treasure hunt – just like the old days. But of course, if I were there, you wouldn't be listening to this. So please will you all take home a present each. From me."

'"Now enjoy yourselves."

'"All my love, Hope."'

Nobody said a word. The only sound was the music still playing in the sitting room. The guests looked uncertain what to do next as a few tissues flashed white among the guests. A nose was blown. Through her own tears, Lucy saw Tom wipe his eyes with the corner of his apron. He looked as if he had been smacked across the face. Beside him Belle was struggling to control herself. Ferdie's inquisitive nose poked up from under her arm as she stroked and pulled at his ears. The mood of the party had changed completely. Was this what Hope had wanted? And why? Just to be centre stage for one last time?

Jo's face was showing mixed emotions: puzzlement, disappointment and anger. Ivy was tugging at her hand again, eager to show her mother something.

'Now what?' whispered Jo, as their guests began to talk amongst themselves.

Her question nudged Tom out of his daze so he faced everyone again. 'I think we should do as she says and enjoy ourselves. So before we all get too maudlin, let's do what she would have done. We'll turn up the music and party on. Come and get your present whenever you want to.'

No one moved.

The respectful murmurs were broken by a shout and a splash as someone leaped into the pool. That was enough to galvanise everyone else. After a controlled rush towards the drinks table, the noise levels began to rise again. Lucy went into the sitting room and turned up the music so Ella Fitzgerald singing 'You Make Me Feel So Young' blared across the garden. Tom was right, they had to do what Hope would have wanted, however hard. And after all the fuss, there were no presents for them after all. Relief all round.

She found Tom and Belle huddled together by the sitting room door. Belle's arms were round him and she was rubbing his shoulders, comforting him. But the moment was short-lived as the party swirled around them and sucked them back in.

'Croquet, anyone?' Belle separated herself from Tom.

'I'll take you on,' called Jimmy from the deli in Gaucín as he put his drink on the table. 'Fran?'

His very pregnant wife shook her head. 'Like this? I wouldn't be able to see the ball!' She stroked her bump with both hands. 'No. I'll find a hammock.'

As they spoke, the party began to fracture into smaller groups again as people decided how they wanted to spend the little daylight left. No one took a present just yet. No one wanted to be first. Alone on the terrace, Lucy dipped into the identically wrapped parcels. She smuggled out one and took it into the sitting room. There, accompanied by the smoky tones of Ella Fitzgerald, she unwrapped it. When she saw what it was she couldn't help smiling.

In her hand lay a cork with a vividly patterned ceramic top. Perfect for any wine bottle. Perfect for any party. And a perfect token farewell from Hope to her friends.

21

'One... two... three...'

Jo was exhausted. Playing hide-and-seek with three four- and five-year-olds was not how she had looked forward to spending her time at a party once she got to fifty. But now that she was, it wasn't as bad as she might have imagined. Her claim that she didn't want children had always been met with disbelief but, a career girl to the soles of her shoes, she had never had that overwhelming urge for motherhood that other women talked about. She had seen Lucy go through so many heartbreaks in her quest for a family, never fully understanding her sister's growing desperation. Her own biological clock had never been wound up. And then, when she was least expecting them, those hormones finally got her – just when it was almost too late. So at last she understood and felt sorry.

'Nine... ten...'

A loud giggle came from down among the olive trees.

One night was all it had taken to transform her life: one drunken night with Steve Masterton, the charismatic American CEO of Ballard Watches. Fairweather and Fowler (more Jo Fairweather than Richard Fowler, in truth) were pitching for the British side of the global business. After a night of champagne-fuelled marketing talk in the Ivy, she had gone back to Masterton's hotel, breaking up her until then inviolable rule of no mixing sex and business. She used the tools she had, flirtation occasionally being one of them – and the one that often helped the ball-breaking businessmen come to the right decision – but until that night she had always known when to bow out of the action. To this day, she had no idea what had made her act so out of character, so unprofessionally. Winning the account would have been a huge coup for the agency. She was not surprised when the phone call came the following day to say they had lost out to Gum, the rivals they were pitching against. She pulled her cardigan tight against the evening breeze as she recalled Richard's shock.

'Fifteen... sixteen...'

He was so used to her pulling in the business she went after that he had been certain they had Ballard in the bag. The second time she had seen him lost for words was twelve weeks later when she told him she was pregnant. As far as he was concerned, her single status and her single-minded devotion to the agency was taken for granted. Children were never part of the equation. Yes, he had three, but that was different. His wife Mandy was one of Jo's closest friends but Jo was his equal, an honorary man. To his astonishment, she had made up her mind – there was no going back. When she was least expecting it, her biological clock had been kick-started into overdrive and she didn't want to miss out on what would probably be her only chance at motherhood. She was experiencing a visceral longing that she had never known. Whether that was down to hormones, a desire for change or both, she didn't know but she wanted the baby, the experience of being a mother, more than anything. *Really* wanted it. The strength of her desire had amazed her as much as it had Richard. She was going to have this baby on her own. Masterton was safely back in the States and they were unlikely to ever meet again. Except... now Ivy was in the world, the situation was less straightforward. Perhaps she owed her daughter the true story sooner rather than later after all.

'Nineteen... Twenty. Coming,' she called. 'Ready or not.'

The purple net skirt was sticking out from under a plaid rug that had a suspicious-looking mound underneath it. One day she would tell Ivy what had happened. One day, when she was old enough to understand. How could Tom suggest she was no different from Hope when she had spent half her life trying to be her own person, not a flake like her mother?

'Where's Ivy? I can't find her.' Jo raised her voice.

Giggles emerged from under the rug as the net skirt was yanked out of sight.

'Chita, Ivy, Manuel . . . where are you? What will we do if we can't find them?' With the help of the indulgent others sitting nearby, she pretended to look everywhere, lifting the corners of rugs, moving cushions, looking round tree trunks. At last she knelt down and pulled the rug in the air to squeals of delight as the three children clutched onto each other.

'Again! Again!'

'No, that's enough. I want to talk to our friends now.' She sat in an empty deckchair beside Ros and Daphne while Ivy leaped to her feet.

Her daughter stood with her hands on her hips, outraged that the game was over. 'I hate the way you treat me sometimes.' She stamped her foot. But before she could go further, Bailey drew her attention by barking at something up a tree. The three children ran off to investigate, Jo's treatment of them forgotten.

Jo was left staring after her daughter in astonishment, with Daphne and Ros laughing. 'She's a character, your daughter,' said Ros.

'I don't know where she got that from,' said Jo, mentally re-scrolling to find the moment when Ivy must have soaked up the phrase. Hadn't she said something like that to Richard the other day over the phone when he was annoyed that she wouldn't be there for the teams who had to come over this weekend with ideas for the rebrand of Flakers Crisps when the client was threatening to leave them? Except *she* had been joking.

'She reminds me of you when you were young. You were a handful.'

'Was I?' That wasn't how Jo remembered things at all. She

watched her daughter ordering her new friends back to the house. There was no question who was boss.

'Drink, anyone?' She took their proffered glasses and returned to the terrace for refills. As she passed the chest, she noticed that most of the little parcels had been taken. At the bottom lay a much larger package that had been completely covered up until now. She couldn't resist taking a closer look. Clearing the remaining smaller parcels to one side, she flipped over the label. There, in her mother's scrawl, was one word. *Jo*.

Tom was half listening to Ramón, their neighbour from higher up the mountain, holding forth about the weather, his favourite topic whenever an English blow-in came within earshot. What else were the English interested in, after all? But while Tom politely nodded and expressed his interest, his surprise, his agreement, his attention was focused on Maria whom he could see over Ramón's right shoulder. She was chatting to a couple Tom didn't recognise. What he did recognise was the slant of her cheekbones, the thoughtful smile that broadened into something sunnier, the way she touched her chin with one long finger when she was thinking, the way she stood like a ballerina, the jut of her hip. As if she was aware of his thoughts, she turned and caught his eye, raised a hand. She excused herself from her conversation, pushing her hair back from her face, and came towards him, throwing one end of her scarf over her shoulder. Tom stepped away from Ramón, who simply turned to the unfortunate woman standing beside him and, without drawing breath, continued his rant about global warming and the effect on the seasons.

Tom felt self-conscious, as if everyone was watching his every move, but he had to talk to her. His movements felt clumsy, his smile too wide for his face, his cheeks burning. As they drew closer, the years fell away. He ran his hand over his head, felt the stubble: a quick corrective. He glanced down then pulled in his stomach: a second corrective. He wasn't what he once was – and that had never been all that much. What could she ever have seen in him? Belle's laugh trilled from somewhere behind him. He stopped. He had thought she was safely inside.

'They look sore.' Maria glanced at his sunburned arms.

'They're fine.' He brushed away her concern, annoyed with himself for not taking Belle's advice and using the suntan lotion – a small act of rebellion on his part that had backfired.

'Are you—'

'Have you—'

They both spoke over each other, then smiled.

'You first,' he said.

'I was only going to ask how long you were staying. Something easy to start us off.'

'Us?' He cleared his throat to bring his voice back down to its natural register. 'Just till Tuesday. We're scattering the ashes tomorrow, on Monday we're seeing the estate agent, then we're done.'

'Just like that.' She looked thoughtful. 'All those good times wrapped up and put away for ever.'

'And the bad.' He had to stop his hand from reaching out to touch her cheek.

'Remember how we were going to go round the world? I was going to sail—'

'Do you still?'

She nodded. 'Yes. We live near the ocean.' A faraway look entered her eyes, then pulling herself to the present, she asked, 'It was never your thing, was it?'

He was about to protest – Yes, it was. How have you forgotten? – but she hadn't finished. 'Back then you were going to take a motorbike and we were going to meet in every port.'

'I'd forgotten that.' Yes, he would have chosen a motorbike over a boat any day. He laughed as the memory surfaced. And with it came the impression of heat hazy days filled with love and laughter. They would speed down to the coast on his motorbike, her arms clasped round his waist, warm wind in their faces. They worked in restaurants on the coast, saving their money to travel to the Far East on a few dollars a day. There, they explored, lay on pristine beaches, dabbled with drugs. They made so many plans that were never fulfilled. And why not?

Because he had been frightened.

For almost two years he had tried, unable to resist her, but eventually he couldn't live with her bohemian unpredictability, the not knowing what they would be doing next, of how they would earn a living, his fear of the unknown. She was too like his mother in many ways, but bolder, fearless. His fear of spontaneity had taken him down a different path. He had picked up his abandoned degree and transferred to Edinburgh. This time he was ready for the student life. This time he felt more sure of himself, able to let the relationship continue through the holidays for another year. By then he had found Belle.

'Hope always said she wanted to come with us.' She laughed. That laugh. 'Do you remember?'

'She would never have left Walter here alone.' As they began to reminisce about Hope and Walter's golden days at the house, Tom began to relax. 'Funny to think they were less than the age we are now.'

'He was a bit older, wasn't he? But they were such a great couple. So much fun.'

'I sometimes wonder what they were like before we were around.'

She put her head to one side, interested. 'What d'you mean?'

'You never know what made your parents who they are, do you? And you can never find out. Not really. You get to meet them a third or a quarter of the way through their lives if you're lucky.' He was surprised at himself. This wasn't the sort of conversation he was used to having. But Maria didn't seem surprised at all.

'I'd never thought of it like that. But you can always talk to them and ask.'

'Most children aren't interested enough in what went on before they came along. I certainly wasn't until now, when it's too late. And mine certainly don't seem to be.'

'You mean they don't know about us, what we got up to.' She lowered her gaze.

'Of course not.' He tried not to sound too appalled at the thought.

'I'm joking, Tom.' She gave him a smile to reassure him.

'Oh.' Everything he did or said in her presence felt so inept. 'All I meant was that we don't know anything much about Mum. Whatever made her the person she was will always be a mystery now.'

'And that's everything that made you who you are, too.'

'I suppose so.' He wasn't sure he really wanted to go any deeper. They had strayed into the territory that Jo felt was so important to the two of them: the territory he had dealt with and dismissed. He shouldn't be discussing it with anyone else. Least of all Maria. 'But tell me about your life. I want to know what's happened to you.'

'In ten minutes? Impossible, but I'll try.' Her laugh lightened the mood between them. 'Then you.'

'Over here then.' Tom gestured to a rug being vacated by two couples heading up to the old barn for a game of table tennis. As the sun set, Jo and Elaine were lighting the candles, the flares and garden lights so the party became more intimate as darkness fell. While Maria sat down, smoothing her dress over her knees, he stacked up the plates left behind and took them to the terrace. When he returned he brought two glasses of wine and handed one to her. 'OK,' he said, squatting down. As he did, he overbalanced and felt the back seam give in his shorts. As it tore, he tipped to the left, his arm out to stop himself from falling.

Holding his glass up high he managed, by a miracle, not to spill a drop. 'Cheers! My mother's son,' he said and burst out laughing.

'No less,' Maria agreed and drank to that.

'Who's that?' Belle had crept up behind Lucy, making her jump. Her breath smelled minty, as if she'd just brushed her teeth. She was clutching a bottle of water. Kneeling down first, she organised a couple of cushions just so, then sat down.

'Where?'

'Over there on the rug.' Belle pointed towards a pair of men, finishing a game of chess on a board set up on a low table between their two bean bags.

'The bald one's Roger Smythe, the architect who helped with the house years ago. I think Mum may even have had a bit of a fling with him once. Do you want an introduction?' Belle's disapproving intake of breath amused her. 'And the younger one with the moustache, that's Bernard Ardant. He runs walking and painting holidays with Sylvie, his partner. He was on the other table in the restaurant last night.' She looked around the garden and gestured towards a tiny, fine-boned woman with dark hair holding court to a couple of men intent on whatever she was saying. 'There she is, talking to Jaime and Joaquín over there.'

'No, no, not there,' Belle snapped, with a flash of her pearly teeth. 'With Tom. The woman in yellow. Maria.' She sounded as if she was testing the name on her tongue.

'Oh.' Lucy followed her gaze to where her brother and Maria were sitting, talking. 'She's an old friend.'

Just then Maria said something and Tom touched his nose. They both laughed.

'I can see that,' said Belle. 'But how do you know her?'

Lucy realised that she should be careful. 'From years ago, when we were growing up. She was a friend of Jo's.' Enough said.

'*They* must have been close friends too,' Belle commented,

making it obvious what she was getting at. 'He's been watching her most of the afternoon.'

'I'm sure you're imagining that.' Lucy willed Jo to finish with the lights and come and rescue her.

'No.' Belle nudged her sunglasses back up her nose. Lucy could only guess what was going on behind them. 'No, I'm not.'

Why shouldn't Belle keep an eye on her husband? If Lucy had been able to keep an eye on Art, things might have turned out differently. She took a deep breath. Belle would only find out the truth from someone else. 'They did have a bit of a thing together once,' she said, as casually as she knew how.

Belle's face froze, then she straightened her skirt.

Lucy hurried on. 'But that was years ago. Years and years. Around the time he chucked in his degree before he picked it up again. As far as I know he hasn't seen her since. None of us have.'

'Oh.' Belle looked as if the air had been let out of her.

For once, Lucy felt almost sorry for her. For a couple that hadn't seen each other for years, Tom and Maria did look unusually friendly.

'You're not jealous?' She tried to make light of it.

As Belle stood up, she seemed to reinflate. 'Of course not! Who he knew before me is none of my business.'

Lucy wished Tom would stop leaning quite so close to Maria. 'Why don't you go over and meet her? I'll come with you, if you like.'

'No, I don't think so. I wouldn't want to interrupt.' Belle smoothed her hair, following the shape with her hand. 'I'll go and catch up with Adam and Val. I hardly spoke to them last night.' She walked towards the couple coming down from the croquet.

Up at the house, soft yellow light filtered through the windows with the sound of music. The various flickering outdoor lights sent shadows darting over the grass. Lucy heard clapping from the house so she went in that direction. In the sitting room, the carpet had been rolled back and furniture pushed to the sides like old times. In the centre of the room Brad and Elaine were jiving in front of a crown of admirers to 'Wild, Wild Young Men'. Who would have thought that the pair of them would be so light on their feet? As the music ended, they came towards the French windows, both looking flushed and happy.

'That was amazing,' Lucy said. 'I didn't know you could dance like that.'

'Neither did I,' said Elaine, out of breath. 'Not any more. But all you need is a decent partner. Oh boy! Where's my drink?'

'I'll get it.' Brad headed back inside to the side table where all the dancers were leaving their half-empty glasses.

Elaine sank into a chair. 'I really enjoyed that.' She fanned herself with a hand, straightened her necklaces with another. 'You've got to grab all the fun you can get at my age. Hope would tell you that.' Elaine winked, allowing a brief glimpse of a streak of peacock eye shadow.

Lucy swallowed. 'I know she would.'

Anything further was prevented by Brad's return. Elaine took her water as the music started up, Elvis this time, and the other dancers took to the floor again.

'Will you?' Antonio emerged from the sitting room, his hand held out to her. His timing couldn't have been better.

'Of course.' They had danced together at every party for the last five or six years. She remembered how Hope would watch them, a smile on her face, not as agile as she would like to be any more.

They left Brad and Elaine and melted into the other dancers, Antonio's touch as light as a feather on her waist. Lucy closed her eyes and let her body respond to the music, let her brain empty itself of thought. As one old favourite gave way to the next, they kept on dancing. It was if Antonio knew exactly what she needed without her having to say a word. They danced fast, they danced slow. They danced together, they danced apart. They danced with a group of friends. All the while Lucy surrendered to the music, letting herself go, detaching herself from her surroundings. Eventually the two of them could dance no more.

They drifted back to the terrace to get a drink. Brad and Elaine had disappeared among the other guests. During a break in the music, Lucy heard the sound of a guitar being played by the pool. A laugh rang out from the olive trees where people still sat out despite the night air growing cooler. She wondered whether Tom and Maria were still out there, whether Belle had gone over after all. Someone shouted from the drive where a game of *pétanque* was being played by the light of the moon. From the barn came the pick-pock of table tennis complete with accompanying gasps and cheers. Everything was as Hope would have wanted it, complete with all the music she loved. That was always the trouble with a good wake – because that's what this really was – the one person who would have enjoyed it most was always the one who was missing. Lucy raised her glass and looked back at the jar on the mantelpiece.

'Here's to Mum.'

Antonio followed suit. 'Hope.'

They drank together.

'Here you are.' Jo came round the corner of the house, carrying Ivy who was draped over her shoulder, her eyes drooping. 'I've been looking for you.'

Lucy's heart sank. 'Why? What's happened?'

'The chest.' She shifted Ivy into a better position. 'There are presents for us in there after all. But I'm going to put this one to bed before I do anything else.'

At the mention of 'bed' Ivy came to, flinging back her head and knocking Jo on the chin. 'No! No bed!'

'Yes.' Jo was firm as she rubbed her jaw. 'You're exhausted, my love. And I want you all bright and sparkling for tomorrow.'

'What if I take you up and read you some more of that story we began last night?' Lucy saw the flicker of relief in Jo's eyes as Ivy twisted round and held out her arms to her. At least this gave her an excuse to absent herself from the party for a while and prepare herself for whatever was going to come next. Although the party was thinning out, there was a reliable hard core who would be here for a few more hours yet. And that was traditionally when things went off the rails.

As she took the weight of Ivy, breathing in her niece's chocolaty, sweaty, earthy smell, she allowed herself to enjoy the moment. 'Come on then.'

'Thanks, Luce.' Jo went to the table and poured herself a white wine. 'At last.'

She flopped into the nearest chair, not objecting when Antonio came to sit beside her.

22

Being aware of Belle's on-off eagle-eyed scrutiny made Tom cut his conversation with Maria shorter than he would have liked. Of course, he could have waved Belle over from where she was saying something to Lucy and introduced the two women properly, but something had stopped him: a feeling of wanting to keep Maria to himself for a little while longer. Once his initial awkwardness had worn off, the years spent apart seemed to roll away, prompting memories he had packed up long ago to return as clearly as if they had happened yesterday. He was enjoying having Maria to himself and didn't want to let go quite yet. As soon as Belle joined the conversation, all that would change. Instead, he tore himself away to talk to their other guests, determined to return to Maria as soon as he could. As he mingled, wherever he stood, whoever he spoke to, only half-listening to their reminiscences of Hope, Maria's yellow dress kept catching his eye, her low laugh sounding in his ear.

Through the people milling about outside, taking a break from the dancing or just up there to top up their glasses, he saw Jo and Antonio sitting on the terrace deep in conversation. Antonio had her hand in his and was talking animatedly, pointing at the house, then returning his attention to her. Tom walked towards them. The music, more frantic than before, more modern, booming into the night prevented him from hearing what they were saying.

'Grab a seat,' Jo said as soon as she saw him. 'Antonio's just been telling me about the plans Mum had drawn up for the house. Did you know about them?'

'She once said something but I didn't take it seriously. You know what she was like, dead set on something one minute and then straight on to the next.' He turned to Antonio. 'I think you may have got it wrong. Anyway, the house is ours now.' He didn't like the idea of his mother confiding her plans in this man and not in one of her family. After all, however proprietorial Antonio might feel, he had no claim on the house now Hope had gone.

'Tom!' Jo was warning him off, but Tom was not in the mood to be told how to behave.

'That may be,' Antonio was implacable as always, ignoring Tom's hostility. 'We often talked about how the house would make a perfect small hotel instead of the B & B. She didn't want to use Roger again so Martin Higueras – you know the architect in Ronda? – drew up some plans. They must be here somewhere.'

'Hotel?! Mum?!' Tom rolled his eyes and gave a scornful laugh. 'That would never have worked. Anyway it's all irrelevant. We're selling up. You know that.'

'Someone else may think it's a good idea though.' Jo gave Tom another of those looks over the rim of her glass. 'We should find them. They might help with the sale.'

'Maybe,' he conceded. The way his two sisters stood up for Antonio drove him mad. What was it about the guy? 'But we've been through most things and anyway that's up to whoever buys the place, not us.'

'Aren't you curious? I'd like to know how Mum thought the old house might be changed.'

'Antonio!' The shout came from the group playing *pétanque* down on the drive.

Offered this timely reprieve, Antonio got to his feet. 'Perhaps I should show them how to play!' He grinned and set off towards the game.

'That man's impossible,' Tom muttered.

'I don't know why you have to be so rude to him. You might at least try. I bet you'll want him to take care of the place till it's sold.'

'Well, I suppose I might,' he admitted grudgingly. 'But I'm still annoyed she left him something when she still owed me several thousand.'

'What are you talking about?' Jo sat straighter, holding his gaze, not letting him look away. 'What several thousand? You've never said anything before.'

'What was the point? I couldn't change her will.' He took a long suck at his bottle of San Miguel.

'Antonio deserved what he got for being such a good and loyal friend to her. Anyway, what did she owe you all that for?' Jo had edged forward until she was perched on the edge of her seat.

'Ages ago, I lent her about ten grand to help do up the house so she could get the B & B going. Remember when she had the plumbing redone and the *casita* knocked into shape?'

'You paid for that?'

'Yes. But she always said it was an investment and that she'd pay me back when the business got off the ground.' Why was Jo making him feel guilty about this? Was he being unreasonable? A deal was a deal, even if it was with his mother. He had known at the time that he'd probably never see the money in Hope's lifetime but he had been banking on her seeing him right in her will at least. Now he thought about it, he realised how daft of him that was. She'd probably entirely forgotten. And he had never been able to bring himself to ask. But he had made that promise to Belle that they would go to Sri Lanka the following spring. Their neighbours, Bob and Alice, still went on about the magical time they'd had there. Belle was determined they should see it for themselves, using her fiftieth birthday as a pretext. Going there in the style she wanted would cost a small fortune. Some extra cash would have come in handy.

'Not all of it,' he justified himself. 'Of course not. But a token would have been nice.' He was embarrassed to hear himself sounding so mean-spirited.

Jo sighed and shook her head. 'I bet she just forgot. Why didn't you remind her?'

So it was his fault? How small Jo could still make him feel without even trying to. Ever the big sister, able to judge and put down. 'I tried, but she didn't want to hear. She did her usual trick of brushing off a conversation she didn't want to have.'

'Well, you'd better look in the envelope she left you. Maybe there's a cheque in it.'

'What envelope?' His grasp on the beer bottle tightened.

'I found it at the bottom of the chest once most of those bottle stoppers had been taken. You've been left an envelope, I've got a box that I daren't open, Lucy's got a smaller one and the kids have all got something too. Ivy's thrilled with a few strings of beads.'

'I'd hoped we'd got away without presents.' The back of his neck was hot with anxiety.

'Antonio did warn us.'

Tom didn't need to be reminded. He stood up and threaded his way through to the chest that had been left where Antonio and Juan had put it down. Its lid hung open. Its contents were exactly as Jo described. He touched the box, then picked up the envelope. 'Isn't one letter enough for the night?' he said to himself.

'What've you got there, Tom?' Adam was at his shoulder, flushed from dancing, his shirt sticking to him.

'A note from Hope.' Whatever its contents, Tom didn't want to share them with anyone except perhaps Belle. She would know what to do. 'I'll open it later.'

He yanked the lid up from where it hung at the back of the chest and banged it shut. He had had quite enough of his mother's dramatics for one day. Silence fell on the terrace as everyone looked round to see what had happened.

Tom shrugged. 'Sorry. Lid slipped.' He folded the envelope

in half, tucked it into his trouser pocket and looked around for Maria, but she was nowhere to be seen.

But if he thought he could forget the envelope, he was wrong. He had to know what was inside. Of course Hope couldn't leave him more money – that had all been dealt with during probate. Except she wouldn't care about that. But hadn't they said all there was to be said when she was dying? Except he had never been able to open up in the way his sisters sometimes did, and he realised that made it difficult for others. Perhaps there was something else that had been left unsaid. He had to know. No one would miss him if he disappeared from the party for a few minutes.

In their bedroom in the *casita*, the noise of the party faded into distant music and the occasional shout. Alone, apart from Ferdie who was dressed in a silly blue-spotted coat and made a beeline for him, snapping at his ankles, Tom sank on to the edge of the bed. He looked around the room. It was just as they had left it. Belle's clothes were strewn over a chair in the corner. The wardrobe door swung open to reveal the padded hangers inside, a couple of Belle's dresses and his linen jacket hanging there, waiting for the next day. The top drawer of the chest of drawers wasn't shut properly. Belle's eyeshade hung over the bedside light, her Kindle beside it. In the corner Ferdie's fleecy bed and a bowl of water were there to be tripped over in the dark.

What was happening to him? He was happily married, for God's sake. At least as happily as anyone had a right to expect. But seeing Maria had brought his younger self to the surface, making him question what he had lost.

And now this!

He pulled the envelope from his pocket, straightened it out and turned it over in his hands. They were the hands of an office worker, soft, short-fingered, one with a plain gold wedding band to match Belle's, squared-off nails and a thin scar at the base of his thumb where he had caught it on barbed wire when he and Jo were once hunting in the woods. He hadn't wanted a ring, thought them faintly sissy, but Belle had insisted. 'It's a sign of our commitment to one another. Wear it for me.'

He lifted Ferdie off his foot and returned him to his basket. The tiny dog tilted his head to one side and gazed at Tom, reproachful. Tom glanced round the room, half-expecting Belle to materialise and mother the creature. He was damned if he could see what she saw in Ferdie. He picked up his San Miguel from the bedside table and took a long pull, feeling the chill of the beer down his throat.

He considered the envelope again and his name in Hope's definitive scrawl. Whatever was in it couldn't amount to more than a sheet or two of paper. He hesitated, recollecting the last weeks of Hope's life. By coming to England to die, she had her chance to say her farewells, to tell her children how important they had been to her. He remembered how, of the three of them, Jo had been the most reluctant visitor, making excuses of urgent work or Ivy. Even when she had been there, she tried not to be left alone with Hope. He understood why. She felt the elephants in the room were too big to bear, knowing that Hope would never tell her the one thing she wanted to know and not understanding why not. And then there had been that mad dash she had made to the bedside from Scotland. Hope had asked for her but she had arrived too late. He and Belle had visited as often as they could, and he liked to think that Hope had warmed to his wife by the end. He would have liked them to have got on better. After all, Belle had done everything she could to help make her mother-in-law more comfortable despite the short shrift she sometimes got in return.

Maria. His thoughts slid to her despite his efforts to pull them away. Hope had always liked her, perhaps because she saw something of herself in her, more than she did in any one of her children. He had to talk to her again while he had the chance. He would find an excuse that even Belle might accept. But first . . . He slid his little finger into the top of the envelope, then paused, preparing himself for its contents. But before the paper tore, the door opened.

'You're here! I've been looking everywhere.' Belle was speaking before she came into the room. Ferdie bolted towards her and up he was scooped. She let the dog lick her face while she cooed over him. 'I saw the light on,' she said, finally tearing herself away. 'I didn't know what to think.'

What could she possibly mean? She couldn't really have thought – not him and Maria!

'I came in here for a quick breather.' He realised he didn't want to share what was in the envelope with her after all. At least, not at that moment. 'What's the problem?'

'I found Ethan with that girl.'

'Which girl?'

'That girl in the shorts. Your *friend's* daughter.' Each word was loaded with meaning. 'He went down to the pool with her and some others during your speech.'

Christina: Maria's daughter. Her mother's legs. Her mother's dark eyes.

'What do you expect, love? He's nearly seventeen. It's not a crime.'

'I'm sure they were drinking – and smoking dope. I could smell it.' He understood her panic after Ethan's disgrace at school. They had managed to keep his expulsion under the rug so far, so no one in the family knew. Everyone believed they had moved him to a new school for sixth form simply because it offered the right A-level combination. Belle didn't want anyone to think they were anything other than a perfect family. But as Ethan's parents, they still had to be vigilant.

Tom patted the bed beside him so that she sat down, Ferdie squeezed under her arm. 'He's old enough to know what he's doing. I don't think even he'd be stupid enough to take any drugs while he's here with us. Where would he get them from?'

'How can we be sure?' A note of panic had entered her voice.

Tom imagined he could hear Ferdie's desperate intake of breath as Belle relaxed her grip of him.

'We calm down and we go back to the party. I'll have a word with him.' He put her hand firmly on her thigh to reassure her, only to remove it smartly as Ferdie snarled at him. There was no question over who owned that particular bit of territory.

'Stop it, you monkey.' She tapped him on the nose before leaning towards Tom, resting her head on his shoulder. Ferdie's growl rumbled softly. 'I knew you'd know what to do.' She inclined her face up to his. 'When I couldn't see either of you, I panicked. The last time I saw you, you were talking to Jo and Antonio, and then you vanished.'

'Antonio was saying Mum wanted to renovate the house. Did she say anything to you? Where would she have got the money?'

'Of course she didn't.' Belle straightened up and went over to the mirror to titivate her make-up, putting Ferdie into his bed. 'But then she wouldn't, would she?' Belle turned to face him, her expression full of regret.

'I guess not.' Though there was a long-held moratorium on the subject, he was all too aware what a disappointment Belle had been to Hope after Maria. And Belle had always been aware that she had never quite passed muster as his wife, although she never knew why.

Belle disappeared into the bathroom and he watched her. She had changed too, no longer the girl he had got to know after clashing heads at their first meeting. They had been in the DHT canteen at Edinburgh. She had stood up from a table, backed into him and sent his tray flying.

'Whoa! Careful.'

'Oh God, I'm so sorry.' Her words were almost lost under her friends' laughter.

'Don't worry.' He'd wiped the mayo from his jeans then bent down to retrieve what he could of his food.

She bent down at the same time to help and their heads banged together.

'Ouch! Double sorry, I guess.' She rubbed her forehead, messing up her artfully arranged (even then) hair. She hadn't worn make-up, hadn't thought she needed it. Her face had been clear-skinned, open and earnest. They began to laugh with every-one else. She offered to wash his jeans. That night they met for supper. Friends at first, their affair took a little time to get off the ground. Belle had no idea of Maria's existence, of how Tom went home to Spain to see her or how torn he would become between the two of them. What a coward he had been not telling her but, for reasons he chose not to analyse, he had kept Maria's existence a secret.

Had he just been keeping his options open? While still smitten by Maria's inexhaustible, irrepressible passion for life, he found himself drawn to the steady domestic harmony offered by Belle. Like Maria, she teased him about his increasing punctiliousness, his timekeeping, his fondness for order. But Belle's teasing was affectionate, not frustrated. She didn't encourage him to take risks he didn't want to take. She tried to understand his limita-tions without pushing him to go beyond them. Life with her was predictable, ordered, secure. For the first time in his life, Tom found himself able to embrace certainty as he began to come to terms with his place in the world.

Eventually, he had been unable to deflect Belle's curiosity any longer. Her questions were becoming too frequent about what he did when he went home, who he saw. When could she go too? He had to make a decision at last. Only after a broken-hearted Maria had disappeared to Boston, did he bring Belle home for the first time. The visit was a disaster. Everything reminded him of Maria, their affair, and how different Belle was from her. There was nothing over which Belle and Hope saw eye to eye. Belle shared his growing discomfort with the spontaneity and chaos that seemed to govern life at Casa de Sueños. Hope, who had always loved Maria, found Belle an uninspiring substitute and made no bones about it to Tom in private, although she did at least have the sensitivity not to refer to Maria in Belle's presence. Eventually Maria had gradually disappeared from the family's consciousness and over years, and two grandchildren, Hope and Belle had arrived at an uneasy truce.

The moment for opening the envelope gone, he slipped it into the internal pocket of his suitcase where it would be hidden. At that moment Belle emerged from the bathroom, looking as fresh as if the evening was starting. In a blaze of remembered affection, he held out his hand to her but she bent down and grabbed Ferdie. 'You go out, then I'll make sure he's shut in.'

He did as he was told, waiting outside, trying not to listen to Belle reassuring Ferdie that Mummy would be back soon. If the dog made her happy, it was a small price to pay. But as shouts rose over the music from the front of the house, he was reminded that before he found his way back to Maria, he must find Ethan. And he thought he knew where to look.

23

Lucy stayed upstairs lying on Jo's bed next to Ivy, reading, until they both dropped off. She woke with a start, immediately aware of the party still going on below the window, of the music beating out of the sitting room doors. Guilty about not being the hostess her mother would have wanted, she dragged herself off the bed and slipped on her sandals before carrying Ivy over to her own bed. For a moment she thought her niece would wake but, as soon as Bampy was back in Ivy's hand, she sucked her thumb noisily, eyes still tight shut and rolled over.

Tiptoeing across the room, avoiding the recently arrived suitcase that was open and spilling its contents on to the floor, Lucy paused in front of the mirror. A gaunt, hollow-eyed mask stared back at her. A hand through the hair and a touch of the make-up that Jo had left scattered on the top of the chest of drawers did little to improve matters. She picked up the glass of wine she'd brought upstairs with her and knocked it back, grimacing at the taste. Dutch courage.

Downstairs, most of the party had come up to the house and was gathered either on the terrace or in the sitting room. The music belted out louder and faster than ever, its insistent beat infectious. She looked around for Antonio, hoping they might dance again. Dancing would numb her feelings as she concentrated on keeping up, keeping going. A flash of yellow caught her eye. Maria was dancing with one of the English expats who had made the journey from Ronda. As they parted, she saw Antonio beyond them dancing with Jo. Jo was laughing as she waved her arms in the air, stopping only when Antonio reached out to take one of her hands and pull her towards him and twirled her under his arm. Lucy looked away.

Outside, she approached the table that was crowded with bottles and glasses. Someone had cleared away the empty plates leaving the remnants of the puddings and cheese. She held up a couple of glasses to the light and picked the clean one, then picked up one bottle after another until she found one with something in it and helped herself.

'Great party. Just like the old days.' Maria had come up beside her and held out her glass. Lucy did the honours.

'I remember,' said Lucy. 'You were always round here, first with Jo and then with Tom.'

That had emerged sounding like an accusation but Maria seemed unperturbed as she shrugged and smiled. 'Wild horses...' she agreed.

'I keep expecting Mum to appear,' Lucy looked towards the house as if Hope was about to materialise at her bedroom window. 'The one person who would have known everyone and enjoyed it the most.'

Maria swayed in time to the music, tapping the rim of her glass with a finger. 'She wouldn't have known Christina. My daughter,' she added by way of explanation. 'I'd have loved them to meet.'

'I think I saw her with the others, sneaking off to the pool during Tom's speech.'

Maria raised her eyebrows. 'She does her own thing. Perhaps I should go and look for her.'

'I wouldn't worry. They're probably enjoying themselves. That's what we used to do, after all.' Late nights round the pool at the height of summer, the only place where there was some relief from the sometimes suffocating heat. She and Hope had once spent the whole night there, sleeping on the loungers, ignoring the others' warnings about mosquitoes – to their cost. But they had lain and looked at the stars and talked about their dreams for the future. As a teenager, she had been full of them. Back then the world had been at her feet, offering up so many paths and choices. Hope had listened and encouraged her, asking questions, offering advice. She couldn't remember many times when she had her mother's concentrated attention for so long.

Maria stopped her tapping. 'Tom asked me to come to the scattering tomorrow. Is that all right?'

'Of course. Why not?' Although Lucy wondered what Belle's reaction was going to be. What was Tom thinking? 'Have you met Belle?' she asked.

'His wife?' Maria shook her head. 'Not properly. Nor his boys, though it's not hard to guess who they are.'

Gabriel from the garden centre in Estepona, a retail opportunity beloved by Hope for years, had made his way through the party to join them. His shirt was part untucked, hair slicked back, sweat blooming on his forehead. He held out a meaty hand to Maria. 'Will you dance?'

'Of course.' Maria smiled and took his hand. 'I'll see you later.'

'Sure,' said Lucy, glad to be on her own again. As she went down the terrace steps, she moved into a world of darkness and shadows. Some of the candles had blown out, the rest flickered in the gathering breeze. The olive trees formed grotesque silhouettes in the moonlight. Rugs and cushions lay abandoned. She picked up one or two of them to make a start on tidying up, then stopped. She didn't want anyone to think she was bringing the party to a close.

'Lucy! Wait!' Jo hurtled down the steps towards her. 'I want to ask you something. Did you know that Mum owed Tom money?'

'Did she? She never said anything to me.'

'Apparently he helped them out when they did up the *casita*. Years ago. And he seems to think we're going to give him extra when the house is sold.'

'She was so specific that we had to sell and split the proceeds equally that she must have forgotten. I don't think we can do anything else, can we?' At that moment, Lucy couldn't bring herself to care as much as Jo obviously did.

'That's what I thought. Anyway, I don't think he can claim anything without proof, do you? I just thought you might know something I didn't. We'll sort it out tomorrow then.' She picked up a cushion and chucked it at the pile. 'I'm going back inside. I don't get much chance to let my hair down with Ivy around.'

'I bet you don't,' agreed Lucy, tamping down a little jab of envy. 'You should make the most of it. I'm going to the pool. I'll remind them there's tons of food left in the kitchen if they're hungry.'

Jo touched her arm, to stop her for a second. 'Thanks, Luce. For all you've done. I know I haven't been the greatest help. Richard and I have got so much going at work this year. We've had rebrandings, launches, consolidating our digital department and . . .' Noticing that Lucy was only half listening, she tailed off. 'What with that and Ivy—'

'You've got a lot on your plate, I know that. Don't worry. Sometimes I've just felt a bit taken for granted, that's all.' There, she'd said it. But she didn't feel the release she'd expected. Instead her heart took a dive as she thought of Art. Would he be back in England by now, she wondered, the affair and the pregnancy splashed all over the papers? Would he be on his way to the house, their house, to take what he wanted?

'Oh my God, but you're not at all. You mustn't feel that, especially not now.' Jo hugged her. 'Once we've scattered the ashes tomorrow, we can start to think again. Let me help you.' She kissed Lucy on the cheek. 'I'll do whatever I can.'

Lucy believed she meant it. Just sometimes Jo didn't think of the effect of what she said or did might be on others. A careless word could be so hurtful, but her heart was with her family, all the more so since she had had Ivy. 'I do hate the idea of us leaving here forever,' she said, suddenly, as another wave of sadness broke over her. 'Of another family taking over the place and doing all the things we used to do here.'

'I know.' They looked towards the house, so familiar to both of them. 'It's such a wonderful old building. No wonder Mum and Walter fell in love with it.'

'And now it's full of our family history and always will be, even if no one else knows it.' Lucy bit her lip hard, warding against more tears. 'If only I'd known what I know now, I might even have left Art ages ago and come back here to help Mum run the B & B. I could have turned it into a good business for her, less hit-and-miss, that's for sure.'

'Really?' Jo was sceptical. 'With Mum and Antonio? Wouldn't you have hated it.'

'Would I?' Lucy didn't know what she thought any more. She had an overwhelming urge to throw herself on to the pile of cushions and sob. Instead she said, 'Go on. You go back to the dancing. Make the most of the evening.'

'Will you be OK?'

Touched by her sister's concern, she said, 'I'll be fine. I've just got to get used to things, that's all. A new start. Exciting.' Except she didn't feel excited at all, just confused and frightened. 'I'm going down to the pool to see what's happening there.'

'If you're sure . . .' But Jo was already backing off, drawn by the music, by the chatter. She didn't want to have a serious conversation now. Lucy watched her go before turning towards the pool.

The click of the latch on the gate provoked a flurry of activity, hasty whispers, a clearing of a throat, another giggle. The underwater lights in the pool were still on, bright in the blue mosaic sides, rippling through the water. A large fig leaf was floating in the shallow end. There was a mutter of voices as Lucy walked towards the deep end where various bodies lay stretched out on the loungers with their backs to her. As she got closer, she saw a couple of bottles of wine, some beer bottles and what looked like a bottle of tequila grouped on the tiles. A plume of pungent smoke rose from the central lounger. A giggle. But this was nothing worse than any of them had done in their youth. If only she could reel back the years and stash away the time.

Ethan was sharing a lounger with Christina, their bodies tipped towards each other so they wouldn't fall off, their legs tangled. Beside them were two other boys, and a girl Lucy didn't recognise. A guitar lay on the ground beside them, half hidden by the large plant pot containing the tree fern. Furthest away, Alex lay apparently asleep.

'Lucy! It's you.' The relief on Ethan's face was almost comical. His hat was flipped to the back of his head, his shirt unbuttoned. He brought his right hand from behind his back, a spliff between his fingers. The rich scent of marijuana floated up to meet her.

'What are you doing, Ethan? Suppose I'd been your father.'

'I know,' he agreed, drawing hard and letting smoke wreath into the air from his mouth. 'Thank God you're not. Want some?'

To Lucy's astonishment, he held the spliff out to her. The only explanation could be that he was as high as a kite. She raised her palm towards him. 'No! Of course I don't. Put it out. Now.' In fact she couldn't think of anything she would like more. That first hit would take the top off her head, steal through her limbs, relaxing her until nothing much mattered. But it had been a long time since she had touched the stuff and smoking with her nephew only yards away from his no-doubt disapproving parents did not seem like the best way to start again, however attractive it seemed.

With mock reluctance, he ground the lit end between two fingers and flicked the burning tip towards the pool. 'There. You won't tell Mum and Dad, will you?' For a second he sounded much younger than he was.

'Where did you get it from?' Presumably from one of these other boys who were strung out beside him.

'I brought a little bit with me.' He pretended to look ashamed. 'It's finished now.'

'My God, Ethan! Are you crazy? What if you'd been caught?'

'Yeah, well I wasn't.' His confidence had returned. Christina giggled again as Ethan slipped the remains of the spliff into his shirt pocket. 'Mum 'n' Dad'll never know, I promise.'

'You don't have to promise *me* anything,' said Lucy. 'I'm just thinking about them.'

As they spoke the three kids she didn't recognise dragged them-selves to their feet, one of them grabbing one of the half-empty bottles of wine and the guitar as they wove their way down the edge of the pool towards the gate, muttering and laughing. Seeing them go, Ethan got ready to follow, keeping a hold of Christina's hand. 'Come on. It's too cold down here now anyway. Let's go back to the house. Is there any food left?' He tipped his hat to the front of his head so the brim ran parallel with his nose.

'Loads. On the table and there's lots in the kitchen too. That's what I came to say.'

Ethan glanced at his brother, who hadn't moved since Lucy had arrived. 'You coming, Alex? Alex!'

Alex didn't reply but lay completely still, one arm hanging off his lounger, his hand touching the paving.

'Is he all right?' Out of concern, Lucy went towards him. 'He hasn't been drinking as well, has he?'

'One or two,' Ethan laughed, dismissive. 'He's a lightweight is all.' He put his arm round Christina's waist and pulled her to him. She didn't resist. 'Alex!'

Now beside the boy, Lucy was relieved to hear his heavy breathing. She shook his shoulder. 'Wake up, Alex. You'd be better up at the house.'

He moved his body a fraction as his eyes opened. 'Wha'?' In the pool lights, she could see his face was the colour of parch-ment. His breath was laced with alcohol.

'I think we'd better get you back to the house for some water and a coffee.' She turned to Ethan who was watching, a grin stretched across his face. 'Come and help me.'

He must have heard her irritation with him and came over to help push Alex into a sitting position with his feet on the ground. Then Lucy took one side, Ethan the other and they tried to haul him to his feet but Alex was a dead weight, slumped between them. Just as Lucy thought they were about to get him on his feet, Alex mumbled something incomprehensible and sank back on to the lounger.

'For God's sake, man! Get a fucking grip.' Ethan shoved his brother's shoulder. If Lucy hadn't been standing where she was, Alex would have fallen sideways.

'There's no point in talking to him like that. He's completely out of it.'

'Alex!' Ethan tried again, this time sounding more worried.

Alex looked up at him, his eyes unfocused as he tried to identify who was speaking to him. A look of surprise came over his face as he raised his hand to his throat. His body swayed before he pitched forward with a groan and was sick on the ground in front of him.

Lucy and Ethan jumped out of the way, leaving Alex doubled up over his knees, retching again. Christina hadn't moved but was watching the proceedings with disgust, pulling her hair back and then round over one shoulder.

As she was wondering whether to get Tom but not wanting to land the boys in trouble, Lucy heard the gate open and shut. All of them but Alex turned to see Belle advancing on them. Her face was set, her mouth tight with anger and concern. She had seen everything.

'What have you been doing to your brother?' She stopped and took in the bottles, mentally counting them, a little bob of the head for each one. 'I asked you to look after him.'

'I have been,' Ethan protested. 'I didn't see him drink that much.'

'Evidently not.' Belle bore down on her younger son still hunched over, groaning. She put a head on his forehead. 'Alex! How much have you drunk?'

He mumbled something none of them could hear and retched again.

Belle faced Ethan who Lucy could see was doing his best to appear stone-cold sober but was swaying from side to side, smiling faintly and using Christina as a prop although she didn't look much steadier. 'Ethan! Go and get your father! He went over to the barn to look for you.' Given an excuse, Ethan took off while he could, Christina in close pursuit.

Belle sat down. 'Kids! I'm so sorry you had to deal with this.' She looked at the ground. 'And your shoes!'

In the drama Lucy hadn't noticed some of the sick had spattered on to her sandals, but she didn't want to make things worse for Alex than they already were. 'These old things? They'll be fine. Don't worry about me.'

Lucy went to the hose. She flinched as the freezing water hit her feet, and watched as it ran into the drain taking trails of vomit with it. Her favourite sandals would be ruined. A couple of shiny blue stones detached themselves and rolled away into the grating before she passed the hose to Belle.

24

Hope's last birthday party was over. The final stragglers had gone, piled into cars and local taxis. The cushions and rugs had been brought in and piled in the hall for sorting out in the morning. Bailey had taken advantage and made himself a bed among them. Ethan and Alex had been sent to bed with threats of groundings, reduced allowances and the confiscation of phones – all to be decided – none of which were taken with sufficient seriousness. The music had been silenced. The lights turned off.

Jo sat by her bedroom window, gazing out into the dark. The lights of Africa were obscured although those closer to home were dotted over the landscape stretching in front of her. The mass of Sierra Crestellina loomed to her left. Looking up, she could make out clouds racing across the night sky. The weather was changing. All she could hear was Ivy's rhythmical breathing, then the odd animal cry outside. When Jo had come up, Ivy had been lying in her squirrel pyjamas, having kicked the thin duvet to the bottom of the bed. She had pulled it up and planted a kiss on her sleeping child's cheek then sat and stared at her, in wonder at the tiny nose, the small mole by her right ear, her slightly open lips. How blessed she was to have this small miracle that had transformed her life. Tomorrow she would fulfil her promise and help her sister make a new start too. That was the very least she could do. She concentrated on folding up Ivy's clothes and putting them in the bottom drawer she had chosen. Only then did Jo take her mother's present to the window.

Like Tom and Lucy, she hesitated to open this last gift. She had noticed how Tom had tucked his envelope away. He would never do anything in public that might involve an emotional response. However much he might want to open it, he would wait to react in private then decide how he would present the contents to the rest of them. She understood only too well because it was exactly how she felt herself.

And now, alone, she ran her hand over the square, box-shaped gift. She held it in both hands, feeling its weight, wondering what on earth their mother had left in store for her. There was only one thing that Jo had ever really wanted from her as an adult – knowledge – and now Hope was dead, she would never have that. She picked up the label, stared at her name, then pulled hard so the label tore from the red ribbon then floated to the floor. She untied the ribbon, taking care to undo every knot and then rolled it up into a tight ball that loosened the moment she put it on the top of the chest of drawers.

Ivy muttered something then shifted position so the duvet slipped off her again. Jo got up to cover her before returning to her parcel.

The wrapping paper was fiercely secured. Jo tackled one end, easing off the Sellotape so the paper didn't tear, then the other. She pealed back the paper to find a faded red tartan metal biscuit tin. Instead of opening it, she took the paper and folded it care-fully, corner to corner just as Hope would have done, then placed it beside the ribbon. She lifted the box, not heavy, and lifted it to her ear, giving it a slight shake. Something inside shifted position.

She pushed at the side of the lid with her thumb until it lifted a fraction. She tried the opposite side. Feeling it give a little, she tried pulling at it from the top, first one then the other side. Suddenly, it flew open, too fast for her to stop the lid crashing to the floor. She looked over at Ivy, but she didn't move. Jo went back to the contents of the box. The first thing she saw was an envelope identical in shape to the one she had opened for Tom earlier in the evening. She lifted it out, registered that it had been left unsealed, and put it on the top of the chest of drawers. Whatever Hope had to say could wait a moment.

Returning to what lay underneath, she stared, mystified. Two pairs of knitted babies' bootees, one pink and one blue but knitted to slightly different patterns, white ribbon threaded through the ankles of the pink pair. Why on earth would Hope leave her these? If she had knitted them for Ivy, she was a little late in the day. If she thought Jo was going to have another child – no chance. One child was quite enough for a single mum of her age, and besides she really was past it now. She picked up the bootees and held them to her face. Soft as angora, they held the faint smell of washing powder.

But there was something else in the box. In the dim light, she almost didn't notice the small square photograph that had been left face down. Curious, she pulled it out. The back of it was spotted brown with age. Turning it over, she saw a picture of two babies, one in a pink cardigan the other in blue with matching knitted hats, tucked head-to-toe in a big old-fashioned Silver Cross pram.

She took the contents of the box and laid them out on the bed. The envelope lay face down, the flap raised, inviting her to take out the contents. Her eyes moved from it to the faded photo, to the bootees. Presumably they had some significance that at the moment totally escaped her. Instinct and cold stopped her rushing this so she left the letter, and its possible explanation, where it was.

Instead she went into the bathroom, brushed her teeth and removed her make-up. Her reflection in the mirror over the basin was pale, anxious. She poured herself a glass of water and drank it in one. She refilled it, took a couple of Ibuprofen from her washbag and knocked them back. Returning to the bedroom, she stripped off and put on her pyjamas, grabbing the sea-green pashmina that had wrapped her mother's ashes and draping it round her shoulders. She took the envelope from the chest, slipped into bed, barely disturbing the objects on it and gathered them on to her knees.

Now she was ready.

Two pieces of writing paper slipped out of the envelope and with them a small, oval-shaped silver locket in a tiny plastic bag that fell on to her legs. She picked it up, took out the locket and flicked the catch. Inside, in either half, was a photo of a baby, one of them obscured by a fine curl of hair. Beginning to feel inexplicably nervous, she clipped it shut and finally picked up the letter and began to read the familiar scrawl.

My dearest Jo,
By the time you read this, I will have told you everything.

But Hope had told her nothing. Jo took a sip of water.

Now you'll understand why I kept everything to myself. At first I didn't want anyone to know what had happened to us . . .

Jo took a deep breath. Her heart beat faster, her pulse pumping at the base of her throat. Was this what she had been waiting for so long?

. . . and I wanted to put it as far as I could behind me. So far behind me that I could believe that nothing had happened. At least I had you to keep my grief at bay.

Grief?

One of the reasons I'm coming to England is to try to talk to you before it's too late. At the very least, I owe you this. I pray I have the courage to do what I perhaps should have done years ago. I'm frightened that I may not or that I may not have time, so I'm writing this just in case. It may be too hard to break such a long silence. I don't know that I can.

Jo had begun to sweat. She tried to steady her hand that was shaking so much she could barely read what was on the paper. During the time Hope was with Lucy, Jo had visited as often as she could, but she had been so busy at work, putting time in with new clients, attending focus groups round the country, and occasionally taking time out to pop in on a shoot, and shmoozing the client once it was over. And, when she wasn't doing that, she was totally preoccupied with Ivy. But there had been that one time...

For once the two of them were alone, Ivy having disappeared into the kitchen. Hope was in her chair, painfully thin, a rug over her knees. Her beautiful hair had thinned so much Jo could see her scalp. She was tired but lucid when Jo tried for one last time. 'Mum, please can't you tell me who my father is now? Before it's too late?' She took Hope's hand, its thin skin loose over the bones and ropes of veins.

Hope had looked at her, tears in her eyes. 'I've tried so hard to forget... perhaps that was wrong.'

The door flew open at that moment. Ivy dashed in and Jo had to grab her so she didn't jump on to Hope's lap. Belle was right behind her. 'Lunch, everyone. Lucy's just putting it on the table.'

Before Jo had a chance to object, to ask for another second alone with her mother, Belle had grabbed the Zimmer frame and was helping Hope to her feet. After lunch, Lucy had helped an exhausted Hope upstairs for a nap. She didn't wake before Jo had to leave for London, none the wiser, but having to settle Ivy with Sue before she took the train to Edinburgh the following morning. But she had seen how relieved Hope had been that Belle's entrance had stopped her from going any further.

When they spoke on the phone, Hope sounded frail but always said she understood Jo was busy and that she would see her very soon. But looking back, Jo realised how selfish she had been after that. She should have stopped resenting her mother's silence about what mattered so much to her and tried harder for a final reconciliation.

Then there had been that last call from Lucy, when she had been in Edinburgh yet again.

'The doctor says it won't be long now, but she wants to see you. Last night she said Walter was with her.' She talked over Jo's disbelief. Hope couldn't die now, not before she had seen her one more time. 'Come as soon as you can. She won't tell me why.'

Jo had dropped everything, confident that Ivy was happy and safe at home with Sue. But by the time she had travelled down from Scotland, Hope had lost consciousness. She never came round again so whatever she might have said to Jo would remain unsaid forever. Staring at the box, Jo understood at last that Hope had wanted to tell her something but her lack of courage and circumstances had conspired against them. The one moment when Jo might have found out all she wanted to know had been taken from them. She punched the bed in frustration. How could she have been so selfish, so stupid? If only she had been more forgiving. She read on.

This box is all I have left of those days. It's been in a case in the attic for years. I didn't want any reminders. But that was cowardly. I should have explained. But as years went by, the harder it became and the less important it really seemed. But at least you now have a photo of Josh. That's the least I can do. Forgive me, dearest Jo. I gave you the best life I could.
All my love
Mum
xx

Jo's deep disappointment at not discovering the identity of her father, the missing piece of her own personal jigsaw, still rankled.

If her father was still alive, she wanted to know. She wanted a chance to contact him and tell him about her life, about Ivy. Didn't he deserve that too?

Jo picked up the photo again. She held it close to the bedside light and stared hard, but the tiny image of the two babies yielded no answers. Was one of them her? Why else would Hope leave her the picture? But if she was, who was the other one? Josh?

She couldn't stay in bed for another minute. Wrapped in one of the dressing gowns from the back of the bedroom door, she tiptoed out of the room and down the dark corridor to Lucy's room. The light was shining through the gap under the door. She knocked but didn't wait for an answer as she turned the handle. 'It's only me.'

Lucy was sitting up in bed holding her wedding ring under the tiny bedside light. She looked up as Jo entered. 'What's wrong?'

Jo had never seen her sister look more sad. The dim lighting emphasised the shadows under her eyes and the gauntness of her face. 'I don't know,' she said, and held out the box to her sister. 'Have a look at this. Move over, my feet are freezing.'

Lucy put the ring down beside the light then shifted across the bed, leaving room for Jo to climb in beside her. 'It's a long time since we've done this.' She jumped as Jo's icy feet touched hers, then took the box.

Jo waited while Lucy read Hope's letter then took out the contents of the box and examined them. 'Did she say anything to you?'

Lucy shook her head. 'I would have told you. My bet's that she chickened out. After a lifetime of bottling it up, imagine how hard it must have been for her to say anything. It would waken so many ghosts, and she must have been worried about how you would react after so long.'

Jo drew her knees up to her chest and pulled the duvet higher, rubbing her feet together. 'What was in yours?'

'I don't know. I couldn't face opening it tonight. I thought I'd wait. I'm glad I have now.' She held up the photo. 'Anyway, why would you be in a pram with another baby? Maybe Josh belongs to a friend of hers . . .' Lucy's voice trailed off.

'Why wouldn't she have mentioned him before? Or the friend?'

'Do you think Brad or Elaine would know anything? They're probably the closest we're ever going to get to her now.'

'Maybe. But if they do, why wouldn't they have said something already? Elaine knows how much you want to know about your real dad. And if Hope could tell her, why wouldn't she tell you? That doesn't make sense.'

'Even if I did know, that still doesn't tell me who Josh is or why he's important.'

Lucy lay back against her pillow and closed her eyes.

'You look exhausted. Shall I go away?'

'I'm knackered.' Lucy didn't move as she spoke. 'It's been quite a day. Not one I ever want to live through again. But not so knackered that I don't want to help you with this.' Her eyes snapped open. 'But why would she have a picture of the two of you in a locket? That doesn't make sense.' She propped herself up, took the locket and snapped it open.

'Maybe Brad knows something. After all he is her half-brother.' Jo was groping towards the answer that kept slipping into her head then out again as she refused to accept it.

'Or maybe he knows someone who does.'

'There's only one way to find out.' Jo flung back the duvet.

'Not now. He'll be asleep.' Lucy put a restraining hand on her arm.

'You weren't.' Jo paused, feeling bad that she hadn't asked how Lucy was. The wedding ring gleamed under the light.

'That's because I can't – too much going round my brain – but don't let's talk about that now. I'm going round in circles. This is much more interesting.' Lucy swung her legs out of bed. 'Hang on, I'm coming with you.'

A shaft of light slanted across the corridor from her open bedroom door, illuminating their way towards Brad's room.

'His light's off.' Lucy whispered.

'But I can't wait till the morning. Not now.' A sense of urgency thrummed through Jo. She felt as if she was so near to solving something of the mystery that surrounded her early life and her mother's. Nothing was more important to her that minute than finding out the identity of this other baby. Why had Hope never mentioned him before? She knocked again and turned the handle.

'Jo, don't!' Lucy was right behind her.

But Lucy's fears were unfounded. There was no one there. The curtains were open, moving in the breeze coming through the open window. Over the chest of drawers hung one of Walter's larger pictures of Ronda. The bed was unmade from where Brad had slept earlier, and it was empty.

'Where on earth is he? He can't have gone far.' Only one thought was driving her: she had to find out what these few clues her mother had left her meant. At that moment, nothing else mattered.

They descended the stairs in the darkness, having been sure to turn off all the lights when they'd gone to bed. The terracotta tiles were chilly underfoot. However, when they reached the ground floor, they found the kitchen door open and the light bright inside. They heard the fridge door open and shut, the chink of china. Lucy grabbed Jo's arm and was immediately shaken off.

'Hallo!' Jo called out. Footsteps padded towards them.

'Damn! Caught in the act!' Brad appeared at the door in a tartan cotton dressing gown and leather slippers, holding a plate. Jo could make out lemon tart, a thin slice of tarte tatin, and a small brownie. 'Jetlag,' he said as if that explained everything. 'Couldn't sleep and all that dancing gave me one hell of an appetite. You don't mind?'

'Of course not, but you frightened the life out of us,' said Lucy, relieved.

'You thought a burglar was raiding the fridge?! Brad looked embarrassed. 'Nope, just me.' He took a bite of the brownie. 'Mm. Now that's *good*.'

They followed him into the sitting room where he sank into the sofa with the mantilla thrown over its back. 'I'm fine on my own, honestly. You go back to bed. You've both had a long day.'

He looked puzzled as Jo sat beside him, while Lucy curled herself up into the red chair, hugging her knees.

'Is something up? Hey, you can really cook,' he said to Lucy as he took another mouthful of brownie. 'We definitely need someone like you in the restaurant. Think about it.'

'We were looking for you,' Jo cut in.

'At this time of night? Whatever for? What can't wait till the morning?' Brad forked a piece of lemon tart, a look of pleasure on his face as he closed his mouth around it. 'This one of yours too, Lucy? It's delicious.'

Lucy was about to reply, her face wreathed in pleasure, but Jo got there first.

'It's this.' Jo held out the tin to him, not giving Lucy a chance to reply. 'Mum's given me this but I've no idea what any of it means.' As she spoke, a half-formed explanation flew in and then out of her mind before she had time to seize hold of it.

Puzzled, Brad put down his plate before taking the tin. 'What is it?'

'I'm hoping you can help. We were wondering if your dad might have said something, anything to you that might throw some light on it.'

'Dad? Well, let me have a look see.'

Both the women watched as Brad went through the contents. His frown deepened as he read the letter, then reread it. Jo picked up the ribboned pair of bootees, rubbing them with her thumb as she waited. Touching them was strangely comforting. Lucy didn't move, her chin rested on her knees, her eyes wide.

Eventually, having examined the photos, Brad turned to Jo,

scratching his head. She resisted the urge to reach out and brush the mini-blizzard of dandruff from his shoulder.

'Dad never spoke to us about Hope, beyond the bare bones that I've already told you.' He brushed at his shoulder. Jo leaned away from him as he did.

'Tell me again.'

'OK, if you really think it might help.' He crossed his legs and leaned forward, an expression of mild indulgence on his face. 'Her mother died when Hope was in her teens. Her dad, mine too, met and married Mum, who was nearer Hope's age than his. She would have been in her twenties then, I guess, and Hope must have been about sixteen. That age difference must have caused a few raised eyebrows at the time. They decided to emigrate to Oz and escape the gossip. Hope didn't want to go, so they decided she was old enough to be left in Epsom with Dad's sister, Jean, until she left school. Years later Jean came out to see us – a real horror, she was, nothing like Dad! Anyway, as soon as Hope could, she moved on to London and as far as I know pretty much lost touch with Dad. If they did have any contact, my parents didn't tell us. That's all I know – thanks to my parents' absurd love of discretion. "What you don't know can't hurt you." That's what they'd say. So wrong. But this...' He held up the photo.

'Yes?' Jo willed him on, despite the nerves fluttering in her stomach.

He spooned up a mouthful of tarte tatin as he considered the babies again. 'Well, it can only mean one thing. You must have thought...'

'What? What must I have thought?' Jo had a sense of knowing and yet not knowing what was coming. She had to hear what he had to say.

Lucy had dropped her knees and was leaning forward, rapt, as light began to dawn.

'Well, I guess there's no point beating about the bush here.

So . . .' He took a breath. 'Don't you think he's your brother?'
Brad sounded almost apologetic as he passed her the photo of
the two babies.

'No! Those babies are the same age. Unless . . .' No, that was
impossible.

'Unless you're a twin.' Brad finished the thought for her.

A twin! She looked down at the two babies, searching their
teeny faces for similarities.

'No!' Jo's hand dropped to her lap. 'That's impossible. Mum
would never have kept that from me.' But what other explanation
could there be? 'What you don't know can't hurt you.' Those
words might as well have been spoken by Hope.

A twin!

'But surely I'd remember? I'd know.'

'Perhaps not if you were separated when you were tiny,' said
Lucy. 'These babies are only months old, aren't they?'

'I don't buy that,' said Jo but as she spoke, the idea brought
an extraordinary sense of release with it, as if a weight she had
been carrying forever had been lifted from her: a weight that she
only realised had been there once it had gone. Yet with this new
possibility came more questions demanding answers. They spun
round her head, like moths fluttering against a light bulb unable
to get at the source of the light, as Lucy and Brad waited for her
to say something. How could they find the truth? Where was
Josh now? What had happened to their father? Who was Hope
that she could keep such a secret from her?

What was it she had written? She looked at the letter again.
*I wanted to put it as far as I could behind me. So far behind me
that I could believe that nothing had happened. At least I had you
to keep my grief at bay.*

So something terrible had happened that coloured the rest
of Hope's life. As if losing both her parents in her teens wasn't
enough. If she couldn't trust them to stick around, who could she
trust? Walter, was the answer. He must have been the rock that

Hope clung to, steady and dependable amid life's uncertainties. He had given her a new life, allowing her to fulfil her dreams. Jo felt new stirrings of admiration for her mother. Overcoming what she had must have changed Hope. But that wasn't all. Something had caused the grief she mentioned, something so devastating she only wanted to forget. Jo had to find out what.

The more Jo turned over Brad's suggestion, the more she felt it had a ring of truth. But as soon as she had almost convinced herself, she remembered Hope. Keeping a secret that was so intrinsic to a child's identity seemed an incredible thing for a mother to do. Now she was one herself, and single, just as Hope had been with her, she was beginning to understand why Hope might have kept her father's identity to herself. Finding the right moment for that sort of truth-telling would be hard. But this . . .

'She might have thought you'd be upset, that it was better not to know.' As ever, Lucy spoke up for their mother.

'But what about me? What about what *I* wanted?' Jo was churning with frustration. 'All we're doing is going round and round in circles. How can we find out whether Brad's right? *Someone* must know.'

'But who? If something that terrible happened to her, moving to Ibiza with you must have been some kind of new start that took her away her from anything that could remind her. Maybe it wasn't that she didn't want to tell you, but that she just couldn't. Maybe she didn't tell anyone.'

'What about *my* mother?'

They both turned to stare at Brad who had been quiet for the last few minutes, listening.

'What about her?'

'Well, she may know something. She and Dad both made the decision to leave Hope behind, but there must have been some contact. We know he kept in touch with Jean. Even if they only wrote once or twice, he might have got news of her from someone else. He wouldn't have stopped caring about her – he wasn't like that. It's last ditch, I agree, but what else have you got?'

'If you're right, there must be birth certificates,' said Lucy. 'But we can't begin tracking them down until we get home. Can you phone her?'

A burst of laughter broke from Brad. 'Phone? Mum has her phone on silent half the time. Besides, it's the middle of the afternoon over there. Bridge, book club, lunch – you name it, she could be at any one of them. But I'll email her and she'll reply as soon as she gets it. She's embraced the digital age that much at least.'

'She sounds astonishing. Couldn't you try now?' asked Jo, impatient to interrupt this human dynamo at whatever she was doing.

'There's really no point. But let me get my iPad.'

While Brad went upstairs, Jo stood up, unable to keep still any longer. 'There might be something here somewhere. Think of that photo I found in her room.' She crossed to the desk. 'Tom's already been through all this stuff but I'm going to look again.'

Lucy pulled herself to her feet. 'Then I'll look through the bookcase. After that we could try her bedroom.'

'You look knackered. I really don't mind if you want to go to bed. I won't sleep just yet so I'll be happy doing this on my own.' Jo took out one of the desk drawers and put it on the table.

'And not help with this? No way. Anyway, if I did, I'd just lie there worrying.' Lucy moved over to the bookcase and began systematically taking out and opening the books one by one, turning them over and shaking them before replacing them.

'You will be all right, you know.' Jo was taking a small drawer from the desk, emptying it and leafing through the papers. If nothing else, the search would be thorough. 'It just needs time. I remember when Jake left I thought I'd never cope on my own, but now I'm fine and I don't regret a thing. In fact I'm happier than I've ever been with things as they are. You know I'll do anything I can to help.' Inadequate comfort perhaps, but it was the best she could manage in the circumstances.

'I know. But let's not think about me just now. This is every bit as important.' Something fluttered from the book Lucy was examining. She pounced on it. 'Look, it's a note to her from Dad.' Holding it at arm's length where it caught the light, she read it aloud, a wobble in her voice. 'Paradise would be lost without you . . .'

Jo took it from her. 'That's sweet!'

For a moment they paused, remembering Hope and Walter, their tumultuous but long relationship. Then Jo broke the silence. 'But if I really am a twin . . .' Just saying those words made her feel very peculiar. 'What happened to Josh?'

'Perhaps your father took him?'

Could they have been divided between the parents? Could their father have taken Josh? If that were true, then there might be a whole other family out there for her somewhere. The thought both alarmed and intrigued her.

'Stop! You're both way ahead of the game.' Brad was back. He opened the fake antique book that contained his iPad. 'Let's get to the truth first and then wonder about what Hope did or didn't do.' He tapped out a message onto the screen while the others watched, then sat back. 'Done. Now all we can do is wait.'

'I don't think much of Tom's tidying up.' Jo was rummaging through another drawer, making a pile of bills, a pile of postcards, and another of letters. 'Look at this.' She held up a tiny diary. She turned the pages. 'Look. The only entries are in January. "Walter's birthday" "Jo – school" "Bunty – vet"' She snapped it shut. 'I'd forgotten Bunty – that gorgeous brown stray that never left. We used to lie on the ground and use her as a pillow. D'you remember?' She had a flash memory of Tom and her lying under a table in a camp they'd made, hiding from the adults, feeding Bunty biscuits.

After half an hour, they had found nothing that had yielded

any clues. Despite refusing to go to bed so he could stay up and help, Brad was snoring on the sofa.

'We should stop,' said Lucy eventually. 'This isn't getting us anywhere, and we're going to be fit for nothing in the morning. Let's go to bed and start again tomorrow.'

Though reluctant to give up, Jo had to agree. The adrenaline that had kept her going so far was being taken over by an aching weariness. The desk had yielded nothing but a few random childhood memories and another note from Walter in his precise handwriting, '*Roses are white, lavender's blue, peaches are sweet, and so are you.*' She couldn't help being touched by this side to her stepfather that she didn't remember ever seeing before. Her knee cracked as she straightened up. They woke Brad who, half-asleep, checked for his mother's reply, but his inbox was empty.

SUNDAY

25

Alone in her room, Jo watched a large moth flutter helpless against the light. She tried to guide it out of the window, but it flew back, its wings battering against the lampshade in vain. She laid Hope's gifts on the top of the chest of drawers before getting into bed. Curled on her side, listening to Ivy breathing, she waited for a moment before turning out the light then lay quite still, letting the warmth of the bed work its way through her. But, despite her exhaustion, sleep wouldn't come easy. She found herself returning to her childhood as random images ran through her mind: Hope teaching her to fry sausages over a bonfire and dropping the pan when it got too hot; her and Tom hiding out in a den while Hope called for them; making sandwiches and going off down to the ruined finca for hours and never being missed. She wondered about how much Hope must have been dealing with that her children had no inkling of. Like most children, they never gave a thought to anything but the present and themselves. Then Walter gave them the chance to go to England and they had each separated themselves from their family to lead their own lives. Not so different from Hope after all.

She finally drifted off as the dawn light began to filter through the curtains. By the time she woke, Ivy was already up, intent on a game with Bampy who was looking grubbier than ever. Through a haze, Jo listened to her daughter's uninterrupted monologue as Ivy got her toys ready for the picnic she was preparing. Jo lay on her back, eyes shut, wondering how awful she'd feel when she got up, when she heard a light knock at the door.

'Who is it?'

'Me, Brad. I've heard from Mum.'

'Hang on a sec.' She flung back the covers, leaped out and grabbed the dressing gown, still doing up the tie as she opened the door. 'Come in.' Her eyelids felt weighted down, her eyes sore. A headache drilled through her temple.

Brad was dressed already, looking none the worse for wear. He shook his head. 'No. I think you should read this without me hanging over your shoulder. I'll be downstairs if you need me.' He held out his iPad, and with his other hand touched her arm in a gesture of support that she appreciated.

'I wanna go downstairs too,' said Ivy as Jo shut the door, her heart thumping against her chest.

'OK. You go and find Brad and maybe Aunty Lucy will be up, too.' All Jo could think about was the iPad in her hand and what the email might say.

'I'm going to make Bampy some breakfast.' The hapless rabbit trailed from Ivy's hand.

'Good plan. I'll be down in a minute to help.'

As soon as Ivy had gone, Jo got some Paracetamol from her washbag and downed a couple, then got back into bed, bracing herself to read whatever Brad's mother had to say. She felt as nervous as she did before a pitch to an important client. She tapped the screen so she could read the message.

Dearest Brad
I got your email when I got back from my Pilates class – new fad which I'm quite enjoying. Joy put me on to it. You know her? Lives two down.

At eighty-something? This was some woman.

What a strange request! Well, of course I remember that
time – it's only my short-term memory that sometimes lets me
down. Although I wouldn't admit that to anyone but you! The
other day I forgot that I'd arranged a meeting of the Women's
League...

Get on with it, urged Jo. Instead of skipping to the point, she
read every word, to make sure she didn't miss anything. After
elaborating in detail all that the Women's League were planning
for their late summer fair, Linda finally reached the point.

Archie and I left in the summer of '61, I think it was. Ten-pound
Poms. Yes, we left Hope in England. Although I was nearer her
age than Archie's, we never really got on. I was only just over
ten years older than her and she came right out, saying I was
too young for her father. Of course, I thought she should be
glad for him and should try harder. But I was too young to
understand. I was upset and grasped at the chance to come out
here - away from all those rows, away from everyone who was
so disapproving of the age difference between us. People can
be very cruel. However guilty we both felt, however much we
wanted to make matters right, Hope made it quite clear that
we would have to drag her onto the boat. She was stubborn
and liked things her way. But who doesn't at that age? We
met our match in each other! Communication between her and
Archie was infrequent. No email or Skype or anything like that
then. Archie was a dreadful letter writer, and Hope was worse.
Too caught up in her own life – and who could blame her? So
was I in mine. But at least he tried. She was so angry and hurt
that he had deserted her. Jean was meant to be keeping an eye
on her but Hope wasn't having any of that. She thought she
could go to London, do her secretarial course, and use Jean's
place like a hotel. Meanwhile Archie, paid her an allowance –
guilt-money, I called it.

And me, wondered Jo. What about me? When do I come in? After a heartfelt tangent about how supportive Archie had been to all his children, Linda found her way back to the point.

> I remember the day we heard she was pregnant. She was only twenty and unmarried, too. The letter from Jean arrived the day I found I was pregnant with you. So what should have been such a happy time for us was anything but as Archie was beside himself. Furious that Jean hadn't watched over Hope better. Furious with Hope. Hope didn't even tell him herself but left that to Jean. Perhaps she was ashamed. Perhaps she was too busy trying to sort herself out. I don't know. A little later, Jean wrote again, saying Hope was expecting twins.

So it was true. Numbed, Jo stared at the words on the screen. *Hope was expecting twins.* She really was a twin. Somewhere she had a brother. *Another* brother. But there was more.

> By then, Jean told us she was caught up in a new crowd and she never saw her. London was buzzing and Hope was too busy with her own life to be worried about how her father might feel. He was thousands of miles away and might as well not have existed.

Jo took a sip of water, uncertain whether to feel sympathy with her mother or disapproval at the way she had behaved. But then again, she hadn't behaved much better herself when she left home. Although she *had* gone back to visit every summer, she reminded herself and at other times too. Contact might have been infrequent but it was not lost. She turned back to the iPad.

> But she did write before they were born and after that they kept in touch – but very on and off. Before the babies, she mentioned someone called Jason, but whether he was the father – who

knows. Those were the Swinging Sixties. Everyone was having
fun. Peace and love and all that. We couldn't afford for Archie
to travel home to see her and next we heard, she had chucked
everything in and gone to Spain with her baby daughter. What
happened to the other twin, I don't know. We were never told.
Back then, I'd say Hope was still angry that her mother had
died, that her father had abandoned her (as she saw it). At the
time, I was angry too. I was angry that she was so determined
not to be happy for us, not to even try to be the happy family
Archie so wanted. I was as selfish as she was. I didn't want to
know about her, I didn't want her spoiling what we had. I didn't
want to help her. It was easier for me to pretend she didn't
exist. I made it easier for Archie to pretend too.

Poor Hope. Jo took the glass of water by her bed and drank. This
family were too good at secrets and pretending people didn't exist.
Even she was herself.

You ask what happened. I can only think that she wanted to
bury whatever happened to her in London and move on. Archie
kept paying her allowance for years out of guilt and worry. He
kept those few letters she wrote, but I threw them out when he
died. I'm sorry. Even when she met Walter and settled down in
Spain, she kept her distance. Sometimes those rifts are too deep
to heal.
     That's really all I can tell you. Please give my love to Jo, Tom
and Lucy. I'd love to meet them too. I'm so glad you have, and
have had a chance to build bridges. They'd always be welcome
here.
Mum xx

Jo couldn't move. Tears rolled down her cheeks. She stared
through them at the email until the iPad went to sleep. Jo had no
idea how long she sat there, immobile, absorbing this momentous

piece of information, wondering how different her life might have been. Why had Josh been given up? Perhaps Hope had been unable to cope with two babies and left one with his father. She couldn't believe Hope would be that cold-hearted. Could he have died? Her head spun with questions.

There was a knock. Lucy put her head round the door. 'You OK?' She came in, a cup of coffee in her hand. 'I thought you might need this.'

'It's true.' Jo coughed as the coffee scalded the back of her throat.

Lucy patted her on the back, then climbed on the bed and hugged her sister, holding her tight. 'Where is he?'

'I've no idea. I don't even know if he's alive, but I'm going to find out.' She wiped her eyes with a corner of the duvet. 'I know we've got to get through the rest of this weekend first, but I'm going to talk to Elaine.'

'But she doesn't know anything,' insisted Lucy. 'I asked her when I collected her from the airport.'

'That's what she says, but where do you think her loyalties lie? She was Mum's closest friend. If Mum confided in anyone except Walter, it will have been her. I still think she may be able to point me in the right direction at least. Could you keep an eye on Ivy just while I get dressed?'

'Sure. Anything.' Lucy went to the door. Opening it, she turned. 'I had a text from Art this morning. He got a flight first thing, having spent the night in the airport. So at least he didn't get much sleep either. The story's in today's papers. I've already had three sympathetic emails from friends and I've had to turn my phone off because of the texts. I know they mean well but I don't think I can bear it.'

'Oh no!' Jo leaped off the bed. Her turn to hug her sister. 'I was so taken up with this. I'm sorry.'

Lucy squeezed her back. 'I don't blame you. We're a right pair.'

'Are you going to be able to get through today?'

'Actually, I feel OK. Tired but OK. I am going to get through this although I'm not looking forward to going home, one bit. I can just see the headlines: WRONGED WIFE OF *EMERGENCY* STAR. And the photos of me looking haggard and wronged as I put out the rubbish.' She shrugged. 'Imagine.'

'I'm going to help you,' said Jo. 'I mean it. Strength in numbers.' They hugged again. 'Come and stay with us.'

'I may take you up on that but not right now. I'm going down to make sure that little monkey of yours isn't up to anything while you get dressed.'

A little later, Jo was downstairs in the kitchen, facing the impressive mountain of plates and cutlery piled up waiting to be put away.

'Elaine and Brad have done an amazing job between them. They insisted on finishing up what we didn't get to last night.' Lucy was drying some glasses, having got Ivy busy at the table sticking pasta shapes and pulses onto a piece of paper, though more had made its way to the floor than onto the paper.

'Love that, Ivy.'

'It's an elephant in a tree,' her daughter explained proudly.

'I can see that.' Jo kissed her on the top of her head, ignoring the surrounding mess. If Sue were here, she would be having a field day, fussing and clearing it all up. But none of that mattered here at Casa de Sueños so the mess could wait. 'Where's Elaine gone?' She would feel much better once she had spoken to her.

'They've gone to Jimena together.' Lucy was piling the plates back on the shelves.

'What? Now?'

'Well, yes. I could hardly stop them. They said they'd be back by lunchtime. I thought that would be OK. Tom wants to scatter Mum during the siesta – feels it would be appropriate somehow. Time of rest and all that.' She raised an eyebrow.

'But I'm bursting to talk to her.'

Ivy twisted her head round to check Jo wasn't actually bursting. Satisfied, she went back to her drawing.

'And as soon as they come back, you can. I expect they wanted a breather from all of us.'

'I guess we are a bit high maintenance this weekend.' Jo looked at Ivy. 'Try not to stick them on the table, my sweet.'

Ivy gave a look of scorn that only a four-year-old could muster. 'Gimme a break!' she said and picked up a bit of penne and dabbed with her glue stick.

Jo and Lucy exchanged a surprised glance and burst out laughing.

26

Despite time ticking by, Tom was delaying getting up. He could hear Belle moving round the bathroom and the sound of running water, electric toothbrush, pots being lifted and put down again as she prepared herself to face the day. He lay quite still, knowing how long it took until she was satisfied with her appearance. He couldn't bring himself to look at his watch despite also knowing that it was almost time for breakfast. At least they had agreed they would forfeit their morning jog this morning. Today was the day his mother's ashes would be scattered. Her party was well and truly over.

He wished he hadn't brought up the question of the money with Jo in such a clumsy way. Otherwise she might have been more sympathetic. Despite her professional success, or perhaps because of it, she had become more canny about cash since she'd made some of her own. He should have waited till they had the sale of the house in the bag and then called a family powwow. That was what Walter would have done. Limit the damage by only dealing with things when they had developed beyond being just a gleam in the eye: the opposite philosophy to the one that made Hope, and now him, charge in like a bull, only to achieve the wrong results.

The bathroom door opened but he kept his eyes shut so he would not have to face the inevitable. He heard Belle leave the room, but she would be back. She would be aware how out of sorts he would be if he missed too much of the day. There was bound to be a discussion about what had happened last night, but before that, she would be checking on Alex and Ethan. Tom thought he heard himself groan as the memory of the previous evening filtered into his brain but he couldn't be sure. Instead of fading as he would like it to, the memory bloomed as one detail overlaid another.

Only the hard core of guests was hanging on when he and Adam had half-supported, half-carried Alex to his room with Belle fussing on the sidelines. She had found Alfonso, the local *médico*, on the dance floor. He had been able to keep his feet still long enough to reassure her that their son didn't seem to be suffering from alcohol poisoning and just needed to sleep it off. Once they had got Alex to bed, a bowl beside him on the floor, Belle had stormed off to vent her rage on the washing-up, leaving Tom to deal with Ethan.

If a lecture had to be delivered, he was always the one left to do it. So, feeling mildly put upon and anxious about but angry with his son, he had taken Ethan to a corner of the terrace. One or two of the guests had looked curious, but no one intercepted them. His son's previous swagger had given way to the sullen defiance that characterised most of their 'little talks'. It hadn't needed Sherlock Holmes to work out that he was under the influence of something. However, he swore that it was just wine and a single spliff. No more. At least he was honest about that. Or at least that's what Tom wanted to believe. But after the episode at Ethan's previous school, he couldn't ignore the prickling of doubt so gave a somewhat halting lecture on the importance of steering clear of drink and drugs.

'Yeah. You've told me before,' Ethan said, his eyes wandering towards the sitting room as if searching for someone.

'Well then, why don't you take any notice? I'm not doing it for fun, but for your own good.' Tom felt the burden of fatherhood weighting him down.

Ethan shrugged. 'Are we done, then?'

Realising this conversation was taking place at the wrong time,

Tom had one last try. Man to man. 'Look, Son. I know how tempting it is, but we don't want the same thing to happen again. Throwing away a decent education would be a mistake.'

'Yeah, yeah.' Clearly not believing that his dinosaur of a father had ever been tempted by anything, Ethan adjusted the position of his hat by a centimetre or two, his eyes wandering over his father's shoulder towards the sitting room where Christina was dancing.

'Your mother would be devastated.' Last card – and a cheap and probably pointless shot.

He was rewarded with a grunt and an eye roll.

'We'll talk again tomorrow.' That was the last thing either of them wanted but it provided a convenient closing gambit. Ethan made an immediate beeline for Christina. Tom retired hurt, cross with himself for not having taken a harder line, for having let Belle down. But being a parent of teenagers could be bloody hard.

Maria had whisked Christina off home shortly afterwards, apparently unperturbed by her daughter's role in proceedings. Tom remembered a time when the two of them wouldn't have thought twice about a joint or two. His hypocrisy when it came to his son's behaviour appalled him. But then, neither he nor Maria had been expelled from school for dealing as Ethan had. They had Hope, the easy-going flower child of the Sixties, and Walter as examples when it came to drink and drugs, not the straight up-and-down Belle for whom more than a unit was virtually verboten. And a cigarette? Out of the question. When Tom had finally tried to introduce Belle to Maria, Belle said something polite and turned to talk to someone else, embarrassing him. The two women were not going to be bonding over their children's misdemeanours. That much was obvious. As a result, he hadn't been able to bring himself to tell Belle that he had invited Maria and Christina to the scattering.

Lying in bed, he took a deep breath, then flexed and relaxed every part of his body from his toes to his top of his head. Done, he imagined walking down the steps of a swimming pool into the warm green water where he lay floating, freeing his mind from his earthly cares. Whoever dreamed up this self-hypnosis lark deserved a medal.

'Tom!'

Belle was back. Floundering in his mental swimming pool, he spluttered to the surface, opening his eyes to find her at the foot of the bed. She looked magnificent, almost warrior-like. Light-grey linen trousers, a leaf-green T-shirt and her hair gleaming in the morning light. Her eyes flashed a warning. She clearly had something to get off her chest. To his horror, he found himself getting a hard-on. Not now, he told himself, not now. But his will was no match for his libido.

'We need to talk.'

'Now?' he asked, lifting the side of the duvet. 'Why don't you get back in here?'

Her expression could have deterred a stampede of elephants. 'This is important, Tom. Don't be silly. Anyway, I'm dressed.'

'You could always get dressed again.' Ever hopeful.

The look she gave him did exactly what his will couldn't. Sex was not on the agenda now, not when it had taken her so long to get ready to face the day.

He sighed. 'Well, give me a minute, then.' He could at least delay proceedings.

In the bathroom, he took as long as he could. A marriage only worked if there was give and take, he argued to himself. So he was taking his time before she gave him the earful he suspected was coming his way. Eventually he could no longer put off the moment. He pulled on his shorts and shirt, and emerged to find Belle sitting in the armchair beside the made bed. In his absence she had tidied the room so comprehensively that it looked as though they had just arrived. Nothing of theirs was on show except for the paraphernalia that came with Ferdie, and their cases. His case! By the time he had eventually got to bed he was so physically and emotionally drained he couldn't face Hope's letter. Remembering it now, it was all he could do not to go over and get it.

'We must talk,' Belle began once Tom was sitting opposite her. 'You promised me you were going to keep an eye on Ethan.'

'I thought he'd be OK here. How was I to know he'd be stupid enough not to check his pockets before we left?'

'Tom! He shouldn't have had any dope in them.'

'Of course. Sorry. I know that.' He felt as if he was getting a dressing-down from his old headmaster.

'I blame that girl.' She nodded twice, her eyes hardening.

'What?' Surely she couldn't shift the blame like that when Ethan was more than likely to be culpable, given his history. 'If you mean Christina, I'm pretty sure she had nothing to do with it.'

'She was all over him when I arrived. He's only sixteen.'

He gazed at her in astonishment. 'Yes, nearly seventeen – almost a man.'

She gaped at him, pushed back her fringe as if to see him more clearly. 'What's wrong with you? Normally, you're on my side.'

He went over to the window and looked out over Hope's English garden. The roses already needed staking. He would mention it to Antonio. But she was right. Something had changed in him. Perhaps meeting Maria had resuscitated some of the old Tom, encouraging him to be less downtrodden, less conformist. He rather liked that idea. He looked at his watch. Breakfast time.

'Oh, Bella.' His pet name for her usually worked a treat. 'You've got to cut him some slack. The expulsion was bad enough and we've succeeded in keeping that quiet from everyone. I agree with you about the drugs – although I also believe him when he says he didn't mean to bring any. But you can't expect him to behave like a monk as well.'

'But he was taking drugs.' She paused between each word as if to make sure their meaning was drilled into him.

'He only shared a spliff. That's a long way from dealing.'

'Only!' Belle's face was scarlet with outrage. She stopped, unable to find the right words. Then, 'I'm disappointed in you.'

That was the most damning criticism in Belle's impressively large critical repertoire. To earn her disappointment meant he had been found guilty of an unforgiveable transgression.

Tom, on the other hand, was surprised by his reaction. Of course he minded what happened to Ethan, and perhaps he should be scared that a single spliff was confirmation that his son was on a downhill slope; that he would drop out of school; fail his exams; become a junkie; drop out of life altogether – but he had to trust his sons. In front of the headmaster – and obviously shocked and frightened – Ethan had sworn that he had been bullied into being part of the drug chain at school, and that he would not get caught up in anything like that again. If Tom didn't trust his son, there was no hope of them ever having the lasting relationship he so badly wanted.

'When we get home, I'm going to make him another appointment with the counsellor.' Belle stood up, as erect as a soldier.

'You can throw as much money at the problem as you like, but he needs to know we're behind him.' Tom pinched the skin between his thumb and forefinger. He wasn't enjoying this at all. 'That's the only way we're going to get anywhere with this.'

'You may be right, but he needs outside help.'

'Perhaps. But let *us* try and support him too.'

Belle picked up Ferdie, who had left his bed to see what the noise was about. She was obviously biting back tears. This was not at all how Tom had wanted the day to start. He tried again. 'They're only kids experimenting. Don't deny you didn't have the odd Babycham when you were a girl.' He smiled, hoping she'd be amused by his reminder of the drink she always ordered when they first met. He was disappointed, but tried again. 'Bet you didn't drink it when your parents were around.' He remembered how her strait-laced, God-fearing parents looked on everything their only daughter did with mild to extreme displeasure. He twisted his wedding ring round his finger.

'No, never.' She looked sad before pulling herself up short. 'But it's hardly the same. If you won't think about it properly now, then I'm going to get us some breakfast. We'll talk about it when we get home.' She didn't give him time to object before she left the room.

The thought of breakfast made his stomach roll after everything he'd eaten the previous night. But his pills had to be taken with food. And everything was better if taken at the right time: his internal clock was expecting them. But he wasn't keen on sitting across from Belle having a stilted conversation or in an uncomfortable silence. He wasn't sure which would be worse. He had no idea how he would break the news that Maria and Christina were expected for the scattering.

He looked around him at the order Belle had imposed on the room. He loved the way she could do that: rescue order from confusion. That's what had made her such a sharp accountant. Even something as insignificant as a tidy room gave him a sense of balance, of things being right with the world. His eyes settled on his case. Taking the envelope from the zip pocket, he ran a finger over the lettering of his name, at the same time remembering his wilful and unpredictable mother. He hesitated, tapping the envelope against his thigh, wondering what she had got in store for him. Whatever it was would disturb him. Of that, he was certain. Throwing the bloody thing away would be so much easier. But what if it contained something that he needed to know or, better still, a cheque?

He flipped the envelope over, put his finger in the opening and ripped it open. Unexpectedly shaken by the sight of Hope's writing, he sat on the bed, disturbing the carefully straightened duvet, and began to read.

281

Dearest Tom

You have been a wonderful son – I couldn't have asked for better. I probably should have said this a long time ago but I was never much good at truth-telling or sentiment, as you know.

He rested his hand on the paper, thoughtful, remembering. The truth was, neither was he.

I have one thing left that I'd like to give you. I know we won't talk about this with Belle there and, if we were to, I don't think I could face the fuss that she'll almost certainly make about why I have never told you before. Because I wanted to forget that unhappy period of my life, is the one simple answer. You may judge me as you will. So – whereas I really don't know who Jo's father is for sure (please don't think badly of me for that), I do know yours...

He stopped, read the line again. So when she brushed Jo off, she had been telling the truth. She honestly didn't know. But why tell him now? Why rock the boat? Especially when he had got used to living without the knowledge, happy with his life and, unlike Jo, didn't have that burning curiosity to find out.

... but it hardly seemed fair to tell you something I could never tell her. However, by the time you get this, I hope Jo will know everything I can tell her. Although I'm afraid I may not have the courage when it comes to it. As for you – Robert was a painter I met in Ibiza. I don't know what happened to him.

He was unsure whether what he was feeling was relief or disappointment.

*. . . I want you to have the portrait that he painted of me
when we were in Ibiza. We went our separate ways – we
were young – but I couldn't let that portrait go. Oh, that was
another life, like a dream to me now. He caught me as my
life was turning a corner and I had you. But then I fell head
over heels in love with someone else. Walter was sent to the
island by a friend of Robert's who thought, as fellow artists,
they might get along. He and I were meant for each other
and we moved back to England with Jo and you. Robert
didn't want the tie of children and was happy to be allowed
to get on with his own life. I couldn't settle in Dorset, and
Walter felt he couldn't live up to his family's expectations
(you know what they were like!) but then, when he came
into some family money, we started a new life in Spain and
bought Casa de Sueños – my House of Dreams. Nobody
knew us here. We left our past behind and came to a place
where we hoped our dreams would come true. Corny, eh?! All
we wanted was a future together. Enough! I know my being
sentimental will embarrass you. So I won't be. The portrait is
hanging in my little room.*

Tom's stomach tilted. Not that!

*I want you to have it as a memento of Robert. He was a
good, kind man, I think, just as you've turned out to be.
But he had a wild streak that, thank God, you've avoided.
I thought maybe you'd inherited it when you took up with
Maria, but I was wrong. You've made a wonderful husband
and father. I'm so proud of you.
All my love to you.
Mum xxx*

Tom rubbed his eyes and sniffed. 'I'm so proud of you.' He had
been waiting for words like that from her all this time. If only she

could have said them when she was alive. But – Robert? Robert who? Was he alive or dead? After all these years of silence, Hope deftly gave with one hand and took with the other. *A good, kind man.* That told Tom zero about the father he had long ago given up on ever knowing: a catch-all description that could be applied to almost anyone. Including himself, apparently. Hope had gone to her grave playing her games to the end without a thought for the effect this news might have on him. He wondered what she had up her sleeve for Jo and Lucy. He smacked the letter onto the bed. Of all the things in the world he did not want – apart from this unsatisfactory and incomplete piece of information – was another painting. Least of all that one. His immediate reaction to seeing his mother posed like that was to look away. And Belle would hate it. Perhaps he wouldn't tell her about it until after the scattering – it would probably only make things worse between them.

He flung himself backwards on the bed, the pillow cool against the back of his head. The day ahead loomed like an unsummitable mountain. Forcing himself to breathe deeply – in, out, in, out – he realised he needed to concentrate his mind and write down what had to be done. Prioritise: that was the thing. He reached for his BlackBerry.

- Sort out boys
- Scatter ashes
- See Maria
- Sort out money with Jo and Lucy
- Make peace with Belle

His finger hovered over the screen. As for his father and the painting – his father could hang himself – perhaps he already had! He hadn't wanted Tom and, equally, Tom didn't want him. Ethan and Alex were what mattered now. He would be the kind of father he never had. Except, he reminded himself, for Walter.

As he was smoothing out the bed, a knock on the door prefaced the entrance of Ethan, who was looking decidedly under the weather. But of course the young bounce back quickly, thought Tom with envy.

'Dad?'

'Feeling OK?'

Ethan answered by pulling a face and rocking his right hand. He sat down on the bed, disturbing its new neatness. 'I've come to say I'm sorry, Dad. I was a dick last night.'

Taken aback, Tom couldn't help himself straightening the edge of the duvet. 'Provided it was a one-off.'

'It was.' Ethan lifted his head. 'I'm not going to get expelled again if that's what you're worried about. I'm not fucking up my life for good.'

'That's great to hear.' He felt a rush of pride in his oldest son, as Ethan stood up. 'So no more dope "accidentally" in your pocket?'

'No more at all. Nothing.'

Tom looked at his son. This boy might go far after all – despite his taste in T-shirts. Presumably that violent-looking logo belonged to some rock band Tom had never heard of.

Ethan removed his hat and examined its rim. 'So is it OK if I go to a club in Estepona tonight?'

Tom jerked to attention. He should have known it was too good to be true. 'Estepona?! Who with? We're scattering Gran's ashes today.'

'Yeah, I know. But that'll be over before it gets dark.' He talked as if he was asking the most reasonable thing in the world, yet he still couldn't look his father in the eye. 'The guys who were here last night are going down. And Christina. They'll take us and bring us back.'

'But you don't even know them!' Tom imagined Belle's reaction if he agreed without mentioning it to her. Which of course was what Ethan was hoping for. 'You'd better ask your mother.'

A cloud crossed his son's face as he replaced his hat on his head. 'God! I knew you'd say that. Why can't you just say yes? Why do I always have to ask her?'

'Because you're only sixteen.' Tom sighed as he longed for the calm of his file-lined office, for the movement of the worker bees on the other side of its glass wall, for the quiet satisfaction of another surveying job well done. 'We're responsible for you, and we don't want anything to happen to you.'

Ethan sprang to his feet. 'Fuck it! OK. But I'll go anyway, whatever she says.'

Stung into action, Tom moved quickly to stand in the doorway, barring Ethan's exit. 'Just one thing. Do you think you could – just for one second – think about what everyone else is feeling today? Just for once. We're all upset and on edge. So today is not the day to cause trouble.'

Unused to his father making a stand, Ethan's face was a picture. Tom stared him out, taking in the red-rimmed eyes, the cluster of teenage spots bright on his forehead, the shy beginnings of facial hair. His son was growing up.

'Sorry, Dad.' Never had anyone sounded less repentant. Ethan shifted his gaze to his bare feet.

Tom stood to one side, glad the moment was over. 'Ask Mum if you must. But don't argue with her.'

'Wha'ever.' Ethan sidled out.

As the door shut behind him, Tom shook his head. A day in the office was so simple compared to this. Problems were solvable in ways that didn't involve other people's emotions. He made a mental note to remember to call in the following day to check that nothing unforeseen had cropped up in his brief absence. Now, breakfast. But first he would check on Alex.

27

Breakfast was not easy. Tom and Belle sat in virtual silence over the meal, popping their pills. He crunched on his muesli and bio-yoghurt while she dipped in and out of another bowl of blueberry-coloured gloop. Something was up. Lucy had been dying to ask Tom what was in his envelope, whether the contents were as shattering as those in Jo's parcel. However, Tom was clearly not in the mood to talk let alone answer her questions. Ethan sat with them, up early for once, as uncommunicative as his parents. Alex had surfaced, made it to the table, toyed with some toast and water and gone back to bed the colour of paper. Lucy couldn't have been more relieved when Tom and Belle took themselves off for a walk to look at the place where Hope wanted to be scattered. Soon afterwards, Jo took Ivy down to the river where they had splashed about so much as kids, keen to fill the time until she could speak to Elaine.

After clearing the table, Lucy took her coffee to the terrace. She and Bailey had the place to themselves again. He flopped down beside her in the shade of the table, his weight on her left foot. From where she sat, the sky dominated everything as always. Clouds had been building up in the west since the early morning with huge banks of charcoal and smoky-grey cumulus looming on the horizon. However, up at Casa de Sueños, the sun still beat down from a sizeable patch of forget-me-not blue sky. Bees hummed among the nearby plants, a couple of lizards ran along the top of the wall and disappeared down the other side. When the sun shone, everything seemed better, more hopeful, even with a storm threatening. The colours surrounding her took on a clarity that they rarely possessed in grey England, the brilliant reds and purples of the bougainvillea and geraniums, the clear whites in the English garden, the varying shades of leaf from silvery olive to deep forest green. Lucy felt more at home here than anywhere else. This was still where she belonged.

Pulling her foot from underneath Bailey, she stretched out her legs, feeling the warmth on her bare skin, and picked up her parcel from the table. It was small, square and Sellotaped to an envelope. She couldn't open it the previous night with so much going on so had waited until she was alone and ready. Having spent so much time with Hope before she died, she couldn't believe there was anything left unsaid between them. They had pored over the old family photographs together, reminiscing, talking about their lives together, making sure the other knew how much they were loved.

She didn't waste time. Within moments the wrapping paper was screwed up on the table. Hope would have straightened it out and put it away for next time, but Lucy had not inherited her mother's thrifty streak. In her hand sat a red ring box, the jeweller's name inscribed in silver on the top: an address in Hatton Garden. Lucy lifted the lid. Inside, the box was lined with black satin but was otherwise empty. She turned it upside down and shook it in case something had slipped into the lining. Nothing. Intrigued, she opened her envelope and took out a letter, the paper trembling in her hand.

Dearest Lucy-doo

Her heart flipped and tears stung at her eyes again. Only her mother called her that.

I know we'll have said all we need to, but I want to be sure you know how much you lit up our lives and gave us so much happiness. Thank you for everything, darling. Not least for having me to live out my final days with you. I'll be leaving here for the last time soon. I can hardly bear to think I'll never see this place again. It's meant so much to all of us, but especially to me and darling Walter.

As a forever reminder of how much you meant to us, I want you to have the ring that he gave me when you were born – you know, the ruby and diamond one. That's the only decent bit of jewellery he gave me (his grandmother's, I think), and the only valuable piece I own. He would want you to have it too. The only snag is – I can't find it. But I know it's here somewhere.

She smiled at Hope's familiar refrain. But what would Belle have to say?

So I'm giving you the box and hoping you can unearth the ring from wherever I've put it. It's yours. Belle did admire it recently and I may have said something that she misunderstood to mean I wanted her to have it – I hope not. But you know what she's like.

Only Hope . . . And now Lucy had done the same thing. She had put it somewhere safe after Tom called her from the car. She held the letter to her chest. Where on earth had she put it? She thought back to being in her mother's bedroom before the others arrived and retraced her steps from there. She must have taken the ring downstairs into the kitchen where she was distracted, making sure she had lunch ready before the others arrived. So much else had been going on, she must have put it somewhere safe, ready for Belle. How silly of Hope to give Belle the wrong impression, leaving Lucy to sort the problem out – so typical of her mother. But she should find the ring first. There had been so many people in and out of the kitchen in the last few days and no one had mentioned seeing it. Perhaps Belle had already found and kept it without saying anything.

She tipped her head back so the sun shone on her face and closed her eyes. Perhaps she should go and look for it anyway – she wanted this keepsake of her mother's more than anything now. Spurred into action, she got to her feet and went indoors.

In the kitchen, it was only a question of elimination. She turned her back on the shelves of plates and bowls, on the cutlery drawer and everything surrounding the sink that had been recently used. She took herself back, trying to recall exactly what she must have been doing when she put down the ring. She opened the fridge, hesitated. Surely not even she … She looked around her, opening the drawers, rummaging through everything. It must be there somewhere. In the larder, she gazed at the rows of home-made preserves, the way past their sell-by-date tins, the empty jam jars, the packets of stale English breakfast cereal Hope once provided to make guests feel at home. All this would have to go. Her eye settled on the dusty jars of herbs and spices and then, in a flash, it came back to her.

She had been looking for peppercorns with the ring in her hand, scared of putting it down and losing it. Rather than leaving it somewhere where it might get lost, she had put it in the jar of dried rosemary. She really had.

'There's rosemary, that's for remembrance.' She had even quoted Ophelia to herself as she had done it. How could she have forgotten that? But so much had been on her mind. She opened the jar and tipped the contents into her hand and there, shining among the dried-up leaves, was the diamond and ruby ring. Instead of risking losing it again, she did what she should have done in the first place and slipped it onto the ring finger of her right hand, pushing it over her knuckle.

Back in the kitchen, she held out her hand, turning it one way then the other, just as Hope used to, so the stones caught the sunlight streaming through the window.

'What've you got there?'

She turned to find Tom and Belle back from their walk. Despite the whiff of suntan cream they brought with them, Tom's forehead and nose were a sore-looking shiny red.

'The ring.' She showed them.

'So you found it,' said Tom, leaning against a chair. 'Where?'

Lucy noticed Belle elbow his arm. 'I'd put it in the rosemary jar. I must have thought it was a safe place and then, well, you know how it is.'

'Not really,' said Belle, her eyes lighting up as she took a step towards Lucy. 'Anyway I'm glad you found it. It looks more valuable than I'd imagined.' She held out her hand. 'Thank you.'

'I'm sorry, Belle, but Mum gave it to me.' Lucy kept her voice level as she clenched her hand into a fist. No one was going to take this ring from her. She was not going to lose this, as well as everything else.

'But she told me that I could have it.' Belle kept her hand out.

'I'm afraid you must have misunderstood.' There was no more to say. Lucy was not going to let Belle have her way over this.

Tom put a hand on Belle's shoulder. 'Not now.'

She shrugged him off. 'Tom, don't interfere. I went to see Hope and she said—'

'Whatever she said to you, she said this to me.' Lucy picked up her letter from the chopping board where she had left it and thrust it towards her sister-in-law. 'I really don't want us to fall out over this, but she must have meant something else or changed her mind.'

Belle hesitated. She took the letter, shook it open and read. 'But she said . . .' There was a catch in her voice as she passed the paper into Tom's outstretched hand.

'You know how confused she got sometimes and worse near the end,' he reminded her.

'But I—'

'Belle! Enough!' Tom shook one finger. 'Please don't.'

'I'm sorry,' Belle said, although she couldn't have sounded less so. If what she was hoping for was a sign that Hope had accepted her at last, she was disappointed. 'Well, if you're not going to support me, I'll go and find the boys, then I'll take Ferdie out.'

'How can I support you when we've got this?' Tom held up Lucy's letter. But Belle wasn't listening. She was already halfway into the hall.

'Oh my God, I'm nearly at the end of my tether.' Tom pulled out the chair and sat down, leaning forward to knock his forehead once on the table. 'I could kill Mum for all this.' As he realised what he had said, he looked up and they both grinned at each other.

Lucy sat beside him. 'For anything in particular.'

'Isn't this crazy weekend enough? Why couldn't she just go quietly like anyone else? Guess what else she's done?' He started straightening the knives and forks that had been left on the table.

'Tell me.'

'She's only gone and left me that painting in her room – that awful one of her that's hanging over the bookcase. It's the last thing I want.'

'Well, let Jo have it, then. She likes it.'

'But it's painted by my father.' He stopped to watch the effect of his words on Lucy. 'She said so in the letter she left for me. I haven't told Belle yet. Thought I'd wait.'

She gaped at him in disbelief. So Hope had finally given Jo and Tom what they wanted albeit in the most unorthodox and disturbing way. Their history. She swallowed. 'Who is he?'

'God alone knows. Someone called Robert. I don't even know his surname. In those days, it was all Peace and Love and anything goes. She probably didn't even know it herself. And we know there's no signature on the painting – we looked.'

'Can I see your letter?'

He pulled it from his shorts pocket. 'Of course you can. I'm going to make some coffee.'

Lucy read and reread, stopping only to stroke Bailey who had come in looking for a drink. He sat beside her, dripping water down her calf as she tickled him under the chin.

'You're going to have to show this to Jo. Has she told you about hers?'

'I haven't seen her this morning. Why?' Tom put two mugs on the table between them, then the jug of coffee. 'Of course I'll tell her what Mum says about not knowing her dad, but I don't imagine that'll come as much of a surprise. Nothing's changed for her. That was the one thing Hope wasn't keeping a secret after all. Poor old Jo.'

'You don't know the half of it.' Lucy got up to get the milk from the fridge as Ivy ran in, flinging her arms around Bailey who sank to the ground with a grunt. As the little girl climbed onto him his tail beat against the floor.

'The half of what?' Jo was right behind her daughter. 'I could kill for a coffee.' She took a mug off the shelf and helped herself.

'I was going to tell him your news. But why don't you, now you're here? You can swap.' She caught Jo staring at her ring. 'From Mum,' she said, wiggling her finger. 'Belle's furious, because she thinks Mum promised it to her, but she must have got the wrong end of the stick. Look.' She held out her letter.

Tom cleared his throat. 'Perhaps you should look at mine first. It's about our real fathers.'

'Are you serious?' Jo stopped the mug halfway to her mouth. 'Ivy, why don't you take Bailey outside?'

'He doesn't want to go.' Out came that pout – the weapon of choice.

'I think he does.' Lucy magicked a fraying tennis ball from the drawer of the kitchen table. 'Bailey!'

The dog looked up with baleful eyes. His tail thumped harder on the floor.

'Come on!'

Ivy scrambled off as Bailey got to his feet and trotted out after

Lucy. The little girl pulled down her sun hat over her eyes and went after them.

'Don't get your hopes up,' Tom warned as he passed over his letter.

His words crushed the blossom of longing in Jo's chest. But whatever the letter said couldn't be more shocking than the contents of hers. She drank some coffee then read what Hope had written while Tom sat, staring into space, not interrupting.

So – whereas I really don't know who Jo's father was for sure, I do know yours . . . She stopped and reread the words slowly, making sure she had understood, as any remaining hope that she might ever find her real father drained away. So Hope had been telling the truth to her all the time. Her father was just one among many men Hope must have known in London, and she was the result of a casual encounter. Hope and she were more alike than she had ever imagined. Except, she reminded herself, Josh was somewhere in this equation too. Where was he? Why wasn't he mentioned?

'So no father, but you get the consolation prize of the painting,' she said. 'And I get a twin.'

Tom swung round towards her, splashing coffee on his shirt. 'What?!' His nose was gleaming beacon red. If what she said hadn't been so significant, Jo would have laughed as her brother mopped at the stain with a dishcloth, only making things worse.

'Yes, she saved the best for last. Apparently she meant to tell me when she came to Lucy's. If only I hadn't had to sort out that client in Scotland, she might have.'

'You can't blame yourself for that. No one knew exactly when she'd go.'

'I wonder if she really would have said anything? I thought she tried that one time but perhaps she would never have seen it through,' Jo consoled herself. 'She didn't to you or Lucy, did she? She must have known that herself or she'd never have written the letters.'

'But a twin!' Tom was stunned. 'Are you sure?'

'Positive. She left me photos of two babies and two pairs of bootees. They're all upstairs. I was up half the night with Lucy trying to work out who they were. In the end, Brad emailed his amazing old mother and she filled in some of the gaps. There wasn't much love lost between her and Mum in those days, but she did throw some light on things.' She hit the table with the flat of her hand. 'This family! Why does it all have to be so complicated? So secretive? Brad had no idea Hope even existed until he was a teenager. Don't you think that's extraordinary?'

'For Mum's parents' generation, no. I suppose people thought having one illegitimate baby was a mistake, but having two or three was something really shameful. And remember that each of hers had a different father – even worse. They probably thought if you didn't talk about it, it would go away.'

'OK. I can understand that of Archie and Linda. But not of Mum. Why not tell us what she knew? How am I ever going to find Josh if I can't find our father?' It was hard to even begin to explain to Tom the aching void that had opened up inside her since her discovery.

Outside, Bailey barked.

Then, 'No!'

Over Lucy's shout, Jo heard Ivy laughing. The idea of giving a child up was unimaginable to her, and yet her mother had done that. Why? What could have happened? Then an earlier though that she hadn't wanted to admit pushed to the front of her mind. Of course, Josh might have died. If Hope really didn't know who their father was then he couldn't have taken the boy. Unless someone else had . . . But who? More than anything, she didn't want him to be dead. She wouldn't accept that as the truth until she had proof.

In the familiar chaos of the kitchen, everything was still except the motes of dust moving through the broad beam of sunlight that fell from the door straight across the kitchen table. Someone had picked some pink geraniums and put them in a vase. A green lizard was motionless on the wall by the back door. Jo tried to put the thought out of her head while she listened to Tom.

'I can understand her making a clean break with Walter. After all, that's what I tried to do when I decided to stay in England with Belle. I suppose we all did, in our own ways.'

'Why did you?'

'In the end, I'd had enough. Mum and Dad were so wrapped up in themselves or each other – or that's how it seemed to me. When you had the beam of Mum's attention, there was nothing like it. But then she'd move on to the next thing, keeping you in darkness until the next time. I never knew what was going to happen next, never felt that security. As a kid, I wanted her to take more notice of me but she always had a hundred things on the go. I guess I wanted more stability and certainty, though of course I didn't articulate that at the time. I must have felt I'd get it when I was away from them. You know . . .'

Jo did. They fuck you up, your mum and dad.

'I thought I'd buried my past. Having it brought up again this weekend is hard. I don't want to think about the other life I might have had.'

'You mean Maria?' Jo couldn't remember Tom ever being so open with her about his feelings.

He nodded. For an awful moment, Jo thought her brother might cry but he blinked hard and then the moment was over. 'But never mind.' He looked as if he wanted to say more, then thought better of it. 'Tell me more about your twin. That's way more important. I want to know everything you know.'

'One second.' Jo poured them more coffee. Then she did.

28

The game of catch was not going well. Every time Lucy threw to Ivy, Ivy dropped the ball so Bailey could race over, pick it up and run off. Once he reached the shade of the olive trees, he'd collapse in a shadow and lie there panting, looking pleased with himself. Whenever Lucy or Ivy attempted to retrieve the ball from between his front legs, he'd snatch it up just as they got there and race off again. Ivy would chase after him, but she was never fast enough.

Standing in the sun, Lucy was aware of the wind getting up, blowing chilly through the olive grove. She looked down at her left hand. Although she had left her wedding ring by her bed, there was an unmistakable groove that ran all around the base of her finger where it had sat for so many years. She rubbed it, pressing hard as if she could magic it away. But the last visible sign of her marriage refused to be removed that easily. On her other hand, Hope's ring glittered.

Lucy dreaded going back to England. She was used to being home alone, but there would be a new emptiness there now as well as the inevitable paparazzi hanging about outside her front door. They would catch her looking abandoned and miserable outside her local supermarket and pair the photo with another of Art and Carrie Flanagan looking all loved up, his hand on her swelling stomach. Then, when they got bored, she would be left to the sympathy of her friends and neighbours who wouldn't know what to say. All the while, she would be trying to build her business back up from rock bottom, thanks to Book the Cooks, or starting another. The reality of her situation was hard to face. This was not what she wanted from her life and, least of all, did she want Art's pity, or anybody else's. The thought of that was enough to strengthen her determination to get through somehow. What did they say? Revenge was behaving better. Well, somehow, that's just what she would do.

'Lucee!' Ivy called. She was standing by Bailey, not quite daring to go near enough to take the ball. The dog was having a grand time, poised, tail in the air, ready to snatch it up again.

As she ran over, Lucy wondered what they were going to do with him if Antonio didn't want him. Perhaps she could take him home to keep her company. But being limited to her pocket-handkerchief of a garden would destroy the poor old boy's spirit. He loved this place too.

She picked up the ball, dodging his dive for it. 'Wait!' she said with as much authority as she could muster. But Bailey hadn't grasped many commands and rarely responded to those he did understand. He was already off after the ball, through the longer grass at the bottom of the slope, picking it up and returning to the shade, lying there, expectant.

'He'll play this all day,' said Lucy. 'Shall we do something else? Shall we go and pick some flowers for Grandma Hope?'

'But she's dead. She won't see them,' objected Ivy.

'That's true. Let's pick some anyway.'

'Does everyone in the whole wide world die?' Ivy twirled around, her dress flaring out round her.

'Yes, they do.'

'Even us?'

'Mmm.' Lucy pretended to be distracted by a pair of yellow butterflies. 'Look at those. Aren't they pretty?'

But Ivy was a single-minded child. 'Does everyone come back?' she asked. 'Will Gran?'

Oh God. Jo would be much better at dealing with this sort of question than her. Her sister always had an answer. Lucy didn't want to say the wrong thing but Ivy was nose to nose with her, waiting for her reply.

'Can I use your phone and speak to her?'

'I don't think she'll answer.' Lucy was relieved to have reached the door of the house. 'I'll just pop in and get some scissors. I'll be one minute. Why don't you wait here?' She darted indoors, leaving Ivy to ponder the mysteries of life, death and the universe.

In Hope's garden, she let Ivy choose the flowers they cut: white roses, larkspur and lupins. There was no point dwelling on what would happen when she got home to Cambridgeshire. Better to try to concentrate on the present and remember this weekend for all the good reasons. And being with Ivy was one of them.

'You know what, Aunty Lucy?' The little girl was staring at her seriously. What was she going to come up with now?

'No. What?'

'I love everybody in the world that's alive but I don't actually love dead people because there's no point, is there?'

Lucy shook her head, amused by the workings of her young niece's mind. 'No, I suppose you're right.' Just as there was no point her holding a candle for Art or her old life either. Absolutely no point at all. She was not going to sit around feeling sorry for herself but would make every effort to move on.

Satisfied, Ivy continued choosing more flowers until they had enough to take inside.

By lunchtime, everyone but Brad and Elaine was present and correct. To Jo's frustration they had phoned to say they were running late and to start lunch without them. The rest of the family were all on the terrace sitting round the table, facing a lunch of leftovers and a salad Lucy had put together.

'Do you think it's going to rain?' Belle nodded towards the thick layer of cloud rolling towards them. It was the first thing she'd said since sitting down.

'We'll be fine,' said Tom, optimistic for once, but even he had swapped his shorts for a pair of trousers. 'It may miss us.'

Jo wondered what was going on between them. Surely Belle couldn't still be holding her disappointment over the ring against him? Jo could almost feel sorry for her brother if she didn't know how much he relied on Belle to make his life run smoothly. What he got in return was the other half of their deal. Other people's marriages were a mystery to her – so much easier to go it alone. She picked at her food, unable to concentrate on anything for more than a minute. Every time she thought she heard a car, she looked down the drive.

'I wish you'd relax,' said Tom. 'You're making me nervous.'

Belle looked up from her salad. 'Is something the matter?'

'Sorry,' Jo muttered, realising she must pull herself together if she didn't want everyone to know what was going on. 'No. Nothing. It's the thought of scattering Mum's ashes that's got me on edge.'

Belle made a sympathetic noise and went back to her lunch.

When Jo had told him all there was to tell, Tom had listened, both appalled and enthralled. He suggested that she could begin her search for Josh online so she had already emailed the General Register Office that morning asking for her and Josh's birth certificates. Now, she could only wait.

A car was coming up the road, turning into the drive. At last. Jo was on her feet immediately, only to sit down when she saw Maria's open-topped yellow car coming towards them. She couldn't help noticing Ethan's face lighting up for a nanosecond, closing down again when he realised Jo and his mother were watching him. 'Sweet,' he murmured.

Jo felt Tom's hand on her arm, as if for support. Then it had gone. Meanwhile Belle's face flooded with colour as she pulled down her sunglasses from the top of her head. They hid her eyes but not before Jo caught her gimlet stare, the muscle working away at the side of her jaw as she watched Tom get up to welcome their guests.

'More cheese?' Jo was on her feet again, wondering how on earth to save the situation.

Maria and Christina were getting out of the car. With their brightly coloured dresses, Maria in an orange wrap and Christina in a green and yellow sundress, they were like two exotic birds landing among a flock of pigeons. Grey, khaki, cream and white were the predominant colours worn by those round the table. Respect for Hope now the party was over.

Jo ran down the steps from the terrace towards the two women, overtaking her brother. 'Hello, again.'

Maria kissed her on both cheeks. 'Tom asked us to the scattering. That's OK, isn't it? Are we too early?' She must have been aware that all eyes were on them. Ivy had hopped off her chair next to Lucy and ran over to join them.

'Not at all. It's great that you could both come.' Jo heard the scrape of Belle's chair on the stone slabs as her sister-in-law got up to leave the terrace. 'We're just finishing lunch, but come up and join us.' They walked up to the table together where Jo embarked on introductions. 'You know us, of course, but did you meet Adam and Val yesterday?'

Val extended a perma-tanned arm that rattled with shiny bracelets while Adam stood up and offered Maria his seat. 'Nice little runabout,' he said with a nod towards her car. 'How many miles to the litre?'

This prompted Tom, who had been silent until that point, into action at last. 'No, no, Adam. You sit down. I'll get another couple of chairs. It's not a problem.' He followed Belle inside.

'And this is Kate, their daughter...' Kate turned and beamed at them. '...And her fiancé, Martin.' Despite his arm being fixed round the back of Kate's chair, he managed a half-swivel and a nod of the head. 'And have you met Ethan and Alex, Tom's boys?'

This last provoked a grin from Ethan who then stood up so

eagerly that he knocked his chair over backwards. He picked it up to a snort from Alex before going round the table to Christina. 'All right?'

She nodded. 'Yeah.'

'Fancy a game of table tennis?'

Christina looked up at him through her fringe and nodded. 'Sure, why not.' The two of them sloped off to the shed, laughing at something Ethan said.

Jo was reminded of Tom and Maria, same height, slim, dark and fair hair, heads close together so no one could catch what they were saying. She wondered if Tom would see the resemblance too. Still at the table, a pasty-faced, red-eyed Alex had barely moved since he sat down except to down a Coke and a couple of ham sandwiches made by Belle. A faint aroma of vomit still rose off him. With no sign of Tom and Belle returning, Jo sat Maria next to her and the conversation round the table sputtered into life again.

'What's she doing here?' Belle had her back to Tom as she leaned over the kitchen table and put coffee cups and saucers on the patterned tin tray.

Although she was trying to sound as if it didn't matter to her one way or another, Tom knew otherwise. He didn't want to upset her but this was not the ideal time to start explaining exactly how Maria fitted into his life. He should have come clean years ago.

'Maria's an old family friend who asked if she could come to the scattering. Of course we said she could.'

'You could have said that it was a private family thing.' She counted the saucers with a finger. 'I don't want that girl near Ethan again.'

'We can't control who he makes friends with.'

'Friends! I don't think that's what we're talking about.' The last cup hit the tray with a clatter.

'Who he fancies then.' With a hand on her shoulder, he spun her round to face him. 'Let it go. If you don't, you only succeed in driving him away.' He was thankful that he'd managed to sound so reasonable when inside his nerves were jangling.

She didn't reply, just pursed her lips.

'Let me help.'

'Thanks but I've almost done it.' She crossed over to the sink and poured water into the kettle. He stared at the back of her head, willing her to look at him, but wishing he was outside with the others, with Maria.

'Actually, there is one thing I haven't told you.' She would be crushed if she found out that she wasn't the first person he had told about the letter. All at once, he realised he had to tell her. What with the whole Ethan and Alex fiasco and her determination to find someone to blame, as well as the dispute over the ring, he'd chosen not to – perhaps because he didn't really want to hear her reaction. But he must.

'Mmm?' She was spooning coffee beans into the grinder but Tom had her attention.

'Mum left us all letters in that chest. Well, you know she left Lucy one, but she left me one too.'

'What? Cufflinks? A cheque for the money you're owed?' When she faced him, she couldn't have looked more scathing.

'Sometimes you're too materialistic. That's not fair.' He wouldn't hear her slate Hope any more even though he knew how let down she felt about the ring. Not the ring itself, but what the gift would have represented: acceptance. She'd talked of nothing else during their walk.

She looked surprised. 'And you're not?'

It took a severe effort of will to stop himself rising to the bait. 'No, not cufflinks or a cheque. A picture.'

She gave him one of those I-told-you-so looks at which she was so expert before returning to the business of making coffee.

'It's in Mum's studio,' he raised his voice to make himself heard over the noise of the grinder. 'You haven't seen it yet but it's quite, er...' He struggled to find the word he wanted and did just as she switched the grinder off. 'Provocative.' The word rang out in the sudden silence. 'I'm not sure you'll like it.'

She sniffed and ripped off a piece of kitchen roll to wipe her nose. 'It doesn't sound as if we'd want it at home. Don't one of the others?' She studied her manicure, picking at the top of one of her nails.

Tom pinched the skin between his thumb and forefinger yet again – did Frank, his therapist, expect him to have such frequent recourse to his methods? he wondered. 'Maybe,' he conceded. 'But the point is, Mum also said it was painted by my father.' He waited.

'Oh my God, Tom.' Belle dropped the spoon, spilling coffee grounds all over the floor. Oblivious to them, she went over and hugged him. He breathed in the lilac perfume that she knew he liked, as his hand wandered up her back, feeling the familiar contours of her body under the loose linen top.

'You always said you were happy not knowing but I never really believed you. Who is he?' She put both her hands on his shoulders as they stood together, faces almost touching. 'How are you feeling? You must call Frank as soon as we get home to talk it through with him.'

Tom shook his head. 'I've no idea.' For once he didn't feel like rushing to his therapist to talk it through. He wanted to digest the news first on his own without help.

Belle's hands dropped to his waist. 'What do you mean? What did Hope say? Please tell me this isn't another of her muddles?' She couldn't help herself from another little dig.

But he ignored it. 'No, not exactly. Apparently he was called Robert, but that's it. I looked with the girls the other night and there's no signature on the painting at all.' For the first time, Tom experienced what he could think of as a sense of loss, as if something he longed for had been held out on offer then ripped away as he reached to take it. But he had believed he didn't care. He had worked through all this with Frank to the point where he was no longer interested in his father's identity. He accepted that Walter had been the one who counted. That's what he had believed for years. Had he been wrong all along? Had Frank?

'Well, you must show me.' Belle stepped back, holding his hand. 'Perhaps you missed something.'

Tom resisted her pull. 'No, no. I went back there alone this morning and checked.'

'But I'd like to see anyway.' She yanked his arm like a small child.

'Not now.' Tom resisted. 'This is to do with me, and I don't want everybody else getting involved and guessing. I had to tell you, but I'd rather save it till later, when everyone except Jo and Lucy have gone. Do you understand?'

'Of course. I should have thought.' She let go of his hand. 'And what about Jo? What did she get?'

Tom gave a resigned laugh. 'Long story. And one she has to tell you herself.'

'But, Tom, we always share . . .' Her face registered hurt before understanding.

'It's not my secret to tell,' he insisted. 'Really. Why don't you finish making the coffee and let's get this day over with. Then we can sort all this out.'

By the time they returned to the table, Ethan and Christina were nowhere to be seen. The sound of their voices and laughter travelled from the old barn. Belle pressed her lips together as Tom took the empty chair beside Maria. He saw but, however much he wanted to resist, he couldn't pull back from the attraction of his old flame.

29

As she talked to Maria, Jo only half-heard what her old friend was saying about how long she was visiting Spain, what she and Christina had been doing, old haunts they had revisited. 'Remember that disco on the edge of Estepona, the one that was completely black inside, just near the main road? You know, the one where I lost you that time when we went there with . . .'

But Jo had tuned out. Brad's rental car was turning into the drive. 'I'm sorry,' she said. 'But there's something I've got to do.' She was aware of Tom taking the seat on Maria's other side as she got to her feet, caught Belle's look of displeasure, heard Lucy's chair scrape back as she began to stand with her. Jo held up one finger to stop Lucy accompanying her. 'No, I'm fine. You don't need to come too. Ivy, will you stay with Lucy?'

Leaving half the table baffled as to what was going on, Jo ran to meet the car as it pulled up. Brad was first out, looking pleased with himself. 'Beautiful place, Jo. Beautiful. And we found a nice little bar where we had an early lunch.'

'How lovely, but I thought you'd never get back. Did you say anything to Elaine?'

He looked blank for a second, then realised what she was asking. 'I didn't think you'd want me to. It's your news. I thought you were going to wait until you get home to do any more digging?'

'Digging? Sounds interesting.' Elaine came round the front of the car. Like Maria, she had chosen to celebrate Hope's life in colour: a red and orange striped dress that floated and swung as she moved. The sun glinted off the chains round her neck and her eyes were shining. 'We're not late, are we?'

'No. You're fine. Tom has it all timed down to the last minute.' Jo nodded towards the table where everyone had returned to their conversations. 'We're just having coffee and waiting for the others, although God knows how Daphne's going to make it to the bit of the wood that Hope's chosen.'

'Think I might go and grab myself something stronger.' Brad touched Elaine's arm. 'Want anything?'

'In a moment. I can tell Jo has something she wants to talk about.'

'Is it that obvious?' Jo was thrown by Elaine's perception.

'I've known you since you were a child, remember? So fire away?' She fanned herself with a hand.

The pick-pock of the table tennis game in the barn was followed by the sound of something hitting the table, then Ethan and Christina laughing.

'I want to show you something. It's all in my room but we haven't got long.'

Puzzled but keen to oblige, Elaine nodded. 'OK, then lead the way.'

Jo was aware of everyone watching them as they entered the house through the kitchen door. By this time she was convinced that Elaine must have the key to the mystery of her twin. Her twin! Although his existence made such strange sense to her, the idea took a huge amount of getting used to. Elaine followed her through the hall, stopping only to get a glass of water from the kitchen.

'What's all this about?'

'I'll tell you in a minute.' Jo almost ran up the stairs ahead of her. Once they were in her bedroom, Jo shut the door and brought over the box from the chest of drawers.

'Why all the cloak-and-dagger?' Elaine sat on the edge of the bed, out of breath. Her outfit billowed out then settled around her.

'I want you to look at this and then tell me what you know.' Elaine looked uneasy, then looked away as Jo handed her the box. 'Go on, please. Mum's left me clues to a mystery that I've got to solve. I think she was trying to talk to me before she died, but...' For the first time, Jo found herself choking up. She cleared her throat. 'You're the only person I know who might know something. You were her friend. Look at these.'

The expression on Elaine's face told Jo all she needed to know. There was something shifty, something knowing there. Elaine's eyes flicked towards the door as if wondering how to escape. She was definitely hiding something.

Jo took the letter and opened the locket before laying them on the bed between them. 'Please. I need to know anything you can tell me. Anything at all.'

Elaine shook her head as she touched the locket, then withdrew her hand as if it was burning hot. 'I can't help you...'

'You *must* be able to,' Jo insisted. 'You knew Hope better than anyone.'

'Better than Daphne and Ros?' Elaine ran her finger round one of her necklaces. 'I doubt it. They've been here, friends with her all the time. Not me.'

'But you were her *best* friend. You must know something – anything – that might give me a lead. Look.' She took the photo of the two babies in the pram and held it out to her.

Elaine hesitated before taking it. She let the picture lie on her lap while she got her reading specs from her bag. She peered at the image. As she shook her head again, she took a deep breath. 'I'm afraid not.'

'At the end, she meant me to know everything. Look at her letter.' She unfolded it and passed it over. 'Brad emailed his mother last night and she's already replied saying that Hope did have twins when she was in London, before she went to Ibiza.

I'm one of them. Elaine, please. Can you imagine what I'm going through? Can you imagine what this means to me?'

Elaine raised her head, passed her hand over her mouth.

Sensing she was holding something back, Jo pressed on. 'I'm trying to understand why she had to keep him a secret. What does she mean by "my grief"? She must have said something. Elaine, I'm begging you.' She passed her the blue pair of bootees. 'Walter was wonderful in every way but he wasn't my real father. And you know I've always wanted to know who was. Mum left a letter for Tom saying she had no idea herself, so I guess I have to be satisfied with that, but if Josh was my twin I want to find out what happened to him. I've got to have the full story to find out who I really am.' She didn't know what else to say to make Elaine talk, but then she noticed her expression had softened. 'Does that sound so crazy?'

'But I swore . . .'

Outside, there was the sound of another car pulling up. Jo glanced at her watch. Tom would start agitating about going soon. But she couldn't go anywhere until this was finished. 'She's dead, Elaine. Nothing you say can harm her now.'

Elaine stopped staring into space and looked down at what was on her lap.

Jo tried one last time. 'She wanted to tell me, I know she did – just read the letter.'

This time Elaine raised the letter from her lap and began to read. When she finished, she folded the paper carefully and returned it to the envelope. She picked up the locket, her hands steadier now.

'We're about to scatter her ashes. Help me be at peace with her when we do.' Emotional blackmail, but that was the only card Jo had left.

'All right.' Elaine raised her hand to show that Jo didn't need to say any more. She got up and went over to the window where she stared out at the countryside, the sun full on her face.

Jo's heart was pounding as she waited for whatever would happen next.

After what seemed a lifetime, Elaine turned round to face her. She removed her specs, letting them hang from the chain around her neck then clasped her hands, rubbing a thumb against her fingers.

'All right. I think Hope would want me to do this despite my promise to her.'

Almost unable to contain her nervous excitement, Jo leaned forward but she knew better than to interrupt.

Elaine walked across the room, turned and walked back. 'Once, years ago, when Hope was expecting Lucy, she did confide in me. She was terrified the same thing might somehow happen again, so terrified she couldn't even tell Walter. Not then, anyway. I don't know if she ever did. She said she would tell you when the time was right and she was ready to face up to what had happened. But she made it absolutely clear to me then, and afterwards, that I was never ever to say anything to anyone including you. It was her story to tell, not mine. So I tucked the whole thing away to the back of my mind and tried to forget. But of course I never quite could, although we never spoke of it again.'

Jo felt sick with anticipation. She moved the curl of hair to one side of the locket so she could concentrate on the two tiny faces that stared out at her.

'I'm not sure that telling you just before we scatter Hope's ashes is the best time.'

'It's *exactly* the best time,' interrupted Jo. 'I've been put off for so long. If not now, when?'

Elaine returned to the bed and sat by Jo, taking her hand and giving it a gentle squeeze. 'May Hope forgive me for this . . .' Elaine's eyes were glassy with tears as she squeezed Jo's hand again.

'He's dead, Jo. He's always been dead. That's one of the causes of the grief Hope was trying to escape.'

Jo gasped. However much she had wanted it, however much

she had known in her heart but pretended to herself she might be wrong, hearing the truth was still a blow. The two women sat silent for a moment, Elaine still gripping Jo's hand.

'What happened?' she asked in a small voice.

'You're sure you want to know now?'

'Yes. Certain.' Now she knew the worst, she needed to know the rest.

'You've got to remember Hope saw herself as abandoned by her family – however *they* might have seen it – so she made up by having fun. Lots of friends, lots of parties, lots of drink and drugs. That's what it was like then and that's why she had no idea who the father was. She never said who the suspects were and I doubt you'll ever find out now. I'm sorry.'

'I know.' Nonetheless, Jo hoped there was more so looked as encouraging as she could.

'Look, I only know the barest minimum. But I'll tell you all I remember.' Elaine shifted to get more comfortable, her sandal dropping to the floor with a slap. 'She was living in a squat – near Russell Square, I think. Anything rather than continuing lodging with her aunt. Do you know about her?'

Jo nodded.

'She was living there with a group of friends, a commune of sorts. I don't know how she met them but they seemed to give her all the support that she needed after you were both born. Then, when you were both only months old, she was persuaded that it would do her good to go out on her own, to get some headspace. You must remember how cabin-feverish you can get with a new baby?'

She certainly did. After Ivy was born, and the celebrations were over, Jo had found being alone in her flat with a tiny baby like a prison sentence. To give herself something to do, she would go to the bookies just down the hill from her flat, place a bet and go back home to watch the race. A couple of times, she had even taken Ivy into the office – something she wouldn't tolerate anyone else doing – until Richard had chased her away.

Elaine had started talking again. 'She went to a friend's, guilty about leaving you both but excited about being out on her own. You know Hope, she lost track of time... When she got home, you were safe asleep in your bed but Josh wasn't. He'd been crying so one of the guys had picked him up, given him a bottle, and laid him on the sofa beside him. He was stoned – nothing unusual – and drifted off to sleep. When he came to, Josh was dead.'

Jo gasped. She pictured a smoky room, a battered sofa, a guitar on the floor, her mother cradling her dead baby. Her shock, her distress and, most of all, her terrible guilt were all too understandable. If only she hadn't gone out... Nothing more terrible could happen to a mother than the death of their child. Now that she had Ivy, she could only begin to imagine her mother's pain and her guilt. 'A cot death?'

'Well, unexplained. She blamed herself, of course. The belief that Josh would still be alive if she hadn't left him tortured her for the rest of her life. That's why she couldn't speak about it.'

So there was no brother to search for. She had gained and lost him again within twenty-four hours. There would be no reunion. This explanation had been so obvious since she had found out about him, but Jo had wanted, more than anything, to believe there would be an alternative happy ending. Instead, her life would go on as before with an extra little space in her memory bank reserved for Josh.

'What happened then?' she asked, hardly able to breathe.

'She took you and ran away as far as she could. She thought if she could start a new life, in a new place, with no one she knew, perhaps she could blot out what had happened. She ran to Ibiza and cut herself off from anything she had ever known and anyone who knew her and what had happened. I think you know the rest.'

Jo picked up the photo, and felt a tear run down her cheek.

Elaine's hand was on her back. No wonder Hope had never been able to tell her. Shame and guilt. 'Poor, poor Mum,' she said. 'And, eventually, she met Walter.'

Elaine smiled and cleared her throat. 'Yes. They met in Ibiza after Tom was born and fell in love. He took Hope and the two of you and gave you a home in England, near his family. I think he probably saved you all. But she could never settle there, too frightened of memories or of bumping into someone who knew. So, when Walter came into some money, they upped sticks and came here to start a new life away from all that.'

'He did that for her?'

Elaine nodded. 'Yes. He loved her.'

Jo was beginning to see her family and their little life here in a whole new light. For the first time she felt that she had come a little way to understanding her skittish, wayward mother. For Hope, trying to start again on her own must have been an almost intolerable burden after her mother's early death, being abandoned by her father, supporting herself and losing a baby so dreadfully. No wonder she wanted nothing to do with her father or his new family. No wonder she wanted her past buried and forgotten. Jo thought of her own life as a single mother. She had moments of wondering whether she was up to it, but her family had been there to support her when she had needed them. Hope had had none of that so Walter must have shouldered everything.

Their rows, the drinking, the need for solitude, the unpredictability, the love – all the tiles were clicking into place. Click. Click. Click.

'Lucy told me how much you wanted to know about your father. But I promised Hope. I hope you understand.'

But Elaine didn't need to apologise. Jo knew about keeping secrets too. 'Of course I do. It's enough that you've told me now. Thank you.' Jo struggled to control everything that was running through her head. 'I can't explain to you how I feel. Angry that she didn't tell me herself – and sad. So, so sad.'

There was a knock at the door before it opened and Lucy put her head round. 'Sorry to interrupt.' She looked from one to the other then at the box and its contents laid out on the bed. 'Are you OK?'

Jo nodded, as the implications of everything Elaine had told her began to sink in. She took the tissue that Elaine had dug from her bag and blew her nose. 'Kind of.'

'Well, Tom's beginning to make noises about setting off. I thought you'd want to know. I've got Ivy safe, so you don't need to worry.'

Safe. Was that what Hope's friends had said to her about Josh? But this was Lucy, the one person in the world to whom Jo wanted to trust her daughter. 'Thanks.' Jo began to put everything back in the box.

Elaine got to her feet and slipped her sandal back on. 'We'll be right there.'

'I don't think there's too much rush. It's going to be a slow old procession with Ian and Bill. Ros has borrowed a wheelchair from the convent for Daphne. Don't ask!'

'Mum would love it, though,' said Jo. 'I bet she's sitting up there somewhere, cheering us on, making us do it all the way she wanted. She couldn't have planned it better.' She could imagine Hope, legs dangling off a cloud, bending over to get a good view and at peace now her secrets were being given up at last. She went over to the mirror and stared at her reflection as she put on her lipstick, remembering a rhyme she once heard:

Mirror, mirror, on the wall
I'm turning into my mother after all.

30

Hope's large extended family meandered towards the wood, accompanying her on her last journey. Like the Pied Piper, Lucy took the lead, clutching the blue-and-white urn as if her life depended on it, glancing over its lid to make sure she didn't trip. She bit her lip in an effort to hold back the tears that were blurring her vision again, just when she thought she had them under control.

Behind her, Elaine and Jo walked together. Elaine's arm was through Jo's, as if supporting her while they chatted, heads bent, intent on their discussion. The others gave them a wide berth as if they knew something important had happened.

Belle was looking after Ivy who was dancing along beside her. Tied to the child's wrist was a red balloon that she was going to let go for Hope at the end of the short ceremony, although she was more excited about having been given charge of Ferdie. The little dog looked like a shrunken, Barbour-wearing member of the country set now that he was kitted out in a ridiculous green waterproof jacket to keep him from getting a chill in the wind.

Ethan and Alex walked on either side of Christina with Tom and Maria behind them. Belle seemed to have separated herself from her family quite deliberately. She had made it clear that she was not about to relax her attitude towards his old 'friend' and her daughter. Maria, on the other hand, had looked bemused, as if surprised by Belle's unfriendliness. Tom was so obviously infatuated by Maria that Lucy found herself sympathising with her sister-in-law for the first time that she could remember. She had wanted to get up and shake some sense into her brother whose behaviour was bordering on embarrassing. He obviously didn't realise what he was doing as he kept glancing at Maria, being over-interested in what she was saying, laughing too loudly if it was something even faintly amusing. She was clearly flattered by Tom's attention and, whether intentionally or not, was encouraging him with that throaty laugh of hers.

The rest of the group chattered among themselves. Brad had struck up a conversation with Antonio who had arrived in the nick of time with a convoluted story about a problem with the chef in the hotel he managed. Lucy had barely spoken to him as she prepared herself for these final moments with her mother, but from the corner of her eye, she saw where he was and to whom he was talking. Adam and his family stuck together, lovebirds Katie and Martin forever entwined, her parents looking on with a mixture of pride and longing for their offspring to tone it down in the circumstances. Bringing up the rear stumbled the old reprobates, all except Daphne who travelled in state in a rickety old wheelchair that Ros was making heavy weather of pushing over the uneven track. Lucy had seen the hip flasks, flashing in and out of their pockets and smiled. Hope would have appreciated such a fitting send-off.

The procession came to a halt at a rusty bed frame on its side tied across the road. 'What's that?' Ivy's voice rose above the rest.

'It's an old bed.' Belle lifted up Ferdie so no one trod on him as the others caught up. 'Sometimes they use them for gates around here.'

'Why?'

Lucy tuned out as Belle embarked on an explanation. She put down the urn and untied the string of the makeshift gate, pulling back the metal frame, scraping it on the track, to let the others through. Not far now.

Hope had chosen to be scattered in a stand of cork oaks, their recently half-peeled trunks a tawny red below the thick, unstripped greyish cork bark. Above, the branches moved in the gathering wind. At times, in the heat of the summer, Hope would come and read here just off the path of one of her favourite walks. Lucy took a breath as she waited for the others to gather round. Jo, Tom and she were going to read short pieces chosen by their mother. Hers was a few of Prospero's lines from *The Tempest*. She almost knew them by heart, taught them by Hope when she was young.

She was about to start when there was a shout as the ancient wheelchair tipped to one side. One wheel stuck out at an angle and Daphne was hanging over the arm, trying to balance the weight so the whole thing didn't topple over. Ian and Bill stepped in to try and straighten her up.

'Sit tight, woman.' Bill had one hand on Daphne's shoulder, his hip flask in the other.

'I can't move, you idiot,' she retorted. 'Ros, help me out of here. You two don't know what you're doing.'

Ros tried to help her companion to safety. 'Put your other foot on the ground.'

'I'm trying.' Daphne stretched out her good leg so that her foot hovered inches above the ground. She remained jammed in the listing chair like a beached whale.

Tom and Ethan came to the rescue, hanging onto the chair as Daphne was hauled out. Ros took her arm to support her but the ground was uneven and she sank to the earth with a loud 'oof'. Belle, Elaine and Jo rushed to help her to her feet. With one arm around each of Jo's and Belle's shoulders and Elaine bringing up the rear, they half-dragged and half-supported her to the nearest tree.

'This chair's buggered,' said Ian with authority, taking a swig from his flask.

'You've an irritating gift for stating the obvious.' Daphne was sitting on the moss-covered earth, her back against the tree trunk, breathing heavily from the effort of getting there.

'We'll have to bring a car to collect you,' said Ros.

Daphne snorted. 'I can't think why we didn't drive up here in the first place. Whoever thought the wheelchair would be a good idea?'

'You said you wanted to be part of the procession.' Ros was miffed that her efforts were deemed insufficient.

'Can we get on with this. Please.' Tom glanced at his watch and then at the rain clouds that were being blown towards them.

'Yes, yes,' said Daphne, accepting a tipple from Bill's flask. 'Please don't let me hold you up.'

Lucy reached into the pocket of her jacket for her verse. She waited until the others were standing quite silently, then began to read her allotted piece of Shakespeare. 'Our revels now are ended...' A tear ran down her cheek as she went on.

As she tipped some of the ashes from the jar, she noticed the red sticker on its base. Belle must have got there when none of them were looking. She removed it as she passed what was left of her mother to her brother.

Tom took the jar from Lucy. He moved to a spot a little lower down the slope. He knew his words by heart. 'Remember me when I am gone away...' As he recited the Rossetti sonnet, he was aware of Ivy asking a shrill question about what that dust was, and Jo whispering back a reply. Otherwise, apart from Daphne's laboured breathing and the odd sniff from Lucy, everyone was silent. Having been surprised by Hope's choice of send-off poem, he found himself enjoying its contemplative tone, its notion of reconciliation with death. 'Better by far you should forget and smile,' he concluded. 'Than that you should remember and be sad.'

As he lifted the lid and tipped the jar, he realised his mistake. The ashes that emerged were caught by a gust of wind and blown back towards him. He jumped to one side avoiding what was left of his mother. Behind him, he heard a startled, 'Nooo!'

Belle had left Ivy with Jo and, despite everything, was standing at his shoulder where, as his wife, she felt she should be. He swung round to find her standing stock still, her mouth wide as she looked down at her dark-blue linen trousers and long grey wrap cardigan, both of which were lightly dusted with . . . well, Hope. As she recovered from the shock, Belle tore off the cardigan and shook it frantically into the wind, beating it with her hand.

He took it from her to finish the job, while she brushed at the little that had landed on her dark trousers but only succeeded in turning it into white streaks. To Tom's horror, she was close to tears, something that he had never seen in public and only once or twice in private. She usually held her emotions well in check. After a lifetime of the over-emotional women in his family, that was one of the things that had drawn him to her. He hated to see her upset. Otherwise, he had carried out everything just as Hope had instructed, even stood where she had asked. The wind hadn't been part of the plan.

The rest of the gathering looked on, suitably appalled, apart from Ethan, Christina and Alex who were smothering their laughter on the sidelines.

Shaking his head at them, Tom passed the last of the ashes to Jo.

Jo looked down at Ivy who was still clutching Ferdie's lead while the balloon floated from her wrist. Her daughter looked back, her little face solemn.

'What are you doing? What's that dust?'

'Shh. Not now. I'll tell you later.' Jo didn't mind about having to explain what the ashes were to Ivy any more. Her original plan had been to take her to one side so she wouldn't be part of the ceremony at all, but she had changed her mind. This was all part of her new resolve to be open with her daughter and answer all her questions, however difficult. When they got home to London she was going to sit her down and talk about her father, answer anything she asked. If she wanted to meet him, then she would even try to make that happen. There would be no secrets between them. So she would explain what the dust was in due course. Just not now.

She took the jar from Tom. The rainclouds were almost directly above them now. This storm was not going to pass them by and it wouldn't be long. She noticed one or two of the others looking up too. Without the sun, the temperature had dropped. In the distance, thunder rumbled.

'Don't cry for me,' she began her reading. At once she realised she was doing exactly that. But why? Tears streamed down her face, her nose was running. She could not stop herself sobbing as a wave of grief engulfed her. Someone (Elaine?) passed her a crumpled tissue. But blowing her nose didn't help.

'I'm sorry,' she said but the tears wouldn't stop. She was dimly aware of Ivy looking up at her in dismay, of Belle taking the little girl's hand and whispering something about Ferdie. Together, they stepped back from Jo.

'Why's Mummy crying?'

She heard Ivy's frightened question, but not Belle's whispered answer. But whatever Belle said could not come close to the real reasons. Jo took a deep breath, blew her nose again, discovering the hole in the tissue for the first time. She had to pull herself together for everyone here, most of all Ivy and herself. If nothing else, she owed it to Hope to carry out her last wish.

She began again. 'Don't cry for me . . .' This time her voice stayed steady, though the words on the card were blurry. She was aware of everyone watching her, holding their breath, of Maria quietly crying. Of Elaine and Brad standing together. Of Tom with his boys: Alex looking as if he might throw up at any moment, Ethan in his new trousers, his eyes moving between Christina and his shoes that were kicking at a stone. Of Hope's old friends: loyal through thick and thin to the very end. Of

Adam and his family, looking on in some dismay at what must have been one of the strangest family gatherings yet.

At last she came to the final lines. 'I am the thoughts, inside your head, While I'm still there, I can't be dead.'

She paused for a moment, allowing them all to remember Hope in their own ways. An image came to her of Hope in her garden, laughing, looking at the sky: a woman content in her small plot in the universe who had done her best to make the best of her life after such a difficult start. Jo was weeping for the loss of her, but also for the loss of her two fathers, the one she had dreamed of for so long and whom she would never know now, and Walter, the man who had so wonderfully filled his shoes. But most of all, she was mourning her twin, Josh, the boy she had never met, never even known existed. He was her other half, lost in the unknown country of Hope's early life. Jo raised a hand to the locket that hung around her neck. Now Hope had gone, she would carry his memory on.

Careful not to copy Tom, she checked where she was standing in relation to the wind's direction, raised the urn with both hands and chucked the last of Hope's remains into the air. As they left their container, the ashes were lifted by the wind and carried into the trees, away into the wood that Hope had loved so much. One last little shake and the urn was empty. Hope had been returned to the land she had adopted as her own. Or, at least, most of her had.

'I'm over.' A familiar voice seemed to whisper in her ear. Hope. 'You must get on with your own life now.'

Jo faced the others. As she did, they burst into spontaneous applause. Belle was busy helping Ivy untie the red balloon from her wrist. They held the string together, while Belle looked at Jo to see if she wanted to take over. Jo nodded, grateful for her sister-in-law's thoughtfulness. She stretched out her hand and her daughter ran to her, leaving Belle holding the balloon.

Jo lifted her on to her hip, only to have one small grubby hand wipe her tears away. 'Don't cry, Mummy.'

'I'm not any more.' She gave her a brave smile. 'Come on, Ivy Rose. Let's go back to the path and let go the balloon for Granny Hope there so it doesn't get caught in the trees.'

Belle passed her the balloon, then brushed at her cardigan again. Poor Belle. The others watched as Ivy was taken to make her own small tribute to her grandmother.

'Do we have to let it go?' Ivy clutched the string.

'Remember what I told you? We're giving it to Granny. So we're letting it go into the sky.'

'Is that where she is?'

'Perhaps. I don't know. But let's think of her as it flies away.'

Together they let go of the string and watched as the balloon whirled up over the treetops and away, as the thunder cracked above their heads and the first drops of rain began to fall.

31

The more-or-less orderly procession out to the wood was re-placed by a mad dash back home during which they all got drenched. Too bad for Ros and Daphne who, having written off the wheelchair, were forced to take shelter under the trees with a near-useless telescopic umbrella and the macs loaned by Bill and Ian, until Tom had returned in Hope's battered old four-by-four to rescue them.

By the time the three of them reached the house, Lucy, Jo and Belle had hot drinks, spirits and home-made cake ready to warm them. The smelly old dog blanket that had kept them warm in the car was removed, towels were provided, showers suggested but refused.

'Do you think she's up there orchestrating the weather? Is drowning us Hope's idea of a last laugh?' wheezed Daphne from her place in an armchair, a medicinal brandy in her hand.

'Or giving us pneumonia.' Ros was shivering despite the rug wrapped tight round her shoulders.

'I could lend you something of hers to wear,' offered Jo.

Daphne looked at her as though she had finally lost the plot. 'Wear Hope's clothes? You're joking? A skirt of hers wouldn't get round my thigh. No, we should go home and change.' She looked up at Ros for a nod of confirmation. 'You must have had enough of us all by now and there'll be a lot to do before you go home.'

Nobody disagreed. So Ian and Bill were prized away, farewells were said, and the three siblings stood on the terrace and waved goodbye as Ros's ancient car choked and sputtered down the waterlogged drive for the last time. Ahead of them, the mass of rain clouds was travelling towards the coast, taking the rain with them. Already the sun was drying out the paving stones, making the raindrops shimmer on the grass and leaves. Shortly afterwards, Adam and his family beat a relieved retreat, promising to keep in touch, wishing them all well and promising visits when everyone was back in the UK that they all knew would never happen.

Only Maria was left. Jo was surprised that she didn't see that she had outstayed her welcome. They had still so much to do and not much time left in which to do it, not least finish the bloody stickering and tidying up before the estate agent arrived the following day. The thought of what lay ahead filled her with a deep gloom. On one hand she desperately wanted to be back at home with Ivy, back at work overseeing the brand relaunch of Flakers Crisps with Richard, back where she could start trying to trace where Josh had been buried. If she was ever to achieve some sort of an ending, or closure, as Tom's shrink, or whatever he was, was bound to phrase it, that was what she would have to do. While talking to Elaine, that had become absolutely clear to her. She would not rest until she had.

'Didn't we, Jo?' Maria had been regaling Brad and Elaine with a story of how the two of them had hitched down to the coast after Maria's parents had said she couldn't go. When they couldn't get back home, Jo had talked her way into them being allowed to spend the night on the floor of a café. 'You must remember?'

Jo was jolted out of her thoughts. 'Sorry, but I don't – not at all.'

Maria looked puzzled. 'You must do. Mum was hysterical, terrified something might have happened to us, but Hope was just thrilled with your resourcefulness. She'd barely missed us.'

Tom laughed. 'Remember that time we—' He stopped as Belle left the room with Ferdie. For a moment, it looked as if he might follow her but then he seemed to think better of it. 'I was thinking about that time we took Lucy sailing...'

'Oh yes, when the mast broke!'

As he and Maria continued to entertain the other three with stories from their shared past, it began to dawn on Jo that Maria was enjoying all this just a little bit too much. She was flirting with Tom, hanging on his every word, laughing in the right places, occasionally touching his arm, admiring. Every now and then she would glance at the door, as if waiting for Belle to return.

After about ten minutes, Belle came back, looking flustered. She glared at the back of Tom's head. 'Has anyone seen the boys?'

Tom didn't even turn round, so wrapped up was he in something Maria was saying.

'Tom!'

'Sorry, darling.' He looked over his shoulder. 'What? No, I haven't.'

'I thought I'd see what they were up to but I can't find them. I've looked in their room, down at the pool.'

'They're probably playing table tennis.' He turned back to Maria to carry on reminiscing. Jo wanted to kick him.

'No, they're not.' Belle's voice went up a notch. 'I've checked everywhere.'

'Don't worry, they'll be around somewhere.' Maria said, her relaxed and confident body language showing who she felt was the incomer here. She glanced at the others, expecting them to back her up.

'They're not,' Belle insisted. 'And neither is your car.'

'Oh well, Christina's probably taken them somewhere then.' Maria stretched out an arm, her hand like a dancer's, long-fingered, elegant. Tom's eyes followed it.

Belle stiffened. 'But I don't want my boys being driven God knows where by someone so young. The roads round here can be dangerous if you don't know them. Especially when they're wet.' She twisted a tissue between her fingers.

'Steady on.' Hearing her distress, Tom got up and went over to her at last. 'I'm sure they'll be fine.'

'How can you be? We don't know where they've gone or when they'll be back.'

'We could call them,' suggested Maria, leaning back in her chair.

'I have. They're not answering.'

'Where do you think they might have gone?' Tom asked Maria, beginning to catch on to Belle's panic.

'I've no idea. She does pretty much what she wants without having to report back to me all the time.'

They all noticed the little jab at Belle. Even Tom, who frowned.

'I don't suppose they'll be gone for long because she knows we've got to get back.'

'Don't you ever worry about her?' Jo couldn't imagine being so relaxed about Ivy. When she thought about the sort of risks she had taken unsupervised as a kid, she didn't want that for Ivy. A mother's job was to watch out for her children – even when they were old enough to vote or drive cars; even when they didn't want you interfering. Wasn't that the burden of parenthood?

Maria threw her hands in the air. 'Good Lord, no. I learned that from Hope years ago. I longed to have a mother like yours who wasn't always keeping tabs on what you were up to. I always thought that if I ever had children, I'd want to be like her, so I try to be. Christina's free to do what she likes – within reason,' she added hastily when she saw how the others looked at her.

Tom was staring at her, taken aback. He might not like crossing swords with his boys, but he had always been quite clear that he and Belle had the ultimate responsibility for them.

'Yes, well that doesn't work for Tom and me,' said Jo, her voice flinty.

Maria looked surprised. 'Really?'

'Nor me,' said Belle, looking gratefully at Jo.

'Well, we've survived just fine,' said Maria. 'And look at you three. You're still here to tell the tale.' Maria drew her legs under her, curled up like a cat. Point made.

'Only just,' said Jo, speaking for all of them. 'Being brought up like that may have had its good points but it had its bad ones too.' She didn't want to share the things they had just found out with Maria, not now that her long-lost friend was beginning to feel more and more like a stranger.

'I never thought I'd hear you say that.' Maria combed her fingers through her hair, sweeping it behind her right ear. 'When you left for England, you were so independent, so strong. I want Christina to be like that.'

Jo was surprised. Anybody who knew her well or with any empathy would have understood how nervous and uncertain she had been, however well she had disguised it. She wouldn't wish that on anyone. Even with the support of Walter's family and Elaine, making her own way had not been easy.

'There's a lot you don't know,' said Tom, standing shoulder to shoulder with Belle who tucked her arm into his.

'Tell me, then.' Maria unfolded herself and leaned her elbow on the arm of her chair, her chin on the palm of her hand. There was no denying that she was quite beautiful, seductive, even. Jo could see why her brother was mesmerised.

'I don't think this—' But Tom was stopped by his mobile ringing. He took it from his pocket and looked at the caller ID. 'Alex.'

Belle reached out for the phone but he raised his hand to stop her as he took the call. He listened for a while, then, 'And where did it happen? . . . All right. All right . . . Alex, calm down . . . Yes, I'm coming straight away.'

He hung up and stared at the phone. 'They've had an accident.'

Belle gave a little scream and clutched his arm tighter. 'No! Are they all right?'

'I think so. They're on the Gibraltar road. Apparently one of those bloody bikes tore round a corner and Christina went off the road.'

'Oh my God!' Belle covered her mouth with her hands. 'She must have been going too fast. I knew something like this would happen.'

'But they're all OK.' Tom was super-calm as he took charge. 'It sounds like the car took the brunt of the damage when it hit a tree. She can't have been going too fast if none of them were injured, thank God.'

'We must go immediately.' Maria was on her feet, slipping them into her sandals, having left her sturdier shoes in the hall to dry.

'I'll drive you,' said Jo. 'Tom, have you got the keys? Ivy, you're coming with us.' She took the keys from him and went into the hall to get her daughter's shoes.

When she returned, Tom and Belle were outside waiting for her, and Lucy was talking to Ivy. They both looked at Jo.

'Ivy and I thought we might watch a film together. You go.'

Ivy nodded fiercely and took Lucy's hand.

'Fine,' said Jo, relieved. 'If you're sure? I hope we won't be too long.'

'Absolutely sure,' said Lucy. 'Come on, let's go and see what DVDs there are.' She led Ivy into the sitting room and to the shelf by the TV that held a few ancient offerings.

'You might need another driver.' Brad had been listening from the sidelines. 'Maria, let me take you.'

Jo thanked God he was sensitive enough to realise that having Maria in the same car as Tom and Belle was not ideal. Although Maria hadn't even asked about Christina she was obviously as relieved as the rest of them when she heard Tom say all three were all right. She had unknotted her fingers and wrapped her arms around herself for comfort, an anxious tic flickering at the right corner of her mouth. Jo had forgotten that too. She kissed Ivy goodbye and rushed out to join the others.

There was a fraught silence in the car broken only by Tom giving Jo unnecessary directions and bits of driving advice. She didn't think it worth reminding him that she knew the road every bit as well as he did. In the back Belle sat rigid, clutching her safety belt and hissing whenever she thought they took a corner too tightly or when they passed an oncoming car. Jo gritted her teeth but stayed silent.

Christina hadn't driven the boys far. They had taken the road up to Gaucín and then left opposite the garage towards Gibraltar. At a point where the road had begun its descent in a series of sharp bends, they found the yellow car, its right front wing smashed into a tree. Tom was out of the four-by-four before Jo had turned off the engine. Belle was right behind him as he raced over to Ethan and Christina. They were sitting on the ground by the car, Ethan with his arm round her, comforting her as she rocked back and forth. Alex stood behind them, kicking at the tree trunk.

As soon as he saw his father, Ethan got to his feet with a grimace, holding his left arm tight against his body. A bruise was blooming on his cheek. He spoke before Tom had a chance to. 'This wasn't her fault, Dad. It really wasn't. The bike took the corner too wide. It came from nowhere. She couldn't have done anything else.' He looked back towards Christina, who responded with a weak smile. At their feet the glass from the smashed right headlight and wing mirror glinted on the ground.

'Ethan! Are you all right?' Belle overtook Tom and stood in front of their son, unsure whether to hold him or not, not wanting to hurt him. Tom understood exactly what was going through her mind. He put his hand on her shoulder, feeling how tense and scared she was, wanting her to know that he was there for her.

'I'm OK. I hit the windscreen when we hit the tree.' Ethan touched his cheek and winced. 'And my shoulder hurts a bit, but that's all. Luckily we weren't going very fast. She's a very good driver.'

'Thank God.' Belle visibly relaxed. 'Are you sure?' She took his good arm and kissed his cheek. 'What about you, Alex?'

'My neck hurts a bit but I'm cool. I was in the back – with my seatbelt on,' he added pointedly.

'Ethan, don't tell me you weren't wearing yours?'

Ethan hung his head. Guilty.

Belle's relief at finding her sons unharmed gave way to anger. 'What were you *thinking*? I thought we'd drummed that into you at least.'

'Shh. Not now.' Tom stepped between them.

Ethan kept looking at the ground. 'Yeah, well, whatever. We're OK, and that's all that matters.' He took a step back towards Christina.

'Ok?! You could have been killed or at least gone through the windscreen.'

Tom put a restraining hand on her arm. She leaned into him, relenting as her anxiety turned to relief.

'Well, we weren't and I didn't.' Ethan sat down beside Christina again. She moved towards him so there was no space between them.

'And you, Christina,' Belle squatted down, 'are you hurt?'

A tear-stained face looked out from the black and blue hair. 'I think Ethan got the worst of it.' She raised her hand to her chest. 'I'm bruised from the safety belt, but that's all.'

'You might have broken a rib. You should probably see a doctor.' Belle looked round at Tom, relying on his agreement.

'I don't think it hurts enough.' Christina managed a smile.

'I'm sure it wouldn't do any harm to have it X-rayed – just to be on the safe side. But your mother's on her way. I'll leave it to the two of you.' Belle turned her attention back to her boys. 'You didn't tell us where you were going. And you weren't answering your phone.'

Ethan and Christina exchanged a look so brief it barely happened.

Belle shut her eyes and shook her head, despairing of them. 'Well, thank God you're all right. That's the main thing.'

Just then Brad's rental car pulled up and an anxious-looking Maria emerged – so not quite as cool as she made out after all. She took in the situation at a glance and, like Belle, went straight to her own child and squatted beside her. 'What happened? Are you hurt?'

Christina didn't look at her, just nodded. 'Bit bruised, but yeah, I'm fine.'

'That's good. How many times have I told you to be careful?' She twisted round to look at the damage to the car. 'What's the damage?'

Tom couldn't believe his ears. Where was her concern for his boys? This wasn't the carefree but loving woman he thought he knew at all.

She bent over the wing of the car to examine the damage. 'At least we're insured.'

'And the boys are OK too,' he reminded her, waiting for her to care. Wanting her to.

'I can see,' she said, straightening up to dazzle him with one of her smiles, except this time he wasn't dazzled at all. 'So no harm done, thank goodness. I'd better call Hertz and ask them what to do now.' She glared at her daughter. 'This will have to come out of your allowance.'

Christina had recovered herself in the short time since her mother had arrived. Her eyes were dark, intense, unblinking as she stared her mother out. Ethan moved in front of her. Tom was touched to see his son being so protective. Not that Christina looked as though she needed much protection. He had rarely seen a young person so defiant, so sure of herself. Yet, looking closer, he thought he detected a certain vulnerability beneath that veneer of self-assurance. In that moment, he felt sorry for her. 'She could have killed herself,' he pointed out, keeping his voice level.

'She could have killed our boys,' Belle added.

'But she didn't.'

He used to tease Maria about that tic at the side of her mouth.

'Thanks be to God,' she added, but too late for it to mean as much as it should have.

Where on earth were her priorities? Something terrible could have happened to any one of their three children. Any one. Her matter-of-factness, her seeming lack of humanity, was shocking to Tom. It was as if his eyes were being opened to a completely different woman from the one he had once felt so passionate about. He had even fallen for the idea that he might perhaps even love her again. But now he saw that for what it was – just a fantasy. Whatever had he been thinking? As Belle came and stood at his side, something shifted back to normal inside him. Either something had changed in Maria or time and distance had put a rosy tint on his memories of their shared past.

Christina walked over to Brad's car and got into the back seat. She didn't respond to Ethan's shout. He waved and held a fist to his ear, thumb and pinkie extended, to suggest they speak on the phone. But all that could be seen of Christina was her hair as she looked away from them all. Tom should have been furious with her, but all he felt was sympathy. He turned back to Maria, aware that Belle was right beside him, hanging on to his every word.

'You'd better sort this out,' he said, as cool as you like. 'We'd better get Ethan to the doctor to have his arm looked at.'

She looked as if she was about to ask for his help, but before she could he added, 'Brad will help you. Won't you?'

Brad nodded. 'Of course. Anything. We can use my car.'

Maria looked as if she realised that everything was slipping away from her, that whatever magic she had briefly exerted over Tom was evaporating. 'We could come back to the house afterwards,' she suggested, 'when we've seen to this. We've all still got so much more catching up to do.'

Tom felt Belle's hand between his shoulder blades, possessive.

'I don't think that's a good idea,' he said, letting go of any lingering regret as Belle pressed a little harder. He knew where he belonged. 'We've got a lot to do before we leave.'

Maria's look was full of a yearning that surprised him and that he hoped no one else saw. But whatever was going on in her life that made her search for comfort in her past had nothing to do with him and he didn't want to know. He had made the right decision all those years ago but had been flattered by her attention, intrigued by the idea of what his life might have been if he had made a different choice. But they would never have worked together. Not then, not now. He turned to his family. 'Come on, Ethan. Alex. Come home with us.' He made it clear there was no option.

Ethan stood up and walked with his brother towards Jo, who had got out of the four-by-four to open the back door for him. He climbed in, still nursing his injured arm.

Tom turned back to Maria. 'You'll be fine with Brad,' he said. 'He'll wait till someone comes and then give you a lift, I'm sure.'

'Of course,' said Brad. 'Let me have a squint at the documentation. That'll tell us who to phone.'

She looked at him with relief and went over to her car, leaning in through the open door to get the rental agreement.

'It's been good to see you,' Tom said. Despite himself, he felt a faint tug of sadness as she came towards him again. Tom heard Belle take a very deep breath indeed as Maria stood on tiptoe and kissed his cheek.

'It was good seeing you, too,' she said.

Belle would never forgive him if he said any more. Their conversation was over. Instead he just smiled, then followed his wife to the car where his family was waiting for him.

They would not see each other again.

MONDAY

32

As soon as Lucy woke up, she knew exactly what she had to
do. After a night of tossing and turning, of staring into
the dark, contemplating a future without Art, she had come to
a decision. The faint possibility that she had at first dismissed as
a fantasy had been growing in her mind for weeks but she had
never thought that it might come true until now.

The sun filtered in through the thin curtains, throwing faint
shadows across the floor. A bee buzzed in through the window
then out again. Bailey barked outside. She got up and went to
the window, pulled the curtains wide and stood for a moment
taking in the all-too familiar view, but the view that she, like
Hope, would never tire of. The rain of the previous day had
blown through, leaving behind a radiant blue sky and air so clear
she could see across the fields and woods, beyond the distant
wind farm and the Rock of Gibraltar to Africa again. With the
scorching summer heat yet to come, the landscape was a blizzard
of different greens freshened by yesterday's rains. She fancied she
could see a pair of eagles circling close to Sierra Crestellina.

As she got dressed, she went through what she had to say
to the others. Getting Jo on her side would be her first task.
Tom would be more difficult, but if there were two of them
to persuade him it might just work. She wondered whether Jo
would be up.

As soon as she opened her bedroom door, it became obvious that Jo was very much up. Ivy's fractured and furious wails

travelled up the stairs from the terrace. 'It's not fair!' she shrieked. 'No, no, no!'

Jo said something Lucy couldn't quite catch.

'You're a very silly girl!' Ivy shrieked. Lucy smiled and ran down the stairs. Perhaps she could help.

At the table, a puce-faced Ivy sat in front of a bowl of cereal. Her hand was on her forehead in best drama-queen style, before she banged it down on the table. 'It's not fair!'

'See what I have to put up with?' Jo nodded a welcome to her sister. 'What's not fair, Ivy? Tell Auntie Lucy.'

Ivy looked up, her blue eyes brimming with tears. 'My whole life's not fair,' she wailed as if overtaken by a great catastrophe.

'I just said that she's got enough sugar on her cornflakes.' Jo sipped her coffee, quiet, calm, scrolling through something on her laptop. 'That's all.'

The only way Lucy could hide her laughter was by going to get herself a glass of orange juice. By the time she returned, the drama was over. Ivy was eating her cereal while Jo tapped something into her laptop as if nothing had happened. She looked up.

'Amazing what a promise of *Frozen* will do.'

Ivy beamed and began singing quietly.

'Lucky I downloaded it – even though it goes against everything I thought I'd want for her. But anything for a quiet life.'

'Can we have a word?' Lucy sat down.

'Provided madam doesn't kick off again, of course. Can you pass me the peach jam?'

'It's about the house.' Lucy passed the jam then spread butter onto a chunk of crusty bread for herself. Someone had clearly been to the bakery in town.

'Mmm?' Jo looked at Ivy, stroking her daughter's hair back off her face with that look of maternal love, then shut her laptop, closed her eyes and leaned back, letting the sun shine on her face. 'What about it? Don't worry. Tom'll have it off our hands soon.' She opened her eyes and looked around her. 'Shame really. I always forget how lovely it can be here.'

'But do we really have to sell it?' Lucy's insides were turning over. The answer could change her life forever.

Jo sat up, looking puzzled. 'It's what Mum wanted,' she said. 'That's all. Why?'

'Do we have to do exactly what she wanted?' Lucy felt almost sacrilegious asking but if she didn't, then no one would. 'She only wanted us to sell because she didn't want us to argue about the place. But if we don't argue . . .'

'Yeees?' Jo was obviously surprised that Lucy was thinking about rocking the boat. Not her usual style.

Ivy jumped down from the table and ran inside. 'I need Posy and Bampy. They have to get ready for a fooneral.'

Lucy waited till she had Jo's full attention again. 'I've been awake all night thinking this through. I've got to find something that will fill my life. No Art, no kids, and a business that needs resuscitating or putting down.' There, she'd said it without tears or self-pity. 'I told you I was thinking of starting a B & B?'

Jo nodded, interested.

'But if we kept this place, I could run it as a small boutique hotel. Don't look so doubtful. I've helped Mum run it as a B & B, so I know the principles, but I want to develop the place into something that's a bit more upmarket and less eccentric – well, less hit and miss. I'll run cookery classes – imagine! – I might be able to hook up with Bernard and Sylvie so that I can offer walking and painting holidays too. And I . . .' She ground to a halt.

Jo was staring at her. With horror? Lucy couldn't tell.

'What? You think it's a terrible idea. I suppose you need your share of the sale? I don't blame you. And I know Tom will want his. That's his payback.' She should have known the idea had no legs, that there was no chance of the others agreeing.

Jo shook her head slowly, a smile spreading across her face.

339

'Absolutely not! I think it's genius. It'll give you a completely new start and, what's more, you'll be brilliant at it. But what about the finances? Won't you need an injection of cash to get it going?'

A tingling excitement began to overrun Lucy's disappointment. Jo wasn't mocking her or being the patronising big sister but encouraging her to go on. 'I can do it slowly, one thing at a time. I've fantasised about how it would work for months but could never do it because of Art and me. But now my life's changed. So I spent the whole night thinking it through. If Art and I sell our house – I don't want to live there on my own now – then I'll have some capital that I can inject into the business. Or perhaps we can organise it so you and Tom have shares. I'm not sure how that could work, but he'll know. How hard can it be?' she asked. 'I know what's needed, you and Tom will have input, and I'm sure Antonio will help me set it up with his hotel experience. Or he'll know someone.'

'Lucy! Not business partners and—'

She felt herself blushing. 'It's way too soon for anything like that. I do like him, though. Don't you?'

Jo shook her head. 'Don't be daft. Not my type. Good dancer, though.'

'Well, perhaps it's my turn for a bit of fun.' She quite liked the idea of that as something coming to her. 'But the thing is, he does know about the business here, having managed the hotel for so long, and he loves this place as much as we do. That's what I'm interested in. I'll start modestly and then gradually put my changes into place.'

'To make a real go of it, you'd need a decent website, a social media presence and some marketing savvy, too. Mum was always rubbish at all that, but for any new business it's a must these days. But I can help you once we've done some research into the market.' Jo's eyes shone with enthusiasm.

'You'd do that?' This was more than Lucy had dared hope. She had imagined a reluctant agreement at best, a deal whereby she could try it for a few months and then have to put the house back on the market if her plans went belly up. Not this!

'Of course I would. Who have you got who's better than me? And Antonio should be able to help there too. You can pay me by giving me and Ivy the odd week or two here out of season. I said yesterday that I'd help you get back on your feet and if this is what it takes – then count me in.' The last words were lost as Lucy smothered her in a bear hug.

'Morning!' Belle breezed through the doors to join them, still in her running gear, with her sun visor pulled down over her eyes. She put down her breakfast bowl and laid her various vitamin supplements on the table, then stood with her hands on her hips, legs apart. 'What a gorgeous day. I love it here when the weather's like this.' Now things had been straightened out with Maria and she had Tom back, her mood had lifted.

'How's Ethan?'

'Sound asleep. He's badly bruised but he'll be fine. The sooner I get him and Tom away from those two women, the better for all of us.' She raised her eyebrows to show she was joking. 'So what's the plan for today?'

The two sisters exchanged a glance. If only they could get Belle onside, then Tom would at least listen to them. He would be out here at any minute. They hadn't long.

Beady as ever, Belle caught the exchange. 'What is it? What are you two dreaming up? I can tell there's something.'

Jo glanced at her watch and began to explain.

When Tom emerged, he was feeling better than he had for days. His run with Belle that morning had gone really well. She might have deliberately slowed down but he had kept up with her the whole way round and the promised endorphins were surging around his body giving him that welcome sense of well-being. The cobwebs had been blown away. He had been an idiot to let himself get so enchanted by Maria. In the clear light of the morning, he saw his reaction to her as the short-lived infatuation that it was: a first love that belonged where he had left it – in the past. And Belle had been so sympathetic when he gave her his long overdue explanation. Not a word of recrimination. Not really. After they had got Ethan back home from the doctor, his shoulder badly twisted but not broken, they had a long talk. Unpacking everything had helped (Frank always said it did). Belle had proved herself to be the most remarkable and understanding of women that he knew she really was, whatever the rest of his family thought.

However, he felt an indefinable sense of foreboding when he saw the three women sitting together at the table. Ivy was playing with her toys on the ground nearby. Bailey was stretched out twitching as he chased more rabbits in his sleep. His sisters had that look he recognised from when they wanted something, from a lift on the back of his scooter, to be driven to a party, to be taken to the coast. Belle was spooning at her breakfast, thoughtful, her earlier enthusiasm for the day on hold.

'I'll just make some of that rye toast,' he said, heading back inside.

When he returned, Belle looked up at him as he approached the table and leaned the pieces of toast against the teapot. 'Lucy's got an exciting proposal.' His sense of foreboding increased. He took his vitamins from their bag and counted them onto his plate.

'Hope it's not going to take too long. The estate agent's coming early so we need to make sure we've tagged everything in the house that we want.'

'That's exactly what I want to talk to you about.' Lucy looked at Jo, then Belle.

Jo gave a little nod before giving her attention to Ivy, who had brought over her toys and was clambering onto her mother's knee.

Tom put a large brown pill in his mouth, followed by a

mouthful of orange juice. He tipped his head back and swallowed before pouring himself some coffee. If he kept up his familiar routines, ignoring the looks passing between the three of them, perhaps whatever it was they wanted to talk about would go away and he could enjoy this last beautiful morning on the terrace. He wondered briefly when the best time would be to phone the office just to check everything was as it should be.

'I wonder if we could reconsider selling.'

Lucy's words broke like a tsunami into his thought processes, obliterating everything else that was going on there. He spluttered his coffee back into the cup.

'But it's all arranged. The house is going on the market this week.' They couldn't do this – not upset everything he had so carefully arranged according to Hope's wishes.

'Well, we thought we might *re*arrange it,' Jo jumped in. 'Lucy's got a plan. You might at least hear her out.'

'Yes, do,' echoed Belle, reaching for a Ryvita. 'I think there may be something in it. For all of us.'

Three against one. Even his own wife was in on it. Her longing to be a real part of the family would have made her easily persuadable. To be included in something the other two were dreaming up represented all she had wanted from the family. Tom conceded defeat with ill grace. 'All right. But make it quick.' He would listen to what Lucy had to say and then dismiss it. Plans should only be changed when absolutely necessary – that was one of the rules he lived by. He leaned back in his chair, admiring the view, while Lucy began to explain what sounded like a totally hare-brained scheme. Keep the house! Run a hotel! With Antonio! Teaching cookery! Oh, please.

'No, no, no!' he said, reaching for the toast and butter. Belle manoeuvred the toast out of his reach, and the packet of polystyrene-like crispbread into its place. 'Hope wanted us to sell, so that's what we're going to do. A rep from Gaucín Properties is coming up this morning and we're going to put it on the market as planned. We're going to sell the place and split the profits, just as Mum wanted. You can use your share to set up a business here if you want to. You can go into something together, if you're so keen, Jo. But I'm not going to go back on everything now.'

Belle had her head cocked to one side as she took on board what he said. She would soon be back in his camp again, once she realised that some of their share of the proceeds would go towards the ridiculously expensive Sri Lankan holiday that she had set her heart on. He took a crispbread, remembering he had another appointment with the hypnotherapist soon after they got back.

'That's not fair, Tom.' Jo jumped in.

He might have known Jo would be difficult.

'You could at least consider the idea. It's the perfect answer for Lucy.'

'I have considered it, and the answer's no. You can't decide to start a business just like that. You need figures, projections, something more than a whim. You know that perfectly well. And this kind of squabbling is exactly what Mum wanted to avoid.' He pushed his chair back from the table, pleased with himself. He was being responsible, acting as the man of the family and making decisions that were for the good of them all. It was time to reassert and prove himself to them. 'Come on, Belle, I want to show you the picture in the daylight.'

As he stood up, he saw the look that passed between Jo and his wife. So this was not over yet. Belle was enjoying the conspiracy. But he would be ready when they next brought it up. Lucy was in her seat, looking as if the world had ended. He felt a pinch of guilt, then brushed it off. She was a resourceful woman. This was a knee-jerk reaction to Art's departure, that's all. There would be other, better opportunities for her that would not be driven by her emotions. He was doing the right thing, sticking to their mother's wishes.

None of them said anything when he left the table. If this was not the end of the matter, at least he had made his thoughts plain. All he had to do was repeat himself. They wouldn't be surprised. He heard Belle's footsteps behind him as she followed him towards Hope's room.

'It's not over.' Jo put her hand on Lucy's wrist. 'I won't let it be.'

'But he was so definite. And he's right. This is exactly what Mum wanted to avoid.' She put her elbows on the table, her head in her hands.

'Well, she's not here, so she won't know. If we don't want to sell the house, there's nothing that says we have to. He can't if the two of us don't agree.'

'I should have known he'd react like that. I should have kept quiet until I'd made a business plan. That's the sort of thing he responds to.' Lucy reached down to Bailey, who had padded over and placed his head on her lap. 'And what about this old boy?'

'It's not over yet. Belle said she'd help – although she might change her mind. Tom can be very persuasive when he puts his mind to it.'

'Do you really think she will?' Lucy paused her rhythmic stroking behind Bailey's ears. 'The fringe benefits of free holidays – not that that'll help my cash flow! – and a profit share seemed to do the trick. Assuming there are any profits ...'

'I hope so, but you know what the two of them are like.'

'Married?' They both laughed.

'Well, yes. A unit. As one. You know.'

'Oh yeah, I remember that. Dimly.' The irony helped in a small way. 'I'm upset, of course I am, but when I think of the way Art's behaved, I feel so bloody furious. Maybe deep down I knew this was coming – just not the way it has – so I was a little bit prepared subconsciously.'

'You're going to be like a phoenix rising from the ashes, that's what I know,' said Jo, licking the honey spoon. 'All we have to do is hope Tom sees sense. We're going to have to count on Belle. Otherwise we're going to have an almighty row.'

'I'm amazed she agreed.' Lucy had never thought she had much in common with Belle, so the fact that she had come round to her way of thinking so readily surprised her. But she had heard them out and understood Lucy's vision for the place. Excited was a word that she didn't associate with Belle, who was normally so measured, but this time she had definitely been enthusiastic.

'She agreed because, although she can be a pain in the ass, she's a decent person at heart. And she wants us to like her – always has, whatever she says. More than that, we've made sure there's something in it for her.' Jo was as practical as if she were pitching for an account. 'Anyway, she only agreed if there was a cap on your making it work. One or two years. So don't get too carried away. She hasn't been as magnanimous as all that.'

Lucy put her finger against her lips. 'Shh.'

They hadn't noticed Ethan come round the corner of the house.

'Ethan! How're you feeling?'

The boy flopped into a chair as if, having been up for all of ten minutes, he was exhausted. The bruise on his cheek had extended into an impressive black eye. He put his phone on the table. 'Yeah, OK. Thanks.'

'You were lucky, by all accounts.'

Ethan grunted his agreement as Lucy slid the coffee towards him.

'What would you like to eat?'

'Whatever. Bread's cool.' he said, stretching his good arm across the table to the breadbasket. 'Jo, you don't have Maria's number, do you? I wanna talk to Christina.'

'I'll do that for you,' she said, taking the bread and buttering it for him.

He nodded. 'Sweet.'

'I could probably get it.' Tom and Belle probably wouldn't be keen if they knew, but what harm could come from it? Besides, Ethan was well on his way to becoming an adult, however much

346

Belle might want to keep him in cotton wool. 'But can't you find her on Facebook or whatever you use?'

'Probably. I just wanted to talk to her after yesterday though...' He flicked at his phone so the screen lit up. 'I can message her, I guess.'

'Might be better,' said Jo. She could hear Ivy playing in the hall, bossing Posy and Bampy about. Jo was grateful that she was never going to have to tangle with bringing up boys.

Satisfied, Ethan tucked into his food, his attention fixed on a game that he seemed able to play at the same time. Ivy came and stood beside him, gazing at the coloured shapes tumbling and exploding on the screen. Jo wanted to pull her away, but she had learned she had to pick her battles, and this was one she had no hope of winning as long as Ethan sat there engrossed.

'Do you mind them going into Mum's room without us?' Lucy asked out of the blue. 'I feel a bit odd about it.'

Jo thought for a moment. 'Actually, yes, I do too. Shall we?'

'I think so. You coming, Ivy? Come and see what's in Granny Hope's special room.'

To Jo's delight, her daughter bent down to pick up Posy and Bampy without objecting and followed, leaving Ethan to it. As they walked round the side of the house, past the *casita*, Alex emerged looking half-asleep.

'Morning! I'm afraid you'll have to get your own breakfast,' Lucy called to him. 'There's some on the table but you can find whatever else you want in the kitchen.'

'Cool,' he said, stifling a yawn then scratching his stomach. 'Thanks.'

'Aren't you glad you had a girl?' Lucy whispered once they were in the back yard. 'My lovely little – unsmelly! – niece.'

33

The small room was flooded with light and air. Belle had raised the blinds and opened the windows. A thin layer of dust that went unnoticed at night coated everything. Belle and Tom sat on the small red sofa staring at the portrait of Hope. Belle's sandals were kicked off in front of her.

'No,' Belle was saying as the sisters walked in. 'We're not having this at home. Imagine explaining to the boys that this is their grandmother.'

'Don't be silly.' Tom leaned forward, staring at the painting. 'They're quite old enough to understand that she was young once too.'

'Not like this!' Belle thumped the arm of the sofa so hard that a cloud of dust rose up, the particles dancing in sunlight. She patted the furniture as if she could force the dust back in again. 'And those muddy colours – they're not the slightest bit mood-enhancing. The only thing that's good about the thing is the frame. I can see that working with a mirror.'

The three of them gazed at her, appalled.

'But it's the only thing I've got of my father.' Tom's protest emerged a little half-heartedly and Belle seized on that.

'Don't be so sentimental, darling. You've managed perfectly well without anything from him until now. You've always said you didn't mind. You don't really like it, do you? What's that?' She pointed a gleaming nail at Jo's yellow spot that was already peeling off at the edges.

Jo took it off and screwed it up. 'Mine. I was going to take the picture until we found out what it was. It's only right that Tom should have it.'

'So you didn't even want it in the first place?' There was a triumphant gleam in Belle's eye as she turned to her husband. She smoothed her hair.

Tom hesitated.

Meanwhile, the naked young Hope smouldered inside the ornate frame, her steady gaze falling on the four of them.

'We're not giving it houseroom except in the attic.' Belle brushed her hands together. Bish bosh. Decision made.

Jo tried to lift the portrait down from the wall. 'Give me a hand, someone. This bloody frame weighs a ton.'

Lucy took the other side and together they hoisted it off the hook and onto the floor. A piece of paper fluttered to the ground that was picked up by Tom. He looked at it. '*Remember me,*' he read. 'That's all it says.'

'She's not giving us much chance to do anything else,' said Jo, as she and Lucy rested the portrait against the bookcase. She tipped it forwards and began tearing off the backing tape, every rip giving her immense pleasure.

'What're you doing?' Tom stepped forward. 'Stop that! You'll damage it.'

'I'm taking the painting out of the frame. Don't worry, Walter showed me how to do this hundreds of times. It's hardly neuro-surgery.' She dropped another bit of tape on to the floor.

Eventually she liberated the portrait, separating it from the frame. 'There,' she said. 'If you guys want the frame for a mirror, there it is. Perfect for the bedroom.' The irony was lost on Belle who just nodded and placed a proprietary hand on it. 'I'll keep the painting for the moment because I love it,' Jo went on. 'If you change your mind, Tom, you can have it. Whenever you like. You only have to ask.' She tipped it towards him.

'He won't,' said Belle, tipping the frame away from her so

she could see it properly. 'This is perfect for us, and a wonderful reminder of your father, whoever he was. Isn't it, darling?'

'Yes,' Tom sounded less certain. 'And I do know where the picture is.'

'You can see it whenever you want.' Jo grinned as she knelt down beside it. 'I know it's not for you, Belle, but I love seeing Mum like this.' The portrait told her of the woman Hope had once been, free-living and free-loving. 'I think I might see if I can have it cleaned up.' She picked at a bit of dirt that had been caught behind the frame where the colours, unexposed to the dust, were much richer than in the rest of the painting, then turned the portrait around. 'Anyway, it's much lighter to ship like this if I can't take it off and roll it.' As she spoke, she noticed something written between the staples holding the canvas to the bottom bar of the stretcher. 'What's this?' She peered closer.

'What?' asked Lucy, bending over her trying to see.

'Tom, you'd better come and look.' Jo straightened up, bumping into her sister as she stepped back. 'I think it's Mum's name and then maybe the name of the artist, your dad.'

As Tom came over, Jo felt a burst of envy. He was about to discover something she never would, now: the identity of his father. Not that it would mean much but at least he would have a name, someone else to belong to, something that would give his life shape, filling in that gap she felt herself. Her brother knelt on the floor, shadowed by Belle who had her arm round his shoulder as she crouched beside him. The frame had been left abandoned against the sofa.

There were footsteps at the doorway. 'So this is where you all are.' Elaine came in, Brad just behind her. 'What's going on?'

'We're just looking at this picture,' Jo explained, preparing to take the impact of Ivy who had had been playing outside in the yard but who appeared behind them, manoeuvred her way past their legs and rushed towards her. Once in her arms, Ivy kissed her smack on the lips. She tasted of strawberry jam. Jo hugged her daughter to her as Tom straightened up.

'Robert Patten,' I think,' he said. 'But I can't be sure.'

Belle leaned in past him, squinting so she could read. 'Yes,' she confirmed. 'That's definitely what it says. Hope Fairweather, then a heart with an arrow through it, then Robert Patten.'

They looked at each other blankly. The name meant nothing.

'Doesn't ring any bells at all,' said Jo, almost wishing it did. Tom looked crestfallen despite his oft-claimed indifference to the identity of his real father. She twisted her head in an attempt to remove her hair from Ivy's fingers as she yanked and knotted it into a new style.

'Let me see.' Elaine came into the room and crouched beside Belle. 'Can I turn it round?' When she saw the portrait, she burst out laughing. 'That's my girl! How gorgeous we were once. Age does us no favours at all. Robert Patten? But I'm sure I recognise that name. There's something familiar...'

'You do?'

Jo heard the hope in Tom's voice as Belle put her arm round him in support.

'Isn't he...' Elaine hesitated, her bangles rattling as she raised her hand to her chin. 'Is this important?'

'Only to me,' said Tom. Belle squeezed his shoulder.

'I'm going back to the house to get my iPad. I must just be sure. I don't want to raise hopes or put my foot in it. Stay here, I won't be a moment.' Off she swirled, skirts flying as Brad came in to look, his eyes widening as he saw the painting. 'That's Hope?' He bent down to look more closely. 'Wow!'

Tom was unsure what to do. On one hand he was repeating to himself what he had always said: he had no need to know who his father was. Yet now he might be so close to finding out, he felt a sudden contradictory sense of urgency. Belle stood close by him while they waited for Elaine's return. He was glad she was there. The picture of Hope didn't matter. If all Belle wanted was the frame, that was a small price to pay for news of his father. After all, if she hadn't made such a song and dance, and Jo hadn't flipped and separated the picture from the frame, they would never have known. He had Belle to thank for that.

His sisters had gone out to the small terrace, Ivy hoisted onto Jo's hip. He could hear her chattering, the other two replying. Ivy wasn't the barrier between his sisters that he had once been afraid she might be, given Lucy's longing for a family of her own. Instead, if anything, she seemed to be bonding them together. His sisters didn't think he noticed what went on between them, but he knew them better than they thought.

'Come and sit down.' Belle led him to the sofa. She shunted the frame out of the way so they could.

'Now, what about Lucy?' She spoke quietly enough for the others not to hear.

'Not now!' He pulled away from her. 'Can't we just deal with one thing at a time?' Didn't she understand how anxious he was feeling? He pinched the skin by his thumb. Breathe. Calm.

'I know, but the estate agent will be here soon. This is so important to her,' she insisted. 'We should at least consider it.'

'Why?'

'Because she's your sister.' She looked at him with a funny half-smile. 'I know I haven't always seen eye to eye with her and Jo, but they're family. And she, out of all of you, deserves something out of all this. Think about what she's lost. At least talk to her, think about it.'

'You've never talked about her or Jo like this before.' Tom couldn't help feeling suspicious.

'Things change,' she said, looking thoughtful. 'I think it's a lovely idea and we'll all miss this place so much if you sell. Lucy knows what she's doing and knows the area. Antonio, too. We'll be able to carry on coming here and you never know, we might make some money out of it as well. That'll be a way of you getting what's owed you. They seem like good reasons to me.'

He laughed. This was more like the Belle he knew and loved. But *we*? This was one decision he would be taking on his own. In fact, a decision he had already taken. In his book, changing one's mind was a sign of weakness not of flexibility. He spent his working life making the right decisions to make the business work, so he was more than capable of making this one. But right now, all he wanted was for Elaine to return with news. He leaned forward, picked up Hope's Sheaffer pen from the table and spun it through his fingers before tapping it on the side of his hand. Belle put a hand out to still it. 'I'm not sure,' he said.

Before they could talk any more, Elaine was back. 'I was right,' she said, breezing in, filling the room with her personality. 'I thought so. Look.' She passed Tom the iPad as the two sisters came in from outside.

'I want to play,' said Ivy, wriggling to get out of her mother's grasp to get to Tom.

'There aren't any games on that iPad,' Jo said. 'Go and bother Ethan.'

Out came that pout again. 'Ethan smells.' She giggled.

'Shh,' said Jo. 'Tom's looking at something important.'

Lucy sat on the arm of the sofa beside Tom, who was intent on what he was reading. 'What is it?'

Ivy climbed aboard Belle's lap, the nearest she could get to the shiny black tablet of treats. Belle gave her a hug.

Tom was lost for words. He scrolled down the Wikipedia entry, reading as quickly as he could, trying to absorb the implications of what he read, scrutinising the picture included in the description.

'Robert Patten's quite a successful artist,' explained Elaine, proud that she had remembered. 'Or was. Not in the league of Hockney or anything like that. but he came to Europe briefly in the late sixties then ended up in the States. This must be by him – look. They're so much of a piece.'

Indeed. Tom was no expert but even he could immediately appreciate the similarities in style of the two portraits. The one he saw on the screen was of a woman, outside this time, walking on a cliff, blown about by the wind, a hand in her hair, smiling. In the background was the glimmering sea, the silhouette of an island.

'You don't think . . .' Tom hardly dared think it let alone say it.

'I do,' said Elaine. 'Now I've see this one for myself, I've no doubt that it's the same woman.'

'Mum,' breathed Lucy.

'It might be,' said Jo, leaning over so she could see. 'That rock's Es Vedra – one of Ibiza's most famous landmarks. And Ibiza's where we lived, where she met Tom's dad. Look at her eyes.'

'It's her,' said Tom. 'It definitely is. But why haven't any of us ever heard of him?'

'His success was brief and years ago,' explained Elaine. 'The only reason I'd heard of him was because he was included in a BBC Four documentary I saw recently about lost artists. I just remembered his name when you said it.'

'I wish she had kept that one and he'd taken this one to America with him,' said Belle merrily. 'I'd happily have that one in the sitting room.'

No one else laughed. They were all staring at the two portraits: one large and very present; the other blown up as big as the iPad would allow.

'Then this might be worth something,' said Lucy. 'If you don't want it, this might be your way of getting the money you're owed.'

'Oh, it must be.' Elaine stood with Brad in the doorway, beaming with pleasure from having helped. 'And it wouldn't be hard to find out.'

'Not that it's for sale,' said Jo quickly. She couldn't bear to think of this memory of her mother in someone else's hands.

'Isn't it?' asked Belle, quick as a whippet.

'No,' Tom handed the iPad back to Elaine. 'No, it's not.' He was quite definite about that. No amount of money would compensate for the loss of this portrait from the family. Even if it weren't in his house, it would be safe with his sister who wanted it.

'But you'll have it valued?' Belle's eyes were sharp.

'Yes, I will. But only for insurance purposes. I'm not selling.'

'I suppose we could put her in the back hall.'

Tom only just suppressed a snort. Now she knew it was valuable, things were different. He could imagine her pointing out the portrait to her friends, and explaining: 'It's by Tom's father, his natural father, the one he didn't know. He was an American artist.' She would like the kudos attached to that, and the story behind it. But that was not how it was going to be. 'No. It's on loan to Jo, because she really wants it, but it belongs to me. Right?' He looked at Jo who nodded her agreement. 'And, Belle, you can do whatever you like with the frame.'

Belle looked regretful for a moment, then accepted what he said with a tilt of her head. Satisfied with the decision, they dispersed back to the terrace. Tom left the others at the table and went to stand by the wall, staring across the landscape under the vast expanse of sky. As soon as he got home, he would find out as much as he could about Robert Patten. His father. The knowledge of him as a real person gave Tom a sense of completion that he hadn't expected. Frank would be interested when he heard that.

'Are you really going to go through with the sale?' Belle had snuck up behind him so that they stood together enjoying the view. 'Imagine never being able to look at this again.'

'Belle, stop it! The estate agent will be here soon.' He turned to her and squeezed her waist with both hands. 'I've made up my mind.'

But Belle detached herself from him. 'You'd made up your mind about your father's identity not mattering. But you were wrong about that, weren't you? I can tell what a difference finding out has made to you already.'

Was it really that obvious? Tom prided himself on being so good at keeping his feelings to himself. Then he remembered how he had behaved with Maria. Everyone had noticed when he thought they hadn't.

But Belle hadn't finished. He should have known she wouldn't give up so easily. She was like a terrier with a bone when it came to getting what she wanted.

'Think of Lucy, then. This is your chance to help her make a new life. This could be her house of dreams now. At least delay things and give her a chance to draw up a business plan. You might think she's got some good ideas. Then, if it doesn't work out within a certain time frame, you can sell after all.'

'And what about Hope's last wishes?'

'Hope's never going to know. And circumstances have changed. Maybe if she'd known what was going to happen this weekend, she would have approved.'

'And Sri Lanka?'

Her inward breath hinted at how much what she was about to say would cost her. 'I hate to admit it but I think my priorities might have been the wrong way round. Giving Lucy this, changing her life, is more important than our holiday. Family is what matters, isn't it? This weekend has shown us that.'

Tom gazed at her. She never stopped surprising him. This was what he had wanted to hear for so long although he knew how difficult it had been for her, without having the sort of warm welcome he would have liked Hope and his sisters to have given her. She had never made it easy for herself. But even so, he reminded himself, change was not something that sat easy with him. Sticking to one's guns was what made the world turn, kept things in order.

'Or perhaps we could take out a loan against the painting.' Her eyes lit up with the idea. 'Or against this place?' Now, they were positively shining. 'And we could still go to Sri Lanka and stay at the Heritance Ahungulla after all.' She couldn't hide the yearning in her voice.

He looked back towards the table where Lucy and Jo were chatting to Elaine and Brad. Was it only him who had such a problem with changing plans? What was the real benefit to him from being so inflexible that a decision couldn't be reversed in different circumstances, and to the benefit of others? The question hit him like a lightning strike. How easy it would be to make them all happy. All he had to do was change his mind for once and give Lucy a chance. And at what cost? He went over to join them.

'Yes, I'm kind of getting used to the idea,' Jo was saying. 'But I feel so sad for Hope. To have lived with those secrets, never to have told anyone. What must that have been like?'

'She managed,' said Elaine. 'She lived her life as well as she could. What more can you ask for? And she had Walter.'

'I've decided that when I get home,' Jo went on, 'I'm going to find where Josh is buried. If nothing else, I need to know where he is. I don't know why that seems so important but it does.'

'But you may never find him.' Elaine looked concerned.

'I will. I absolutely will, if it's the last thing I do,' said Jo. They all knew when she got an idea in her head what she could be like. As intransigent as himself, Tom thought.

'You mustn't set too much store by it,' insisted Elaine.

Jo gave her that look.

But Elaine was undeterred. 'Seriously. You may never find it. And anyway, in the great scheme of things, does finding Josh's grave really matter?'

Jo looked shocked. 'To me. Yes.'

'Think about it.' Elaine removed her sunglasses to make her point, screwing up her eyes against the sun. 'I understand what a shock it's been and that you want closure, especially now you know about your father, but you have your own baby now. Ivy means everything to you, doesn't she?'

Jo inclined her head. 'You know she does.'

In the shade of the house, bored by the adult conversation, Ivy was trying to plait Bailey's hair. The old dog lay in the heat, his tail thumping on the paving stones, enjoying the attention. He snapped at a passing butterfly.

'Don't let your love for her be swallowed up by this, because she's what's important now. Your own family and the present are what matters, not what's in the past.'

There was a scraping sound as Lucy moved her chair and got up to go inside. Although her hands were raised to push her hair off her face, Tom spotted the loneliness and the loss in her expression. He didn't need anyone to interpret for him. What struck him even more forcibly was the idea that it was within his gift to make her feel better.

Elaine and Belle were right. Family was what mattered. Without them, what else was there?

From the upstairs corridor, Lucy could hear the murmur of Tom and Jo talking in the sitting room. Belle had taken the boys and Ivy down to the pool. The occasional shout and splash drifted up to the house. Otherwise everything was still and quiet in the heat of the day. Elaine and Brad had taken their coffee and were lying in the two hammocks among the olive trees. Brad would be leaving soon to meet Amber in London. And Elaine, who had been such an important part of their family and of this weekend, would be going too.

Left on her own, Lucy was besieged by memories and child-hood ghosts – the obstacle races she and her friends ran up here in the winter, dressing up in Hope's discarded clothes, being huddled with friends in her room listening to music, trying out make-up, the sound of laughter and shouting outside on the terrace, the pet cemetery near the woods: all the things that had made her who she was – all of them about to disappear under the imprint of a new owner. The estate agent would be here soon.

What she could have done with this place! Her vision for it had been so clear. Instead, all of them would soon have left for the last time. The idea of returning to such an uncertain future and a house she didn't want to be in was daunting. But somehow she would find the strength she would need to cope alone. She stopped in front of one of Walter's early seascapes, not too abstract but painted long before he thought about painting for the tourist market. She loved its energy, the way he managed the light on the water. She traced the faint line of a fishing smack with her finger. Perhaps she would take this home to remind her. She pulled out her packet of stickers.

'Lucy! Where are you?' Jo's voice rose up the stairs.

'Up here.' Her hand dropped to her side.

'You've been up there for ages. What are you doing?'

'Come down. We've got something important to talk to you about,' Tom called. 'It's about the house.'

Hardly daring to hope, Lucy went to the top of the stairs to find her brother and sister looking up at her, grinning.

'Hurry up, before I change my mind!'

'What do you mean about the house?' But their faces said all she wanted to know. 'Really? We're not going to sell?'

Jo was nodding like a madwoman. 'Tom's called the agent and put him off.'

Lucy felt her jaw drop as she looked down at her brother's face to check that this was really true.

'If you're going to make a go of this, perhaps you'd better get Antonio up here so we can have a proper discussion about what's going to happen.' Tom raised his hands, palms upward, as a sign of defeat. Bringing Antonio into the equation must have cost him a lot. 'After all, he's the one who knows what Mum had in mind. He knows how to run a hotel and he's got the local contacts and, most important, he knows this place inside out. We should hear what he has to say. Those plans might be useful after all.'

'Or you might just want to throw them away and start again,' added Jo.

'I'm not going to do anything without discussing it with you.' Lucy felt her smile splitting her face as she went downstairs towards them. The three of them stood together in a circle, arms around each other. For the first time that weekend, Lucy felt safe, secure – as if, whatever she did in the future, she would have all the support anyone could need.

'Family hug, darlings.' Lucy could hear Hope calling them together. 'Family hug!' Something she couldn't remember them having since they were children, but she had a feeling that, if everything went according to plan, this might not be the last one. As soon as she got home to England, her house would go on the market. She would pack up what she wanted, sell the rest and move here to fulfil her new dream. Things were just beginning after all.

Acknowledgements

There's always a long list of thank-yous that comes with any book. In this instance, my huge thanks are due to:

My indomitable agent, Clare Alexander, who has encouraged and supported me since day one of my writing career.

My editor, Kate Mills, who has the beadiest editorial eye, and the terrific team at Orion with a special shout-out for Jemima Forrester and Juliet Ewers.

Sue James and Tessa Hilton for their unstinting support.

Lizy Buchan, the best writing buddy I could ask for.

Hugh and Jane Arbuthnott, Diana Paget and Paul O'Neill for being so generous with their time and help.

Four-year-old Scarlett Arnstein, Bo Bennett, Florence Gray, Daisy du Cann, Sophie Ingham, Fiamma Roberts and Lily Tobias – for their wit and wisdom. And to their mothers for bothering to write it all down for me.

And, of course, to my dear family and friends who make everything possible.